Half Circle Creek 2

D1528131

WORTH THE

WAIT

Millie Shepherd

Millie Shepherd

For my not so little, little brother, Eli

"When I got what I got, I don't miss what I had
The old me before you belongs to the past."
— Jason Aldean "Got What I Got"

Chapter

ONE

"I'M TRULY SORRY FOR WHAT I'M ABOUT to tell you all." Eli Blager slowly shut his Bible on his pulpit in front of him, his tear-blurred gaze taking in the many eager faces that made up his congregation as they waited patiently for him to continue. He took a deep breath to calm his nerves and emotions before he quietly said, "I've decided to resign from my position as pastor."

A hushed—yet somehow knowing—silence settled over the small church. His eyes darted from face to face, taking it all in since this was going to be his last time behind the pulpit that had been his Sunday companion for the past five years. Everyone's expressions held neither pity nor anger, and his shoulders relaxed as relief seeped into his bones. He'd been so worried that they wouldn't understand his decision, but the calm and compassionate looks peering back at him told him they not only understood, but were expecting his resignation.

1

Why are you surprised?

Ever since his wife Cherish's death three months prior, things had been heart-wrenching, and he'd forever be grateful for the men who had stepped up to take his place for church services. But once he came back, he discovered it was too difficult to raise his five small children alone on top of attempting to keep up with writing sermons, visiting members of the congregation, and everything else that was involved in running a church. A rogue tear rolled down his cheek, splashing down onto the wooden structure beneath him, and he got his bearings back.

Don't get emotional here, Eli. Not in front of nearly the whole town.

He hastily cleared his throat, the sound rumbling deeply in his chest as he gestured to a small family sitting in the front pew on the left. "I'd like to introduce to you your new pastor and my good friend, Phineas Carmichael."

The older man stood, glancing around the room with a nod and smile to the congregation. As he sat back down, Eli continued, "Since he was looking for a church to pastor and I've known him for years thanks to sharing a pew with him back in Carson City before either of us were in the ministry, I knew he was the perfect fit. I hope you all make him, his wife, Elsie, and their daughter, Lotta, feel at home. They generously traveled here sooner than they'd planned so that he can take over services next week."

Eli took in the crowd in front of him as a silence settled over the room. He made eye contact with Abe Askingly. The burly, middle-aged man sat with his wife and adult son in the right row of pews, three from the front. Abe gave him an encouraging smile, and the tension in Eli lessened in response with the knowledge that he had Abe's support.

"Alright then," Eli laughed, attempting to lighten the mood lest he fall into the constantly swirling pit of his emotions. "If you'll all stand, please turn your hymnals to page eighty-five."

The congregation rose as one, and the fluttering of pages being flipped filled the stuffy room. He lifted his arm as the melody of "Come Thou Fount of Every Blessing" flowed from the piano in the corner where Laura Nelson sat gently making the keys do her bidding. Eli's hand swayed lightly as he led the congregation for the final time in a hymn. As they sang, he gazed from pew to pew, a calmness he hadn't felt in years settling in his heart.

Yes, this was the right decision to make.

After Cherish's death, his minute passion for the church had faded and a heavy burden took its place. And he found that even if he could keep up with the parenting and ministry work, he didn't feel like he was qualified to be a pastor anymore. Without Cherish, who had been the reason he'd ever joined the ministry, he knew it wasn't possible to continue without her. Him being a pastor had been her dream—not his. She'd been passionate about serving others and him being in the ministry brought her larger opportunities, so he'd done it because he loved her and wanted to make her happy. Yet he'd always desired to live the simple life of a farmer, and now that his children needed him more and the church had taken it so well, he was content to just warm a pew instead of grip the pulpit while following that dream.

The beloved hymn ended, and he dismissed the people in front of him. Weaving his way through them, he shook their hands like he always did after every service, yet this time accepting words of farewell for his resignation as he went. Iris, his oldest daughter at nine years old, carried Jared snuggly against her chest as she led her three younger sisters behind her to stand by Eli's side. He smiled down at her as he took the three-month-old babe from her arms and lightly stroked her cheek with the fingers of his other hand.

"Thank you for keeping them all quiet during the service, Iris."

"You're welcome, Pa." She returned his smile, her grin the spitting image of her mother's. Sorrow tightened his chest. It always made him miss Cherish more when he looked at Iris and Jared, the only two children who'd inherited their mother's looks. But before he could dwell on his wife, a hand on his shoulder distracted him. Turning to look at the person wanting his attention, he glanced up into the face of Jack Klister, the town deputy. His wife, Bella, stood by his side, hand tucked into the crook of his arm.

"Eli, we wanted to tell you that we'll miss you behind the pulpit." Jack shook Eli's free hand with a small smile that slowly stretched larger as he continued. "I'm really thankful you waited until after you officiated mine and Bells's wedding. It wouldn't have been the same if you hadn't done it."

"I'm glad I waited, too. It was a blessing to be able to marry you two." Eli nodded at the young couple who had only been married for two weeks, a smile tugging at his own cheeks. They had nearly been separated by an evil-minded outlaw a couple of weeks before their wedding, so he was thankful that there had even been a wedding to officiate. Yet it had been difficult to join two people in marriage when his own had been horrifyingly destroyed. He'd had to bury his emotions deep down that day to make sure to keep a happy appearance for Jack and Bella's sakes.

"Can I hold him?" Bella asked quietly, pointing at the baby in the crook of his arm.

"Of course." He gently placed Jared in her arms and smiled as she snuggled him close, his face in the bare curve of her neck above the bodice of her pale green dress. Her face glowed with bliss. Eli glanced up at Jack and found him watching his wife with a loving smile and pride shining out of his dark eyes.

A loud, deep laugh bounced off the white-washed walls of the church, drawing Eli's attention from the young couple and his son. Abe stood a few feet away talking with Doc Adams and his son Gabe, whose arm was wrapped around the shoulders of his petite fiancee, Dolly Nelson. Glancing back at Jack and Bella, Eli quickly said, "I'll be right back. Do you mind watching the girls and Jared for a moment?"

"Of course not," Jack answered, shaking his head.

"Thanks." Eli squeezed past Jack and another church member. "I'll only be a few minutes."

Stepping up to the small group of men and Dolly, Eli caught their attention with a wave. He quickly shook all three of their hands and nodded to Dolly before turning to Abe. "Thank you for all you've done these past three months. I don't know how I'll ever repay you."

"Don't even try." Abe shook his head, his blonde curls falling over his brow as his blue eyes sparkled.

"But thank you doesn't seem like enough," Eli sighed, the same peace that had come over him behind the pulpit sweeping in once again. He let his gaze take in the other two men standing beside them. "I appreciate you all helping me

5

out during this time more than you'll ever know."

"It's the least we can do," replied Doc Adams, reaching out to gently squeeze Eli's arm. Doc glanced over Eli's shoulder, watching something behind him as a small infant's whimpers swept toward them. "It looks like your son is giving Bella a little bit of a hard time over there."

Eli turned around and looked at the babe in the girl's arms. Jared's face was slightly puckered like he was about to cry, but Bella started rocking him gently in her arms and his face smoothed. Shaking his head, Eli said, "I better go get him and round up the girls to take them home. I'm sure they're all hungry by now."

"Alright, we'll see you later, Eli." Abe nodded as Eli glanced back at him. "You go take care of that family of yours."

"Thanks again, Abe."

"Don't mention it." Abe shook Eli's hand a final time. Eli wove his way back through the crowd to where he left his children with the newlywed Klisters.

Rubbing the back of his neck, fingers brushing against his curly hair that was in need of a trim, Eli walked down the short hall and into his cozy living room. Only it never felt as cozy as it used to. If the room's four walls could talk, they'd tell tales of hours spent laughing, cuddling, and chatting, but most importantly of love. Now it was lonely and almost cold, so continuing on through his small house, he stepped into the dimly lit kitchen and plopped down in a chair at the table.

All the girls were safely tucked in bed in their shared

bedroom at the end of the short hall, and Jared was peacefully sleeping like a rock in his crib in Eli's room. The announcement he'd made at the end of the morning service had started what turned into a long, hard day. Both Tulip and Petunia had cried more than once, and he was still trying to figure out how to console four- and two-year-old little girls. He'd always been close to his children, yet at times without Cherish, it was nearly impossible to get them calmed down.

Of course today had to be one of those days.

Some days were better than others, but that day had been the worst they'd had in the past couple of weeks. Almost as soon as they had gotten home, the tears started flowing and it had taken both Iris and him to get the younger girls settled. He hated leaning on Iris so much since she was only nine, yet she'd grown up and become a responsible little woman faster than he could blink. That hurt nearly as much as Cherish's death. Iris was still very much a child, and she needed to be able to be carefree and have the time to play, but instead now she was cooking, cleaning, and tending to her siblings like a young woman.

Dropping his head down onto his bent arm lying on the table, he let all of the emotion that had built up throughout the day drain. His sleeve dampened as his broad shoulders shook under the force of his deep sobs.

Why me? I can't raise the girls and Jared alone.

His body continued to rack with cries, and he shifted in his seat until his sopping cheek pressed against the smooth wood of the table. Fisting his other hand, he halfheartedly pounded the table several times. Slowly but surely, his tears ceased and he could breathe easier once again. The pain still throbbed horribly in his chest, yet his body wasn't as tense with held-back emotion anymore.

He tried his best to not break down in front of the girls. It would only make things harder, and he couldn't let that happen. They'd already been through so much that he wouldn't allow his own cracked and bleeding heart to cause them more pain. He'd seen their grief-glazed eyes the first several weeks after Cherish's death when he was close to losing it. That look and the mewing newborn were the only things that made him pull himself together.

Only he wasn't pulled back together. Not even the tiniest bit. The smiling, collected father his children and the town saw was just a mask covering a very broken, lonely, and desperate man, whose heart ached for the wife he'd loved for ten long years despite not always getting along with her. But the worst part was that he didn't know how to pick up the shattered pieces to fix himself.

He'd visited Cherish's grave often during the first few weeks to see if it would be of any aid, but instead of making things better, it made it all worse. He quit going and didn't plan to go again anytime soon in the future since it felt odd because she truly wasn't there, and a soulless body under six feet of dirt did little to comfort an aching heart.

Through many sleepless, pain-filled nights, his Bible had been his constant companion accompanied by long tear-filled prayers. Those things helped soothe his soul, but only to a point. He'd finally drift off to dreamland with a sense of peace, then wake up the next morning to the whole vicious cycle once again.

He needed something more. Something only a fellow human could give him. But he couldn't figure out what that was.

Lord, please show me the way.

Lifting his face off of the table, he wiped the moisture off his cheeks and rubbed the tabletop dry with his sleeve. He knew sleep wouldn't come for many more hours, so he leaned back in his chair, gray eyes darting from one corner of the kitchen to the next as if in search of answers in the dim room.

The lamp on the table cast a warm, yellow beam of light on the newspaper lying open beside it. Reaching over, he grabbed the corner of the paper and slid it toward himself. He flipped it over, having already read the front page that morning when he was the only one awake, and a small advertisement on the bottom left corner caught his attention.

Mail-order-brides? Who would want to "buy" a bride?

Not giving the advertisement another glance, he opened the paper to read the articles inside, but no matter how hard he tried to concentrate, his thoughts kept drifting back to the three-word title on the other side. Curiosity finally getting the best of him, he flipped the page back over, and read the whole advertisement:

Mail-Order-Brides

Need a wife? Send a letter to Miss Prudy's Mail-Order-Bride Agency and Miss Prudy will find you a bride!

Please include in your letter your likes and dislikes in women, and you'll be matched with someone who fits your desires.

He laid the paper back down on the table and scrubbed a hand down his face. Cherish's final gasping words that forced him to promise to remarry had haunted him since that mournful night. Despite that promise, he never really intended to go through with it, at least not for many years anyway. His heart was still wrapped up in Cherish, and he didn't think he could ever love another woman like that again even if he tried. His deceased wife's words seemed to echo from all the corners of the room as he stared at the advertisement in front of him. "Promise me…That you'll marry again, for the children and for yourself. I want you to be happy."

No, I can't marry for myself. But I will for the children.

The children needed the love and nurture of a mother, something he couldn't give them no matter how hard he tried. A mother's touch was unique and unlike any other–it wasn't physically possible for him to unleash it from somewhere deep inside of him. The only problem was that there wasn't a single woman in Half Circle Creek who he could marry even if it was just for the children. All the single ladies of the town were either way too young, already in a relationship, or old and widowed. None of them would do, yet the advertisement glaring furiously at him from the table just might be the solution to all his problems.

But is it the right thing to do?

Something inside of him told him it was. Why else would he have found it right after praying for an answer so desperately? And why else would it be bothering him so ferociously?

There's no harm in trying.

He rose from the table and quietly made his way to his room. Opening the top of the small desk in the corner near the door, he silently fished out a piece of paper, envelope, and pen and ink. His heart hammered against his ribs as he tiptoed in his socks back to the kitchen table and the glowing lamp. Sucking in a deep breath, he attempted to calm the sudden nerves swirling in the pit of his belly. It helped a little as he slowly let a deep sigh slip past his parted lips.

Dropping back into his still warm chair, he scooted

the newspaper out of the way, and laid out his letter writing supplies in front of him. He smoothed a trembling hand over the cool paper and wetted his pen in the jet black ink. Once more glancing at the advertisement, he nodded to himself, then pressed his pen to the paper.

Here goes nothing...

Chapter

TWO

Tuscaloosa, Alabama
Late October 1865

RUBBING A TINY BIT OF LARD INTO her cracked and raw hands, Lisa Fullerton walked up the narrow staircase to her midget-sized quarters in the attic of the boardinghouse. She shut the door behind her as she entered her chilly room. Being careful not to smack her skull on the low, arched ceiling, she slowly lowered her aching body onto the edge of the bed that nearly took up the whole room. Her stomach rumbled despite the meager meal of leftover black-eyed peas, cold creamed corn, and one slightly stale biscuit. The boardinghouse's leftovers were her meals, and some days she went hungry while others she had enough to keep her stomach from rumbling.

Lisa rolled her shoulders to try and relieve the tension from being bent over a washboard all day. As she shifted, the letter in her apron pocket rubbed against the coarse fabric, a swishing sound signaling the movement. With a slight frown, she pulled the unopened missive from Miss Prudy's Mail-

Order-Bride Agency out of the pocket at the front of her tan, flour sack apron.

It had been roughly a month and a half since she asked Miss Prudy–an old widow friend of her mother's–to add her to the list of women willing to marry strangers. Lisa wasn't happy about it, but she had no choice. She could serve tables day in and out and scrub laundry until her hands bled for room and board. Or she could marry someone she'd never met. There was a risk with the latter, but one she was willing to take if it could get her out of her war-destroyed hometown and away from the haunting memories the place surrounded her with.

Momentarily forgetting about the letter between her raw and bleeding fingers, she let those memories sweep her away. Her mother's smile flashed before her, Pa's laugh echoed in the corner, and her brothers' teasing tickled her ear. Even Mammy's bossing seemed to call to her from down the hall. Shaking her head, she quickly came back from the past.

Gone. All of them.

The War Between the States had slowly but surely, stripped her of each and every one of them. Year by year, one by one, her father, three older brothers, mother, and mammy had been taken from her by either fatal wounds or an illness.

It had only been a little over a month since Lisa had not only lost Mammy, the sole loved one left, but also her childhood home. Fullerton Manor, their house in town, had been damaged by the war just like the University of Alabama where her father had worked as a professor for nearly twenty years. But the damages weren't the cause of its loss. Lisa was nothing-to-her-name-dirt-poor, and the bank took the house after she failed to pay the overly expensive taxes on the property. Mammy had died two days before Lisa had to leave, and it still broke her heart to think of the older woman's labored final words. "Now, Lisie Marie, don't ya fret, chil'. The good Lord has plans fer ya. Mighty big plans. Ole Mammy can feel it in her bones. Don't cry for me chil', we'll see each other again in Glory."

Mammy, maybe this letter has those plans you always talked about in it.

Running her thumb gently over the still sealed envelope, she took a deep breath. Tearing open the letter before her nerve left her, she pulled out not only one, but two papers. She tossed the empty envelope onto the bed and glanced at the handwriting at the top of each letter, trying to identify which one was Miss Prudy's.

Gently laying the second, unexpected note on the bed beside the envelope, she hungrily read Miss Prudy's loopy pencil scratchings.

She found me a match!

Pressing a shaking hand to her now warm cheek, she switched the papers and slowly began the letter from the man Miss Prudy had matched her to.

His handwriting is strong looking and extremely neat. Surely that's a good sign!

Lisa's eagerness to learn about this strange man took her by surprise. She hadn't expected Miss Prudy to find a man willing to give her the time of day since she was very much a spinster at twenty-eight. Thanks to her overprotective brothers and somewhat shy nature around men that had plagued her younger years, she'd never had a beau or been courted. Yet the letter in her trembling hands seemed to seep a new chance through her skin deep into her core. Tears pricked the back of her eyes and her stomach did somersaults as a marvelously encouraging sensation filled her. She directed her gaze back to the black ink peering expectantly up at her from her lap.

Dear Miss Fullerton,

This is a very awkward type of letter to write since I have to describe myself and my family with the possibility of marriage to someone I've never laid eyes on before, but I will do my best.

My name is Eli Jared Blager, and I'm about to turn thirty-one. I am a newly widowed father of five. My wife, Cherish, made me promise to remarry moments before she passed away, so I'm trying to keep that vow for her and my children.

Lisa's brows nearly reached her hairline.

Five children?

She had always wanted to be a mother, and thought she'd left that dream behind her years ago, yet now it was within reach. Shaking her head in amazement, she continued reading.

I have four little girls, Iris, Hyacinth, Tulip, and Petunia, and one son, Jared. They're nine, seven, five, two nearly three, and five months. I'm very proud of them! They are well behaved children, yet the sudden death of their mother at Jared's birth has shaken them tremendously, causing them to be emotional at times.

I wanted you to be well aware of this since if we were to wed, it would be for them. Not me. But because I would be your husband, I figure you want to know more about me than my children.

I am of average height, roughly five feet eleven inches, and I have dark gray eyes and brown, curly hair. If I had a photograph of myself I would include it in this letter, but since I don't you'll have to try to use your imagination.

I used to be the pastor of the church in my town but resigned my position at the end of August since my children are my main priority. I hope you are a religious young woman, and in the hopes that our beliefs might be similar, I'll quickly explain the doctrines I hold dearly to.

A wide smile slowly stretched across her face as to her surprise, his Christian beliefs and values lined up nearly exactly to hers. Despite the fact that she had no experience with children—let alone a baby—since she was the youngest child, everything else was lining up miraculously. Only one paragraph left to the story, she sighed happily as her dark brown eyes continued down the page.

Now that I am no longer pastoring, I'm going to be turning my small piece of property into a farm. I've decided to grow a crop of alfalfa and raise pigs since you can't grow much else in Nevada, and both of those things fetch a fair price. I won't be rich and funds might be scarce at times, but I will work myself nearly to death if I have to in order to provide for my family.

I hope you decide to send me a letter in response, so we can further converse, and decide what we want to do.

Sincerely,

Eli Blager

Laying the letter down on the bed, she stood and hastily began to get ready for bed. Everything in Mr. Blager's letter swarmed through her mind so fast she had to set her hand on the slanted wall above her head to steady herself. If his writing style was any way of telling, he seemed like an educated man, yet the black words on the creamy paper also rang out as if he had a hard time writing them. *The poor man just lost his wife and now he's looking for a new one just for his little ones. Of course it had to be hard to write!* Gently removing the pins from her hair where it was coiled into a tight bun at the nape of her neck, she shook it loose, and the long, black strands fell around her face. She sat back on the bed and reached over to grab her brush from the small nightstand, the only other piece of furniture in the cramped room. Pulling it through her locks, she stared at the letter beside her, trying to decide what to do.

After her one-hundred strokes were completed and the black thickness braided out of the way, she reached inside the thin box on the nightstand. Pulling out a single piece of paper, since she had very little, she angled the page toward the little bit of light coming from the round window above her cot.

Lisa closed her eyes briefly, the seriousness of her decision sinking in as she took a deep breath. She sat the tip of the thin pencil to the top of her just as thin paper and quickly jotted down, "Dear Mr. Blager."

Alright, Lisa, this is it.

As her pencil scratched lightly against the textured paper, she wrote out a letter very similar to Mr. Blager's before she changed her mind or the dim light disappeared. In loopy, yet neat letters, her reply read:

As you said, this is a strange sort of letter to write, so I'll get straight to the point.

Your family sounds wonderful, but I will forewarn you that I have no experience with children. Yet I will try my best should this situation go past letters.

Since I know you're probably curious about the woman holding this pencil, I'll tell you a little about myself. My full name is Lisa Marie Fullerton, and I'm currently twenty-eight. I have black hair, dark brown eyes, and a large amount of freckles on my face. I'm very average looking, truth be told. Ever since the end of the war, I have been working at a boardinghouse. I wash dishes, scrub laundry, and wait tables in exchange for meals and a place to sleep.

I'm also very glad to inform you that our religious beliefs are identical, and I am sorry that you had to give up your ministry. But I will say I'm happy that you found a new profession in order to provide for your children.

Thank you for the letter. I hope there will be another.

Signing her name with a flourish at the end, she stared at her own handwriting for a moment, the realization hitting her in the gut like the smack of an angry sibling.

There was a possibility her life was changing, that she was getting a new beginning. A new home. And all far, far away from Tuscaloosa.

Thank goodness!

Chapter

THREE

Half Circle Creek, Nevada
Early April 1866

"ALRIGHT, GIRLS, BE GOOD FOR MRS. ASKINGLY, you hear?" Eli kissed Petunia's cheek before he sat her in the chair beside Iris at Abe and Abby's kitchen table.

"Yes, sir," Iris and Hyacinth chirped, eyes wide and excited for what the day was bringing.

"I'll be back in a little bit to get you all." He tousled Tulip's already messy curls with a small shake of his hand. Three of the girls had inherited his curls and even though it had been ten months since Cherish's death, he still hadn't figured out how to tame and fix their hair since it was so much longer than his. Stepping away from the table, he nodded at Abby where she stood near the stove with Jared happily resting on her hip. "Thank you for watching them for me today, Abby."

"Don't worry about it." She smiled then shooed him out of the room toward the front door. "You better get a move on it if you don't want to be late to catch that stage."

"Yes, ma'am." He laughed as he stepped out of the door, sliding his tan hat on his head. Climbing onto the seat of his buckboard, he paused to run a trembling hand down his red, checkered shirt. The curtain stirred on the Askinglys' front window, moving from the inside.

Probably Abby looking to see if I've left yet.

Snapping the reins, he put the horses in motion. The stage was often late, but he wanted to be there early just in case. There was no sense in being tardy when he was meeting the woman who was going to be his new wife, especially since he wanted to make a good first impression.

He and Lisa Fullerton had been exchanging letters since November, and after their third letter, she decided she wanted to come west. Eli bought her the tickets for the long trip involving ships, a train, and a stagecoach, and now, three weeks later, she was nearly in Half Circle Creek.

To say he was nervous was an understatement. He wasn't sure if the breakfast he'd had a few hours before would stay down, and his palms were embarrassingly slick with sweat. Tightening his jaw to keep his teeth from clacking together from his jitters, he took a deep breath as the stage station came into view.

Lisa hadn't been able to send him a picture just like he hadn't been able to send her one, so the only thing that he knew about her was that she had black hair, dark brown eyes, and freckles. It was a very loose description, yet it shouldn't be too difficult to spot her since the stage could only hold so many, and she'd likely be the only young woman traveling alone.

Pulling back the brake and wrapping the reins around

it to keep it in place, he climbed over the wheel. Eli's feet hit the ground, and he stepped over to the small platform in front of the station. He shifted nervously on the wooden floorboards as he took off his hat, holding it at his waist, and swiped a hand through his hair to smooth it.

Rattling wooden wheels, clopping horse hooves, and a hoarse, manly shout signaled the arrival of the stagecoach. Eli's stomach churned and he pressed a shaking hand to it as the stage slowly came to a halt.

Everything is going to be alright. You can do this.

The stage driver climbed down, his boots stirring up a small cloud of dust as they thumped onto the ground. He grabbed a teeny stool and sat it on the ground before swinging open the door on the side of the red stagecoach as he called out, "Half Circle Creek! Anyone here for Half Circle Creek?"

The sound of a small ruckus spilled out of the stage, then the driver lifted his hand to help an elderly lady step down. Eli tried to glance past him and into the stage, but he couldn't see around the lady.

What if Lisa didn't come? What if she used the funds for the tickets on something else and everything was just a way to get money?

Like the drop of a hat, the station abruptly became silent. In the hush, the driver assisted another passenger from the stage. Eli's breath caught in the back of his throat, and a low whistle sounded from somewhere behind him, but he couldn't tear his eyes from the young lady leaning out of the stagecoach to find out who had made the noise.

With black hair coiled at the nape of her neck, a splattering of freckles on a creamy white, elegant face, and dark brown, soulful, yet sad eyes, the woman who had to be Lisa

Fullerton stepped down to the wooden platform in front of him. Blinking to make sure he was still awake, Eli slowly grinned.

Striding forward, his eyes skimmed over her cream-colored blouse and burgundy skirt, and he was once again surprised. But this time by her height. She had to be roughly five-foot-seven, slightly tall for a lady.

Definitely not what I was expecting!

Clearing his throat, he got her attention, and offered her his hand to shake. "Ma'am, might you be Miss Lisa Fullerton?"

"Yes, sir that I am." She gave him a small smile, her bare hand rough against his as she shook it. "And you are?"

"Eli Blager." He nodded and surprise flitted across her face, but she hid it with an even wider smile.

"It's a pleasure to finally meet you, Mr. Blager." Her slightly husky voice had a slow, smooth, twang to it like he'd never heard before, and it sent a pleasant shiver up his spine.

"Please just call me Eli."

"Of course," she paused with a shy look, "but only if you'll call me Lisa."

He nodded and offered her his arm, walking her to the buckboard. "I have four little girls who're so excited to meet you. They're probably bouncing in their seats right now at my friend's house."

"They're excited to meet me?" She looked down at him from the seat, wonder and surprise in her brown eyes.

"Yes. Very excited. It's all Iris and Hyacinth could talk about this week." Eli laughed, and her eyes widened slightly at the sound. Multiple thumps vibrated the wooden platform as the driver tossed the luggage down from the top of the stage. "If you'll tell me which of those bags is yours, I'll fetch it and we can be on our way."

"Oh, of course, I nearly forgot." She looked away from him to the pile of carpet bags and assortment of trunks. One slender finger, which he couldn't help notice was rough and raw, likely because she'd spent the whole winter scrubbing dishes, pointed to a small, flowered carpet bag at the top of the pile. "That little one is mine."

He had it in hand within seconds and carefully tossed it into the back of the buckboard before climbing up on the seat beside her. With a click of his tongue and snap of the reins, they were off.

Glancing over at the dark-haired beauty beside him, Eli realized his nerves had vanished, and that somehow their silence wasn't strained or awkward.

What a relief!

Things had started out on steady footing and would hopefully continue that way.

"Do you think you'll like it here?" he asked, breaking the silence with his deep, rumbling voice.

"Yes. Yes, I do." She hastily glanced from place to place, like she was trying to take it all at once. A grin tugged at his lips at the childlike glee on her face. "It's all so different from Alabama."

"Is that a good thing or a bad thing?"

"A good thing." She finally looked back at him, a smile on her face, but he saw the sadness in her eyes that her pleasant expression couldn't quite hide. He'd heard about how destroyed the South had become in the war, and he didn't want to even think about what she might have witnessed.

Hopefully she wasn't involved too closely in the brutality of it all.

"I'm glad." He nodded, his smile never wavering. Settling back into a peaceful silence, they pulled up into the Askinglys' front yard. He turned on the seat to face Lisa, his palms suddenly slick against the reins which he wove nervously between his fingers. "Lisa, I really hope you'll like my family."

Her name slipped past his lips easily like he'd been saying it for years, and the feeling was strange yet extremely likable.

"I'm sure I will, Eli." She gave him a small smile, the freckles bunching on her lifted cheeks. Her husky voice added an unfamiliar but pleasant sounding twang to his name, and it sent a shiver up his spine.

Eli clambered off and stepped over to her side of the wagon to help her down. Her feet had barely touched the ground when the front door swung open and his two oldest daughters bolted down the porch steps. He raised his eyebrows at them in warning as they screeched to a halt in front of Lisa and him. Their chins bobbed down to their bodices as shy blushes colored their cheeks.

"Lisa, I'd like you to meet my oldest daughters." Eli pointed first to the girl wearing her red locks in braided pigtails, then to the other, whose brown hair was styled the same way. "Iris and Hyacinth. Girls, this is Miss Lisa Fullerton."

"Nice to meet you both. I've heard a lot about you." Lisa offered her hand to first Iris, then Hyacinth.

"Ma'am." They nodded, shaking her hand.

"Please, call me Lisa. If that's alright with your father." She glanced over at him, and he nodded with a small smile.

"Lisa, you can call me Cinthy." Hyacinth took a step closer and laid a tentative hand on Lisa's cream colored sleeve.

"Alright, Cinthy." Lisa smiled down at her, brushing her fingers lightly over Cinthy's round cheek. Glancing over at Iris, she asked, "What about you, Iris? What would you like me to call you?"

"Oh, everybody just calls me Iris, ma'am." Her face beamed, half of her mouth lifting in a grin.

"You don't have to call me ma'am. It makes me feel like a little old lady." Lisa scrunched her nose, winking at Iris. A giggle slipped past the hand Iris pressed to her mouth. The giggle that Eli hadn't heard nearly as often in the past ten months as he used to.

Good!

"Eli, are you going to invite your new lady friend in the house so your other children and I can meet her, or do I have to?" Abby's laughing voice called across the yard. Eli looked up to find her standing in the open doorway on the porch wearing a wide grin with Jared propped on her hip. Petunia, his shyest child, peeked out from behind her full pink skirt while Tulip was nowhere in sight.

"We're coming, Abby!" Waving for Lisa to follow him, he walked toward the porch.

Somewhere between the porch steps and the buckboard, both Iris and Cinthy had each grabbed one of Lisa's hands, and he let the three of them stride up the four small stairs first. Abby swept Lisa into the house, and he followed with a low chuckle.

Good ole mother hen, Abby.

Lisa and Abby exchanged 'hellos' and introduced

themselves as he scooped up a shyly blushing Petunia. He kissed her forehead, rubbing his smooth chin against her cheek to make her giggle. Lisa bent down to eye level with ten-month-old Jared, and quietly talked to him. He stretched out his arms to her, and she took him from Abby with a surprised expression. Lisa tucked her arm under his bottom, cradling him against her side. She did it so naturally it surprised Eli, especially since she'd said she had no experience with little ones. He'd been nervous about what it would feel like to see the woman who'd possibly become his children's new mother holding Jared, but as he watched Lisa give Abby a questioning look, he relaxed. He had expected pain but instead was getting happiness.

"He's been passed back and forth so much that he will nearly go to any one who gives him attention," Abby explained as she stepped away and went into the kitchen, returning a moment later with Tulip.

As Eli moved closer to Lisa, Petunia buried her face in his neck, trying to hide. He rubbed a comforting hand up her small back. "I see you've already met Jared."

"Yes, but who might this little sweetheart be?" She peered curiously at the cowering three-year-old in his arms.

"This is Petunia." He lifted his shoulder a little to make her look up, and she moved her face away from his neck just enough to look, her thumb finding her mouth.

"Nice to meet you, Petunia. I'm Lisa." She smiled, and it turned into a grin as Jared plopped his head down on her shoulder with a deep, relaxed sigh.

"Now, don't you forget about this sneaky little one who was hiding in the kitchen." Eli glanced behind him to find Abby gently pushing a teary-eyed Tulip toward them.

He hastily bent down, stretching out his free arm for her to come to him. He scooped her up and stood again. Tulip–the five-year-old of the bunch–was the most emotional out of the girls and he expected a few tears from her, but her chin quivered dangerously.

Kissing her cheek, he buried his face in the messy curls along the side of her face and whispered in her ear, "It's alright Tulip. Lisa isn't going to hurt you. She just wants to meet you. Dry your tears now, sweetheart."

She did as she was told, and as Eli turned to face Lisa, Tulip's quivering chin slowly turned into a watery smile.

"What's your name, little one?" Lisa asked quietly, a gentle smile playing on her lips.

"Tulip."

"That's a very pretty name. I'm Lisa." She rubbed Jared's back and he sighed again.

"Pa?" Iris tugged on his sleeve and he looked around Tulip's head to see her clearly.

"Yes, sweetheart?"

"Is Lisa going to be our new ma?"

Lisa glanced up at him with hesitant eyes. They'd agreed not to make any final decisions until after they had all met.

"We'll see, Iris. We'll see."

Chapter

FOUR

"THANK YOU FOR LETTING ME STAY AT your house, Bella," Lisa said a few hours later, smiling at the younger, curly-headed, blonde girl standing by the stove several feet away.

"Of course." Bella glanced over her shoulder to grin at Lisa where she sat at the kitchen table, a cup of hot coffee between her hands. "You can't stay with Eli since it wouldn't be proper, and Jack and I are Eli's closest neighbors, so it just made sense. There's no reason for you to stay at Lola's Boardinghouse when you would have to walk across town to come talk to Eli and the girls."

"Thank you anyways." Lisa laughed. "Eli and I are going to try and figure everything out this week, so I should be out of your hair by Saturday."

"You're not a bother."

"Bella, any person living with a newly married couple is a bother." Lisa rolled her eyes with a giggle. She really liked Bella, but she couldn't help feeling like she was imposing on their hospitality.

"Lisa, you're not a bother." Bella turned around to face her, one hand on her hip while the other one continued to stir the stew on the stove. "Anyways, you'll be so busy over at Eli's that we'll probably only see you at supper time."

Before Lisa could answer, the front door swung open and a tall, dark-headed man stepped into the house. He tipped his hat at her with a smile but strode past her and the table to Bella. Pulling her close, he gave her a quick kiss. He turned back to look at Lisa, one arm still around Bella's waist. "Hello. I'm guessing you're Lisa Fullerton."

"Yes, I'm Lisa." She smiled.

"Nice to meet you, Miss Fullerton. I'm Jack Klister." He stepped away from Bella and toward Lisa, hand out-stretched. She stood to shake his hand. He was a kind-look-ing young man and rather handsome.

No wonder Bella fell in love with him.

In the last half an hour that Lisa had been with Bella, the younger woman had told her all about the town and her husband. They seemed like a nice couple, and Lisa was glad they were Eli's closest neighbors. She'd been nervous about meeting new people in a strange place, yet she appeared to have made a friend, so the closeness was going to be nice when they wanted to visit each other.

"You best get cleaned up, Jack. Supper will be on the table in a few minutes," Bella called after him as he walked back toward the front door to hang up his hat on the rack beside the door.

"What are we having?" he asked as he came back into the kitchen side of the wide room that was half living room and half kitchen.

"Beef stew, biscuits, and I have an apple pie cooling in the window."

Sorrow trickled into Lisa's heart at the mention of apple pie. It had been her father's favorite and always reminded her of him. But not wanting to appear sad for Jack and Bella's sakes, she pushed the emotion to the side.

"Sounds good." He washed his hands and slightly dusty face at the sink.

Lisa hid a smile behind her coffee cup as she quietly watched the exchange. Jack could barely keep his eyes off of Bella and she kept glancing over at him with a sweet smile.

That's the kind of love I want.

But she wasn't sure if she'd ever get it. If she did marry Eli, it was only to be a mother to his five precious children, who in just a few hours had already captured her heart. Despite her inexperience with babies and children, something deep down inside her told her that she'd be alright. That she could be the mother those little girls and boy needed.

Bella moved over to the table and set down the dishes of food. Both Jack and Bella were soon seated and the meal underway. Sleep pulled at Lisa's eyes, but she tried to keep up with the questions Jack asked her.

"Jack, will you stop pestering her with questions," Bella laughed lightly, resting a hand on Jack's forearm where it lay on the table next to her. "She's had a long day and I'm sure she's too tired to want to talk."

"I'm sorry, Miss Fullerton. I get a little carried away sometimes," Jack apologized with a sheepish look.

"It's alright. And please just call me Lisa." She hid a yawn behind her hand, her sleepiness growing.

"Maybe you should just go to bed," Bella suggested.

"I think I will. It's been a long three weeks of either being on a boat, train, or a stagecoach. I'm not even sure when the last time I had a full night's sleep was." Lisa laid her napkin beside her empty plate. Slowly standing up, she started toward the bedroom on the kitchen side of the small house that Bella told her was hers while she stayed with them. "Good night."

"Good night." Jack and Bella's voices echoed behind her.

The chirping of birds and bright sunlight shining through the window at the end of her bed woke Lisa the next morning. Rolling over onto her back, she rubbed the sleep out of her eyes, then rested the back of her hand against her forehead with a sigh. She hadn't slept that well in a long time. Her eyes had closed as soon as her head had hit the pillow, and she hadn't stirred the whole night.

Glancing around the small bedroom, she took in the light brown, wooden walls and silver mirror above the table by the door that her carpet bag sat on. A decent-sized nightstand stood beside the bed, and lacy white curtains covered the single window. It was a mansion compared to the cramped attic back in Tuscaloosa.

A deep, manly voice followed by a girlish laugh slipped under the closed door. Lisa sat up and swung her feet over the edge of the bed.

What time is it? I must have overslept!

Bare feet quietly brushing the smooth, wooden planks of the floor, she walked across the room to the door. Silently opening it, she peeked out.

Standing at the stove once again, Bella said something softly to Jack who was putting a coffee cup in the sink. He stepped up behind her and wrapped his arms around her waist, pulling her close against his chest. Bella turned her face toward him, and he kissed her soundly before burying his face in her neck.

Lisa's cheeks heated as she realized they didn't know she was watching. Hastily, yet without a sound, she closed the door again. Wanting to give them the privacy they deserved, she grabbed the brush out of her carpet bag and made quick work of fixing her hair for the day in front of the mirror.

She unbuttoned her nightgown and slipped it over her head, the sun from the window warming her bare skin. Swiftly pulling on her layers of undergarments, tightening the back of her corset, and buttoning her blouse and skirt, she was ready for the day ahead.

Folding up her nightgown, she put it back in her bag. Her fingers skidded across the thin, off-white fabric, and her cheeks heated again in embarrassment as she realized she'd nearly presented herself to two complete strangers in her night clothes and bed-mussed hair.

Heavens to Betsy! The lack of sleep must really have addled my brain.

The sound of the front door opening then clicking shut echoed in the other room. Lisa gave herself a final look-over in the small, oval mirror. Smoothing the lace collar on the same cream blouse she'd worn the day before, she fingered her mother's wedding band that she wore on a thin chain around her neck.

The best I can do for now.

Opening the door, Lisa stepped out into the kitchen. Bella looked over with a smile. "Good morning, Lisa. Did you have a good night's sleep?"

"Yes, I did. I slept like a rock. I was worn slap out." Lisa walked over to the table as Bella gestured for her to sit. Placing a cup of hot coffee in front of her, Bella went back over to the stove.

"Worn slap out?" Bella asked, bringing a plate full of food back to the table, which she gave to Lisa.

"Oh, it's something we say back home. It just means you're extremely tired," Lisa explained, glancing at the fried eggs and thick ham slice. "What time is it, anyhow?"

"Nearly eight." Bella sat down across from her.

"That late? I really did oversleep!"

"It's alright. You needed your rest after taking a journey like that." Bella smiled. "I hope you don't mind being alone later because Jack and I are going on a picnic outside of town for lunch, and I won't be home to keep you company."

"Don't worry about it." Lisa set down her fork to wave away Bella's concern. "Eli has something planned this afternoon, so I won't even be here."

"Good!" Bella nodded. "I felt bad about leaving you to fend for yourself when you're a guest."

"I've had to fend for myself for a while now, so it's nothing new." Lisa shrugged. A comfortable silence settled over the room as Lisa continued to eat the breakfast Bella had kept warm for her.

"Lisa," Bella quietly said after a moment.

"Yes?" Lisa gazed over at the blonde woman.

"I hope everything works out for you and Eli."

"So do I." Lisa smiled softly, reaching over and patting Bella's hand where it rested on her folded arms on the table.

Chapter

FIVE

"HERE WE ARE." ELI PULLED THE BUCKBOARD to a halt by a tree next to the creek on the far side of town near the schoolhouse. The grassy area around the tree had been used for years by people young and old as a picnic spot, so he figured it was the perfect place to take Lisa and the children for the picnic he had planned.

Iris unlatched the back of the buckboard from her seat in the wagon bed, and Eli glanced over his shoulder just in time to see her clamber down then help Tulip and Cinthy to the ground. Petunia sat between him and Lisa, who held Jared snugly on her lap.

Hopping off his side of the wagon, Eli circled around the back to Lisa's side, and took Jared. She placed her hand in his offered one and carefully climbed down. She tried to get Petunia to come to her so she could get off the wagon seat, but still shy around Lisa, Petunia scooted farther away.

"If you take Jared back, I'll get her," Eli offered. Lisa nodded and took back the babe, stepping out of the way.

Leaning his chest against the side of the bench, he reached for the painfully shy three-year-old. She came willingly and hid her face in his neck, thumb in her mouth. "Pet, there's no reason to be so shy. Lisa is a nice lady and we're all going to have fun today."

Petunia didn't answer, but she did lift her head off his shoulder to peer at Lisa where she stood next to him. He turned to Lisa, who gave Petunia an encouraging smile, and nodded toward where the three older girls were waiting patiently by the tree. "After you."

Lisa led the way, Jared propped on her hip. He couldn't stop the smile that tugged on the corners of his mouth as he watched her walk in front of him. She looked so comfortable and at ease with Jared.

And to think she told me she didn't have experience with children.

In her very first letter, she had made a point of saying that she knew nothing about raising children but that she would try her hardest to do a good job. And so far in just the several hours she had spent with the girls and Jared, he could see she was serious. Not only was she serious, she was doing a good job at it.

On top of that, Lisa and all the children except Petunia had made an instant connection. It had nearly been love at first sight. It was such a relief since he wasn't sure how they would take to a new woman in their lives, especially the older girls, who could still vividly remember their mother. He knew, though, that Petunia was young enough and enough time had passed that Cherish was doubtlessly becoming a foggy memory for her. It saddened him to realize that Cherish would eventually just turn into a name and someone they all talked about, but there was no way for him to change it. Now he just had to hope that Petunia would eventually warm up to Lisa.

As soon as he set the small girl down, she scampered over to Iris and hid behind her blue skirt. Opening the basket, Eli pulled out the large blanket he had packed. As he traced his thumb along a seam, remembering all the hours Cherish had spent making it, pain knocked lightly on his heart. Not wanting to dwell on it, he unfolded the quilt with a snap. He attempted to get it all smoothed out with one flourish, but it didn't work.

A tug on the other end brought his gaze up from the blanket corners in his hands. Lisa snatched one corner of the other side and pulled it straight, all the while still balancing Jared on her hip. She did the same with the last messy corner, and the blanket was smooth.

Lisa glanced up at him, and a smile sparkled in her eyes. He gave her a small, closed mouth grin in response. Waving the other girls over, she settled down on the blanket and plopped Jared gently into her lap.

Eli quickly pulled out the dishes of food from the basket. There was a variety since he'd asked Granny Lola, the older lady who ran the town boardinghouse and restaurant, to surprise him.

"Is that cherry pie?" Iris asked, eyes wide with glee as she pointed to the dish nearest her.

"It looks like it." Lisa leaned closer to inspect the gooeyness peeking out of the cracks in the golden crust. "Is it your favorite?"

"Yes!" Iris bounced slightly.

He looked up with a smile and raised brow. "Well, you

have to eat lunch first before you can have any pie, young lady. Let's see what else Granny Lola packed for us." He lifted the towel on the bowl closest to him. "This one is shredded roast beef. What's in the one beside you, Cinthy?"

"It's a loaf of bread," she chirped.

Lisa tucked a wriggling Jared a little closer, then leaned over to grab the stack of plates beside Eli and flipped up the towel on the final dish. "I reckon this is potato salad. I've never seen it made like that before."

As she sat back up, Eli peered in the dish that was filled with potato chunks, chopped ham, tiny pieces of celery, and sliced boiled eggs mixed in a creamy whiteness. "Yes, it's potato salad. Granny Lola has a special recipe that's different from any other I've had before, and it's really good."

"Well, since we have the beef and a loaf of bread, we can make sandwiches," Lisa suggested, picking up the loaf of bread. "You'll have to cut it though since I can't do it safely with Jared in my lap. I don't want to let him go since we're so close to the creek."

"Of course." He took the loaf and sliced enough for them all to have a sandwich. She took the pieces from him and slapped the sandwiches together on the plates beside her. Jared squirmed around in her lap, yet she kept a tight hold on him as she passed a plate to each of the girls sitting around her and one to Eli.

Eli hastily made up Jared's plate with chunks of bread and the potato salad cut into smaller pieces, then took the wiggling boy from Lisa. He kept him on his knee as they both ate. Once Jared was finished, he set him on the blanket beside him, making sure to keep his leg in front of him so he couldn't crawl away.

Lisa talked with the girls as they ate, and he took the opportunity to watch her while she wasn't paying attention. She tilted her head to the side as she giggled at something Iris said, the sadness in her dark brown eyes replaced by a sparkling happiness. He didn't know the cause of that sadness, yet he hoped to find out soon. Her laugh was high yet husky, and her full lips parted in a wide smile, making her freckles bunch on her cheeks. She had a willowy sort of build and appeared to be a little too thin like she hadn't eaten properly in a while. The jet black hair that had been coiled at the nape of her neck the day before was pinned back in the same style again. He couldn't help but wonder how long it was and what she looked like with it all down.

She glanced over and caught him looking, and she smiled curiously at him. His mouth curved into a grin, and she turned her attention back to Cinthy.

Lisa looked so different from Cherish. They were nearly opposites. Where Lisa was dark, willowy, and thin, Cherish had been light, on the short side, and filled out. Cherish hadn't been heavyset, yet birthing children had left its mark on her.

What would Cherish think of Lisa?

Cherish had been a friend to all, so Eli knew the answer to that question.

"Lisa, can we play a game?" Iris's voice pulled him abruptly from his thoughts before they had a chance to pull him completely under. Thankfully, enough time had passed that thinking of Cherish didn't hurt as much anymore, but there was always still a throb in his heart when he allowed himself to get engulfed in the memories.

"Of course, hunny. What would you like to play?"

"The Key of the King's Garden. That is if you know how to play it."

"Aah, yes! I loved to play that with my brothers when I was a little girl." Lisa nodded enthusiastically with a big smile, but he caught the sadness that flickered through her eyes as she mentioned her family. "Alright, everyone sit in a circle."

The girls circled around her, and she scooted back into the empty space they left her. She glanced over at him, the question in her eyes nearly as loud as her spoken words. "Eli, will you join us?"

"I'd love to!" He scooped up Jared and sat him in the center of the circle before he squished himself into the gap Tulip and Lisa made for him on Lisa's right side. His hand accidentally brushed against her thigh, the touch sending the tiniest of a spark up his arm. He froze, expecting her to stiffen or at least shoot him an unpleasant look, but she just continued like it had never happened.

Thank goodness I didn't upset her!

Able to breathe again, he watched as Lisa pointed to Cinthy, telling her to begin the game. Eyes roaming mysteriously over the rest of them, the ever dramatic Cinthy leaned toward Iris on her right and made her voice deeper as she said, "I sell you the Key to the King's Garden."

Giggling, Iris looked down at Petunia, and continued the game. "I sell you the bag that held the Key to the King's Garden."

"I thell you the thring on the bag that held the Key to the King'th Garden." Petunia nodded, her lisp floating in the air. Turning shy eyes to Lisa on her right, she whispered, "Your turn, Litha."

"I sell you the twine that made the string on the bag that held the Key to the King's Garden." Lisa slowly reached an arm around Petunia, and pulled her close. Petunia surprisingly let her and even cuddled into Lisa's side, finally at ease with her. Lisa's brown eyes found Eli's, and her face was lit with joy.

Returning her smile, he added to the sentence circulating through the group. "I sell you the flax that made the twine that made the string on the bag that held the Key to the King's Garden."

"I sell you the ground that grew the flax that made the twine that made the string on the bag that held the Key to the King's Garden," Tulip exclaimed after sitting silently in thought for a moment. "Now, finish the sentence Cinthy."

"I sell you the horse that plowed the ground that grew the flax that made the twine that made the string on the bag that held the Key to the King's Garden." Cinthy waved out her hand with a flourish with the last word, making everyone laugh. "Can we play again?"

Lisa glanced up at him, one brow slightly raised. He nodded, then said, "Iris, you start this time."

They continued another whole round, but they had barely gotten halfway through the third when Jared began to screech. Eli scooped him up, calming him down. Petunia yawned from where she now laid with her head in Lisa's lap.

"I think it's naptime for these two," he laughed.

"I'll start picking up everything." Lisa gently slid Petunia off her lap and stood up. With the girls' help, she quickly had all of the picnic things gathered, in the basket, and tucked back behind the buckboard seat.

She took a nodding off Jared from Eli as he lifted

Petunia onto the bench. The older girls clambered into the wagon bed, quietly bickering about who would sit where. Grinning with a small shake of her head, Lisa handed Jared off to Eli as he assisted her up onto the seat beside Petunia. Once on her lap again, Jared snuggled his face into Lisa's chest with a contented sigh.

Almost like a slap to the cheek, it dawned on Eli that should things work out with Lisa, she would be the only mother Jared ever knew. The thought took Eli's breath away, yet at the same time filled his chest with a sense of calm. From what he'd seen so far, he really liked Lisa and the feeling was mutual with his children. He still wanted to keep Cherish's memory alive for them as much as possible, but he didn't want to live in the past. Lisa appeared to be the gate to their future, and if she was willing, Eli would stride down the path with her by his side.

Walking around to the rear of the buckboard, he closed the back and latched the door in place. He tousled Tulip's loose, messy curls as he strode past. He grabbed the side of the bench and pulled himself up and onto the seat. It shifted under his weight and Petunia slid toward him, but she scooted back over to Lisa. Petunia leaned her head on Lisa's arm and popped her thumb into her mouth with a sigh. Lisa stared down at the curly head propped against her with a mixture of happiness and wonder.

"If you don't mind, I was going to make a quick stop at Granny Lola's to give her back her dishes." Eli unwound the reins from the brake, then snapped them over the horses' backs, putting them in motion.

"I don't mind," she answered, glancing over at him.

"Abby also agreed to watch the children for a few

hours again today so we can talk and figure out what we want to do. We can swing by her house and then I'll take you over to my little farm and show you around."

"That would be nice," she said, her words nearly whispered. Finding her lowered voice odd, he turned toward her and found both Jared and Petunia asleep against her. Lisa smiled over at him, her dark eyes twinkling with bliss and her cheeks a rosy pink. "They sure fall asleep fast."

"Sometimes, but not always," he whispered, his voice pitching lower. They shared a smile, and she leaned down to brush a gentle kiss on top of Jared's strawberry blonde tufts of hair. Looking back toward the road in front of them, Eli released a contented sigh.

Chapter

Six

L ISA GRIPPED ELI'S HAND AS HE HELPED her off the buckboard in front of a small house with white siding and a porch that took up the length of the front of the house. Eli stood patiently at her side as she scanned the yard, taking in everything with eager eyes. It was her first time seeing it all, and her stomach swirled with excited nerves as she realized it could be her new home.

A decent-sized brown barn stood just behind the house. The sound of a pig's snorts and the distinct clucking of what sounded like quite a few chickens scurried through the air from beyond the barn. Turning to look at the other side of the cozy-looking, square house, she saw a cleared field in the far corner of the property. The top of a tree swished back and forth in the breeze behind the house.

A gentle touch to her elbow brought her gaze back to the handsome man standing beside her. He smiled gently as he asked, "Would you like to look around outside first?"

"Yes. It would be nice to stretch my legs after sitting

all that time through the picnic and then the ride here." Lisa watched him out of the corner of her eye as he led her toward the barn. She'd been considerably surprised when she met him since he wasn't what she expected.

She wasn't entirely sure what she was expecting, but it sure wasn't an incredibly good-looking man with a deep, rumbling voice that reminded her of distant thunder. She let herself fall a few steps behind him and studied his figure. He was built like an upside-down triangle—he had broad shoulders, was narrow at the hip, and his legs were long. If he hadn't told her about his previous work in the church, she would have never guessed that his muscular arms and thick chest had stood behind a pulpit.

But, of course, a preacher doesn't have to be plain or ugly.

They came to a stop in front of the barn, and she pushed all triangle-comparing thoughts out of her head. He swung open the tall, wooden door, and gestured for her to step in. The scent of fresh hay tickled her nose, and the low moo of a cow echoed toward her.

It only took her eyes a second to adjust to the dimmer light. She saw two empty stalls on her left and another empty one on the right, but the fourth was housing a black and white spotted cow. Tipping her head up, she spotted a loft nearly half full of hay.

Eli stepped around her and walked toward the lonely cow. She followed, reaching out and letting her fingertips skim across the top of the stall door on her right as she went past. He glanced at her as she slid up beside him. He rubbed the top of the cow's head, and she couldn't help but giggle when she saw the cow close its eyes and huff out a breath that almost sounded like a sigh.

"She's a little spoiled," Eli laughed with a shrug.

"What's her name?" Lisa asked, reaching out a tentative hand to stroke the cow's back. Since she'd grown up in town and purchased everything from the mercantile, her family never had any livestock, so this was completely new territory for her.

"Don't be scared. She won't hurt you." He gently grabbed her hand and rested it on the cow when she tucked her palm back into the folds of her skirt, taking a step back. "The girls named her Milky."

"Seems fitting." She lifted one side of her mouth in a smile, Eli's hand still covering hers. His touch sent a warmth through her arm all the way to her chest where it stayed and filled her with an unfamiliar, yet pleasant emotion.

"We best continue on with the outside part of the tour so we can get inside the house and figure things out," he chuckled.

"You're right. Lead the way."

They walked back out of the door they had entered, then circled around the right side of the barn. They paused momentarily at the chicken coop which was quite large. Roughly twenty or so chickens pecked around the ground. Occasionally, one of them let out a loud squawk or darted at one of its relatives.

"The white ones are for meat and the gray ones are the laying hens. There's also one rooster," Eli explained as they continued through the feathered creatures toward the back of the barn.

As they rounded the corner, the snorts she had heard earlier became louder. With a flourish very much like Cinthy's during their game of The Key to the King's Garden,

Eli pointed to a mud-filled pen with a fat, light gray pig in it. The pig snuffled along the ground, completely ignoring them.

Eli rested his foot on the bottom rung of the fence, putting his elbows on the top one. Lisa followed suit and leaned against the fence beside him but kept both feet on the ground. She expected to feel out of place or overwhelmed by all the new things surrounding her, but instead she found herself comfortable and strangely at home. Glancing over, she watched his excited expression as he said, "She is going to have a litter of piglets in a few weeks and then I'll have quite a few plump pigs to sell this fall."

"I'm sure the girls will love the piglets."

"That they will," he sighed, then abruptly pushed off the fence. "I'm sure you don't want to stand here looking at a big ole fat pig all day when there's a whole house for you to explore."

They walked silently back through the yard, but when she caught sight of the cleared field again, she asked, "Is that where you're going to plant the alfalfa?"

"Yes." He nodded, looking at the field as he tucked his hands into the pockets of his dark brown pants. "I plowed last week, and I'll plant the seed here in about a week or two."

"Is this your first time growing alfalfa?" She reached out and touched a bud on the azalea bush by the porch steps. It reminded her of the azaleas that had surrounded Fullerton Manor and an ache settled low in her stomach.

"I've always had a garden, but never anything larger. So, yes, this is my first time." He gestured for her to walk up the steps ahead of him. A comfy-looking swing hung from the porch roof to the left. It appeared to be well used if the chipping white paint on it was any telltale, yet it seemed to be built sturdily. Eli opened the front door, bringing her attention back to him. "I didn't show you the garden bed, but it's on the other side of the house in the backyard."

They stepped into the house, and he sat his tan hat on a tiny table by the door. He turned to her as she glanced around. "It's not much, but it's home."

It was small, but it felt spacious and large compared to the room in the boardinghouse attic she had lived in for more months than she cared to remember. Out of the corner of her eye, she caught Eli shifting nervously on his feet as she glided over to the dark red settee in the center of the room. Gently running her fingers over the striped cushion along the back of it, Lisa peered around the rest of the room, taking in the sturdy coffee table between the settee and large fireplace with a gray stone mantel. A rocking chair sat in the right corner of the room with a pink and purple quilt draped over the back of it. The sun shone through half-opened, lacy, white curtains on a window beside the table where Eli had put his hat.

Everything had a feminine touch, making the fact that this was another woman's house all the more obvious. She had already known she would be picking up the pieces Cherish left behind, but it sank in deeper as she glanced around. A heavy weight attempted to settle in her chest, yet she shoved it away, determined to make things work instead of doubting herself.

Feeling the nervous tension seeping out of Eli where he still stood in the doorway, she turned to him with a smile. "It's lovely, Eli. Cozy, warm, and very much a home."

His shoulders drooped as he let out a sigh. "You've only seen the living room, I'll show you the rest."

Eli took off toward a hall behind her on his left. She quickly followed him, her boot heels clicking lightly on the smooth wooden floor. Two bedroom doors met her, one on each side of the whitewashed walls of the hall. He swung open the one on the left and pointed inside. "This is the girls' room. Tulip and Cinthy sleep in the bed on the right, and Iris and Pet in the other."

Lisa leaned in the doorway, taking in two large, feather beds on either side of the room with a nightstand stuck between them. Lacy, white curtains just like the ones in the living room adorned the window above the nightstand. A table sat to the left side of the door, while a dark brown wardrobe stood tall on the opposite side.

The door on the other side of the hall clicked open and she slowly spun around on her heel. Eli gestured to the interior with a small smile. "This is my room. Jared bunks with me right now, but as soon as he's old enough, he's going in there with the girls."

She slid up beside him and looked through the open door. Her eyes immediately went to the crib and chair along the wall, but as she slowly scanned the rest of the room, her stomach dropped slightly. A bulky, red quilt covered bed sat in the far corner along the left wall, taking up nearly half the room.

Of course there's only one bed. Why would there be a separate one just for you?

Quickly swallowing down the awkward realization that should they marry, they would share a bed, Lisa swiveled back around to look at Eli. He gazed at her expectantly with a question in his eyes. Summoning a pleasant expression, she pulled her lips into a shy smile as she quietly said, "It's all very nice, Eli."

"I'm glad you think so." Relief swept across his face. "The kitchen is the only thing left. We can sit in there and talk with a cup of coffee if you like."

"That would be nice." She nodded then followed him back down the short hall.

Eli led Lisa into the kitchen and gestured for her to sit at the table as he walked over to the cabinet next to the door. He pulled out two coffee cups and set them on the counter below the cabinet. Glancing over at Lisa as he filled the coffee pot with water at the sink, he watched her dark eyes flick from corner to corner of the room. She gazed at the stove next to him, then stole a slow peek at the back door farther to Eli's right where another cabinet sat. The clunk of the coffee pot on the stove echoed loudly through the tense, silent room, and he cringed at the sound.

I really need to start some sort of conversation before this gets even more awkward than it already is.

He cleared his throat, and she jumped slightly, turning to look at him as he leaned his back against the sink. "I'm glad Petunia finally warmed up to you today."

"She's such a little sweetheart." A bright smile lit up Lisa's face. "I knew her shyness would eventually disappear. She just needed some time. I used to be painfully shy when I was her age, so I know what it's like."

The awkward tension dissolved out of the room as the

sound of Lisa's slow drawl swirled through the air.

"You don't seem like the type who would've been shy as a child." He laughed lightly, stepping across the room toward her. The chair he pulled out from the table squeaked across the floor quietly as he turned it around and straddled the seat, resting his arms on the top of the back.

"The only way to keep up with my older brothers was to quit being shy, so my shyness was very short-lived." She smiled, then quickly glanced out the window by the table before meeting his eyes again. "My brothers and I were very close."

"It must have been hard for you to leave them to come out here then." A bubbling sound came from the stove and he jumped up to get the coffee before it burned. He poured the black liquid into the cups on the counter, peering over at her. She stared down at her folded hands on the table. His stomach fell with dread and regret.

Did I say something wrong?

"I don't have any family left in Tuscaloosa," she whispered as he put a cup in front of her.

"I'm so sorry." He watched her above the brim of his cup, trying to read her expression, but she kept her face tilted down as she took a drink. He didn't know how badly Alabama was affected by the war, but he had a feeling it was one, if not the main reason she decided to leave. "What happened? That is unless it's too painful to look back on."

"No, it's alright. It would actually be nice to talk about it. I've been holding it all in for so long." She leaned back in her chair with a deep, shuddering sigh, eyes glittering with tears. "I guess I'll have to start at the beginning so it'll make sense. It might be a long story."

"I don't mind listening. And take your time. I know it's hard to talk about loved ones who passed away." He stood up and turned his chair back around to sit in it the right way. He leaned his elbow on the table, swirling his coffee in his mug.

"My father was a Latin professor at the University of Alabama, but he quit to join the war. He and my three brothers all enlisted as soon as the call for troops came to Tuscaloosa. My oldest brother, Will, was killed in the Battle of Rich Mountain. Matthew and Louis died roughly a year apart in the Battle of New Bern and the Battle of Dover. And then an infected wound took Papa at the beginning of '64."

She wiped away the errant tears streaming down her cheeks, and he wanted to comfort her somehow but didn't know what to do. The raw pain on her face tore his heart in two. Her shoulders quivered as she took a deep breath and continued. "Almost a year ago, Mama got sick and she slipped away before I could do anything. After that, it was just my mammy and me in a too quiet house. Mammy had actually taken care of not only myself and my brothers, but my mother, too, so she was quite old. At the end of September last year, she got sick just like Mama and passed away. Two days later, the bank took Fullerton Manor since I hadn't been able to pay the taxes. Ever since then, I've lived in a little boardinghouse where I scrubbed laundry and waited tables for my room and board."

And here I thought it was hard losing just Cherish!

"I really don't know what to say," he whispered, emotion clogging his throat.

Lisa looked up at him with sorrow-filled eyes. "You don't have to. You know what it feels like to lose someone you love with your whole heart, and that's comfort enough." She smiled sadly at him, cleaning the last of her tears off her face. "Now you know all about me, so tell me about yourself."

"Well, my story is similar, yet very different from yours." He rubbed the back of his neck, the pain he kept buried slowly coming to the surface as he started his own tale. "At the beginning of June last year, Cherish went into labor, and things were fine at first. Right after Jared was born, she began to hemorrhage and there was nothing either Abby or Doc Adams could do to stop it. She was gone within the hour. Before she died, she made me promise to remarry for the children."

His voice cracked and he couldn't continue. Tears blurred everything in front of him and he desperately fought to press down the emotional whirlwind in his heart. A rough, yet tender hand pressed against his on the table. Glancing up, Eli saw Lisa peering at him with new tears shimmering in her soulful eyes. He turned his hand over, and squeezed her fingers in his with a grateful smile.

"Well, that's enough of all that sad stuff. Let's talk about what we're going to do." She grinned lightly, taking her hand back.

"Alright. You've met my children, seen my house, and heard part of my story, so what do you think?" he asked. His question sounded strange after he spoke it, and his cheeks burned in embarrassment. She laughed lightly, breaking the sadness still hanging in the air.

"If you don't mind me being blunt, I think we'll be a good fit." Lisa plopped her chin on her hand, squinting her eyes slightly at him.

"So do I." His cheeks split in a grin. "Will you marry

me and help me raise my little ones?"

"Yes. Yes, I will." She nodded, a grin tweaking up the corners of her lips.

Eli's heart seemed to come clean out of his chest and float to the ceiling as happiness filled his ribcage. If he were a small boy, he would've clapped from joy, but he satisfied himself with a wide, nearly painful smile instead.

Chapter

SEVEN

THE NEXT DAY, LISA PUSHED HER HEEL off the floor, setting the rocking chair in Eli's living room into motion. A sleeping Jared lay curled against her chest, his warm breath tickling her neck. Petunia's brown curls hung off the settee where she was napping, her petite form curved into itself. Quiet sucking sounds came from her where she nursed her thumb, eyes closed peacefully. Iris sat on the other end of the settee darning a sock, gaze intent on her work. A small squeal drifted in from outside where Tulip and Cinthy were playing while Eli tended to some chores in the barn.

How does it already feel like home?

School had ended the week before Lisa's arrival which meant Cinthy and Iris were now home during the morning and afternoon. Lisa realized how much responsibility was on Iris's shoulders, so she walked the short distance from Jack and Bella's house to help ease the nine-year-old's burden.

"Lisa?" Iris asked quietly, looking over with bright

blue eyes so different from Eli's dark gray ones.

She must have inherited them from her mother.

"Hmm?"

"Are you excited about the wedding on Saturday?"

Lisa wasn't sure how to answer.

How do you explain a marriage of convenience to a little girl?

"A little I guess." She shrugged her left shoulder, hoping the answer would satisfy Iris. "What are you going to wear?"

"My Sunday dress." Iris set down the sock in her hand in her lap and her eyes widened in excitement. "It's the prettiest dress I have."

"What color is it?" Lisa smiled, enjoying the girl's obvious pride in the dress.

"It's light green with little white flowers all over it. Do you have a wedding dress to wear?"

"Unfortunately, I don't. Before I came here, I had to sell my house and almost everything in it, including my mother's wedding dress. I had always planned to wear it on my wedding day." Lisa looked past Iris, staring off into the distance at the memory. Parting with her mother's wedding dress had almost been harder than losing the house, but she was grateful to still have her mother's ring.

"Do you have anything else besides the outfit you're wearing right now?" Iris's hushed question brought Lisa's attention back to her.

"I was able to save one of my favorite dresses. I'm going to wear it, but sadly, it's not white."

"Not everyone gets married in white. Miss Bella didn't." Iris laid the darning on the settee and walked over to Lisa's side. She rested her hands on the empty armrest of the rocking chair.

"She didn't?"

"Nope. Her dress was light blue. It was her Founder's Day dress from last year. It makes her look like a princess. She let me try it on one time, but, of course, it's too big for me." Iris explained, eyes sparkling. "What color is your dress?"

"A dark copper." Lisa's lips turned up, her cheeks pushing toward her eyes. "I'll have to ask Bella to borrow her iron so I can get all the wrinkles out."

"I can't wait to see it!"

"I can't wait to wear it again!" Lisa laughed. "I haven't worn it since the last dance my mother hosted at our house, and that was years ago."

"Can you remember it?"

"Oh, yes." Lisa gazed at the floor, letting the happy memory sweep her away as she told the tale. "There were close to fifty people at that dance. All the women had on the prettiest dresses. Back home, women wear crinoline under their skirts so they are big and full. The drawing room was filled with bright colors, tasty smelling food, and cheerful laughter. I always loved the dances Mama hosted. She would let me help plan everything, and then I would sit in the kitchen and watch Sally, our cook, fix all the food. I would get a new dress made just for that night, and then dance till I thought my feet would fall off."

"Sounds like that was a wonderful night," a deep voice rumbled from the front door.

Lisa jumped, exclaiming, "Land's sake!"

Glancing over, she saw Eli standing in the doorway with a wide grin on his face. She shook her head with a small smile as she said, "I didn't hear you come in."

"Sorry, I didn't mean to scare you." He tossed his hat on the table near him.

"It's alright."

"You must have come from a rather rich family if your mother hosted dances like that." He stepped over and bent to look at Jared nestled against her before turning to do the same with Petunia.

"We lived comfortably since Papa was one of the most senior professors at the University, but we weren't exactly rich. We had a lot of friends, and once a year Mama would throw a large dance," she explained. She tilted her head to the side, peering up at him as he moved back to her side. "What does your father do for a living?"

Her eyes left his face as she bit her bottom lip, instantly regretting the words as they left her mouth.

Please, let his father still be alive. I'd hate to cause him any more pain by bringing up another dead loved one.

"My parents run the largest mercantile in Carson City. They've had the store since '54 when we moved to Carson from Boonville, Missouri, my hometown." He smoothed a palm over the top of Iris's straight, strawberry blonde hair.

"How long have you lived in Half Circle Creek?"

"Since '55 when Cherish and I got married. Her family was from here, and I met her when they came to Carson City on business."

"I know I'm probably pestering you with all these questions, but does her family still live here?" Lisa gently rubbed Jared's back as he shifted in his sleep with a quiet snort.

"You're not pestering. I asked the first question after

all," he laughed lightly, crossing his arms over his broad chest. "And, no, her family is no longer living here. Both of her parents passed away in '59, and her older brother is a sea captain on the East Coast."

"Oh." She fell silent, pondering on what he just told her. Glancing back up at him, she asked one last question. "How often do you see your family?"

"My parents, two younger brothers, and their families come up every year two weeks before Christmas and stay through New Years."

"That's nice. Too bad they can't visit more often."

"Grandpa can't leave the store that often and Grammy doesn't like to take long trips," Iris explained with a shrug.

"I can understand that!" Lisa laughed. "Long trips are no fun, especially when they're by stagecoach."

"Iris, why don't you go play with your sisters outside? I need to talk to Lisa about the wedding for a moment." He gestured toward the front door with a tilt of his chin.

"Sure thing, Pa." Iris quietly walked across the room to the still-open door. Right before she strode out, she sent them a mysterious grin over her shoulder.

What was that look for?

Eli's brows creased for a moment, but with a small shake of his head, he looked down at Lisa again. "I talked to Pastor Carmichael this morning, and he said he can easily perform the service on Saturday morning for us. I explained to him how we agreed to have a very small ceremony and nothing else. He understood, but asked who were going to be the witnesses. I thought we could have Abe and Abby do it for us."

"Yes, that would be nice, but could we maybe invite

Jack and Bella, too?" Lisa scooted up in the rocking chair, a small cringe on her face. Her backside and legs had gone numb several minutes before and her right foot was beginning to tingle.

"Of course." He nodded, then reached out and took Jared from her. The baby surprisingly stayed asleep. "Let me take him. I'm sure you're stiff from sitting in that chair for this long. It's not a very comfortable seat, and I've regretted sitting in it for too long more times than I care to remember."

"Thanks." She slowly stood, her legs stiff under her weight. She took a step away from the chair and swayed as the feeling came back to her limbs. Eli's hand shot out to steady her. She thanked him with a small smile, then asked, "Do you want me to come over and help get the girls ready on Saturday morning before the wedding?"

"No, there isn't any need. Iris and I do a pretty fair job of getting everyone ready in a reasonable amount of time." He grinned, clearly proud of his little brood.

"Alright then. Now, I just have to make sure I'm not late."

"Are you still sure you want to go through with this?" Eli asked, brows scrunched as his eyes scanned her face.

"Yes, I'm sure." She reached out and squeezed his shoulder. "I really like your family."

I don't know how I got so lucky to end up with these wonderful people.

"Thank you for doing this. I can tell the girls already love you." He smiled and grabbed her hand lightly in his.

"You're more than welcome," she laughed lightly.

Chapter

EIGHT

"**I**RIS, WHERE'S TULIP'S OTHER SHOE?" ELI SHOUTED across the house. Tulip sat at the table, dressed, haired fixed, and all ready to go except for the missing boot. He still needed to change Jared and fix Petunia's hair, and they were supposed to leave in less than ten minutes. He wanted to get to the church before any of the few guests they invited arrived. "Iris, did you hear me?"

"Yes, sir. I can't find it!" She ran out of their bedroom, ribbon-tied pigtail braids flying out on either side of her head.

"Did you look under the bed?"

"Yep."

"In the wardrobe?"

"Yep," she repeated. Except this time, it was accompanied by a bobbing nod.

"How about under the nightstand?" He sighed, his shoulders drooping.

So much for being able to get everyone ready in a reasonable time.

Jared normally slept like a rock at night and nearly nothing would wake him except for hunger, yet he'd fussed most of the night. A tooth was the culprit. Eli had spent practically the whole night either rocking him or pacing the floor until he'd finally just tucked the baby into bed with him and they'd both dozed off. Waking up that morning had been a struggle, and Eli had accidentally overslept by two hours. It had been close to chaos trying to get the girls fed and ready quickly.

"I forgot to look there!" She spun around, her green dress swirling widely about her legs. A few seconds later, a muffled yell proclaimed, "I found it!"

Iris's boot heels clacked across the floor as she hurried back into the kitchen. She tossed him the boot which he deftly caught. Stepping up to Petunia's chair, she lifted the brush in her other hand and made quick work of fixing the smaller girl's hair.

"Thanks, Iris." He glanced up from where he knelt in front of Tulip, tying her boot laces. Iris nodded, then scooped Jared up out of his highchair, which was beside Cinthy. She strode back past him and toward the living room, but Eli stopped her with a question. "What are you doing with Jared?"

"I'm going to get him ready for you. You still have to get the buckboard hooked up and if you don't hurry, we're going to be late," she exclaimed with a shrug before continuing on her way.

"Thanks again, Iris," he called after her, shaking his head.

"No problem." Her voice came from the other side of

the wall in his room.

She's so much like her mother.

"Alright, Tulip, you're all ready and so are you, Pet." He slowly stood to his feet, glancing at his three daughters sitting patiently at the table. "I want you three to sit here quietly while I go get the buckboard hooked up."

"Yeth, Pa." Petunia answered as Cinthy, who had been one of the first to be ready, and Tulip nodded.

He strode out the back door and rushed toward the barn. Opening the barn door, he swiftly hitched his two horses to the parked buckboard in the center of the aisle. His hands trembled as the nerves he'd been too busy to pay any mind to slowly but surely reared their ugly head in the pit of his stomach. He tightly gripped the side of the wagon bed, resting his forehead on the sturdy wood as he took a long, deep breath.

Everything's going to be alright.

But everything wasn't. He was about to marry a woman he'd known for less than a week. Granted, she had been relatively open about her past with him, but he still didn't really know her.

This new step in his life scared him more than he cared to admit. A drop of sweat trickled down his spine, making him shiver. He'd said 'I do' to another and slipped a ring onto a womanly finger before, so he knew there wasn't much to it. But this time was different.

Very different.

He'd loved Cherish, and all he felt for Lisa was what was probably the beginning of a friendship. Nothing more. Just thinking of Cherish reminded him of why he was even going through with all of this.

I'm keeping my promise, Rish.

Lifting his head, he clenched his hands into tight fists until they quit trembling. He stepped up to the front of the buckboard and grabbed the bridle on the horse closest to him. Gently tugging them forward, he moved the buckboard out into the front yard. Stopping them with a quiet 'whoa', he walked through the front door just in time to see Iris carrying a newly dressed Jared back into the living room.

"Is everyone ready?" He grabbed his hat off the table by the door.

"Yes, I think so. Here you take Jared, and I'll go get the girls." She darted into the kitchen. Eli shifted Jared onto his left arm and patted his right pants pocket with his free hand.

Good, it's still there.

Lisa had given him her mother's wedding band for the ceremony. She wanted to use it instead of a new one since it was special, and he was scared he'd lose it somehow before he had a chance to put it on her finger.

Jared patted a chubby fist against Eli's shirt, drawing his attention back to the baby. He looked up at him with bright blue eyes and a drooling, toothy smile. Shaking his head with a grin, Eli brushed a kiss on the boy's head.

"Well, Jared, aren't they the prettiest little blossoms you've ever seen?" Eli asked, using Cherish's pet name for their daughters, as the girls walked back into the living room. All of them were dressed in their best and their hair was prettily smoothed and fixed. "All of you turn around so I can see the full effect."

All four of the girls spun, an assortment of green, pink, blue, and purple skirts swirling, boot heels clicking on the floor.

How did I end up with such beautiful children?

They continued to spin, and he called out, "Alright that's enough. We don't want you to get all dizzy. Anyways, we need to get a move on it. We can't be late."

With a serious nod, yet mysterious sparkle in her eye, Iris grabbed one of Petunia's hands and led her and the other girls past him out the door. Slapping on his hat, Eli followed, making sure to close the door behind him.

Within minutes, they were all in the buckboard–the youngest ones tucked safely in the back and Cinthy on the seat with him–and headed down the road. As they drove along, he noticed several wagons going in the same direction as him toward the church.

That's strange.

Eli pulled the buckboard to a halt in the church yard, eyes flitting to each parked wagon. It looked like nearly a quarter of the town was there.

What is going on?

Spotting Pastor Carmichael near the front of the church, Eli wound the reins around the brake. He glanced back at the children as he climbed down, saying, "You all stay here. I'll be right back."

He slipped through the crowd, passing women carrying plates of food which they took toward the back of the church building where tables were set up. Pastor Carmichael's seventeen-year-old daughter, Lotta, swept past with a grin. Finally reaching the pastor's side, he gripped the middle-aged man's shoulder as he leaned in close and quietly questioned, "What is going on? Abby, Abe, Jack, and Bella were the only ones supposed to be here today."

"I know, but Abby, a few of her friends, Bella, and my wife wanted to give you and Lisa something special and not just a simple ceremony." The pastor slowly smiled. "I tried to talk them out of it, but you know what it's like when a woman sets her mind to do something."

Eli didn't know whether to be pleased or angry. His first wedding had been a big ordeal and it hadn't bothered him since he was too in love to care how things were done. Now he was having to do it all over again without the love, and it was a little overwhelming. Yet he found himself more worried about what Lisa would think about the fuss being made over them than anything else.

Hopefully it won't upset her.

"Oh, Eli, there you are!" Abby exclaimed, striding up, a bouquet of flowers in the crook of her elbow as Pastor Carmichael slipped away to talk to someone calling for him. "I hope you aren't mad that we wanted to surprise you and Lisa."

"No, it was just the last thing I expected." Eli blew out a breath as he peered around the full church yard. "I just hope Lisa doesn't mind."

"Bella is going to tell her before they get here, so she isn't completely shocked." Abby looked past him at his buckboard. "Your oldest daughter is a pretty good secret keeper."

"Iris was in on all of this?" His jaw dropped as he glanced over his shoulder and caught Iris's eye. She gave him a smile, her cheeks blushing.

"Bella accidentally slipped while Iris was in the room a few days ago when we first started planning, so we told her what we were going to do." Abby nodded, then turned toward the open church door. "Well, I'll talk to you later. I need to go put these flowers where they belong."

"Alright." He tossed her a wave and wove his way back through the crowd to his wagon. Reaching up for Cinthy, he proclaimed, "We best get inside."

Taking a shaky breath, Lisa traced the fingertips of her right hand over her bare collar bone above the off-shoulder neckline of her dress. It felt strange to not be wearing her necklace. Within the hour, her beloved mother's wedding band would be adorning her finger instead of resting on her bosom.

Is every bride this nervous?

The dark copper silk of her skirt quivered around her as she trembled all over with nerves. Lips pursed, she released a deep breath, her stomach doing a tipsy turn. Her face heated as nausea crept up her throat.

She never thought she would get married, let alone to a man she'd only known for a week. It was nerve-racking, terrifying, and exciting all at the same time. But the main thing that kept swirling through her mind was whether or not they could eventually fall in love. As a child and young woman, she'd watched her parents, and she wanted a love like they had shared. Yet she wasn't sure if an affection like that could grow from a marriage of convenience.

Dipping her fingers in the cool water-filled bowl in front of her on the small table, she swiped the wetness on the back of her neck. A small drop fell on the edge of her puffed sleeve along her bare shoulder, darkening the fabric slightly. Her attempt to cool herself failed, and she hastily pressed one hand to her queasy stomach as her other palm fell to the table.

No, you can't get sick.

Swallowing loudly in her quiet, borrowed room, she closed her eyes, breathing slowly, yet deeply. Slowly but surely, the nausea faded and she could breathe normally again. A knock rattled the closed door as Bella's voice drifted through the wood. "Lisa, are you almost ready? We need to leave really soon."

"I'm as ready as I can be," Lisa answered, her voice coming out wobbly.

"Are you alright?"

"Yes, I'm fine." She glanced at herself in the mirror, and the pale face staring back at her didn't look like someone who was fine.

"Can I come in for a moment? I need to tell you something."

"Of course. The door's open." The knob turned and the door slowly swung into the room. Clad in a light blue dress trimmed in black lace, Bella peered up into Lisa's face, her expression going from happy to worried in seconds.

"Do you feel alright?" She reached out and grasped Lisa's arm lightly.

"I guess I'm just a little nervous." Lisa laughed, patting Bella's hand on her upper arm. "What was it you needed to tell me?"

"How about you sit down for a moment? You look awfully pale. I don't want you to faint." Bella led Lisa over to the edge of the bed and gently pushed her down to sit. "I know we should have told you before, but Ma, a few ladies at the church, and myself invited some of the town to the ceremony and planned a picnic for afterwards."

"Oh," Lisa whispered, not sure what to think. All her conflicting emotions were suffocating, and she just wanted to be able to come up for air.

"Please don't be mad. Even though yours and Eli's marriage is going to be different than most, we thought it would be nice to at least try and make the day special for you," Bella hastily explained as Lisa stayed silent. "If you don't want all those people there and just Ma, Pa, Jack, and me instead, I'll send Jack down to the church and he can tell everyone to leave."

"No. No, don't do that." Lisa snatched Bella's hand as she turned to leave the room. "It's fine. I don't mind having everyone there. To be honest, I've always dreamed of having a big wedding with some sort of picnic afterwards. I just didn't think I would be able to with...well, with this sort of marriage."

"You're not upset then?" Bella's light blue eyes studied her face intently.

"No, I'm not upset." Lisa patted Bella's hand that was still in her grasp. "I'm actually thankful. Despite the fact that I never thought I'd marry like this, at least now a small part of my girlhood dreams are coming true."

"I'm glad I could do that." Bella smiled, tears shimmering in her eyes. "We better get a move on it or Eli is going to think you've gotten cold feet."

Lisa nodded, standing up, her nearly forgotten nerves sweeping back in lightly. Only this time, she attempted to keep a tight rein on them, and she managed to curb the nausea from returning as she rode in Jack and Bella's buckboard to the church.

The yard in front of the small, white church was filled with roughly twelve wagons, not a person in sight. Jack assisted her down, and Abe stepped out the tall, open doorway, briskly walking up to them. Lisa shook the wrinkles out of her full bell-shaped skirt as he stopped momentarily to kiss Bella's cheek.

"You look very pretty, Lisa," Abe complimented, turning to face her.

"Thank you, sir." She ducked her chin, a nervous grin pushing up her cheeks.

"Everyone is ready inside. Since your father isn't here and I doubt you want to walk down the aisle alone, I can give you away if you want." He looked down at her with gentle eyes the same shade as Bella's.

His face blurred as tears filled Lisa's eyes. She missed her father more than normal that day since he wasn't able to be the one giving her away, so Abe's generous offer meant more than she could ever express.

"That would be lovely. Thank you." Her voice quivered as she took his offered arm. She hoped he didn't notice her palm was sweaty and that her fingers were trembling. He laid his larger hand over hers and gave it a friendly squeeze as Jack and Bella slipped into the church.

"Ready?"

Not really, but it's time.

"Yes," she whispered and they walked toward the wide open wooden door of the church.

A slow, sweet piano melody rang through the air, but she only heard it faintly as everything around her blurred and nerves buzzed through her. Knowing she would either be sick or faint, she hastily found one thing to focus on. Her eyes connected and latched hungrily onto Eli where he stood on the small platform in front of the pulpit.

He smiled gently at her, and the corners of her mouth twitched up in a halfhearted attempt at returning the gesture. She tried to keep her eyes only on his face as the gap between them narrowed, but her gaze slipped as she took in his attire.

His broad shoulders filled out a black suit coat, and a white shirt peeked out above the small opening above the half-closed jacket. The loose ends of a black string tie curled against his chest.

Her feet halted as Abe stopped in front of Eli. She glanced away from his face to look up at Abe with a tiny nod of thanks. A slow smile stretched across his cheeks as he stepped away, disappearing from sight behind her.

Eli stretched his hand toward her and she put her trembling one in his. His palm was slick against hers and her eyes darted to his. Half of his mouth twitched in a closed-mouth grin. Looking closer at him, she saw him hurriedly clench his jaw as his cheek twitched.

He's just as nervous as me!

Somehow that realization settled and calmed her shaking insides. Neither of them was sure about this, yet they were willing to try and make it work.

They turned toward the preacher, hands clasped in front of them, an arm's length of space between them. The pastor's voice seemed to drift to her from a distant corner, but he was really right next to her. With his voice ringing quietly in her ears, she held Eli's nervous, emotional gaze.

Her mouth moved to say the words required of a bride and her own southern drawl swirled around her, yet she somehow felt like she wasn't even awake. The nerves and realization of what she was doing left her numb and dazed. Eli's deep voice rumbled through her as he vowed to be tied to her till death parted them. The warm metal of a ring slipped onto the finger next to the pinky of her left hand.

He must have had Mama's ring in his pocket.

Loudly announcing them man and wife, Pastor Carmichael proclaimed, "You may kiss the bride!"

Lisa froze, eyes widening. She'd been so nervous that the kiss to seal their vows had completely slipped her mind. One of Eli's dark brows twitched as a pained look flitted through his gray eyes. Leaning closer, he brushed an extremely chaste kiss on her right cheek.

A cheer rose from the crowd in the pews, and she finally saw them as she peeked to the right. A blush warmed her cheeks as she and Eli turned their backs on the pulpit and faced the congregation quickly standing to their feet. Her hand was still in Eli's and he gave it a gentle squeeze as he glanced over at her with a smile. A small grin flashed across her face, and they walked back down the aisle hand in hand.

She squinted at the bright morning sun as they stepped out of the church. Eli led her around to the back of the church building where tables were set up with food as everyone slowly poured out of the door behind them. The crowd was soon swarming around, chatting and eating. It appeared to be a regular shindig.

Except it isn't. I just got married.

The children rushed over to them. As Eli took Jared from Iris, snuggling him close, and Petunia tugged gently on Lisa's skirt to get her attention, all her nerves slipped away like a leaf on the breeze. A sense of peace filled the vacancy left by the vanished nerves, and her gaze flitted across the five children, who she was now mother to, and her new husband. *Everything's going to be alright. I can just feel it.*

Chapter

NINE

ANDS ON HER WAIST, ELI LIFTED LISA down from the buckboard bench so they didn't wake Jared up by switching him back and forth. It had been a long day with the wedding, which lasted until nearly three in the afternoon, and now Eli was exhausted. The many hours spent behind the church had been filled with eating, laughing, dancing, and quite a bit of talking. Abby had invited them over for supper, so after returning home to let Petunia and Jared nap and get everyone changed out of their fancy clothes, they headed to the Askinglys' house. Jack and Bella had joined the crowd, and the conversation had lasted so long it was dark by the time they left. All the children had fallen asleep on the way home, and Eli hoped they would stay that way through the transfer to bed.

"I'll go put Jared in his crib and then I'll come back for Petunia," Lisa whispered to him through the darkness surrounding them like a cloak.

"Alright. I'll stay out here until you come back just in

case one of them wakes up."

A beam of moonlight fell on Lisa as she glided toward the front porch, chin tucked down as she snuggled the top of Jared's head against her cheek. The front door clicked open and five minutes or so passed before she walked back out. Her skirt rustled quietly as she made her way back to the wagon. Circling around to the rear, together they silently unlatched and opened the back.

He climbed in the wagon bed, cringing as it shifted with a loud creak under his weight. Scooting forward on his heels, he gently scooped up Petunia where she lay curled up with her head pillowed in Iris's lap. Lisa took a step closer to the bed and leaned her chest over the edge, arms outstretched. He carefully gave the small girl to her, and Lisa pulled her tightly to her. She soothingly kissed the top of her head and whispered "ssh" as Petunia stirred before Lisa pitter-pattered back into the house.

She already loves the children.

After several minutes and a few more passes between the house and wagon, he and Lisa had all five children in the house. They thankfully stayed asleep when they were tucked safely in bed, but now the house was too quiet.

A stifling silence filled the air, sweeping between Lisa and him where they stood awkwardly in the dark living room. Striding over, he lit the lamp sitting on the wide mantel above the fireplace. The room slowly glowed to life, but the light didn't chase away the tension pacing nervously between the furniture and where Lisa stood stiffly in the hall entryway.

He cleared his throat, the sound abnormally loud in silence. Running his fingers through his hair, he glanced over at her. "I was thinking about making some coffee. Would you like some?"

"Thank you, but no." She shook her head, a piece of hair slipping free from where it was pinned on top of her head. She pushed it behind her ear and out of the way. "If I drink coffee this late, I'll never be able to sleep tonight."

"Well, make yourself comfortable. I'll be in the kitchen," he stammered, his voice quivering.

"Alright." Her chin ducked in a jerky, quick nod. "I think I'll just go to bed. It's been a long day."

She swirled around on her heel and darted into the bedroom before he had a chance to say a word. The door clicked shut, and instead of the relief he expected now that she was no longer in sight, his nerves came back with a force so strong his knees nearly gave out under him.

Swiftly turning toward the kitchen, he hurried into the homey room on weak legs. Rejecting the idea of coffee, he collapsed into the nearest kitchen chair. His elbows propped on the table, he let his face drop into his hands.

She won't expect anything of me tonight, will she?

He had nearly panicked when he remembered that wedding vows were sealed with a kiss. Cherish's sunken, dull blue eyes framed in an unnaturally pale face had flashed before him, and for a moment, he had slipped back to that night. The night he'd pressed a final kiss on the lips of the love of his life.

But he'd quickly gotten a hold of himself and just barely brushed Lisa's cheek instead of her mouth. As his vision had cleared, he'd seen Lisa's eyes reflecting the same frozen fear.

No, she won't want a regular wedding night.

No sound filtered through the kitchen wall from his

room, but he waited a few minutes longer before standing up. Walking down the hall, he slowly cracked the door open and peeked in. The room was cloaked in darkness since there was no window, but once his eyes adjusted to the new lighting, he could make out her outline on the bed.

Lisa lay curled on her side as close to the wall as she could get, the blanket up to her chin. Her black hair puddled around and behind her head. She faced the wall, but he could tell she was awake by the way the covers trembled lightly.

She's terrified.

His shoulders drooped with sadness at the realization. The last thing he wanted was her to be scared of him, yet he understood. They had only known each other for a week, and she likely didn't know what to expect from him once they were alone. Some men were animals behind closed doors, but he wasn't, and he hoped she would realize that soon.

Slipping into the room, Eli grabbed his nightshirt from where it was draped over the footboard. He stepped back into the hall, closing the door behind him, and quietly stripped out of his clothes. The cool fabric of his nightshirt slid over his head, and a sigh released from deep inside of him, taking his nerves with it. The fact that Lisa was as uncomfortable about sharing a bed with him as he was with having to share it with her strangely calmed him despite her fear.

He opened the door again, scooping his discarded clothes off the floor. Moving quietly through the room, he tossed his clothes on the chair beside Jared's crib. Silently bending to peek at the sleeping babe, he smiled softly. Jared lay curled up on his stomach, fisted hands beside his cheek. Tentatively, Eli reached down one finger and gently stroked his silky smooth forehead. Jared didn't even stir in his sound asleep state.

If only I could sleep as soundly as you, little man.

Taking two steps to the left toward the big bed that somehow now seemed smaller than usual, he pulled down the blanket on his side. The idea of sleeping on the settee flicked through his mind, but as he bit back a yawn, it disappeared. He was too tall to stretch out on it, and he had no desire to sleep curled up in a tight ball all night. Not when he wanted to be able to move the next day. As he climbed under the covers, his weight deeply sank his side of the mattress. Lisa's sharp intake of breath as she slid in his direction echoed loudly in the awfully quiet room. Her fingers lightly knocked against the wall as she scooted back over.

Not sure whether or not to say anything, Eli decided to stay silent. He rolled on his left side, back facing her, as he shifted as far away from her as he could. His chest and arm nearly hung off the edge, but they both wanted space, so he just closed his eyes.

Despite the fact that he was exhausted from being up with Jared the night before, sleep wouldn't come. He was overly aware of Lisa's every tiny movement as she drifted off to sleep. Of how the quilt slowly stopped trembling and her deep, soft breaths seemed to fill every crevice of the room. Her presence beside him flooded him with memories of all the nights he'd slept with Cherish curled against his back. He fisted the blanket as tears threatened to spill down his cheeks. Scrubbing a hand across his wet face, he gradually calmed himself down.

A few hours later just as sleep was finally pulling him under, she rolled over and her hand pressed lightly against the middle of his back. His slowly closing lids flicked open at the touch, sleep completely forgotten.

It's going to be a very long night...

Chapter

TEN

T HE CROW OF A ROOSTER WOKE LISA the next morning. Her eyes fluttered open and confusion filled her as she stared up at an unfamiliar whitewashed ceiling. A quiet, deep snore beside her swept in realization. Shifting her head on her pillow, she looked over at Eli where he lay sleeping on his back.

His red pinstriped nightshirt-clad chest gently rose and fell as he breathed heavily. The brown curls on his head were tousled like he had run his hands through them, but it was probably only from where he'd tossed and turned in his sleep.

Lisa had woken up to him shifting in his sleep many times throughout the night. When he'd bumped her, she knew he wasn't awake, so it didn't bother her, but she was thankful they had stayed on opposite sides of the bed.

Despite the fact that Eli didn't appear to be a demanding sort of man, she had been terrified he would insist on having a wedding night. That was something she wasn't sure she could give him. They didn't love each other, and that type of relationship was for lovers. Not strangers.

Hopefully he'll continue to stay on his side of the bed.

Deciding to get up to start her day, she glanced down at the foot of the bed. Eli was blocking her from getting out of bed the normal way, but if she was quiet and didn't jostle the mattress, she could climb over the footboard without waking him. Inching the blanket off herself, she silently scooted down toward the sturdy, wooden footboard. He didn't move a muscle, even when she accidentally bumped him as she swung one leg over and put her bare foot on the floor.

Grabbing her old, light blue robe from her carpet bag at her feet, she slipped it on before gliding quietly out the open door. She tiptoed down the hall, through the living room, and into the kitchen.

The chair squeaked on the floor as she pulled it out from the table, making her cringe. Sitting at the table, she smoothed her wild hair with one hand as she decided what to do that day.

Today's the first day of being part of a real family again. I've got to make sure I do it right.

One of Lisa's deepest desires was to be a part of a family again. And not only just a part of a family—a needed individual. After her own family had been stripped from her one at a time, she realized what it was like to feel alone and a burden to society. Granted, her services had been needed at the boardhouse back in Tuscaloosa, but it was her scrubbing abilities that were desired. Not her.

She knew the Blagers needed her as a mother, yet she wanted to prove that they desired her for *her*. Whether or not it would be a large task to accomplish, she was willing to give it her all.

Surely they could want me for more than the obvious?

Standing from the table, she walked over to the cabinet beside the sink. She silently opened the cupboard door and peered inside, looking for the coffee. The tin sat nestled next to a small collection of spice jars.

As she filled the empty coffee pot with water, the swish of bare feet on the wooden floor announced the arrival of someone behind her. Expecting one of the older girls, she turned to find a sleepy looking Eli standing in the doorway. He rubbed a palm across one eye and covered a yawn with the other one. "Good morning. I didn't feel you get up."

Still garbed in his knee-length nightshirt, he stepped over to the stove and opened the bottom. Using the stick resting beside it, he stirred the glowing embers within the middle of the black metal.

"I tried to slip out without waking you." She shrugged, setting the coffee pot on the stovetop that was beginning to warm up. "What would you like me to fix for breakfast?"

"It'll have to be something quick since we have to leave for church in a few hours, and everyone has to get ready." He stood, brushing his palms together. "Maybe just simple scrambled eggs and bacon."

"Alright." She nodded, then turned to pull two cups out of the still-open cupboard. "Care to join me for some coffee?"

"I'd like that." A slow grin spread across his face.

Within minutes, they were seated at the table together, a calm, relaxed silence filling the cozy kitchen. It surprised her that they could somehow feel so at ease with each other when just the night before the awkwardness and tension between them had been thick enough to choke.

"Did you sleep well last night?" His rumbling voice echoed in his mug as he asked the question.

"Yes." She nodded, a sense of shyness spilling through her. "Did you?"

"Uh-huh." He copied her gesture and nodded. "Quite a bit better than I did the night before. Jared has a tooth coming in, and he was really restless. He's normally an extremely sound sleeper. Almost nothing wakes him up. We had an instance just a few weeks before you arrived that Cinthy woke up screaming bloody murder because of a nightmare, and he didn't even twitch."

"I wish I could sleep like that," she laughed lightly.

"Don't we all?" He grinned, leaning back in his chair as he swiped a hand over his messy hair.

"Were any of the girls like that?"

"No." His lips pursed into a tiny frown as he crossed his arms over his chest and rested his cup on his left elbow. "Cinthy was the worst. Cherish and I both spent more nights awake than we did asleep when she was a baby."

From everything she'd heard about Cherish from Bella and Abby, Lisa knew the first Mrs. Blager had been a wonderful lady, yet she needed to hear Eli's side of the story.

"What was she like?" Lisa whispered, curiosity getting the best of her. "Cherish, I mean."

"Cherish..." He took a deep breath as the pain that flitted across his face was swiftly replaced by a tender look.

Apparently she still has a tight grip on his heartstrings.

"She was a friend to all and enemy to none," he

continued, his tear-glazed gaze staring at the wall above her head. "Iris not only looks just like her, but their personalities are nearly identical. So when you look at Iris, you're really seeing a smaller version of Cherish. After her death, it was hard to look at Iris since they're so much alike, but as time has gone by, that pain faded."

Lisa understood Eli's pain since she had felt the same way every time she looked in the mirror after her parents' deaths. She was the perfect combination of both of them, so she saw them in her own face.

Lisa took a drink of the hot brew in her cup, her mouth filling with gritty liquid. She swallowed it with a grimace, nearly shuddering at the awful taste as coffee grounds stuck to the back of her teeth. A deep chuckle brought her eyes up from the dark, disgusting substance in her mug.

"You look like you swallowed a bug." Eli's teeth flashed white in his slightly tanned face.

"Why didn't you tell me the coffee tasted awful?" Her brows scrunched together as she set her mug on the table. Pushing it away with one finger, she cringed at the bad flavor still in her mouth.

"I didn't want to hurt your feelings." He shrugged, his cup clanking lightly down beside hers.

"Telling me I make coffee even a pig would turn its nose up at is not going to hurt my feelings." She laughed.

"I'll go get dressed and then come make a new pot if you'll start waking up the girls," he offered, slowly standing up.

"You've got a deal." She nodded and they shared a grin.

That night, Eli pulled the blanket up to Tulip's chin and bent to press a kiss on her forehead. She gave him a sleepy smile and cuddled deeper into the mattress next to Cinthy. Leaning over a little farther, he brushed the curls off of Cinthy's brow with a tender touch. A quiet sigh escaped her lips as she closed her drooping lids.

He stood back up and turned around to bestow a goodnight caress on his oldest daughter where she lay in the other bed alone. Walking toward the door, he paused and glanced back at his three oldest daughters. "Good night, my little blossoms."

"Goodnight, Pa," Iris murmured.

He strode quietly into the living room. A soft baby snore drifted up from where Lisa, Jared, and Petunia all laid in a pile on the settee sound asleep. Tiptoeing around to the front of the human sandwich, he slowly shook his head with a smile.

It had been a rough day from the very first. Lisa had accidentally burned breakfast, so they'd gone to church hungry. She admitted on the ride there that she had no experience in the kitchen since she had grown up with a cook who didn't like anyone in her territory. Eli wouldn't have been honest with himself if he didn't admit that he'd found it a slight disappointment. Cherish had been an excellent cook and she'd never once made gritty coffee, but he knew this was only a bump in the road with Lisa. A bump he was sure they could figure out and conquer.

Then, as soon as they'd gotten home, Petunia had fallen in the yard and scraped both knees and her left palm.

She'd been a sobbing mess for over an hour, and once the tears had stopped flowing, she'd clung to Lisa for the rest of the day. Eli had scrounged up something for both lunch and supper since Lisa not only had Petunia clinging to her skirt, but Jared had been extremely fussy thanks to his tooth and didn't want to be put down. And to make an already hard day even worse, Tulip had had the temper tantrum of the century. Neither Lisa nor him knew what triggered it, but it took both of them to get her hysteria calmed.

Lisa had ended up curling up with Jared and Petunia on the settee after supper. One by one, they'd slowly drifted off to sleep. After an hour or two, he'd carefully shifted Lisa out of her sitting position so she was lying down and wouldn't get a sore neck. She'd woken up slightly, but fell back to sleep with a soft sigh.

Jared was curled snugly against her right arm along the back of the settee while Petunia lay stretched out with her cheek resting on Lisa's chest. The only thing keeping her on the settee was Lisa's arm wrapped tightly around her back. Her stocking-clad legs draped over Lisa's waist and her arm was tucked beside her as she sucked her thumb.

Carefully, so he didn't wake any of them, Eli lifted Lisa's arm off Petunia. Neither of them stirred as he slowly peeled the small girl off. Carrying her into the girls' shared room, he tucked her in bed beside an already sleeping Iris. He blew out the dim lamp on the nightstand and tiptoed back out of the dark room, half closing the door as he left.

Lisa and Jared looked quite the pretty picture spooned together on the settee. Eli hated to have to break it up, but they both needed to get in their proper beds. Tentatively slipping his hand between Jared and Lisa's stomach, his knees nearly bounced off the edge of the settee as his heart pounded wildly in his chest. Besides moving her on the settee, he hadn't touched more than Lisa's hand since they met, and it sent an unpleasant fire up his arm. Wanting to pull his hand back, yet not daring since the movement was likely to wake them both, he closed his eyes tight with a shaky deep breath.

He wasn't touching Lisa intimately, but it still felt wrong. It was like somehow he was being untrue to Cherish, and he hated himself for it.

I'm so sorry, Rish.

Yet almost as soon as the apology drifted from his mind, the second half of Cherish's last words echoed eerily through his head. "...and for yourself. I want you to be happy."

He pushed it all away, not wanting to think about it as he delicately lifted Jared off Lisa. The back of his hand where it had rested against Lisa's blouse-covered stomach was burning like he had set it on the top of the hot stove. He fought the urge to rub it on his pant leg as he shifted Jared against his chest. The boy stirred, letting out a breathy sigh, but thankfully didn't wake up.

Eli carried the baby to his crib. Tucking the small blanket around his lower body, Eli brushed a lock of the thin, red hair away from Jared's forehead.

Needing to steady himself for a moment, Eli gripped the side of the crib with both hands, his knuckles going white. Lisa had only been his wife for one day. How was he going to deal with this new, unwanted emotion for the rest of his life?

Logic told him there was no reason to feel guilty since Cherish was no longer alive, yet it didn't change the fact that his insides were churning with that very emotion. Squinting his eyes in the darkness surrounding him, he willed away the swirling in his gut. But he failed miserably as it swept back in even more forcefully as Lisa's pretty smile appeared in his mind.

If only she wasn't so beautiful.

Lisa's love for the children and innocently sweet, almost childlike ways were more than pleasant to watch, and she lit up a room when she walked into it. Cherish had had the same effect, but with Lisa it was different. The graceful way she carried herself drew his immediate attention while the slow, smooth twang of her husky voice made him hang on to her every word. It still left him reeling with shock that in such a short amount of time, she'd managed to become a light in his dark and dreary world.

It just feels so wrong...

Letting go of the crib, he took a deep breath and headed back out to the living room. Even though he didn't want to, he needed to wake up Lisa so she could go to bed. The settee wasn't the most comfortable thing to sleep on, let alone in the awkward position she was lying in. She would end up sore, and she didn't need that added to a long, hard day.

He swiped a hand nervously through his hair, accidentally tousling his curls messily. Stepping in front of the settee, he watched her sleep for a moment. Her long, black lashes fanned along the top of her freckled cheeks while her hair was partially undone from how she had it pinned back behind her head on the settee cushion. He didn't think he could ever fall in love again, yet this woman was making him begin to doubt himself.

This woman is going to either break me or hate me when it's all said and done.

His biggest fear was that somehow, someway, she'd fall in love with him as time went on, but he wouldn't feel the same way, and he'd break her heart. She'd already been through so much. He'd hate himself if he hurt her even more and added to her pain.

Slowly reaching down, he rested his hand on her upper arm, thankful when his hand didn't burn off like it almost had minutes before. He gently shook her shoulder as he quietly said, "Lisa, wake up."

"Huh?" She stirred, blinking up at him. Her eyes skittered over his face, then flitted down to her blouse, which was no longer covered in a toddler and babe as he removed his hand. "Where's Petunia and Jared?"

Her voice was even huskier than normal in her sleepy state, and he hastily swallowed before answering. "I put them to bed. It's after nine."

"Already?" She quickly sat up, swinging her feet to the floor as her hand went to her messy hair. He shifted back a few steps to give her space. "Why didn't you wake me up?"

"You looked cozy all cuddled up with Pet and Jared. Plus I didn't want to wake them up since they had finally calmed down." He shrugged with a half smile.

"I still can't believe I fell asleep like that." She shook her head with a light laugh. "I haven't done that since I was a child."

"It was a hard day. I would've fallen asleep, too. Actually, I have fallen asleep on the settee more times than I can count." His half smile slowly stretched into a full-out grin.

"It's not the most comfortable thing." She rolled her

neck to the side, kneading it with one hand. "Or I'm just turning into a little old lady."

"It's the settee. Cherish used to complain about it, too," he chuckled quietly, the deep sound rumbling in his chest.

"You're just saying that to make me not feel old," she joshed, standing up.

"No, I wasn't." The smile on his cheeks didn't falter, but the one on the inside did. Little did Lisa know that literally moments before she'd put him in a dilemma with his conscience, and now she was joking around with him.

What would she do if she knew what she's beginning to put me through?

"Well, I guess I should go to actual bed now." Her voice whipped him from his thoughts. "I have a feeling tomorrow is going to be another hard day."

"There's a large possibility of that." He nodded. "I'm going to read for a few minutes and then I'll come to bed as well."

"Alright." Her lips twitched in a smile before she glided toward the bedroom. The door clicked shut behind her, leaving him alone with his own thoughts and nightly Bible reading and praying ritual. Sighing deeply, he plopped himself into the rocking chair. He watched the closed bedroom door for a moment before flipping open the Bible on his knee to the place he'd left off two nights previously.

If only I knew how this is all going to turn out.

Chapter

ELEVEN

FTER THREE WEEKS OF A TEETHING BABY, nearly daily burnt meals that turned into going to Granny Lola's for supper, and somehow creating a routine that they'd all fallen into, Lisa stood at the kitchen counter beside the stove. Jared cooed from his highchair at the table, another little tooth peeking out of his partly gummy grin. She glanced over her shoulder at him with a light laugh as he carried on a gibberish-filled conversation with himself. "You're getting too big for your britches, little man."

He squealed lightly, banging the wooden ring in his chubby hand on the tray attached to his chair. His thin, red hair—that was beginning to curl like Eli's—stuck out wildly in all directions. Jared was an adorable little baby, and she loved him to pieces.

"Litha?" Petunia's high lisp drifted in from the living room where she sat playing with Tulip. The two oldest girls were spending the afternoon with some of their friends in another part of town, so Lisa only had three children under foot for a few hours.

"Yes, hunny?" she replied, stepping away from the counter where she was chopping up potatoes to fry for lunch. They sadly reminded her of her beloved mammy, who had loved fried "taters" more than any other food, but Lisa couldn't let herself dwell on the pain.

Hopefully I don't burn them this time.

Lisa would've asked Abby or Granny Lola for some help, but she felt like she would be a bother, and she didn't want to be a burden. Plus she figured that she'd eventually get her footing in the kitchen.

"I'm hungry." The padding of Petunia's feet signaled her arrival.

"Well, lunch will be done here soon. You'll have to wait just a little longer." Lisa wiped the potato juice off her hands on the new flowered apron Eli bought for her. He had not only bought her the apron, but also a new set of clothes. She still continued to wear her old cream blouse and burgundy skirt every day, using the new outfit for outings and church. When he'd taken her to the dress shop to order the clothes, she'd been pleasantly surprised by the gesture. His thoughtfulness and the fact that he cared warmed her heart.

"Alright." Petunia sighed, turning back around and skipping into the living room.

The solid thump of an ax smacking something hard was quickly followed by a loud crack as Eli split firewood in the backyard. He'd been working at it for an hour and had only stopped once to come get a drink of water. Glancing over at Jared, who was contentedly gnawing on his ring, she grabbed a tall glass from the cupboard. She filled it at the sink then opened the back door, slipping outside. A soft breeze lapped at her face and the bright sun warmed her cheeks.

She walked the few feet to where Eli stood, arms raised above his head about to swing the ax again. The glass cool in her hand, she silently watched him slam the sharp metal into the half-chopped chunk of wood sitting on a small stump in front of him. It flew into two pieces as the ax head crashed into it.

"I brought you some water," she called out quietly.

He swiveled around, then smiled softly. Her heart sprouted wings and fluttered briefly at the sweet expression. Resting the ax down against the stump, he swiped his fore-arm across his sweaty forehead. The sleeves of his red check-ered shirt were rolled up past his elbows. Eli took a step closer to her and carefully grabbed the glass out of her hand, his fingers brushing hers lightly. "Thanks, Lisa. I was actually about to come get a drink."

"You've been out here chopping for a while now. Why don't you come in and take a break for a moment?" Lisa sug-gested, a small smile parting her lips.

"I want to finish this stack first." He gestured with a nod to the petite pile of wood still needing to be chopped be-hind him. Lifting the glass, he drank all of the clear liquid in a handful of swallows.

"You do know that it's only the end of April and that you have all summer to chop firewood for next winter, right?" She laughed lightly, crossing her arms over her chest.

"I know, but I'm going to be busy with other things so I wanted to get a head start." He shrugged, a half grin on his face as he handed the empty glass back to her. "When's lunch going to be done?"

"Here shortly." Her heart plummeted, though, as his

brows twitched ever so slightly that she doubted he even realized he moved them. "And I'll try not to burn it this time. I never told you I was a good cook."

"No, you didn't." He smiled hesitantly.

"I'm trying to get better, but somehow my attempts just keep failing." She frowned, and Eli reached out, squeezing her shoulder softly.

"It's alright. Sometimes things take time to learn. It hasn't even been a month yet. Give yourself some slack." His smile morphed from hesitant to encouraging.

"Thanks, Eli." She nodded, patting his hand where it rested on her arm. "I better get back inside and finish cooking so I can feed the hungry people houndin' me for food."

Lisa turned on her heel and strode back into the house, Eli's deep, rumbling laugh following her. Stepping over to the counter where the chopped potatoes laid, she fought back a grin. The last three weeks had helped change things between her and Eli, and she liked where they were at in their relationship.

That is if it can be called a relationship.

They had settled into a nice friendship and were quite comfortable with each other. Eli already knew how to make her laugh and she him. He'd even made her blush a time or two. Yet the best part was that after they'd been married for a week, the awkward tension that reigned over them at night had thankfully fled. They no longer laid in bed stiffly and as far apart as they could be. Somewhat quickly, they'd realized that neither of them expected or wanted anything from the other, so a sense of ease had settled over them when it was time to get some shut eye. Not only had a feeling of contentment come between them, they sometimes chatted quietly before drifting off to sleep, and she'd even woken in the middle of the night to find his arm draped over her. At first it had startled her, but once she realized how nice it felt, she relaxed and scooted in closer, snuggling against his chest.

Her thoughts swiftly migrated back to the task at hand. She didn't want to burn this meal, so she needed to give it her complete attention. The large cast iron skillet she'd put to warm on the stove before peeling the potatoes sizzled loudly, but she wasn't able to give it the watchful eye it deserved since Jared let out an abrupt cry. Swiveling around, she found his trembling lower lip was puckered and his blue eyes glimmered with unshed tears. His wooden ring–the only thing giving his sore gums relief–was discarded on the floor beside her chair.

"There's no reason to cry, little man." She hurried over and scooped up the lost toy. He took it with a happy squeal and small, bouncy giggle in his seat. Laughing, she smoothed a hand over his wild hair as she bent to press a kiss to his chubby cheek.

A loud pop followed by a quiet roar filled the space behind her. Lisa twirled around so fast, she nearly fell over. Bright orange flames shot out of the grease-filled skillet on the stove.

Panic pounding through her veins, she rushed across the room, grabbing the nearest towel as she went. She beat the cloth in her shaking hand over the burning pan, attempting to put out the flames. Only her endeavors backfired as the towel was instantly engulfed in flames.

Hastily letting it fall to the floor before her hand and sleeve caught on fire, she glanced with terror from skillet to burning towel. Without even giving it much thought, yet knowing she had no other choice if she didn't want the house to burn down, she screamed for Eli.

Panic soared through Eli, causing his heart to nearly pound out of his chest as Lisa's scream tore through the air. He bolted toward the back door, ax falling to the ground. The door crashed against the wall as he threw it open. Lisa stood near the stove, a burning towel at her feet while flames climbed out of the skillet on the stovetop.

What on earth?!

Rushing forward, he gently shoved Lisa back and stamped out the burning towel with his boot. Jared's scared sobs were the only thing that echoed through the room as Eli snatched the pan lid sitting on the countertop. He slammed it down on the flaming skillet, his chest heaving. A sizzle slid out from under the lid as the small grease fire was swiftly put out.

Swinging around, he faced Lisa, angry words bubbling up in him thanks to the fear thrumming through his whole body.

Cherish wouldn't have let this happen…

But every thought slipped away as he saw the wild terror filling her dark eyes. His gaze slipped to the living room doorway where wide-eyed Tulip and Petunia stood before bouncing to the wailing baby. Unsure of who to comfort first, he stepped around Lisa and scooped up Jared. He buried his face in Eli's neck and his sobs turned to hiccuping breaths.

Striding back to Lisa, Eli peered into her face, but her

fear-glazed eyes didn't see him as they stared at the mess the fire had made. Tears slowly began to streak down her cheeks. His heart clenched at the sight.

She's so frightened.

Eli reached out and grasped her arm. She turned to him with a quiet, deep sob, and he immediately took a step closer to her. Tugging her carefully toward him, he pulled her to his chest. Her head fell on his right shoulder as one hand gripped the front of his shirt and her other arm circled around his back, holding him tight.

Despite her violent sobbing, she was soft against him. Part of him wanted to like it while the other half hated the whole situation. The guilt that he'd been keeping on the back burner attempted to sweep in, but he hastily swallowed it down, shoving it away. He glanced down at Lisa and tentatively reached up, smoothing his palm over her hair.

I'm just comforting her. Nothing more.

With no reason to continue standing in the middle of the room, he walked them toward the kitchen table. He put Jared, who was no longer crying, back in his highchair. Kicking out a chair with his heel, Eli slowly lowered himself onto it and pulled Lisa down into his lap. She didn't protest, and even scooted in closer, burying her face in his neck. Her sobs didn't slow any, and he worried that she'd never calm down.

He gently rubbed his hand up her back, resting his cheek against her warm hair as he murmured, "Lisa, it's all over. Everything's alright now."

"I almost burnt your house down, Eli. Everything's not alright!" she cried, shuddering against him. "The girls and Jared could have been seriously hurt or even killed."

"Hey." He grasped her shoulders lightly and tilted her

back so they could see each other. "The fire was put out before anything could happen."

"That's not the point!" Tears dripped off her chin onto her lap, and both of them shook under the force of her sobs. "I can't cook and now I've nearly burnt down your house. You probably wish I had never answered your letter."

His heart sank with sadness. He didn't know how she'd come to that conclusion, but he needed to snuff it out immediately.

"Lisa, don't say that." He gently grabbed her face in both his hands, forcing her to look at him. Her tears streamed over and between his fingers as he looked deeply into her red-rimmed eyes. "I have never once regretted our decision to marry. In just the short amount of time you've been here, you've become one of the biggest blessings. Who cares if you can't cook! That's not why you're here. If I wanted a cook, I would have hired someone. Lisa, this is *our* home, and you are part of this family."

As the words left his mouth, a sense of peace settled in him as the guard he'd put around his heart slowly cracked, falling away. Eli stared at her as the realization that in the few weeks they had known each other, she'd become special to him. He didn't know what type of special she was, but that was something only time could tell. All he knew was that he wanted to prove to her that she was more than just a hired hand under the guise of marriage.

Lisa's breath hitched, and her hiccuping cries slowed until a final droplet dripped from her lashes to the hesitant smile that barely lifted the corners of her tear-swollen lips. He grinned back, drying her sopping cheeks with his thumbs. She gently pushed his hands away and leaned forward until her forehead rested in the curve of his neck. His arms went around her back, and he pulled her tightly against him. Her quiet sobs faded until they turned into shallow, shaky breaths with the occasional shudder.

Soft, pattering bare feet drew his attention from the woman in his lap to the two little girls slowly creeping across the silent kitchen toward them. He opened his left arm, and they ran the rest of the way to him. Tulip buried her face in Lisa's burgundy skirt, her shoulders trembling with her small cries, while Petunia curled into his side, snuggling in with a shiver against him.

Lisa didn't lift her face, but her hand reached down and rested on Tulip's head. She smoothed Tulip's messy curls as she murmured, "It's alright, Tulip. There's no reason to cry."

"Then why you cry, Litha?" Petunia leaned over Tulip, attempting to peer into Lisa's face.

"The fire scared me, but that's not a very good excuse." She sighed heavily, then sat up. Eli's arm slid down her back to rest around her waist as she dried her damp cheeks on her sleeve. She pulled Tulip into her lap, and the small girl threw her arms around Lisa's neck. The force of the embrace nearly knocked Lisa off balance, but Eli tightened his grip so they both didn't smack the table behind her back. Tulip's cries turned into sobs, and Lisa stroked her back as she whispered, "Ssh, it's okay."

Petunia watched from where she was still curled against his arm. She stood on tiptoe, reaching up a hand to pat Tulip. "Tulip, pleathe don't cry."

Jared let out a shriek from his highchair, and Lisa's head swiveled to glance at him. A smile spread across her face, but it turned to a look of shock as she looked back at Eli. Her gaze darted down to where her body sat firmly against his and back up to his eyes. She blushed deeply as if she'd just then realized she had been in his lap the whole time.

A deep chuckle rumbled in his chest at her wide, surprised, dark eyes. She blinked rapidly a few times, her mouth a round circle, but she swiftly gave her head a small shake and the look disappeared. Shifting slowly, she scooted off his lap. His heart dipped with disappointment as his arms felt strangely empty. Tulip still clung to her, but her sobs had slowed enough that she no longer needed to be held.

Lisa set Tulip down and moved toward Jared, but Eli stopped her as he leaped out of the chair and gently grabbed her arm. She peered up at him with lightly scrunched brows and a tiny frown. "I'll take care of Jared. Why don't you go wash your face? It'll make you feel better."

"But what about lunch?" she questioned as she turned to leave the room.

"I'll take care of it." He waved off her concern, his back to her as he scooped up Jared.

"Eli?"

He glanced over his shoulder at her whispered word. "Hmm?"

"Thank you."

"For what?" His brows creased.

"For letting me be part of your family." She smiled softly, her eyes still glimmering and puffy from her previous tears. "It means more to me than you'll ever know."

Taking flight, his heart soared with a happiness he hadn't felt in a long time.

"You're welcome." His lips mirrored hers. "You're most welcome."

She slipped into the living room, and he sighed.

What did I do to deserve not only Cherish, but Lisa as well?

Chapter

TWELVE

"L ISA! LISA, WHERE ARE YOU?" IRIS'S VOICE shouted from outside two days later.

"In here, Iris!" Lisa called back, sitting back on her heels from where she sat crouched, scrubbing the living room floor.

"You'll never believe what I just found." Red braids swung into view as the young girl crashed through the open front door.

Lisa threw up a hand, stopping her before she could go any farther. Laughing, she exclaimed, "Land's sake! I've been mopping all afternoon. Don't even think about tracking those dusty boots across my clean floor, young lady!"

"Yes, ma'am." Iris's blue eyes sparkled brilliantly with happiness. She kept her hands tucked behind her back, but she shifted like whatever she was holding was moving.

"What's behind your back, Iris?" Lisa raised one brow, waiting for something absurd to be pulled into view. All the girls were adventurous and a little on the tomboyish side.

Iris slowly brought her hands around in front of her. A tiny, cream-colored, long-haired kitten rested contentedly in her grasp. With a meow that was barely audible, it began to squirm and Iris had to wrangle it back against her so it couldn't get away. She looked expectantly down at Lisa. "Can we keep him? Please?"

Lisa took a shallow breath, not sure how to answer. She really wanted to say yes to make Iris happy, but at the same time, it would only add more work to their already full plates.

"I don't know." Lisa shook her head. "We already have a lot going on with the crop, pigs, chickens, other animals, and all of you children. And anyways, where did you find it?"

"He was wandering around behind the barn," she explained, then begged, "Please? I'll take care of it all by myself. I can do it."

"I know you can do it, but I'm not sure what your pa will think of it."

The kitten wiggled from Iris's arms and thumped gracefully to the floor. Head cocked to the side, caramel-colored eyes wide with curiosity, it slowly crept up to Lisa. She reached out her fingers to it, and it sniffed them before rubbing its jaw on her bent knuckles. A quiet purr rumbled lightly from its small, fuzzy chest. She stroked one finger down its soft back, and it arched up, quivering with pleasure.

"Please?" Iris's plea drew Lisa's attention from the kitten and back to the nine-year-old.

"You'll have to ask your father." She picked up the purring fuzzball, cradling it against her bent legs. Memories of her childhood cat flooded her, and she hoped Eli would grant Iris's wish. "I'm not agreeing to anything unless he does."

"Okay!" Iris spun on her heel. "He's in the backyard. I'll go get him."

Iris was gone in the blink of an eye, leaving Lisa alone with the cream-colored cat. She rubbed her hand across its side as she lowered herself to sit on the floor. It curled up in her lap, and she watched its eyes close. The loud purring slowly drifted to a stop as the kitten sighed contentedly.

Well, I'll be! You sure fell asleep fast.

Eli's voice drifted through the open door, then he appeared, Iris dragging him by the hand along behind her. Apparently forgetting Lisa's warning about the floor, Iris stepped all the way into the living room. Both her and Eli's boots trailed dirt across the floor, and Lisa cringed inwardly.

Eli's gray eyes darted from the kitten in her lap to the bucket of water at her side then to his feet. His free hand grabbed the back of Iris's dress, and he pulled her along with him as he stepped back into the doorway.

"Can we keep him?" Iris turned to look up at her pa's face, eyes sparkling with a wide smile and her clasped hands tucked under her chin.

"I'm not sure." Eli rested his hand on Iris's shoulder. "Lisa, what do you think?"

Lisa blinked, surprised that he wanted her input with the decision. She figured he'd just say yes or no, but the fact that he asked for her opinion warmed her heart with gratitude. "I told her she had to ask you."

"And I told her we had to ask you," he laughed.

"Well, it looks like we have a bit of a problem." Lisa

shook her head with a grin, her hand resting lightly on the sleeping kitten. "Are any of the girls allergic to cats?"

"Not that I know of." His lips pursed into a tiny frown. "And I'm not either. I actually grew up with cats since my mother loves them. How about you? Are you allergic?"

"No. I grew up with cats, too, and they've never bothered me."

"Does that mean we can keep him?" Iris bounced on her toes, her voice pitching higher.

Eli caught Lisa's eye, and she could clearly see the question he was silently asking her. She gave a small nod, and his right brow twitched up as the barest hint of a smile tugged on the corner of his mouth.

Since when can we have a conversation without words?

The thought startled Lisa. Things had changed even more between them since two days before when she'd nearly burnt the house down. But the switch was in him, not her. It was like he'd had a guard up she'd never even noticed, yet now it was gone and he acted a little different. He seemed more carefree and like he wasn't trying to hold her at arm's length anymore. They'd been comfortable with one another nearly from the get-go, but now it felt more relaxed and the little bit of tension that had remained was now long gone.

"You can keep him." Eli's voice yanked Lisa out of her thoughts. Iris jumped up and down with a squeal before throwing her arms around his waist. He rested his hand on the back of her head as she squeezed him tight. "But he's your responsibility. You have to take care of him and clean up all of his messes. I don't want Lisa picking up your slack or even having to do it myself. Do you understand?"

"Yes, sir. I understand." She tilted back to look up

at him again, and even though Lisa couldn't see her face, she knew Iris was grinning.

Iris let go of Eli and twirled around, hurrying over to Lisa. Iris soon had the sleeping kitten in her hands again and rubbed it gently against her cheek. Lisa tilted her head with a laugh as Eli reached out and reeled Iris back to the doorway. "Iris, your shoes! I'm sure Lisa doesn't appreciate you getting dirt all over her clean floor."

"Oh, I'm so sorry, Lisa!" She peeked over the kitten's ears at Lisa with an apologetic look.

"Don't worry about it." Lisa waved away the apology, Iris's happiness wiping away her frustration before it could begin. "What are you going to name him?"

"Well, he's almost the same color as the cookie dough Ma used to make at Christmas time." Iris's eyes squinted in thought as her fingers wove into the kitten's long fur. "I think I'll call him Cookie!"

"That's a very nice name. It fits him just right." Lisa nodded with a grin.

"I'm going to go show him to the girls." Iris squeezed past Eli and bolted out into the yard. Eli's deep chuckle filled the room as he bent and slipped off his boots.

He stepped into the living room and snatched the broom from where Lisa had left it propped against the wall. With quick strokes, he swept the dirt Iris had tracked in back out the door. Lisa peered up at him from where she still sat cross-legged on the floor. "What are you doing?"

"I'm cleaning up Iris's mess." He looked back at her as he tossed the broom against the wall.

"You don't have to do that. I'm already down here." Lisa protested with a shake of her head. "Anyways, I'm nearly done. I just have a little section over here left."

"Slide the bucket over here, will you?" He squatted down so he could reach the floor, completely ignoring her objection. Shaking her head again, but this time with a grin, she did as he asked. He snagged the small, bristled brush out of the cloudy water and began to scrub the section of the floor Iris had walked on.

Lisa crossed her arms over her chest with a sigh. "You're stubborn, you know?"

"Sometimes, but not always." He glanced over with a wink and grin.

"You do realize that as soon as the children come back in the house, this floor is going to look like I never even cleaned it to begin with?"

"Yes, but that doesn't mean I can't help you finish and clean up the part that was dirtied again." He scooted his sock-clad feet across the floor, his somewhat large frame still crouched down, and she giggled at the funny sight. Fingers bent over the back of the wooden handle in the brush, he made quick work of cleaning the section of floor by her side that still needed to be mopped. "There! Now it's all done and you got to take a break."

"Thanks, Eli, but you didn't have to." She nodded at him as he slowly stood.

"My pleasure." A grin spread across his face as he reached down a hand to help her up. A tiny spark shot up her arm at his touch, and she bit back a smile. She was soon on her feet, and with a swift swish of her skirts, she settled them properly around her again.

"Do you have something you need to get back to outside?" she asked, snagging the bucket and walking toward the kitchen. He followed behind her close enough that she could feel his warmth.

"No, I was actually on my way in the house when Iris came to get me. Here, let me dump that." He took the bucket from her and stepped out of the back door. The splash of water smacking the grass echoed from the yard after he disappeared. He set the wooden bucket beside the door as he strode back inside.

They rarely got a quiet moment to themselves, and she found herself craving his company. She spent most of her time with the children, so she wanted to be in another adult's presence if only for a little bit of time. She sucked in a shaky breath as she pushed away the sudden nerves in her stomach.

"Petunia and Jared are still napping, so I have a few spare minutes without anything to do. I was going to have a cup of coffee. Do you want to join me?" She glanced over her shoulder at him as she filled the coffee pot, anxious for his answer.

"That would be nice." He nodded.

They were soon sitting at the table, filled coffee cups in hand. A steady, comforting silence wrapped around them as they sipped on the black brew. Lisa sneaked a glance at him while he watched something out the window. Hiding her small smile behind her mug, she took in the sculpted, smooth lines of his side profile. She fought down a contented sigh as she relaxed against the back of her chair.

How did I get so lucky to end up with such a gentle, kind man like him?

Later that night, Lisa climbed silently to her side of the bed. Eli followed behind her and flopped the blanket over both of them. She let out a sigh as she snuggled down onto her pillow. It had been a hard day once again, yet the soft bed felt like a cozy embrace.

"Thank you," Eli murmured quietly beside her.

"What?" Confused, Lisa turned to look at him in the darkness.

"I said thank you." The bed bounced slightly as he nodded.

"Please tell me you haven't already fallen asleep and are having a conversation with me while you're in dreamland. You aren't making any sense!" Lisa laughed quietly. She had discovered that when Eli had a hard day, he talked in his sleep, and she'd even caught him sleepwalking once. That had scared the living daylights out of her since she wasn't sure where he would go, but thankfully he'd only gone to the kitchen then come straight back to bed.

"I'm awake." A deep chuckle rumbled in the air. "Thank you for agreeing to let Iris keep the kitten today, and thank you for just being you."

She'd never been thanked for being herself before, so it left her somewhat stunned. A silence settled between them as her throat tightened with happy tears and she struggled to find an answer. Her voice hitched, giving away her stirred emotions, as she whispered, "How could I not agree? Not only was she super excited, but Cookie is adorable."

"Hey, you aren't crying, are you?" He rolled over on his side and propped himself on his elbow as he leaned in close to try and see her face. His breath stirred the loose hair framing her face, and a quiver ran up her spine. Even though they were only friends, whenever he got really close, she couldn't calm her pounding heart. He was very much a man—a handsome one at that—and she a woman.

At least he doesn't notice…and if he does, I haven't caught on.

"No, I'm not crying." She cleared her throat as it croaked again.

"You're not lying to me, are you?" Even in the dark, she saw his brows scrunch.

"I would never lie to you." She shook her head to emphasize her point. "I promise I'm fine."

"Okay." He lowered himself onto the bed but didn't roll over. His eyes burned a soft place into her skin as she felt him staring at her in the dark.

She slowly turned over, facing the wall as she said, "Goodnight."

"Night," he whispered.

Within moments, the sound of his deep, heavy breathing filled the quiet room. She relaxed and closed her eyes to drift off to dreamland. The journey was almost complete when something unexpectedly thumped onto the end of the bed near Eli's feet. Lisa's eyes flew open.

What was that?

She stiffened as the blanket moved while whatever creature walked closer to her. Her heart beat wildly in her chest, but she slowly rolled onto her back. Reaching over, she gripped Eli's shoulder. She gave it a sharp squeeze and shook him lightly as she hoarsely whispered, "Eli, wake up! There's something on the bed."

"Huh?" He sat halfway up. "What did you say?"

"There's something on the bed."

Eli sat all the way up, and reached down to the foot of

the bed. She pulled the blanket up to her chin, cowering slightly in her fright. A combination of the darkness pooled around them and his large hands around the culprit kept it from sight until he abruptly plopped it onto the center of her chest.

She gasped loudly and started to lift the covers to knock it off until Eli's rumbling chuckle vibrated beside her. "Lisa, it's only the kitten."

"Oh!" Her cheeks heated as she realized he was right. "Now I feel so foolish."

"Don't. How were you supposed to know it wasn't something else?" He flopped gently back onto his pillow as Cookie began to purr loudly.

"I thought he was in the girls' room." She stroked the kitten's back as he rubbed his little head on her cheek. A giggle escaped her throat and she felt Eli looking at her in the dark. She turned her head to glance over. His teeth flashed in the dark as he smiled.

"Apparently he wanted to sleep with you instead." Eli teased with a yawn. He picked up the fluffy tail swishing near his arm and rubbed the soft fur gently between his fingers. Letting go, he rolled over with a sigh and with another whispered, "Goodnight".

He was soon asleep again as was the kitten curled under her chin. Shifting the warm ball of fur, she curled up on her side, face to Eli's back. She tucked the kitten between them and gave into the heavy pull of her tired eyelids.

Chapter

THIRTEEN

THE NEXT MORNING, ELI HEADED DOWN THE road toward Jack and Bella's house to ask Bella a favor. One which he hoped she would be willing to give him. His boot heels clicked lightly on the steps as he strode onto their small front porch. He swiped off his tan hat and knocked soundly on the door.

I hope this works out.

Jack opened the door seconds later. "Hello, Eli. Come on in."

"Thanks." He followed the younger, yet taller man into the kitchen of their cozy home. Eli nodded politely at Bella, who sat at the table with a half-finished plate of food in front of her. "I'm sorry I interrupted your breakfast."

"Don't worry about it." Jack waved a hand, gesturing to a chair. "Have a seat. I'm sure you have a reason for dropping by this morning."

"Yes. Yes, I do." Eli settled into the pointed out chair, and set his hat on his knee as Jack plopped back into his seat beside his wife. "Bella, I was wondering if you could help me with something."

"Of course. What is it?" She stood up and moved over to the cabinet behind her where she pulled out a mug. "Would you like some coffee?"

"Thank you, that would be nice." He nodded. Nerves and guilt took turns nagging him since he felt bad for asking Bella to give up a little of her time. "We have a slight problem with Lisa's cooking. She nearly burns everything she touches. We've had to go to Granny Lola's so often that now she just expects us. But I've noticed that Lisa is very willing to learn new things, and that when she tries, she puts her all into it and is successful. And because of that, I feel like she just needs a little guidance in the kitchen, and then she'll be as good of a cook as anybody."

"You want me to come over and help her, don't you?" Bella smiled as she set a full, steaming cup of coffee in front of him.

"Yes, I would really appreciate it if you could. I would've asked Granny Lola, but she's been extremely busy with the boardinghouse lately." He took a sip of the hot brew and let the smooth, flavorful liquid slide down his throat.

"Does she know you came over to ask me?" One of Bella's brows raised slightly and one side of her mouth twitched like she was trying to rein in a grin.

"No." He glanced down into the blackness filling the mug in his hands with a sheepish look. "I planned to tell her once I got home. We had a little incident earlier this week with a small grease fire, and she was pretty upset. I wasn't exactly sure what she'd think of the idea of me asking some- one to teach her how to cook."

"Oh, boy. You'll be sleeping on the settee tonight." Jack shook his head sadly, but his dark brown eyes sparkled with a smile. "She might get mad at you for doing this behind her back."

"I'm not doing this behind her back," Eli protested, beginning to feel uncomfortable.

"What did you tell her when you came over here?" Jack questioned as he leaned his elbows on the table.

"I just told her I was coming to see how you two were since we hadn't seen you in a few..." Eli stammered to a halt as the realization of what he'd just done hit him in the gut. A memory of a time he'd done something similar with Cherish when she couldn't figure out a sewing pattern flitted through his mind. His forehead dropped into his open palm, a groan rumbling in his chest. "I'm a complete idiot."

Someone please kick me in the seat of the pants

"No, you're not. You just made a mistake, is all." Bella reached across the table and gently squeezed the forearm he had resting on the table.

"Things have been going so well, and now I've just taken three steps back." He set his mug on the table as a frustrated sigh escaped his lips.

"Not necessarily." Bella's face was halfway hidden by her coffee cup as she took a long drink. "She could take it fine or it could really hurt her feelings."

"I feel so foolish asking you two for advice, but to be honest, I don't know what to do." Eli rubbed his fingers against his temple, pressing deeply into the flesh. "Lisa is so different from Cherish that it leaves me clueless sometimes."

"Your best bet would be to just simply not say anything." Jack shrugged, resting his arm along the back of

Bella's chair. "Bells and I will never mention it. It can be our little secret."

"Jack." Bella shot him a glare, gently elbowing him in the ribs. He rubbed his side with a sheepish look. "That is not the answer."

Eli leaned back in his chair, hands falling limply into his lap. "I should just come clean and tell her. I've already dug myself a hole, and I'd really like to fill it up by being honest instead of making it bigger. An apology seems like the safest route."

"I agree." Bella nodded, then pursed her lips in thought. "But be careful how you go about it. Something about Lisa makes me feel like she's a lot more sensitive and insecure than she shows. I've watched her after church multiple times, and with the way she takes care of the children and helps out anyway she can, it's almost like she just wants to feel needed."

"I've noticed that, too." Eli nodded as he rubbed one palm across his pant leg distractedly. "I really do need her, and I want to prove it to her."

An invisible weight lifted off his chest, warmth taking its place as the words left his mouth. She'd completely wiggled her way into his life and now he wasn't sure if he could live without her.

"Just make sure you need her for the right things," Bella interjected. Eli cocked one brow up, not entirely understanding what she meant. "Like any person, I'm sure she probably wants to be needed for *her*, not for the work she can do or the skills she possesses."

"You know you're way too wise for someone your age," Eli laughed lightly.

"I wouldn't say wise. Maybe just observant and a little cautious now." Bella shrugged.

"Well, I guess I better get back home and start fixing this mess I've made of things." Eli slowly stood up from the table.

"Wait, I didn't give you an answer." Bella stopped him before he could even get halfway to the door.

"You don't have to worry about it. I have to make sure I didn't just ruin everything between Lisa and me." Eli smiled sadly.

"If everything is fine between you and her and she would like the help, you come tell me. I'm more than willing to teach her how to cook." Bella's head bobbed in a nod.

"Thanks, Bella." Reaching out, Eli gave her upper arm a gentle, friendly squeeze. "I really appreciate it."

"Of course. That's what friends are for. And I consider both you and Lisa as friends." Bella's face split in a wide grin as Jack stepped up behind her and offered Eli his hand to shake.

"I second that. If you ever need anything, and I mean anything, don't think twice about coming to ask us." Jack tightened his grip on Eli's hand to emphasize his words.

"I'll remember. Thank you two for being the type of friends who always have my back." Eli put his hat on his head, waving to them as he stepped out of the door.

His boots puffed up small clouds of dust on the dusty road as he walked back in the direction of his house less than half a mile away. His thoughts were a guilty whirlwind.

How could I have been so stupid?

Coming up on the house, he circled around to the backyard to slip in through the kitchen door. His hand trembled as he gripped the doorknob. The gentle clank of a pot being set on the stove drifted through the closed door. Sucking in a deep breath, he turned the metal knob and opened the door.

Lisa glanced over at Eli with a smile as he walked through the back door. She brushed the flour from her attempt at making a loaf of bread off her hands on her apron. Looking closer at Eli's almost guilty expression, she studied him for a moment before saying, "How were Jack and Bella this morning?"

"Oh, um, they were fine," he stammered, tossing his hat on the cupboard beside the door.

What's going on? He hasn't acted nervous like this since the first week of our marriage.

"Is there something wrong?" she asked, her right brow cocking up slightly.

He opened his mouth like he was about to say something, then snapped it closed. He swallowed visibly, and something in her stomach curled tightly, leaving her queasy. The way his eyes darted back and forth, avoiding her, made an uneasy quiver run up her spine. Her apron swished back down over her skirt as she dropped it.

"Eli?" Her question was laced with wariness and a sense of dread.

He finally made eye contact with her, but his gray eyes gazing into hers didn't give her any relief. He took a step closer and reached out like he was going to touch her, but his arm dropped back to his side. Panic fluttered in her chest as the seconds ticked silently by. She was about to burst out with another question when he abruptly said, "I'm sorry."

"Sorry for what?" Confusion raged through her racing heart, settling in with the panic and uneasiness already moseying about.

"I went to the Klisters' today because..." His voice drifted quietly to a halt. He cleared his throat with a shake of his head as his chin tilted down. "I should have asked you first, but I went to see if Bella would teach you how to cook."

The words slapped her across her face, leaving a burning sting on her cheek.

He lied!

Her eyes watered and her mouth opened and closed several times before she finally managed to whisper, "You said you didn't care that I couldn't cook."

"I know that, and I meant it!" He closed the space between them, hands reaching for her shoulders, but she took a step back, avoiding his touch.

"Then why?" She swallowed the rogue sob rising in her throat. "Why did you act like you were only going over there on a neighborly visit? Why didn't you ask me if I wanted help?"

"I don't know, Lisa. I don't know." He ran a shaking hand through his curls, making them stand up in a few places. "I hate seeing you struggle like this and figured that maybe with a little assistance, you could become an excellent cook. I just didn't think it all through like I should've, and I'm so sorry. I never meant to hurt you. All I wanted to do was help."

He was cloaked in a watery film thanks to her tears, yet she could still make out the genuine, truthful look in his eyes.

No, he didn't lie.

"I know I messed up and went about it the wrong way. I truly am sorry." His hand stretched toward her, and this time she let him touch her. And strangely, his gentle grip on her arm calmed her pounding heart as she took a deep breath. "Please, give me a chance to make it up to you."

She nodded, and before she could say anything, let alone blink, Eli pulled her into his arms. His hand rested on her lower back as he held her tightly, somehow settling her stirred emotions even further. His heart hammered beneath her ear, and as she listened to its melody, she realized he was as upset about this as she was. She fisted the back of his shirt as she wrapped her arms around his waist, burying her face in his chest. A blush warmed her cheeks as her self-confidence soared to new heights.

He has faith in me.

Leaning back, she peered up into his face. Dark gray eyes searched hers imploringly, and she tried to ease the worry flashing in them with a small smile. His expression relaxed slightly and her whole body slumped with a sigh. "Despite the fact you didn't exactly go about it the right way, it was very sweet of you to want to help."

"I never wanted to upset and hurt you like this. I hope you understand that." His arms squeezed her a little tighter.

"I realize that now." The small upturn of her lips turned into a full-fledged, genuine grin.

"So, am I forgiven, then?" His brows raised expectantly.

"Yes, you're forgiven." She laughed lightly, the tears still clogging her throat making her voice huskier than normal.

"That easily?" His chest vibrated against her as he spoke, and she fought the shiver trying to crawl up her spine.

"Uh-huh." She nodded. Her gaze darted down to his full lips, desire to feel them against hers causing her breath to stick in the back of her throat. The seconds ticked by slowly as she looked back up at his eyes. They darkened and her heart pattered excitedly in anticipation that he might lean down and kiss her.

Jared screamed from the other room, and she swiftly stepped out of Eli's arms. A chill settled over her, and if not for the squalling baby—who she couldn't help but be annoyed with—she would have never left his calming embrace. Eli smiled at her before she hurried across the room, but she stopped just inside the living room as a sudden thought filled her mind.

Leaning lightly against the doorframe, she stuck her head back in the kitchen. "What did Bella say about teaching me how to cook?"

A look of shock flitted across Eli's face, but it vanished as he answered, "She said she would love to help you."

"Good, because I would appreciate her help. Could you go back over later and tell her that?"

"Sure thing." Eli nodded with a wide grin.

Chapter
FOURTEEN

LISA TIED ON HER APRON THE NEXT day as she glanced over at Bella, who was doing the same, Cookie weaving in between her feet, his purrs loud. "Thank you for being willing to help me find my footing in the kitchen."

"Of course." Bella nodded. "I love to cook, and I haven't had too much to do the past few days, so I'm glad to be able to help."

"Where do you think we should start?" Lisa asked. Excitement buzzed through her, making her bounce lightly on her toes.

"What areas do you need the most help in?" Bella pulled a small pad of paper and pencil out of her apron pocket.

"The only thing I don't burn is coffee. And I used to burn that until Eli showed me how to do it the right way." Lisa admitted with a sheepish look. "But if you show me the basics, I'm sure I'll be good to go. I can typically pick up on things pretty quickly once I'm shown how to do them."

"I guess we'll start with a simple meal." Bella tapped the pencil on her chin. "How does beef stew and biscuits sound?"

"That sounds perfect!" Lisa's face split in a wide grin.

"I'll write down the recipe for you and several other simple ones to start you off. If you need any others, just ask me and I'll give them to you." Bella scratched out the recipe for both the stew and biscuits as she told Lisa what ingredients were needed.

Lisa skittered from one side of the kitchen to the other gathering the items, but halted suddenly when Bella stammered. Looking closely at the shorter, blonde girl in the kitchen with her, Lisa noticed that Bella's face was milky white and that she swayed. Lisa reached out and grabbed her arm, bending to peer in her face. "Are you alright?"

"I just…I just got a little dizzy, is all." Bella pressed a palm to her abdomen. "And my stomach doesn't feel the greatest."

"Why don't you sit down?" Lisa gently led her over to the table and made her sit in a chair as she pulled it out. "I'll get you a cup of coffee. Maybe that will help?"

Within seconds, Lisa had a steaming mug in Bella's hands. The younger woman stared warily at it a moment before finally taking a drink. Her hands shook lightly, stirring the dark liquid, but she didn't drop it or fall over in a faint.

"Feel any better now?" Lisa scooted out another chair and sat next to her, worriedly studying her face. "Do you want me to have Eli get Jack? Eli's right out back in the alfalfa field, so it would only take a moment for me to go fetch him."

"No. No, I feel better now." Bella shook her head.

"I've been having these little spells here recently, but I'm hoping they'll go away. Jack doesn't know, well at least I don't think he does. It would only make him worry and that's the last thing I want him to do."

"Don't you think you should let him know you haven't been feeling well? Something could happen and then he'd be surprised."

"I was hoping it would just go away, but it's been happening every day all week." Bella shook her head with apprehensive eyes.

"If you don't mind me asking, what feels off?" Lisa stood and walked over to get herself a cup of coffee.

"Well, I've been sick multiple times a day and the smell of certain foods makes me gag. I get hit with dizzy spells nearly every morning after Jack leaves for work." Bella leaned her elbow on the table and propped her cheek in her palm.

Lisa didn't know much about medical things, but all of Bella's symptoms rang a bell in her mind. She knew Bella's mother, Abby, was a midwife, so it surprised Lisa that Bella hadn't come to the same conclusion.

Yet she could have and just not mentioned it.

Sitting back down, Lisa took a sip of her coffee and watched Bella over the brim of her mug for a moment. Her face was no longer pale, but Lisa could practically see the wheels turning behind Bella's light blue eyes. Tentatively reaching across the table, Lisa rested her hand on Bella's arm. "Do you have any idea about why you might be feeling this way?"

Bella nodded her head, her eyes shining with tears. "I do. But I'll have to go see Ma to make sure."

"I'm guessing you hope your hunch is right?" Lisa smiled, the tender girl's happy tears warming her heart.

"Uh-huh." Her lips trembled, but they curved up into a beautiful smile.

"Do you want to put off our cooking lesson today so you can go see your mother?" Lisa asked curiously, not at all caring if Bella decided to leave.

How could I insist on her staying? She's about to burst with happiness.

Yet a thread of sadness filled Lisa's heart. Being around the children day in and out only deepened her desire for a sweet smelling newborn, but the state of her marriage made it unattainable.

"No. I told you I was going to teach you how to cook today, so that's what I'm going to do. I can wait to go see Ma." Bella nodded with a serious expression, but her eyes still shone with awe and elation. "And we might as well get started so that you all don't have a late lunch."

Chapter

FIFTEEN

TUGGING HER APRON BACK INTO PLACE, LISA stepped into the backyard a week later. With confident strides, she made her way around to the chicken coop along the side of the barn. Her cooking lessons with Bella had gone well, and Lisa now had a hang of cooking. But one thing she had yet to fix was fresh chicken, specifically fried chicken.

Good crispy, fried chicken was one of her favorite foods. Many times as a child, she'd watched their cook chop, bread, and fry up chicken legs and breasts. It had been years since she'd had a decent piece of fried chicken, and now she planned to surprise Eli and the girls with it for supper.

Snatching up a spare stump and a hatchet, she set them up in the yard near the coop. The thought of having to chop off a chicken's head then pluck and gut it made her stomach churn lightly. With a hard, deep swallow, she shoved the disturbing thought away.

Walking through the crowd of chickens, she set her hands on her hips.

Which one should I grab?

Remembering that Eli said the white chickens were for meat and the gray ones for eggs, she picked out a plump, white-feathered creature. She grabbed her skirts, lifting them slightly above her ankles, and swished them at her chicken of choice. A chase began, the squawking fowl running frantically away as she followed hotly after it.

It screamed, taking flight a few feet off the ground. Seeing her chance, she dove for it. She tripped right as her arms encircled the flapping bird, and she skidded several feet across the ground. A small cloud of dust engulfed her and she coughed the dirt out of her throat. Leaping to her feet, she wrangled the chicken under her arm. It let out another loud, squealing squawk, but she determinedly tightened her grip on the feathered beast.

Walking toward the stump and hatchet, she glanced at the other chickens, which had gone back to their calm pecking in the dirt. Their quiet clucks seemed like the wrong sort of death march for their fellow coop-mate who was about to be beheaded. She shook her head as a small shiver traced her spine.

Her trembling left hand snaked out to grab the hatchet propped against the stump. The afternoon sun glinted off the silver blade. Lisa's eyes darted from the weapon to the panting chicken under her right arm.

I can't do this!

Her arm slowly began to loosen its grip on the bird, but Iris and Cinthy's laughter drifted to her from where they were playing with their hoops in the front yard. The tinkling sound strangely calmed her nerves as Eli's handsome face flashed through her mind. Taking a deep breath, she straightened her shoulders bravely. This was a chore that had to be done if she wanted to surprise them with a fried chicken dinner.

You can do this, Lisa! If Bella, Abby, and Granny Lola can all butcher chickens for their supper tables, so can you!

Putting down the hatchet so she could use both hands, she lowered the chicken. With her tight grip never lessening, she carefully placed its writhing body on the flat surface of the stump. It attempted to flap, but she kept it still. She slowly peeled one hand away once she was sure it couldn't get away from her. Snagging the hatchet once more, she lifted it, making sure the blade was going toward the proper beheading place on the chicken before she tightly closed her eyes. A loud crunch followed by a croaking squawk floated through the air right before something warm and wet sprayed her in the face and drenched her hands.

Her eyes flew open as the dead chicken's body squirmed in her grasp. A deep gasp escaped her throat as her grip loosened and the little headless body thumped to the ground. Blood sprayed everywhere, coating her thoroughly as the chicken's blood-spattered legs pumped, making it run around the yard.

Land's sake!

Blinking rapidly, her sticky hand slowly rising to her face, she glanced down at her feet. Lifeless, glassy eyes stared up at her from the decapitated chicken's head where it lay on the other side of the stump. A scream tore from her open mouth as she rapidly backed away, attempting to put as much space as possible between her and the horrid thing.

Her legs gave out from under her and she crumpled to the ground. Trembling violently, sobs welled up and out of her as she pressed her palms against the grass.

Stomach dropping in fear, Eli leaped to his feet where he was bent inspecting his alfalfa and tore through the field toward the barn where the scream had come from. His emotions swirled all over the place as his thoughts ran rampant. Lisa's scream had been filled with so much terror that he didn't know what to expect this time.

Please, don't let her be hurt.

He was halfway there when Iris and Cinthy came running in his direction from his target. Iris nearly plowed right into him, but catching her by the shoulders, he kept her from falling.

"Pa, it's Lisa!" Her blue eyes were wide with fear.

"Where is she? What's wrong?" His heart hammered against his rib cage.

"She's over by the chicken coop. She's covered in blood and crying. I…I don't know why. I was too far away to see anything except the blood." Iris's voice shook and tears filled her eyes.

"Stay here." Eli darted past the young girls and took off at a dead run for the side of the barn.

Oh, God, please don't let her be hurt!

The frantic, yet heartfelt, prayer had barely left his mind when he skidded around the barn, almost falling, and caught sight of Lisa. She was sitting on the ground, shoulders shaking, palms buried in the grass.

His knees collided with the ground as he bent in front of her. Reaching out, he grabbed her shoulders and tilted her up from her hunched position. His breath caught in the back of his throat as he saw her blood-covered face and clothes.

Too much blood. Too much blood!

Images flashed through his mind of the blood-soaked mattress he'd had to burn after Cherish's death and the stain on the floor under the bed where the life-giving, red liquid had seeped through and dripped onto the wooden planks. He frantically shoved them from his memory so he could concentrate on the situation in front of him.

His hands flitted over her as he searched for the source of all the blood, but surprisingly, there wasn't one. She shook in his grasp, and red tears dripped off her chin. Gazing at her blood-stained face, his panic slowly calmed. "Lisa, what on earth happened?"

"I..I...Oh, Eli, it was just awful!" She threw herself forward with a sob, and he held her tightly against his chest as she sobbed.

"Ssh," he murmured, rubbing a hand comfortingly up and down her back. Glancing around in search for the cause of all the blood since it wasn't coming from her, his gaze fell on a discarded chicken head beside the stump. On the ground beside the stump, his hatchet lay with a bloody blade. It only took him a moment to realize what had taken place, yet he didn't see the chicken's body.

Lisa slowly stopped shuddering against him, and she leaned back to look up at him. Her blood-covered face was tear-streaked and her dark eyes red-rimmed and swollen. His hands slid up her back and around to her face. Wiping the tears off her cheeks with his thumbs, he cradled her face in his palms, the sticky feeling of her skin strangely calming him all the way down.

"You've never killed a chicken before, have you?" he asked.

"No. I wanted to surprise you and the children with fried chicken for dinner." Her voice still shook and was tear-clogged, but she was no longer violently shaking. "I came out here to get a chicken, and…it ran off without its head!"

She shuddered against him, and he fought the grin wanting to push up his cheeks.

"Well, I guess this is my fault for not asking you if you've ever handled a chicken so I could warn you about that." A small, sheepish smile parted his lips. "When you kill a chicken, you have to tie them down first or else they'll run off."

"Why do they do that?" Her brows raised curiously.

"I'm not sure." He shrugged. "It's like if you chop off a snake's head. Their bodies will still twitch and move for a while."

"I wonder where the chicken went to then?" She shifted slightly away, pulling her face from his hands as she leaned back to look around.

"I don't know, but you don't need to worry about it. I'll take care of it." He stood, biting back a relieved laugh, and offered her his hand. "Do you think you can walk?"

"Yes, I'll be fine." Her grip in his was a little weaker than normal, but she didn't sway once she was on her feet. "What are you going to do with the chicken when you find it? That was what I planned to make for supper tonight."

"I'm going to take care of it." He looped her arm through his just in case she were to suddenly sway. She'd gotten quite the scare, and he knew she couldn't feel all the way normal. She began to protest, but he interrupted, "When a chicken runs around like that, it makes the meat tough, so there's no reason for you to use it to fry. But I'll see what I can salvage from it since there's no reason to waste the whole thing."

They walked toward the house, and Iris and Cinthy, who had obediently stayed like they were told, scurried up with worried looks. Lisa started to reach a hand to Iris, but stopped, and instead gave her a smile as she said, "I'm alright Iris. I just had a little accident while trying to chop a chicken's head off."

"You aren't hurt, are you?" Iris's quiet voice was laced with worry. "You're covered in blood!"

"The chicken's blood," Lisa informed her. "I'm not hurt, but that chicken sure is."

A chuckle rumbled in Eli's chest as he led them toward the back door.

How can she go from a sobbing mess to joking?

He opened the door and waved for them to enter the house ahead of him. The girls ran through to the living room, and seconds later, the front door slammed shut, the sound of their chatter silencing with the bang. Lisa glanced over at him, brows raised as she pushed a piece of hair off her forehead with the back of her hand. "Did they just walk with us around the back of the house only to run out the front door to the part of the yard they could have easily just circled around to?"

"Yep!" He laughed, going over to the sink to wash the blood off of his hands.

"Since I won't be making fried chicken now, what do you want me to fix for supper instead?" she asked, stepping over to the sink beside him as she stared at her hands with a cringe.

Stepping out of her way, Eli stood and silently watched her for a moment. Despite the fact that she was coated in partially dried chicken blood, she somehow was just as beautiful as ever. He felt bad that she'd had to go through something like this. It had to be a little on the traumatizing side, especially since it was likely the first time she had to willingly kill a living being.

Even if it was just a chicken.

Cherish had been able to kill chickens without even thinking about it. It was how she'd been raised; therefore, it wasn't a big deal, yet Lisa had an entirely different upbringing with servants and a cook. He didn't blame Lisa one bit for her reaction.

An idea formed in his mind and he said, "Don't worry about supper tonight."

"What?" Her brows scrunched over confused eyes as her lips parted.

"You're a mess and need to get cleaned up, so why don't I heat up some water so you can take a bath." He nodded.

"Eli, you're confusing me." She began to put her hands on her hips, but stopped when she glanced down at her soiled apron and skirt. "That doesn't answer my question about supper. You and I aren't the only ones who need to be fed. There's five little ones who will want something in their stomachs, too."

"I know." He slowly grinned, a thrill stirring in his chest as he saw the light blush that he'd noticed brighten Lisa cheeks whenever he would smile at her that way. "That's why we're going to go pay Granny Lola a visit."

"But I am fully capable of cooking now. There's no reason for us to go down there." She lifted her chin stubbornly.

"I know that, too." He crossed his arms over his chest, copying her stubborn attitude, which he got a kick out of. "I just thought considering what happened today, you'd like a small break."

"I don't need a break." Her eyes narrowed.

"Well, I think you do." His right brow raised, a challenging tension rising between them. Her head cocked to the side as she stared quietly at him for a moment.

"You know what I think? I think you're scared I'll burn the house down if I attempt to fry something." Her dark eyes flashed with anger, but he caught the small flicker of fear before it disappeared.

"That's not why I want you to take a break. Yes, there is a possibility that a grease fire could happen, but that's not the reason." She stiffened and her hands fisted at her sides. He could tell she was prepared to argue back, but before she could say a word, he continued, "You want to know the true reason? It's already three-thirty. By the time you finish getting cleaned up it will be close to five, and that leaves you very little time to have supper on the table at our regular dinner time at five-thirty. I will admit the reasoning is slightly selfish since I would really like to be able to eat earlier than later. It's been a long day and lunch seems like it was hours ago. My stomach has been growling for a while now."

The stubborn set of her shoulders relaxed as a bright smile cracked her stiff expression. A small, light laugh escaped her throat as she shook her head. "Of course. You're a man, and it's a known fact that men think with their stomachs instead of their heads."

He patted his stomach with a grin as it growled loudly, appearing to make her statement true. His chest rumbled with a deep chuckle as he asked, "You want me to start heating that water for your bath?"

"Yeah." She nodded, her face lit with a wide, genuine smile. "A bath would feel brilliant."

Chapter

SIXTEEN

"**I**S EVERYONE READY?" LISA STUCK HER HEAD into the girls' bedroom three weeks later, Cookie slipping past her and jumping on one of the beds. It was Founder's Day, and they were all about to leave to join in the festivities in town. Not only was it Founder's Day, it was also Jared's first birthday. The day was going to be cheerful, yet Lisa could sense some emotional tension stirring in Eli. Even though she'd only known him for two months, it had been long enough that she was able to tell when he pulled up a cheerful mask to cover the tumult within his heart, and he was doing it that day.

But, of course, he has every right to feel pain today. It's the first anniversary of Cherish's death.

After Lisa had first arrived, she'd noticed Eli presented his false happiness on days he struggled, yet as time had gone by, the fakeness was slowly replaced with real emotion. She figured he would have a hard time that day, but it was still painful to know he was hurting and there was nothing she could do to ease his pain. It wasn't like when one of the children would fall and scrape a knee, or if they misbehaved and she had to take a paddle to their backside. She knew how to comfort them during those moments, but she had yet to figure out how to ease Eli. As his wife, she felt like it was something she should know how to do, but it was difficult to help him when he was mourning the woman who he'd been married to before her.

The woman I'm sure he still wishes was his wife instead of me.

The thought stung, but she wasn't entirely sure why. She knew their marriage was only one of convenience, so she didn't expect him to feel the same way toward her as he had toward Cherish.

"We're all ready, Lisa." Iris's voice jerked Lisa from the sad place her thoughts had drifted. The four girls lined up in front of her, all dressed in their Sunday best with their hair tamed.

"Well, I'll be! You girls are pretty as a peach." Lisa smiled, pushing the last of the dreariness in her heart out of the way. The children deserved to have a good day no matter what she and Eli felt like inside, especially since she could tell by Iris and Cinthy's occasional melancholy expressions that they were struggling, too. "We better get a move on it. Your pa is already outside waiting on us in the buckboard with Jared."

"Yes, ma'am." Iris nodded and grabbed Tulip's hand as Lisa scooped up Petunia. They all walked through the house and out of the front door, which Lisa closed behind her.

Lisa helped the girls into the back of the wagon, and

Eli assisted her up onto the seat before handing her the squirming birthday boy. Glancing over her shoulder at the other children, she questioned, "Did you girls remember your hoops and toys?"

"Yeth, Litha." Petunia's distinct lisp met her ears as the bench tilted under Eli's weight.

"Good. We don't want to have to come back for them." Lisa nodded, turning to face forward again. With a snap of the reins, they were off and headed toward town.

They were in the heart of town before she knew it, and the swarms of people milling around surprised her. Eli must have sensed her surprise since he glanced over at her and said, "Founder's Day is one of the busiest days of the year for Half Circle Creek. People come for miles around to join in with all the fun."

"Oh." She murmured, her eyes darting from place to place, the now-familiar town strangely unfamiliar with so many people. "I know there's going to be a hoop race and a three-legged race since the girls are in those, but what else draws so many people to town?"

"Near the mercantile, there's always food and clothing booths set up. Ladies enter their baked goods and canned things in competitions. But the schoolyard and the area where we went on that picnic is where the party is at," Eli explained. "There's all kinds of games. From wood-chopping contests to flapjack eating competitions. You name it, and it's probably going to be done today."

His grin was wide as he spoke and it matched his cheerful tone, yet as Lisa gazed into his eyes, she saw the pain he was desperately attempting to hide from them all. Not wanting to make him uncomfortable by acknowledging it in any way, she smiled as she replied, "What are you going to participate in?"

"I wasn't going to. I figured I'd just watch the younger children so you could have a good time." He shrugged.

He's struggling pretty badly today.

One thing that Lisa had quickly learned was that Eli loved to have fun and goof around, so even though she doubted he realized it, his statement only showed how deeply pained he was. Tilting her chin up, she cocked her right brow, giving him a challenging stare. "Young man, that's not acceptable!"

"Young man?" Both of his brows rose, nearly disappearing in his curls. "For one thing, I'm older than you, plus I doubt many people would consider thirty-one to be young."

Happiness over the fact that he was playing along with her gentle teasing pitter-pattered through her heart.

"I don't see any gray hairs or wrinkles on your face." She gazed intently at him like she was searching for the two thieves who uncompassionately stole youthful looks. "And I'm pretty sure that makes you young. And you have to have some fun today. I insist."

"And if I don't listen?" His tone was serious, yet she caught the twitch of his lips that meant he was fighting a smile.

"Then I'll make you." She nodded, echoing his false seriousness. "And it just might cause a scene."

"Well, we can't have that happen." He pulled the buckboard to a halt, and glanced over at her with the slow grin that made her insides warm. "I surrender."

Lisa smiled at a red-faced and sweaty Eli a few hours later as he collapsed beside her on their picnic blanket spread out in the grass. He'd participated in the wood-chopping competition then helped set up the tables for the arm-wrestling contest behind the schoolhouse. Iris and Cinthy ran up from where they had been playing with some other children across the field. Nearly the whole Blager family had split up with the two oldest girls playing with their friends while Eli was off having fun of his own. Abby had swept Tulip and Petunia away to show them a display of fancy dolls that Estelle Fabre, the town dressmaker, had sewn to sell. Lisa was left to only tend to Jared, whose dimpled, chubby hand she'd held onto as he stumbled along beside her as they walked around for a little bit before getting their picnic blanket set up for lunch.

Eli laid on his back beside her, chest heaving with a sigh as Abby walked up with the youngest girls. They both had a new doll tucked under their arm. A thought popped into Lisa's mind as the town midwife got closer, and she wondered whether or not Bella had spoken to her mother. Lisa looked up at Abby with a smile and a shake of her head as the middle aged lady reached her side. "Abby, you didn't have to get them dolls."

"I know, but I wanted to!" She grinned, the expression nearly identical to her daughter Bella's. "They never asked, but I saw the way they kept looking at them. I couldn't resist!"

"Thanks, Abby." Eli sat back up, reaching over to pull Petunia into his lap. "I'll pay you back for them."

Abby waved away the offer. "They were a gift, and gifts are supposed to be free."

"Alright." Eli nodded. Abby echoed the gesture and

turned on her heel to leave. She was soon out of sight as the crowd swallowed her up.

"Who's hungry?" Lisa asked, looking up from the open basket sitting at her side.

"I am!" All four girls plus Eli's voice morphed together, and Lisa laughed at their eager faces.

"What did you bring?" Cinthy leaned forward, gray eyes wide with anticipation as some of her curls escaped from one of her braids.

"Ham slices, boiled eggs, a loaf of bread so if anyone wants to make a sandwich with the ham, and some apples. I know it's not much, but I figured we'd end up snacking on things throughout the day since there's food everywhere." She pulled the dishes out one by one and laid them on the blanket within reach of Eli and the girls yet out of Jared's way. Lisa had cooked it all herself and was quite proud of the results. One towel-covered plate remained in the basket's belly, but she didn't take it out. "I actually have a little surprise, but everyone has to eat lunch first."

"What type of surprise?" Cinthy, who was the closest to her, attempted to look into the basket, but Lisa snapped the lid shut before she could get a peek.

"If I told you that, then it wouldn't be a surprise anymore." Lisa laughed. "Now who wants a sandwich?"

As the three oldest girls and Eli piped out their answer, Lisa made quick work of putting thick pieces of ham between slices of bread. Passing them around, she caught Eli's eye and blushed lightly as he sent a wink her way. Despite his seemingly pleasant expression, she could tell his happiness was still forced by his dull gaze. Knowing there was no changing the mood he was attempting to hide, she fought back a frown as she cut up a slice of ham into small pieces for Jared and Petunia.

I wish there was a way I could make him feel at least a little better.

She'd thought joining the town's excitement might help, but so far nothing had made any visible difference. He appeared to be enjoying himself, and she was sure he was, yet there was a sense of sadness shadowing the sparkle in his eyes. She didn't blame him for mourning Cherish a little harder that day, especially since some days she missed her family more than others.

Jared crawled over to her, and she handed him a bite of the ham as she listened to the quiet conversation about past Founder's Days stirring between the girls and Eli. For some strange reason, she felt like she was an outsider and like she wasn't truly a part of the family. It had happened occasionally before when their past lives were brought up, and it always left her with an eerie feeling. A sense of dread filled her heart as she fed the one-year-old sitting in front of her.

What if I end up being just the helping hand and never anything more?

She shook her head to clear the thought. More than often than not, she felt like she truly belonged with the Blagers, yet her insecurities liked to try and squash out that pleasant feeling. Her shoulders lifted and dropped in a silent sigh as she gave Jared a half smile.

"You alright, Lisa?" Eli's voice abruptly brought her gaze up. He was watching her with a slight frown and lowered brow, worry flickering through his eyes.

"Yeah, I'm fine." She nodded, hoping her smile made her words ring true. Shaking off the unease wanting to settle in her bones, she dug into her own lunch and inserted herself into the conversation around her.

Nearly as soon as the final bite of their lunch was taken, the girls started to hound her to reveal the surprise. She flipped the lid of the basket back open and pulled out the covered plate with a flourish, nerves and pride fighting for a place in her chest as she proclaimed, "Since I knew we'd be busy all day, I brought along the cake I secretly made for Jared's birthday."

The girls squealed and clapped as she set it on the blanket in front of all of them. Shifting his position, Eli caught her attention. Her eyes met his and he mouthed the words 'thank you'. She nodded in response before pulling out a knife to cut the cake covered with white icing. "I'm not sure how good it will taste, but hopefully it's at least a little bit tasty."

"I can't wait to eat it. I love cake!" Tulip said as she bounced on her knees.

Lisa swiftly cut them each a slice and passed them around on their lunch plates. She set a piece in front of Jared and he buried his fist into it. Pulling it back out, he shoved it in his mouth and smeared icing all over his face. They all laughed and dug into their own cake.

As if on cue the tink of multiple forks colliding with tin plates echoed around Lisa. She paused with her first fork-ful of cake halfway to her mouth as dread drooped her shoulders. "It tastes awful, doesn't it?"

"No!" Iris exclaimed, seemingly having found her voice first. "It's delicious!"

"Really?" Lisa's brows rose, and she shoved the bite of cake still balancing on her fork in her mouth to see for herself.

"It really is! It's probably the best cake I've ever had," Eli exclaimed as she discovered that he wasn't lying. The moist, fluffy chocolate cake practically melted in her mouth, and she fought to keep her eyes open as a soft sigh escaped her throat.

How on earth did I make something that tastes this good?

"Are you sure Granny Lola didn't make this?" Iris teased, her eyes sparkling as she talked around the cake in her mouth.

The joke stung a tiny bit, but Lisa shoved aside the discomfort before it could settle. The last thing she wanted was to be angry with them over her previous cooking failures.

"No, she didn't. I made it yesterday while Jared and Pet were napping and everyone else was outside. Then I iced it this morning before anyone was up." Lisa snatched Jared before he escaped off the blanket, his cake smashed and forgotten about.

"Lisa, I know it sounds silly, but well done." Eli nodded, scooping up another piece of cake from the plate. Lisa's cheeks heated as she wrangled a squirming Jared back into the circle they had made on the blanket.

"Thank you!" Her heart swelled at the compliment. She'd discovered weeks earlier that to have Eli think highly of her in any way was one of the things that gave her both great comfort and happiness.

He smiled brightly at her, and for a moment, it seemed his eyes were all sparkle and no shadow. Her cheeks ached lightly as she grinned back, her heart happy and her stomach full of food she hadn't burnt.

Chapter

SEVENTEEN

TANDING IN THE KITCHEN WAITING FOR LISA to change into a fancier dress for the Founder's Day dance, Eli nursed a cup of coffee. His heart had been heavy all day despite how hard he tried to be genuinely happy. Guilt swirled in his stomach. It felt wrong to be sorrowful on a day that should be happy since it was Jared's first birthday and the town's largest party, but his last glimpse of Cherish's pale, hollowed-eyed face kept flashing through his mind.

In the recent months, the pain had dulled to where he could think about her and it no longer hurt. He could remember all the good memories fondly and without a pang of pain, yet all that sorrow had swept back in that day. Realizing that she had indeed been gone for a whole year and that it was only the first out of all of his life was still hard to swallow.

Lisa's cheerful laugh as she talked to Granny Lola in the other room drifted to him in the kitchen, and he smiled sadly. He'd caught Lisa looking worriedly at him throughout the day and he knew she had seen right through his mask of cheerfulness. Somehow, she'd learned how to read him quite well, and he wasn't entirely sure what to think of it.

Once he'd become the pastor, Cherish had thrown herself wholeheartedly into serving the community and congregation. Her new responsibilities combined with taking care of the girls and their home had taken nearly all her time, and since he didn't want to burden her with his problems, he hid his emotions. And thanks to her always being so busy, she never noticed. At first it stung since she'd always been there for him when he'd had a bad day, but as time passed, he became used to it. So, of course, it came as a great surprise when he discovered within the first few weeks that Lisa was able to see straight through his emotional mask.

At times, it complicated things since for so many years he'd felt like his emotions were a burden to others, and that was the last thing he wanted to be to Lisa.

She already has enough to take care of, and she doesn't need my feelings to add to that load.

He could tell that all day Lisa had been going out of her way to make him feel better by keeping a steady conversation going, encouraging him to enjoy himself, or just being by his side. It made him feel bad, yet at the same time it was a comfort. Even though he didn't exactly like the fact that someone could see what he wanted to hide, it was nice to know that she cared enough to want to soothe his aching heart.

Lisa had a way with the children and could comfort them quite well, but the way she went about trying to make him feel better was different. She was motherly with the little ones while the comfort she gave him was almost wife-like instead. Well, as wife-like as she could be considering they didn't have a real marriage.

"Eli?" He was shaken back to the present by the husky twang of her voice.

"In the kitchen," he called back, setting his empty coffee cup in the sink.

Within seconds, she was standing in the doorway, and the sight of her took his breath away. She was wearing the same copper-colored dress she'd worn on their wedding day, and her black hair was piled high on her head instead of coiled at the nape of her neck. He slowly took in the length of her. The dress clung to her curves, and the exposed, milky skin of her shoulders and neck caught and held his attention, causing an emotion he hadn't felt in a long time to stir in his chest.

Stunning. Absolutely stunning!

He hastily cleared his throat as she noticed him staring and raised her brows at him. "You look lovely, Lisa."

"Thank you." She nodded with a small smile and faint blush. "I'm ready to go."

"So am I." He walked toward her and they went through the living room, pausing momentarily to tell the children goodbye. He ruffled Jared's hair as he said, "Thank you for watching them for us, Granny Lola."

"Of course," she laughed. "I haven't gone to the Founder's Day dance in several years since my knees aren't the same as they used to be, so I'm glad to have something to do tonight while everyone else is out dancing their feet off. It also gives me a small break from the boardinghouse. Now you two better get a move on it or you'll be late!"

Stepping out of the house, they made their way to the empty field on the back side of town that was quite close to

their house. Lisa's swishing skirts was the only sound between them as they walked side by side. He glanced over at
her and, on a whim, reached down and snatched her hand.
Her head swiveled as her surprised eyes locked on him. With
a small smile, he tucked her hand into his elbow. Even in the
dim light, he saw her wide grin and caught the slight droop
of her shoulders as she sighed silently.

A warmth that started where her palm rested against
his shirt sleeve traveled up and didn't stop until it settled
within his heart. It chased away the chill of sorrow that had
had a hold on him the whole day. He wasn't sure if it would
stay away for the rest of the evening, but as they got closer to
the lantern-lit field full of people, a sense of calm finally
washed over him.

It's going to be a good night. Well, at least for now...

Lisa felt the tension release from Eli as they walked into the
crowd of people staying out late to dance. She smiled to herself, glad she had apparently comforted him somehow. Even
though he had snagged her hand—which sent a pleasant tingling sensation up her arm—nearly as soon as he'd tucked it in
his elbow, she noticed him finally relax for the first time all
day.

A flash of pale blue caught her attention, and she
looked over to find Bella standing next to Jack where they
were talking to her father. Lisa hadn't seen the young couple
during the festivities earlier in the day, and when she asked
Abby where they were, she told her that Bella hadn't been
feeling well. And Lisa hadn't talked to Bella since their last

cooking lesson several weeks before, so she wasn't sure if her assumption about the younger girl's sickly feeling was true or not.

Bella glanced up and caught Lisa's eye with a smile. Lisa waved lightly, then rested her hand on her stomach, the action asking a question. Bella nodded, her grin brightening her whole face.

Good for her!

Even though Lisa was happy for Bella, a spark of jealousy lit in her heart, making the desire for a baby of her own even stronger.

Before Lisa had a chance to slip her hand out of the crook of Eli's arm to go over to congratulate the mama-to-be, a fiddle's tune filled the air. Eli leaned down toward her, his breath stirring her hair as he whispered in her ear, "Would you like to dance?"

The tiniest of shivers climbed her spine at his closeness. She had assumed they would share a dance since they'd come together and was filled with glee over the fact that he asked anyway.

"That would be lovely." She nodded, looking up at him with a grin.

He led her toward the center of the field where a group of dancers, including Bella and Jack, prepared to begin. The fiddlers kicked off a lively version of "Shady Grove," and Eli's hand rested on the small of her back, steadying her yet making her heart pound with its warmth as he twirled her around.

She'd hadn't danced in years, and as her feet remembered the steps, a laugh slipped out of her throat. A chuckle rumbled out of Eli, and they wove through the other dancers, smiles lighting their faces as a sense of happiness engulfed them.

She glanced up at him and his gaze connected with hers. A look of admiration and something else she couldn't place filled his eyes, and a warmth stirred her heart. Before they'd left the house, she'd seen the expression on his face as he stared at her where she stood in the kitchen doorway. A strange emotion that she'd never felt before had filled her belly and heated her cheeks.

Maybe things can change between us…

After dancing to several more songs, Eli led her out of the crowd in search of something to drink. Her hand was once more in the crook of his elbow, and deciding to be bold and deepen their touch, she tentatively leaned her head on his shoulder. He glanced down at her, but a shadow was across his face and she couldn't see the emotion in his eyes. Yet a smile spread across her face as he shifted, pulling her hand from his elbow to wrap his arm around her shoulders. A bubbling, joyful sensation filled her to the brim, and she briefly closed her eyes with a silent, happy sigh as they waited in the punch line.

His arm slipped away as he poured her a glass of punch. She nodded her thanks as she took it from him, their fingers brushing lightly. The happiness she felt seeped from him, yet something deep within her told her that it would likely disappear as soon as they left the cheerful crowd and were back home since he'd been struggling all day and things got worse at night. A sense of sadness attempted to sweep away the glee in her heart as the hunch shifted through her, but she shoved it out.

I'm going to take advantage of this happiness while I have it.

Even if it's only for a few moments.

Chapter

EIGHTEEN

A FEW HOURS LATER, LISA FOLLOWED ELI quietly into the house, her eyes adjusting to the new lighting. Granny Lola looked up with a smile from where she sat in the rocking chair, a knitting project and Cookie in her lap. She lifted her fingers to her lips, signaling them to be quiet since it was nearly midnight and all the children were asleep. The older lady slowly rose out of the chair, bundling up her yarn and needles, and walked toward them where they stood in the entryway still.

"Were they good for you?" Eli asked her, his deep rumbling voice a whisper.

"Yes. They were little angels." She nodded, a pleasant smile on her face.

"It's late and I'm sure you're tired and ready for bed. Would you like me to drive you home?" Eli offered. "It'll only take me a few minutes to get the wagon hooked up."

"There isn't any need. Caleb and Emma said they'd swing by and take me home." She waved a hand, dismissing his offer. "They should be here any second."

As if on cue, the rattle of a wagon rolling up outside echoed through the open front door. Lisa peeked out into the darkness and made out Jack's younger brother jumping down from the wagon bench. Granny Lola grabbed her small bag off the settee and gave both Lisa and Eli a brief hug before stepping into the night air.

"Thank you again for watching the children," Lisa quietly called after her.

"Don't mention it!" Lisa saw a flash of white in the darkness as Granny Lola waved her hand. Eli shut the door with a click, and the wagon rolled out of the yard a few seconds later.

Just like Lisa had figured, it only took a few minutes for Eli's genuine cheerful demeanor to fall away and the false happy mask to slip back into place. Her shoulders drooped as she watched him skirt around her and hurry toward the kitchen despite the fact that it was way past their normal bedtime.

I guess it would be hard to go into that bedroom tonight.

A shiver traveled up her spine as she remembered that Cherish had died in the very room she, Eli, and Jared—whose crib hadn't been moved in with the girls yet since Eli still wanted him close—shared every night. Eli had assured her the mattress had been replaced, but it was still an eerie feeling to know she slept practically in the same place the first Mrs. Blager had died.

Shaking off the unpleasantness filling her bones, she went into the kitchen. Eli stood at the sink where he was filling the coffee pot with water. As he shifted to the side, she caught sight of his trembling hands just as a small rattle of the lid on the pot echoed through the silent room.

He's about to break down.

In the hopes of distracting him, she quietly called out, "Don't you think midnight's a little too late to be drinking coffee?"

He jumped, the pot nearly escaping from his grip as he twirled around to look at her. His gray eyes were rimmed in red, but he was far enough away that she couldn't tell if they were from tears or tiredness. But she'd put money that it was the first thing, and not only just tears, but tears he was probably desperately holding back.

"I'm sorry. I didn't mean to startle you," she apologized with a smile.

"It's alright." His voice was tight and rough.

Choosing to ignore the emotional battle she knew he was trying to hide from her, she pointed to the coffee pot in his hand. "You know if you drink that this late, you'll never be able to sleep tonight. Why don't you drink some warm milk instead?"

"I guess you're right," he sighed, his chest heaving heavily with the expelled air.

"Better yet, why don't you just go to bed?" His mask slipped slightly as a look of mournful pain flitted across his face, and she fought the urge to pull him into a hug. She knew if she were to do that, he'd likely break, and the last thing she wanted to do was humiliate him, which was what would likely happen. So instead, she stepped over to him and laid her hand on his arm. She expected him to pull away from her touch, but instead he leaned toward her. "It's been a really long day, and I can tell you're exhausted. Just go to bed."

Please, don't attempt to stay in the kitchen all night.

His chin bobbed in a nod. "You go ahead and change into your night clothes. I'll come to bed in a few minutes."

"Alright, but you better come or else I'll come back out here to find you." She smiled lightly, hoping to lighten the mood. His lips twitched in the briefest of smiles, and she took it as a tiny win.

Several minutes later, she climbed under the covers after checking on each of the children, switching her fancy dress for her nightgown, and taking down her hair. With the blanket pulled up to her armpits and lightly tucked around her, she listened for any sound coming through the wall where Eli was still in the kitchen. After a moment of dead silence, the heavy click of his boot heels on the floor echoed through the house. A deep sigh escaped her and she briefly closed her eyes, thankful he wasn't putting off coming to bed.

A dark shadow filled the doorway as Eli stepped into the room. He made his way to the chair beside Jared's crib where he kept his night clothes. She rolled over to face the wall to give him privacy as he undressed despite the fact that the room was pitch black and she couldn't have seen him if she wanted to.

It was so quiet that the swish of his boots as he pulled them off and set them at the end of the bed with a small thump was deafening. The buttons of his shirt clicked lightly against the chair as he draped it over the back, and the rasp of metal echoed through the room as he undid his belt and switched his dress pants for the light ones he'd taken to wearing to bed instead of his nightshirt as the days got warmer. She scrunched her eyes tightly closed, fighting the urge to peek at him. His bare feet rubbed against the floor as he made his way toward the bed, and she shifted onto her back once again. The bed tilted as he climbed under the blankets beside her. She slid toward him, her arm brushing his bare shoulder as his weight sank his side of the mattress. Neither of them spoke.

Tired from a full day of excitement and making sure Eli was alright, Lisa slowly drifted off to sleep. Dreamland had nearly taken her captive when she was suddenly jerked wide awake as a deep sob echoed through the room. The bed trembled lightly as Eli's chest heaved heavily.

Oh, Eli...

Not sure what to do to comfort him, yet desperately wanting to, she slowly slid her hand across the mattress until she found his where it lay at his side. He jerked, apparently surprised she was awake, as her fingers brushed his. She pressed her hand into the mattress, sliding it under his. His fingers instantly intertwined with hers and she gave him a squeeze.

Knowing it wasn't enough, and not caring if she was being bold, she pulled their clasped hands onto her stomach as she scooted closer to him. She rolled onto her side, pressing herself against him. A fiery heat warmed her where she connected to his bare chest, but she ignored the sensation, needing to soothe him more than wonder why he made her react that way.

To her surprise, he didn't push her away and instead rolled onto his side, practically curling into her. His free arm wrapped around her waist as he shifted closer and buried his face in her neck. Not able to put an arm around him, she drew circles on the back of his hand with her thumb as his tears wet her hair and neck.

The force of Eli's deep, racking sobs shook her, but

she didn't care. All that mattered was that he was finally letting it out and allowing her to hold him while he did.

She untangled her hand from his as he pulled her even closer. Running her fingertips lightly up his back, she smoothed her palm over his hair as she murmured, "It's alright."

He shuddered against her as he took a deep breath. "I'm sorry, Lisa."

"There's no reason to apologize for crying. I know you've been holding it back all day and there's nothing shameful about shedding a few tears." She buried her fingers in his curls, closing her eyes at their softness. "No one—and I mean, no one—should ever feel bad for crying for any reason, especially for a lost loved one. It only hurts more when you keep it all inside instead of letting it free. Trust me, I know the feeling."

"I know," he sighed, his sobs slowing into shuddering breaths. "It just makes me feel weak and like I'm not in control anymore."

"Hey, look at me." She pushed him back so he would do as she said. He was close enough that even in the dark she could see the tears glistening in his eyes and brightening his cheeks. "Never feel that way. God wouldn't have given us tears if He didn't want us to cry. Eli, letting yourself cry and feel things makes you strong. And no matter how hard you try to hide what you're actually feeling from me, I'll always see past that mask you pull up. So please don't put it on."

"I don't know if I can promise you that." His cheek lifted as he gave her a half smile.

"I'm not asking you to promise anything. I know that this is just a way you cope with things, but I want you to know I'll be here for you should you ever need a listening ear or a shoulder to cry on." She pulled her hand out of his hair, moving it down to his smooth face. Swiping her thumb lightly over his cheeks, she wiped away all the tears still dampening them.

He shifted his face toward her, and for a startled moment, she thought he might kiss her. She stiffened but relaxed with a small smile as he brushed a kiss on her forehead and murmured, "Thank you."

"You're welcome," she whispered back, suddenly aware of how she was pressed against his bare chest. Warmth spread through her face, heating her cheeks and settling in her chest. Her heart hammered on her ribcage.

Hopefully he can't feel it.

"I'm sorry if I woke you up." He rolled part way onto his back but didn't let go of her. His hand rested on her waist, his grip on her loosening, leaving her with a feeling of loss, yet she didn't know why. He reached up with his other hand that still rested on her stomach, and he pushed her hair away from her face. His fingertips lightly brushed her jawline and she fought against the shiver attempting to climb her spine.

"It's alright. I wasn't all the way asleep yet." She smiled in the darkness as she dropped her head down onto his shoulder, snuggling in against him.

Might as well take advantage of getting to be this close to him while I can.

The thought nearly made her jump.

Since when do I want to be close like this with him?

"I still feel bad about keeping you from going to sleep." His chest vibrated against her as he spoke.

"Don't. It doesn't bother me, and I'm glad I could help

you when you needed me to." She rested her hand on his chest beside her face with a sigh.

"Well, I don't plan to cry anymore, so you can go back to sleep."

Leaning up, she gazed at his face in the dark. "Are you sure you're okay now?"

"Yes, I'm fine. I actually feel a lot better." He shrugged. "I guess I just needed to get it all out."

"Alright." She laid her head back down, satisfied that he meant what he said and that it wasn't masked Eli talking. "Then please do me a favor."

"It depends on what type of favor you want." His chuckle was light and loud in the quiet room.

"Go to sleep."

"Yes, ma'am." She felt him shake his head, and knew he was grinning. "But only if you do."

"Don't worry about that," she murmured, her eyes drifting closed, "I'm already halfway there."

"Goodnight," he whispered, voice soothing in the dark as sleep pulled her under.

Chapter
NINETEEN

WO WEEKS LATER, ELI CREPT INTO THE empty house, guilt swirling in his chest as he silently made his way to his bedroom. One thing he didn't know about Lisa was when her birthday was, but he didn't want to come out and ask her since he doubted she would tell him. So that only left him with one option: look in the front of her family Bible that she kept on the nightstand beside their bed.

Lisa had taken the three youngest children with her to the mercantile, and Iris and Cinthy were playing in the front yard, so he was the only person in the house. The click of his boot heels on the floor was loud in the unusually quiet house. The silence deepened his guilt, but he pushed onward determinedly.

There's no reason to feel guilty. I'm only going to open her Bible to find out her birthday.

He shoved the uneasiness away, the feeling reminding him of the last time he'd done something behind her back. Lowering himself to sit on the edge of the bed, he reached over and grabbed the black, leather Bible from off the nightstand. His thumb rubbed across the smooth cover as a deep sigh unfurled from within him, heaving his chest.

Ever since Founder's Day night, he and Lisa had gotten closer. It was like one of the many walls separating them had crumbled. Instead of avoiding touching each other if it wasn't an emergency, they would now intentionally brush up against one another when they passed, and he would occasionally rest his hand on the small of her back if he slid up behind her. He liked where their relationship was, but something deep inside of him told him that he still couldn't have more.

Despite the barriers that had fallen, there were still a few more surrounding his heart. The heart that continued to beat faithfully with love for Cherish. He wasn't sure if he could ever love Lisa the same way, but he was extremely thankful for her friendship and genuine care for him and the children. There was something special about Lisa, and he'd hate himself if he were to somehow hurt her by not being able to move past friendship.

He'd noticed how her cheeks would brighten when he smiled at her and how her breath would hitch when he'd get really close. At times, he couldn't read the emotion shining out of her eyes when he caught her watching him when she thought he wasn't looking, and it worried him more than a little.

Surely she isn't falling in love with me?

If she was, he desperately wished he could stop it somehow. He wasn't ready to love again. He wasn't sure if he even could.

Remembering the Bible resting in his rough hands, he

glanced down. He slowly lifted the cover with his thumb, flipping past the first page to find the family tree. His index finger ran down the aged page as he searched for Lisa's name. A slow smile spread across his face as his eyes found the carefully written entry.

Lisa Marie Fullerton born safely to William Jonathan Fullerton Jr. and Lydia Marie Fullerton on June 21, 1837.

He stared at the words for a moment, the guilt in his chest fading as a plan formed in his mind. Her twenty-ninth birthday was only in two days, and he was grateful he'd decided to find out when it was. Missing her birthday and not doing a single thing for her to make the day special would've made him feel awful. She deserved to have a fuss made over her for at least one day, even if she did protest. And he knew she would.

Placing the Bible back on the nightstand, he stood up. He turned and walked back out of the room and into the kitchen.

Lisa would be home soon, so he needed to start putting his plan into action. Opening the back door, he leaned in the doorway and looked out. It was a pleasantly warm, summer day, and he chuckled as Iris and Cinthy ran through the yard, playing with their cream-colored cat. He hated to interrupt them, yet he needed their help, so he shouted, "Girls, come here for a minute!"

Iris scooped up the kitten, who had wormed his fuzzy little self into all of their hearts, and she followed Cinthy toward the house. They both slipped inside, cheeks pink from romping around.

"What do you need, Pa?" Iris asked, looking up at him as Cookie squirmed from her grip and plopped on the floor.

He slithered over to Eli and rubbed against his dark brown pant leg. Bending at the waist, Eli picked up the fur ball and cradled him on his arm against the front of his red-checkered shirt.

"Lisa's birthday is the day after tomorrow, and I want to surprise her with something special," he explained, fingering the kitten's velvety, pointed ears. "I didn't know when her birthday was, so she doesn't know we know."

"Then it'll be an even bigger surprise!" Cinthy exclaimed, her gray eyes widening with glee.

"What's the plan?" Iris walked over to the table and pulled out a chair, which she promptly sat in. Eli and Cinthy followed her and took seats at the table.

With the kitten balanced on his lap, he told them the idea he had. They both nodded seriously and swore to keep it a secret.

"We'll have to get a move on it since it's only in two days. Which one of you wants to go to Granny Lola's for me?" He looked between his oldest daughters. "Lisa will be back any minute now, so if I were to leave, it would make her suspect something odd is going on."

"I'll go," Iris offered with a shrug as she leaped out of her chair. "If I go right now, I can swing by the mercantile, too, and get the other things we need."

"Alright, but make sure you don't run into Lisa. We can't have her finding out."

"I know, Pa." She stepped over to him and gave him a small hug. "I'll be back soon."

She ran through the living room and out of the front door, leaving him and Cinthy at the table. He looked over at her with a smile and passed her the kitten as he stood up. "If we want this surprise to be a success, I have work to do. I'll be in the barn if you need me, alright?"

"Yep." She nodded, her grin wide. "I'll go play with Cookie in the front yard until Lisa gets back."

They split ways, and within seconds, Eli was in the earthy-smelling barn.

Now, hopefully Lisa will like the little surprise we have planned for her.

Chapter

TWENTY

RUNNING A BRUSH THROUGH HER LONG, BLACK hair, Lisa sat at the table in their bedroom. She twisted all the strands together and coiled them at the nape of her neck, slipping pins into the knot to hold it in place. A sigh drooped her shoulders as she stared at herself in the mirror.

Today's my birthday and no one even knows it.

Her family had always made a fuss over birthdays, yet since they were all gone, it was now just another day. She was thankful to have reached the ripe old age of twenty-nine, but it also filled her heart with a sense of sadness. So many young men during the war had never gotten the chance to see twenty-nine, and even Cherish had died months shy of her twenty-ninth birthday, which Lisa only knew thanks to Bella telling her.

Leaning back in the chair, her hands fell to her lap as she let her dreary thoughts leave her melancholy for a moment.

If only my family were still here…

A knock on the doorframe startled her out of her gloom, and her eyes darted to the open doorway beside her. Eli leaned against the wooden frame, a soft smile on his face. "I didn't disturb you, did I?"

"No. No, you didn't," she answered with a small shake of her head.

"Well, if you're all ready for the day, breakfast is on the table." Flashing her a wink, he disappeared back down the hall before she had a chance to say a word.

He'd gotten up earlier than normal that morning, but she hadn't known he was making breakfast. Not a sound had drifted through the wall from the kitchen. Apparently not only had he cooked breakfast, he'd also taken care of the children when they woke up, telling her to stay in bed a little longer.

Strange.

Quickly standing, she strode through the small house and into the kitchen. The aromas of coffee, fresh biscuits, scrambled eggs, and bacon aroused her senses, making her stomach grumble lightly. All five children sat around the table, and Eli stood behind her chair, which was pulled out and waiting for her.

Her head cocked curiously to the side as she looked at each of their smiles. Crossing her arms over her chest, she stopped halfway to the table. "Alright, who wants to tell me what's going on? You're all acting funny."

Eli glanced at Iris with a nod before turning back to Lisa. As if on cue, they all exclaimed, "Happy birthday!"

What?!

"How...how did you know?" she stammered out, more than surprised. "I never told anyone."

"I looked in the front of your Bible." Eli smiled sheepishly as he rubbed the back of his neck. "I hope you don't mind."

"Of course I don't mind." Her voice cracked, and she bit her bottom lip, fighting back tears. A happiness settled in her heart, blooming onto her face as a few rogue tears slid down her cheeks.

Eli sidestepped the table and hurried over to her. He paused in front of her for a moment, a hesitant expression on his face. The look disappeared and he pulled her into a hug. His touch sent a thrill through her and soothed a small place in her heart she didn't know needed consoling. She wrapped her arms around his waist and buried her face in his shirt, overcome with a strange mixture of sadness and joy. Sniffing back tears before she began to sob, she muttered, "You know you didn't have to surprise me. It's just a birthday."

Yet even as the words left her mouth, she knew it wasn't the truth. It was just a birthday, but they were meant to be special, not dreary and sorrowful. The fact that Eli cared enough to sneak around and look in her Bible just so he could acknowledge the special day that was entirely her own stirred new, unnamable emotions in her heart.

"In this house, birthdays are celebrated. They're not just days for people to ignore and not tell others about." He leaned her back, lifting her chin with a finger, a stern look on his face. The sternness cracked as he smiled down at her, and the same expression lifted her cheeks. "Now, birthday girl, may I escort you to the table?"

"Yes, you may." She nodded with a light laugh, laying her hand in his offered one. He led her to the table and seated her in her chair, which he gently pushed in after she sat. She glanced around at the smiling faces of Eli's children, and a sense of contentment settled in her bones.

To be able to be a part of this family is the best birthday present I could have ever asked for.

Cheerful chatter swirled around the kitchen as the plates full of food were passed from person to person. Fork halfway to her mouth, Iris turned to Lisa with a grin. "Did we really surprise you?"

"Yes, you did!" Lisa laughed. "I never suspected anyone knew. Y'all are very good at keeping secrets."

"Cinthy and me were the only ones who knew today was your birthday. We didn't tell Tulip and Pet just in case if they slipped and said something around you." Iris nodded, apparently proud of her secret-keeping skills.

"I will say that it was a very pleasant surprise." Lisa looked up and met Eli's dark gray eyes. "Thank you."

"Oh, this is just the beginning!" He lifted his fork and pointed it at her with a chuckle. "You, young lady, are going to be taking it easy and having fun today."

"What do you mean?" Her brows rose at his jest at her calling him a young man not too long before.

"The girls and I are taking care of all the chores, including the cooking, and we have a picnic planned for lunch. The only thing you're allowed to do today is relax and enjoy yourself."

A grin parted her lips as she shook her head, eyes blurred with happy tears once again as she said, "I don't know what I'm going to do with all of you. You're going to spoil me rotten today."

"It's our pleasure." Eli's eyes darkened with a mysterious emotion she couldn't place, and his voice dipped a tone lower than its normal bass. "You deserve more than a day's worth of spoiling."

Her eyes darted away from him as her cheeks heated, heart fluttering like a caged bird's wings in her chest.

What is that supposed to mean?

"And Granny Lola is making you a special cake!" Cinthy bounced in her seat, her expression filled with dramatic glee.

"Cinthy!" Eli and Iris's voices blended in the air.

"Apparently you aren't a very good secret-keeper after all." Iris shook her head, disapproval lightening her blue eyes. "That was supposed to be a surprise for the picnic."

"Oops." Cinthy's hand went to her mouth. "I forgot. I'm sorry"

"It's alright, Cinthy. Now I know to make sure I leave room for dessert." Lisa reassured her with a wink and lopsided grin. Cinthy's discouraged face lit back up, and her wide smile so like Eli's returned.

The children chattered among themselves as they continued their morning meal while Eli made sure Jared's food ended up in his belly instead of on his shirt. Lisa's gaze took in each of them, and she thanked the Lord for bringing them all into her life.

I don't know what I'd do without them.

Eli slipped into the bedroom after making sure the girls were asleep. He was exhausted yet heart-happy. His surprise had been successful, and Lisa's obvious cheer throughout the day was payment enough. Glancing at the bed, he smiled in the darkness as he made out the faint outline of her curled under the blanket, her hair partly spread out behind her on her pillow. She'd left his side of the covers flipped back for him. He could tell she was still awake by the way she shifted lightly, attempting to get in a comfortable position.

After a quick change of clothes, he slipped under the blankets beside her. Like every night, his weight on the mattress made her slide toward him, but she strangely shifted hastily away. His brows creased as confusion swam through his veins.

Strange. She never moves away anymore.

"Lisa, what's wrong?" he whispered, turning his head to look at her in the dark.

"Nothing." Her voice cracked.

He lifted himself onto his elbow and leaned toward her to see her clearly. "No, something is wrong. You sound like you're trying not to cry."

"I said I was fine." She rolled away from him and faced the wall, curling into herself.

Shaking his head with a sigh, worried that he had somehow upset her, he flopped back down onto the mattress.

Should I leave her be or push her a little to find out what really is the matter?

The memory of her comforting him not that long before flashed through his mind, and he decided to do the latter. Pushing himself up to a sitting position, he reached over and laid his hand on her shoulder. She was trembling slightly, and his heart clenched in his chest at whatever was causing her pain. "Lisa, I know that's not the truth. I'm not going to go to sleep until you tell me what's wrong. I thought that you had a good time today, but maybe I was wrong."

"No, you weren't wrong. Today was wonderful." She still wouldn't turn toward him, so her quiet, quivering words bounced off the wall.

"That still doesn't explain why you're trying not to cry. And, yes, I can tell that's what you're doing." Tugging lightly on her shoulder, he attempted to roll her gently to face him. He didn't want to impose on her personal space or feelings, yet he felt a desperate need to console her anyway he could. And he couldn't do that when she wouldn't even look at him.

"I'm sorry," she murmured, letting him shift her part of the way onto her back.

"Hey, why are you apologizing? You're the person who just told me that it's alright to cry." He leaned down to peer in her face. It was too dark to see much, but he caught the slight lift of her cheek. "Are your tears happy or sad?"

"Sad." Her voice dipped so low, he barely heard her answer.

"Want to talk about it?" He scooted up the mattress and leaned his back against the wooden headboard, giving her some space yet still being close enough he could touch her.

"Do you really want to listen?" Her question was hesitant and soft.

"You told me you would be a listening ear and shoulder to cry on when I had a problem, and I have every intention of being the same for you. So, of course, I want to know what's bothering you on your birthday."

"It's just that it's my first birthday that all of my family are gone." She sat up and scooted herself next to him, her nightgown pressing against his bare arm. "Last year was really hard since Mama passed away just a few weeks before my birthday, but I at least still had Mammy. This year, I don't even have her."

He wrapped his arm around her shoulders and pulled her close against him as she allowed the dam to break and her tears to flow. She quivered against him, her sobs calm shudders instead of racking heaves. Scooting in toward him, she laid her damp cheek on his bare chest just below his collarbone.

A warmth filled him at the connection of their skin, and he swallowed down the sudden emotion rising in his throat. It was beginning to get hard to ignore the reaction he was having to her when she got all close and personal with him. He wanted to keep her at arm's length, yet that arm was slowly but surely getting shorter without his permission. Taking their relationship past friendship felt wrong and just the thought of it swirled guilt in his gut.

Yet it's not wrong. Cherish is gone. There's nothing standing in my way of loving Lisa.

Close to panic lest the thought take root and he put it to action, he shoved it from his mind. She shifted against him, pulling him completely from the scary place his drifting thoughts had taken him.

Her sobs had slowed, and she leaned back, tilting her face up toward him. Peering down at her in the darkness, he whispered, "You feel any better?"

"Yeah, a little." Even in the darkness tightly cloaking them, he saw her half smile. "It's just hard sometimes when I remember everyone is gone."

"I understand. At times, grief sweeps in and takes you under when you least expect it or on days that you want to be cheerful. It is a merciless little rogue of an emotion." He lightly squeezed her shoulders.

"That's for sure," she sighed, her whole body heaving with the force of it. She turned her face away, staring past him into the dark room. "I just feel so alone at times."

Her admission sent a pang through his heart. Reaching out his free hand, he gently grasped her chin and tilted her face back toward him. His voice deepened, taking on a husky tone without his permission as he whispered, "Even though you might feel alone, you aren't. We're your family now, and we'll always be here for you when you need us. All you have to do is say something, and I'll be there. Please, don't think you have to struggle alone. I'd hate to think of that. Everyone needs someone to lean on, and that's what I'm here for should you ever need a crutch."

"Thank you so much, Eli." Tears trickled down her cheeks into his palm as her words came out with a sob. Despite his earlier thoughts and wanting to avoid those feelings at all costs, he tugged her close. Her arms slipped around his back as she held onto him, pressing her face against his chest and snuggling into the embrace. It felt right to have her in his arms once again, and something inside him never wanted to let go.

Chapter

TWENTY-ONE

"COME ON IN, BELLA." LISA WAVED THE younger woman into the house a month later. "I'm so glad you were able to stop by for a visit today."

"It feels good to get out of the house." Bella smiled, her face slightly pale.

"You're still getting sick?" Lisa led her into the kitchen where she gestured for the curly blonde to sit. Before she lowered herself onto the chair, Lisa sent a curious glance down her form. Bella's green, off-shoulder dress was snug around her abdomen, which was in the beginning stages of what would soon be a firm, round belly. Shifting lightly on the chair, Bella tugged her dress to give herself a little breathing room before resting her hand on the swell of her stomach.

"The dizzy spells thankfully have stopped, but I still get sick every morning, and my stomach stays sour pretty much all day." She sighed, rolling her shoulders. Her fingers smoothed the bunched fabric around her hips as a quiet laugh escaped her throat. "I didn't realize this dress was so tight already! By the time I discovered it, I didn't have time to change since I didn't want to be late."

"I wouldn't have minded if you were late." Lisa smiled, walking over to the stove to grab the hot coffee pot. "Would you like some coffee?"

"Yes, that would be very nice."

Within moments, they both had steaming mugs in hand and were chatting quietly about different recipes. Bella glanced around the room, her blue eyes curious as they searched for something. "Where are the children? It's too quiet for them to be in the house."

"Eli has them outside. He knew you were coming today, and since he was taking a break from tending to the crops, he decided to keep them out of the way for me." Lisa took a long drink from her cup. She was proud of him for how hard he was working to make the farm a success. Both the alfalfa and pigs were growing splendidly, and they surprisingly hadn't had any bumps in the road so far.

"That was nice of him." Bella stared down into the dark brew filling her mug, but suddenly glanced up with a hesitant look on her face. "I've been meaning to tell you this for a while, but it's a little awkward."

"What is it?" Lisa's head cocked to the side, curiosity filling her. "And don't worry about being awkward."

"Well, it's about Eli."

Something inside of Lisa began to panic. "What about him?"

What if she knows something about him I don't know yet?

"Don't worry, it's nothing bad," Bella assured as she leaned up and rested her hand over Lisa's. "It's just that you've changed him. Jack and I were talking about it last

174

night. After Cherish's death, for months, Eli was so sad. Even though he did a good job at hiding it, all you had to do was look in his eyes and see the truth. One thing about him that always pulled people toward him was the sparkle in his eye. It had a way of letting you see he was enjoying life. After he lost Cherish, that sparkle completely disappeared. But a few weeks after you two got married, it came back."

Lisa's shoulders relaxed as a shy grin spread across her face. Bella squeezed her hand lightly, her blue eyes watery. "You gave him back his happiness, Lisa."

"I haven't done anything but take care of his children and his house," Lisa whispered, the words practically an admission that their marriage wasn't a real one. Her gaze focused on Bella's hand where it rested on top of hers, cheeks warming in embarrassment to have been so honest with a girl ten years younger than her who had a man's love.

"I know you and Eli don't have a bond like Jack and I do, but you do have a wonderful friendship. A friendship that gave Eli something else to live for besides his children." Bella leaned down and caught Lisa's eye. "That type of friendship is something precious, and it often grows into more. But just like a garden, you have to wait to see that growth."

"How on earth can you read me so well?" Lisa asked, shocked that somehow Bella had realized her deepest desire.

Her feelings for Eli had slowly but surely been growing, and she was desperately trying to fight against them. Yet it was becoming a losing battle.

If only I knew whether or not this will end with me being broken-hearted.

Lisa's greatest fear was that if their relationship would

turn into something more that she would disappoint him. Or that he would always compare her to Cherish and want the old back more than she knew he already did.

"I could tell by the look in your eyes when I said his name." Bella smiled knowingly. "I remember how it was when I realized I really liked Jack, but we were just friends. It was hard, and patience at times was my enemy."

"I just wish I could foresee the future," Lisa whispered, tears clogging her throat. "I don't want to get hurt or hurt him."

"And that's the hardest part about love." Bella stood, pulling Lisa into a warm hug. "It's a risk every time you let someone in your heart, but sometimes that risk is worth it."

"I guess I'll just have to be patient and find out if this is worth the wait." Lisa leaned back, sniffing as she dried her cheeks with her sleeve. "Alright, enough of this! You came over so we can talk about happy things, not so I can cry on you."

"I don't mind the tears." Bella smiled as they both sat back down.

Lisa shook her head with a small grin as she swiftly changed the subject. "So do you think the baby is a girl or a boy?"

"Jack thinks it's a girl, but I'm guessing it's a boy." Bella laughed, lifting her half empty mug to take a drink. "But obviously all we care about is whether or not it's healthy and that the birth goes alright."

Lisa winced, deftly hiding it behind her coffee cup. Bella's word hit a nerve in Lisa, reminding her that the only reason she was having this conversation was because Jared's birth had gone horribly wrong. But before the thought could settle and make her uncomfortable, Lisa shoved it to the side.

The conversation slipped into baby names, newly walking one-year-olds, and ways to tame curly hair as they laughed cheerfully and sipped their coffee.

"Come on, you can do it, little man," Eli chuckled as held out his arms for Jared as he walked on wobbly legs toward him. Jared shrieked out a laugh as he plopped down on his bottom instead of continuing the full three feet. Stepping forward, Eli scooped him up and tossed him in the air a few times. "You'll get a hang of using your legs sooner than later, and I'm pretty sure Lisa would like it to be later."

Ever since Jared had begun to crawl, he'd been getting into everything, so it would only get worse once he was fully mobile. Lisa had pulled him out of many dangerous situations, and she often went to bed exhausted at night thanks to being kept on her toes nonstop.

A calm breeze blew through, stirring Eli's hair and slightly easing the hot, sticky day. He puffed a tendril out of his eye while his gaze left the redheaded boy in his arms. Cinthy raced around the base of the tall, black oak tree in the backyard that he and all the children were settled under. Her curls were beginning to escape from their braids, and her blue skirts billowed out around her as she ran. Tulip was hot on her heels, reaching out to snatch her older sister's dress. A grin spread across his face.

Whoever thinks that children aren't a blessing obviously has never spent time with them.

He would be forever grateful that Cherish had given him a large family even though doing so had taken her life. Despite the fact that Lisa wasn't the children's mother by blood and that they called her by her first name instead of the customary "Ma," she had completely filled Cherish's shoes. She doted on them and gave them more love than he ever expected her to. It was wonderful to watch their relationships blossom.

If only my relationship with…

"Pa!" Iris's frantic call abruptly interrupted him midthought.

"What's wrong?" He hastily rounded the tree to where she was standing, staring up into the wide branches. She pointed to a branch about halfway up, and he spotted something cream-colored. "What is it?"

"It's Cookie! He climbed up there and can't get down." She looked at him with wide, scared eyes. "You have to help him down."

"You want me to climb up there and get him, don't you?"

"Yes!" She nodded enthusiastically.

He looked from her to the cat in the tree, then back to the girl standing in front of him. His shoulders heaved in a sigh as he handed Jared to her. "Here. Watch your brother and I'll get Cookie."

"Really?" she asked, apparently shocked that he actually agreed as she set Jared on her small hip.

"Yes, really." Grabbing the lowest branch, he hoisted himself upward. He looped his leg over the limb, straddling it like a saddle. A drop of sweat slowly rolled down his temple from his hairline before dripping off his jaw as another gentle breeze swirled around him. It only took him a few moments to reach the trembling cat. Stretching out his hand, he murmured, "Come here. I'll help you down."

Cookie crept over to him and let him scoop him up. Tucking him close to his chest, Eli began the descent back to the ground. He was about halfway down, his legs wrapped around a branch, when he bounced as a loud snap rang through the air. The kitten dropped from his hand as air gushed under him, and Eli's arms flailed. His children's faces flashed through his mind. A strong, overpowering love for them filled his chest as his eyes snapped shut.

I can't leave them. Not like this.

With a solid crash, he landed on the hard ground. The wind was knocked out of him and something cracked in his side. Fiery pain burned across his chest, and each of his gasping breaths jarred his ribcage, increasing the flames.

Iris's terrified face appeared in front of his tear-blurred vision. He could barely concentrate, but he made out the other crying girls crowded around him. Sobbing, Iris rested her hand on his shoulder as she asked, "Pa, are you alright?"

"Go…" he rasped, the pain making it hard to breathe let alone talk. "Get Lisa. Now."

Her distraught face disappeared, and he blinked, his surroundings darkening around him. He fought to keep his eyes open, but the fierce pain won the battle and everything went black.

Chapter

TWENTY-TWO

T HE BACK DOOR FLEW OPEN AND SLAMMED against the wall, making Lisa jump. She spun around in her chair as Bella's cup rattled onto the table in surprise. Iris stood in the doorway, tears streaming down her face, chest heaving.

"Land's sake! What on earth is wrong, Iris?" Lisa leaped to her feet and hurried over to the young girl. Grabbing her by the shoulders, she studied Iris's face.

"It's Pa," she gasped. "He fell out of the tree and he's hurt bad."

Lisa's heart dropped to her shoes as her heart attempted to escape through her ribcage.

No!

She darted past Iris and sprinted through the yard, both Bella and Iris on her heels. Jared sat on the ground next to Eli, who lay on his side, face pale and eyes closed. He was all too still.

Please, don't let him be dead.

But as she looked closer, she saw his chest rise and fall. Relief swirled through her, yet his right arm was curled around his chest like he was in pain.

Her knees hit the grass beside him as she reached out a trembling hand and gently touched his cheek. His eyes fluttered open, and the gray depths were filled with pain. She hastily bit her lower lip as it began to quiver, and whispered, "What hurts, Eli?"

"Ribs," he gasped, panting lightly. "Think I broke them."

"We need to get you in the house to see what you've done to yourself. Do you think you can stand if I help you?" She shifted onto her heels, prepared to help him stand when he said the word. She didn't want him laying in the yard while she went to get Doc Adams.

"I'll try." He lifted his arm, and she ducked under it, her shoulder supporting his weight as he slowly sat up. A deep groan ripped from his throat at the movement, and when Bella stepped closer to help him on his left side, he waved her away. "Don't want you hurt. Lisa is enough help."

Lisa shifted under him as he made it all the way to his feet. The weight of him nearly crumpled her, but she kept her footing.

Heavens to Betsy, he's heavy!

"Bella, would you grab Jared, please." Lisa called over her shoulder as they slowly limped across the yard to the open back door. The distance seemed monumental with Eli sucking in pain-filled breaths at each of his movements. All the crying girls followed closely behind, and Bella trailed at the very back, Jared on her hip.

Eli nearly fell as they stepped into the doorway, and

he pushed her against the doorframe as he got his footing back. Despite his injuries, his up close and personal presence made her heart beat wildly. Especially since she was pinned between him and the doorframe, his form practically curled around her. She shoved herself away from the wood pressing against her right shoulder, giving them both the just the right amount of momentum to make it into the kitchen.

Eli tried to lead her toward a chair at the table, but with a slight change of course, she got him to head for the kitchen doorway as she said, "You need to lie down, not sit at the table."

He grunted out a small answer, but it was so warbled, she wasn't sure what he said. It felt like hours had passed, yet it was mere minutes, when she finally got him to the bed. Helping him lower himself to the mattress, she shifted his legs until he was half sitting, half laying down. His arm curled back around his chest and side as pain flitted across his face.

"You hold still now. I'll be right back." She squeezed his arm lightly, her caress completely hiding the panic hiding inside of her. Turning on her heel, she exited the room. Bella looked up from where she stood with Jared by the table, her light-blue eyes filled with worry.

"Do you think he'll be alright?" Her voice was tight like she was holding back tears.

"I'm pretty sure he has a few cracked ribs." Lisa pressed the back of her hand to her forehead. Tears pricked the back of her eyes, but with a deep breath, she willed them away. "He really needs to see a doctor to make sure nothing is wrong internally."

"I drove the wagon today, so I can go get Doc Adams for you," Bella offered as Iris took Jared from her.

"Would you?" Relief swept through Lisa, drooping her shoulders.

"Yes." Bella nodded, walking toward Lisa, and giving her arm a light squeeze. "I'll be back soon."

Thank goodness I don't have to leave him.

The front door clicked shut as Bella left the house, leaving Lisa alone with her injured husband, who was only that because they exchanged vows, and his five young children. Closing her eyes, she took a deep breath to calm the panic before it rose to the surface and showed itself.

You have to stay calm. No matter what.

"I need you all to either go outside or to your room and play quietly, alright?" Lisa looked between the oldest girls. "Your pa needs it to be quiet while we figure out how badly he hurt himself."

"Do you think he'll be okay?" Iris whispered, her voice quivering.

Realizing how terrifying this was for them since they'd already lost their mother, Lisa bent down and opened her arms. They all rushed over and collapsed against her, Jared nearly falling from Iris's grip. Lisa caught him before he hit the ground and pulled the girls as close as she could. "Your pa's going to be alright. He just needs to be fixed up by Doc Adams, is all."

As the words slipped from her mouth, she hoped they were true and that they wouldn't come back to bite her. Swallowing down the thought, she asked, "How did he fall out of the tree? No one has told me that yet."

"Cookie got stuck and Pa went up there to get him down. He never would've climbed the tree if I didn't ask him. It's all my fault!" Iris exclaimed, a sob escaping her. Lisa gently pushed back the other girls so she could shift Iris closer.

"Hunny, none of this is your fault. It was just an accident." Lisa stroked her hair as she murmured in her ear, a sudden thought filling her mind. "If your pa was getting the cat out of the tree, where did Cookie go?"

"I don't know. He went flying through the air when Pa first started to fall, but I didn't see him afterwards." Iris leaned back, wiping her face.

"Well, why don't you take your sisters outside and find him while Jared and I tend to your pa." Lisa slowly stood up and propped the little boy on her hip.

"Alright!" Tears and worried look surprisingly gone, Iris did as she was told, and the house was soon emptied.

"Little man, let's go check on your pa now." Lisa hurried back to the bedroom, where she found Eli once again with his eyes closed. Sitting extremely carefully on the edge of the bed, she placed Jared in her lap as she reached out and softly squeezed Eli's hand. He stirred lightly, eyes opening as he returned the caress. "You feel any better?"

"No. Still hurts." He cringed.

"Bella went to get Doc Adams, and they'll be back soon." She smiled lightly, attempting to overcome and cover up the sudden emotion swirling through her.

"Good." His lips twitched in a grin.

Hastily standing, she stepped away from the bed, her back to him. Tears flowed down her cheeks as she set Jared in his crib, her arms trembling too much to hold him safely any longer. She could feel Eli's eyes watching her, but she didn't turn around. She gripped the crib's edge, her knuckles whitening under the force. A shuddering breath shook her shoulders as she fought down the sob welling up in her.

I could have lost him.

The image of Eli lying on the ground, still and pale flashed through her mind, fear swirling through her once more. The thought of losing him caused her more terror than she ever imagined it could. It wasn't like she hadn't lost anyone she'd loved before. She'd already gone through that more than once. Her closed eyes flew open as it dawned on her, the realization settling deeply in her chest.

I'm in love with him!

Like a slap to the face, she knew that what she'd just discussed with Bella was true. She had moved past friendship and wanted more. Only she wasn't sure if Eli had made that shift.

I'll have to wait and see.

"Lisa?" Eli's voice was rough thanks to his pain, and it only made her tears flow faster. "You alright?"

She nodded, hoping that it would be a good enough answer. The bedframe creaked as Eli let out a deep groan. Swirling around to face him, tear-soaked cheeks forgotten, she found him attempting to get out of bed. Her mouth dropped open as she tried and failed to speak. Head shaking, she hurried over to him, gently pushing him back against the headboard. Her throat constricted under a sob as she swallowed it back down to be able to talk somewhat clearly.

"What do you think you're doing?" Her voice cracked with a husky rasp, and Eli's eyes studied her face, his brows creased the slightest bit.

"You're not alright. You're crying," he growled. Reaching up a hand, he grabbed her arm and tugged her carefully down on the bed beside him. His fingers swiped away the loose tears on her cheeks, and instead of calming her, it only made her cry harder. "Lisa, what's wrong?"

"You just scared me, is all." She turned her head away, looking anywhere but him lest he see her true feelings, which she was sure were shining out of her eyes. "I...I thought you were dead!"

Grasping her chin with a tender touch, he tilted her face back toward him. Her eyes darted down to the buttons on the red-checkered shirt he always wore. "Look at me."

Doing as he asked, she made eye contact with him, and a sense of calm filled her heart as she saw the tender–almost loving–emotion shining out of Eli's gray eyes. His hand left her cheek, traveling down her neck before he buried his fingers in the hair at the nape of her neck. She fought against the shiver rising up her spine as he pulled her closer, resting her face in the curve of his neck. Careful not to jar his ribs, she tangled her fingers in his free ones where they rested along his side. His chest vibrated against her as he said, "I'm sorry, Lisa."

"It's alright. I'll get over it," she murmured, her heart pounding at his nearness.

"That darn cat had to climb the tree," he grumbled. She smiled despite her tears, glad he was grouching instead of crying in pain. Sniffing, she slowly backed up, not wanting to move away, yet knowing she needed to before she said or did something foolish that she'd regret.

"Iris and the girls are outside looking for him. Iris said he flew through the air after you dropped him." Lisa smiled, drying her cheeks with her sleeve as she tried to lighten the mood.

He grinned, a soft chuckle which swiftly turned into

a cringe escaping his throat. His hand now resting on her shoulder instead of woven into her hair, he drew his thumb up her throat. She couldn't hold back the shiver this time, and leaped to her feet, needing to put space between them.

Why does he have to touch me like that?

Part of her hoped it might mean he loved her back, yet it confused her tremendously and made her thoughts spin. Friends didn't caress each other.

Or did they?

She didn't have a clue since she'd never been close friends with a man before, so this was completely new territory.

Jared fussed from his crib, raising his arms above his head. She went over to him and scooped him back up. He giggled, pushing his fists against her upper chest. "You, little man, are just plain rotten."

Eli's eyes burned into her back as he continued to watch her. She wasn't sure if he felt the connection between them that seemed to get stronger each day. She couldn't help but wonder if their marriage would one day become real, and if it did, how soon that future day would be.

The front door creaked open as Bella's and Doc Adams' voices floated through the house. Glancing back at Eli, Lisa skirted out of the door and into the living room. Bella looked up with a sheepish smile as she said, "I hope you don't mind that we just came in and didn't knock."

"That's alright." Lisa nodded, then turned to Doc Adams. "He's in the bedroom."

The older man slipped past her and into the bedroom as she thanked Bella before she headed for home. Lisa's boot heels clicked lightly on the floor as she made her way to where Doc Adams' voice mingled with Eli's roughly spoken words. Stepping into the room, her cheeks warmed a few degrees as she caught sight of Eli's now shirtless chest. He'd had his shirt off many times in her presence, but it had always been dark, so she'd never realized how tan his skin was or how sculpted his muscles were. But the attraction fizzled out into dismay as her gaze flickered over the swollen, bruised skin across his side. It looked worse than she'd expected, and she hastily swallowed away the tightness in her throat.

Eli's gasp of pain as Doc Adams felt his ribs pulled her out of her thoughts. Sliding up to the footboard, she caught Eli's gaze and gave him a small, encouraging smile. He didn't smile back, but she noticed that he relaxed a little.

Digging around in his small, black doctor's bag, Doc Adams shook his head. "You sure did a mighty fine job at cracking several of your ribs."

"Can you fix 'em?" Eli grunted, shifting his shoulders along the uncomfortable headboard.

"I can bandage you up, but your body will do the fixing," Doc Adams chuckled. "I'll need you to sit with your legs hanging off the edge of the bed so I can reach better."

With the doctor's assistance, Eli did as he was asked. Despite many grunts and moans of pain, his ribs were soon wrapped tightly in white bandages. Out of breath, Eli turned on the bed and collapsed gently onto his back.

"You'll have to stay in bed for several days, and then take it easy for at least four weeks so your ribs heal properly." Doc Adams tucked the leftover bandaging back in his back and snapped it shut.

"But the alfalfa needs to be harvested within the next few days," Eli exclaimed with a pain-filled gasp as the deep breath it took to speak jarred his sore ribs.

"It'll have to wait or you'll have to hire someone to do it for you," Doc Adams replied, his face a mask of seriousness.

"I can't afford to hire someone." Eli squinted his eyes, rubbing a hand over his forehead.

"Is this your first or second crop?" Doc Adams asked.

"Second."

"I don't know what to tell you, Eli, but you can't risk it. There's a possibility that you could delay the healing process or even fall again in the field and make the break worse. If that happened, it could puncture your lung, and I don't want that on my hands." Doc Adams crossed his arms over his chest. "It looks like you'll have to take your second crop as a loss. But at least you still have your pigs to fall back on. They'll bring a pretty penny when you sell them."

Eli closed his eyes with a groan as he pressed his head further into the pillow. Lisa frowned, an idea forming in her mind.

I doubt he'll let me do it, but it's worth a try.

"Well, Eli, I've done all I can for you, so I best be on my way." He reached down and gave Eli's shoulder a gentle squeeze.

Eli opened his eyes and whispered, "Thank you."

Turning to Lisa, Doc pointed at her as he said, "Now, young lady, I want you to make sure your husband follows my orders and rests."

"Yes, sir, I'll make sure he does just that." Lisa nodded with a smile, eyes never leaving the curly, dark-haired man lying in bed in front of her.

"Alright then, I'll just let myself out and be on my

way."

"Thank you, Doc Adams." Shifting Jared to her other arm, Lisa stuck out her hand for the doctor to shake. "We really appreciate it."

"My pleasure. I'm just doing my job." He glanced back at Eli one more time. "And, Eli, don't even think about trying to harvest that crop."

"Yes, sir," Eli replied, a frustrated scowl marring his handsome face.

Chapter

TWENTY-THREE

STRUGGLING TO SWING HIS LEGS OVER THE bed, his arm wrapped tightly around his middle, Eli finally succeeded to sit up on the edge of the mattress. Breathless from the effort it took to move with cracked ribs, he placed his palms on either side of him as he carefully got his breath back. It had only been a day since his accident, but he couldn't stay in bed any longer.

I have a crop to harvest.

Taking the crop as a loss wasn't something he was willing to do. Not when he had a family depending on him to take care of them.

He had the house to himself since Lisa had taken all the children with her when she'd left to run errands after breakfast. Hoisting himself off the bed, he gasped as fiery pain shot through his side. His teeth gritted together so hard he was surprised he didn't crack a tooth.

Hobbling to the footboard, he grabbed his shirt off the wooden structure where Lisa had draped it the day before.

He carefully pulled one arm into a sleeve, a hissed breath escaping through his teeth. It took him an embarrassing amount of time to finally get his other arm in its sleeve, and by the time he was done buttoning the front, he was breathless and in more pain than he'd care to admit.

Got to hurry. Lisa will be home any minute now.

His backside plopped back onto the bed as he sat to pull on his boots. Growling in the back of his throat, he nearly gave up when he discovered yanking on his shoes was harder than his struggle with his shirt since he had to bend over to shove his foot in the boot. Dread swept through his pain filled chest.

How am I supposed to harvest an alfalfa crop when I can barely get myself dressed?

Pushing the discouraging thought from his mind, he concentrated on getting his feet boot clad. A satisfied grin broke out on his sweaty face as he finally succeeded. With a careful shove to the mattress, he stood back up.

His steps were slow as he made his way to the kitchen. Seeing the coffee pot still on the stove, he poured himself a cup of the dark brew to give himself a little break before continuing on outside where an extremely hard day's worth of work waited for him. Not daring to sit at the table lest he struggle to get back up, he leaned his back gently against the countertop behind him. His eyes slipped closed as he took a long drink, but they shot back open as the front door creaked.

Oh no.

Lisa's familiar footsteps echoed through the living room and to the bedroom. He cringed as they practically ran back down the hall. Her form filled the kitchen doorway, dark eyes wide with fear. He shifted away from the counter as she caught sight of him, her expression relaxing with relief. But it was swiftly replaced with a strange combination of anger and concern.

"Why are you out of bed?" Her voice was calm, the complete opposite of her face.

"Where are the children?" he asked, avoiding her question and her eyes as he stared into his mug.

"Abby is watching them for the afternoon for me." She watched him for a moment before pointing her finger at him, her other hand on her hip. "And don't you avoid my question because I know that's what you're doing. What are you doing out of bed? You know you aren't supposed to get up."

A sheepish feeling swirled through his gut, but he fought to keep it from crossing his face.

"There's a crop outside that needs to be harvested," he answered bluntly, meeting Lisa's gaze. Her mouth dropped open in shock as she stared unbelievingly at him.

"Please, tell me you're joking!" Lisa exclaimed, finally getting her voice back. Eli was obviously in pain if the sweat beaded along his brow and pale face were any telltale. His shirt clung to shoulders, and she knew that it had likely been a little bit of a struggle for him to get on.

"I'm as serious as I've ever been." His eyes darkened and his brows lowered.

"Well, I don't care how serious you are. You aren't leaving this house." She crossed her arms over her chest, anger and fear mingling like friends inside her. The last thing she wanted Eli to do was injure himself further.

"Like you can stop me?" A challenge shone out of his eyes as his chin tipped up and his jaw tightened in frustration.

Worry flitted through her since she wasn't sure how far he'd push it. Fighting with him was the last thing she wanted to do.

"I'll drag you back to bed if I have to." She shot him a look. Lisa knew this was turning into an argument, but it was an argument she wasn't willing to lose.

I can't lose because if I do, he'll go outside and hurt himself worse.

"You can't do that and you know it!" He laughed harshly with a cringe. "You were barely able to help me to the house yesterday. And that was with me helping. How do you expect to forcefully shove me back in bed when I'm fighting against you?"

Her eyes narrowed as anger seeped into her bones, the temper she kept deep down and in control surfacing.

"All I have to do is flick you in the ribs and you'll crumble just like that and do my will." She lifted a hand, snapping her fingers to emphasize her point. His brows shot up, nearly disappearing in the curls messily scattered across his forehead.

"You wouldn't dare," he growled.

"Just watch me." She took a step closer to him and he set the mug in his hand down on the counter behind him. Holding up his empty hand, he gestured for her to stop, and she did, not really wanting to hurt him even if it was for his own good.

"Lisa, you don't understand!" His voice rose a few tones, but it wasn't quite a shout.

"What don't I understand?" She looked up at him, eyes pleading for him to explain.

"I have to get that crop harvested. I can't take it as a loss."

"But we have the money from the first one and in a few months the pigs will be sold. That's a decent amount." She threw one hand out.

"I have to think about the future, Lisa. This isn't about the present. Whatever money I make this year has to last until next year's first crop." He dragged a hand through his hair, making it stick straight up. "This is my first year as a farmer, and I can't fail."

She clenched her shaking hands into fists as she took a deep breath, barely keeping the reins pulled tight on her temper. Her voice lowered, a husky rumble in the back of her throat as she said, "So, this is about you, isn't it? You just don't want the word 'failure' associated with you."

"This isn't about me!" He roared, fury flashing in his eyes. He flinched, wrapping an arm around his jarred ribs. She took a step back, surprise spurring her movement as her own anger evaporated.

I went too far…

"I want to be able to provide for this family. For you." His voice cracked. "I know hard times will come, but I don't want to have to face them my first year. I want to be able to make sure my children don't go to bed with hungry stomachs. I want to be able to get them new clothes when they need them. This has *never* been about me."

Tears streamed down his pale face, and there was a telling wetness on her own cheeks. Stepping up to him, she choked out, "I'm sorry. I'm so sorry. I should have never said that."

Without a word he reached out and offered her his hand. She stepped closer and carefully wrapped her arms around his waist, making sure to stay clear of his sore ribs as she rested her head on his shoulder. His fingers tangled in her hair, messing up the pinned-down coil, but she sighed at the caress. His cheek fell to the top of her head as he murmured, "I should never have yelled at you like that. I'm the one who should be apologizing, not you."

"It's alright," she whispered, her voice muffled by his shirt.

"No, it's not. I was mad at myself and my stupid ribs. I should have never taken it out on you." His grip tightened on her back, and the nearness of him intoxicated her senses, setting her heart to pounding. "But no matter how much you protest, I have to harvest that crop."

She pulled away from him and stared up at him. Shaking her head slowly, she pleaded, "Please, don't. You getting hurt again would be one of the worst things that could happen."

"Lisa, I have to." He looked away, but she gently grabbed his chin and turned his face back.

"If you could have seen the girls' faces yesterday, you wouldn't still insist. They were terrified, Eli. They can't lose you, too. Not after already losing their mother." Unable to stop herself, she ran her thumb along his jawline. He hadn't shaved in a few days, so his face was rough with stubble. The feeling sent a tingling sensation all the way down to her elbow.

"I don't have any other choice."

"Yes, you do." She nodded, knowing he wouldn't like

what she was about to propose. "I can do it."

"No!" His tone was urgent, yet he spoke gently to not cause himself more pain, and he shook his head. "No, I won't have my wife out in the fields doing a man's work. I won't allow it!"

"Like you can stop me?" She cocked up her right brow, purposely echoing his words from earlier. His lips twitched as he realized what she'd done. The argument had completely turned around on its head with it now being about her not doing something instead of him.

"I'll tie you to a chair if that's what it takes to keep you from going out there in the fields." Eli looked at her with stormy eyes and a frown, yet there was also a strange emotion in his gaze that she couldn't place. It swirled a fuzzy feeling through her stomach.

"Eli, why do you think I took the children to Abby's? Yesterday I decided that I would harvest the alfalfa nearly as soon as Doc Adams told you that you couldn't do it. I can do this. Please, let me do it." She whispered, her tone pleading. "I don't want this to come between us because I lo…Not when we've already come this far."

How far have we even come though? And did I just almost say "I love you"?

He stared in silence at her for a few moments, the fact that he was thinking clear by the look in his eyes. His fingers slipped from her hair as his other hand left her waist. He rested both of them on her shoulders near her neck. Closing the space between them, he leaned down toward her, and for an extremely desirous moment, she thought he was going to kiss her. But instead he rested his forehead on hers, his cof-fee-scented breath warm on her face as he said, "I'll let you, but only on one condition."

"What condition is that?" she asked, her eyes slipping closed with a silent sigh. Everything in her screamed to tilt her face forward and kiss him, but she quieted the shouts, not wanting to do something foolish.

"You have to promise me that you won't do anything that will end up getting you hurt. I can't have anything happen to you...I need you." The emotion in his voice surprised her, yet it made something floating around inside of her finally settle down with satisfaction.

He needs me. He actually needs me!

"I promise."

Chapter

TWENTY-FOUR

A FEW MINUTES LATER, ELI WAS SITTING AT the kitchen table, refilled cup of coffee between his hands as he waited for Lisa to change into different clothes. Despite her promise to be careful, he still hated the fact that she was going to be doing his work. It didn't feel right, yet he couldn't help but wonder what Cherish would have done if it were her instead of Lisa in this situation. The more he thought of it, he actually wasn't sure if Cherish would've been able to physically do it. She had been a delicate flower of a woman.

Lisa was the opposite, and he knew she could harvest the crop. She had the gumption, determination, and just enough of a stubborn streak to keep her going.

I bet she could do anything she put her mind to.

The difference between how his life was with Cherish and how it was now was tremendous. He hated himself for it, but he liked the new better than the old. With Cherish, he was just the calm, collected preacher man who was always there to comfort and help out his flock. He would still willingly go if anyone wanted his help, yet there was a sense of freedom he had with Lisa and his new farming occupation that was missing during his time in the ministry and first marriage.

He wasn't sure how it had happened, but Lisa somehow knew him better in just roughly four months than Cherish had in the last years of their marriage. At first, he hadn't been sure how he felt about Lisa being able to see past his emotion mask, but as time had gone by, he discovered that it was actually a comfort. To be able to have someone to lean on and console him again when he was having a rough time was something that he'd never realized how much he'd missed having in his life.

Yet Cherish is the one who still holds my heart.

Even as the thought flitted through his mind, he wasn't sure how true it was anymore. He loved the friendship he had with Lisa, but he kept finding himself desiring to touch and hold her more and more. Friends didn't want to hold each other close and feel the other's heartbeat against them.

Well, at least they shouldn't.

Lisa's clicking heels on the wooden floor as she walked down the hall pulled Eli out of his thoughts. As he looked toward the kitchen doorway, a warmth spread in his chest as he waited for her arrival. Her form filled the opening separating the living room and the kitchen, and he nearly choked on his coffee.

"What are you wearing?" he exclaimed, brows shooting up.

"What's the matter? You don't like it?" She laughed lightly as she smoothed a hand down the front of a tan button-up shirt before adjusting the waistband of the dark brown pants she was wearing. Both looked strangely familiar.

"Where did you get those?" He couldn't drag his eyes away from her. The pants fitted her legs in a way that would tempt any red-blooded man. His cheeks heated as his thoughts slipped onto a road they had no right to travel down.

"They're your old clothes. I found them in the back of the wardrobe. I stayed up late last night to alter them to fit me." She smiled, but the expression vanished as she caught him staring at her. A blush blossomed on her face, and he swiftly dropped his eyes back down to the cup in his hands.

"That's why you didn't come to bed last night," he murmured as a strange tension filled the room between them, its grip nearly making him gasp for breath. He'd always thought she was attractive, but as more time went by, it became overwhelmingly noticeable. The thoughts he occasionally allowed himself to think were always shoved to the side in haste. He still felt guilty to think of another woman the way only Cherish had ever filled his mind.

"I did come to bed, but it was a little after midnight. You were already asleep." She stepped over to the table, her eyes looking at anything but him, and he did the same—not daring to glance at her lest he stare again and do something foolish.

Snap out of it already, Eli!

"Do you know what to do with the alfalfa?" he asked, wisely changing the subject for his own sake.

"You cut it down with the sickle and then load it into the back of the buckboard so it can be sold. That's what you did with the first crop, right?" She rubbed a hand on the back of her neck, finally making eye contact with him.

"Yep." He nodded, a small smile twitching the corners of his lips up. "But you have to make sure that you don't pull up the roots or sod when you cut it."

She stood in front of him, listening intently as he described the process in full. The tension evaporated slowly from the room and the normal ease that was always between them replaced it. Gently sighing so not to jar his bound chest, he let himself relax.

"Now, young man, you need to get back to bed. You've been up long enough and I'm not going outside until I know you're tucked in safe and sound," she said, her tone serious, yet her sparkling eyes a display of mirth.

He never thought he'd love being called a young man, but the jest from Lisa's lips sent a flutter of happiness through his heart.

"Yes, ma'am." He rolled his eyes with a grin as he carefully pushed himself to his feet. Her fingers encircled his arm just above his elbow. Heat radiated through him, and he swallowed abruptly, hoping she didn't hear. Leading him to the bedroom, she gently eased him to a sitting position on the bed.

"I don't even want to know how long it took you to put these on." She shook her head as she pulled off his boots. His eyes glued to her form bent in front of him, and once again he could breath or look away.

Why is she making me feel this way?

"Then I won't tell you," he whispered, his voice strangely lower than normal and husky. The sound made him cringe, but he hastily wiped away the expression as she glanced up with just a touch of surprise lighting her dark eyes.

She slowly stood to her feet, hands resting on her thighs. Swirling her finger, she gestured to his legs. "Alright, get all the way in bed."

Doing as she commanded, he lifted one leg at a time onto the mattress, his arm instinctively snaking around his chest. A quiet grunt of pain rumbled in his throat. Lisa shifted beside him and he looked up in time to catch her shaking her head. "And you thought you could harvest a whole crop of alfalfa in that condition? You wouldn't have even made it to the barn, let alone lasted five minutes in the field."

Instead of answering since what she said was the truth, he just stared up at her as she crossed her arms over her chest. A smile played on her lips and his own moved upward to match hers. "You're a very stubborn man!"

"And you, young lady, are just as stubborn." He cocked up his right brow, his grin turning saucy. She tilted her head back with a laugh and the room filled with the husky, tinkling sound. Yet again for what felt like the hundredth time that day, a warm emotion spread through his chest, but this time leaving him with a pleasant feeling instead of guilt. "The day is slowly ticking away. You better get a move on it."

"Yes, I better," she sighed, her shoulders drooping before she straightened them. "I have a lot to do and a short amount of time to do it."

She walked across the room and into the doorway but paused before leaving the room. Her eyes found his, and she smiled softly as she quietly called, "I don't want to come back inside to find you in the kitchen again. You stay in bed this time."

"I won't move." He nodded, his expression turning tender. "And, remember, be careful."

"I will." Her voice dropped to a whisper as a look he couldn't read settled over her face. She tossed him one last smile before slipping into the hall and out of sight.

Resting his head against the headboard behind him, he listened as she made her way through the silent house and outside. He wanted to watch her out the window in the kitchen but didn't dare. Exhaustion was his steady companion, plus Lisa would have his hide if she found out he got out of bed right after he told her he would stay put.

A full-fledged grin spread across his face as he thought of the dark-headed beauty likely already in the barn, but it slowly turned into a frown as he realized his predicament.

What am I supposed to do with these new emotions when my conscience tells me they're wrong, yet at the same time they feel so right?

Chapter
TWENTY-FIVE

WITH A DEEP SIGH THAT DROOPED HER shoulders, Lisa pushed her sweaty hair off her forehead. She had only started harvesting the alfalfa plus doing all of Eli's chores on top of the housework that the oldest girls couldn't do the day before, and she was exhausted. Eli hadn't asked any of the neighbors for help, which she figured was due to stubborn pride, and she still felt like too much of a newcomer to ask herself, so she was on her own. Putting the sickle back on its hook, she grabbed the pitchfork from on the wall beside it.

The horses nickered from their stalls as she walked toward them, pitchfork dragging along the ground behind her. She was too tired to expel the extra energy to lift it to her shoulder, yet she somehow had to muck the stalls before she could go get the children, who Abby was generously watching again. After she came back home, she had to fix supper, then get everyone ready for bed.

If only it could be bedtime already…

Even with all the days she'd spent scrubbing laundry and waiting tables, Lisa had never been this tired. She didn't think it was possible to fall asleep while standing up, yet now she wasn't so sure. Her eyes burned with the need to close her lids for many hours, but she had a while to go still before her head could sink into her soft pillow.

Leading out one horse, she hooked his halter to the stall door. The open blisters and raw places on her hands rubbed painfully on the pitchfork handle as she hefted it to clean out the stall. Her burning arms grew weaker with each fleeting second, but she managed to clear out all the soiled hay. Breathless and head dully throbbing, she moved over to the other stall and did the same. It took her double the time that it had the day before, but she was finally finished with all the chores.

Her hand reached instinctively to rub the soreness at the base of her neck between her shoulders as she walked across the yard to the house. Pausing momentarily to gaze at the alfalfa field, tears stung the back of her eyes.

So much, yet so little time.

Despite working for hours in the field for two days, she'd barely managed to harvest a quarter of the crop. At a distance, the field looked small, yet when she walked through it, cutting down the alfalfa as she went, it was quite large. It felt like such an endless task, and she couldn't go fast enough. The alfalfa needed to be completely harvested within days in order for it to be sellable, yet she'd never make it.

Fighting back the tears welling up thanks to feeling like a failure–and being beyond tired–she continued on to the house. The back door opened easily, and she stepped into the silent kitchen. Eli was still bedridden and would be until the

end of the week, so she had been alone all day, and the lone-
liness was beginning to get to her. She slowly pumped water
at the sink, washing the dirt, sweat, and dried blood off her
hands. The cool water stung her torn up palms, and a hiss
slipped past her sun-chapped lips. A single tear dripped off
her chin into the water below her and she failed to stifle the
sob as it escaped her throat.

I can't do this! At least not alone.

Emotions battled inside her, and her shoulders shook
as she quietly let it all out for a couple of minutes. Bare feet
shuffled on the wood floor in the hall, and she hastily dried
her face. Apparently Eli had heard her cry through the wall.
She sensed him as his form filled the doorway behind her, but
she didn't dare turn around until she had a hold of herself.
Gentle hands rested on the tops of her shoulders and she was
carefully spun around to face the man who she didn't want to
see her tears.

His gray eyes skittered worriedly across her damp
face, taking in the tears, smeared dirt, and sunburn. He lifted
one hand and cupped her cheek. She leaned into his touch
with a sobbed sigh as he wiped away the wetness on her face
with the top of his thumb.

"You're working too hard, Lisa." His voice was a
warm breath across her face as he leaned down and rested his
forehead on hers. "You're going to make yourself sick if you
don't slow down. And that's the last thing I want."

"I don't have a choice." She shook her head, but he
stiffened his wrist, stopping the movement. "You said it yourself. That crop has to be harvested."

"It's not just that, you're doing *all* of my work, and it's
way too much for you to handle." He backed up, looking

deeply into her eyes. The gaze warmed her chest and fluttered her stomach.

He cares so much…But why can't he love me?

"I've decided to just hire someone to help out until I get back on my feet." He let go of her, shifting back a little.

"But we can't afford that!" she exclaimed, tears warbling her voice.

"It's a sacrifice we'll have to make. I don't want you dealing with all of this anymore. It's not right!" His voice deepened a few tones like it always did when he was being serious and wanted to make his point clear.

"I just need a few days to adjust and then I'll be fine. I can do this, Eli."

"Well, maybe I don't want you to do this." His eyes narrowed and he leaned down until their faces were inches apart. "Do you realize how hard it is to lay in bed all day knowing you're outside working yourself to death?"

"I'm not working myself to death," she insisted, backing up a step before she did something foolish. Despite the fact that they were bickering, being that close to him was all too tempting. All she had to do was shift slightly and her mouth would be on his, shutting him up and successfully ending their little spat. Things had shifted for her the past several days, and she now wanted to take their relationship places it had never been, yet she had to be patient since she didn't want to push things and ruin everything.

"Lisa, you were barely capable of changing into your nightgown last night, you were so tired! I don't even think your head had touched the pillow yet and you were already sound asleep. It's not good for you."

"It's not the first time I've been tired, and I was fine

then." She pursed her lips, her tiredness bringing out frustration. All she wanted to do was get through the next several hours with as few issues as possible, yet it didn't appear to be happening.

His brows creased dramatically as he gave her a dark, worried stare. He grabbed her hands faster than she could blink, a pain-filled grimace crossing his face as the motion jerked his ribs. Lifting them to chest level, he turned them over to expose her palms as he growled, "Look at them, Lisa! Blistered and raw."

"I'm just not used to the work, is all." She attempted to curl her fingers in to cover the marred flesh, but his thumbs abruptly stopped her.

"These aren't the hands of my wife–these are the hands of a field hand. And that's something I *never* want my wife to be. Your place is in this house, not out digging in the dirt and throwing slop to the pigs. That's my job."

"Well, you can't do your job right now, so I have to." She jerked her hands out of his and pushed past him, walking toward the living room.

"Where are you going?" he asked, confused as he followed after her, albeit a little slower.

"I have to change so that I can go get the children from Abby."

"Which will be a long walk since the buckboard can't be used until the alfalfa is all harvested." He leaned against the bedroom door frame as she took her hair down.

"How else do you expect me to get them home? You know what happened yesterday when Iris tried to get them all home. Petunia, Jared, and Tulip were all crying by the time they got here. And Abby has baking to do today, so she can't leave the house to walk the several blocks over here." She dragged the brush through her black locks, then braided it to the side, not having the energy to pin it back up.

"Once I hire someone, you won't need Abby to watch them since you'll be back to your normal routine." His voice rumbled, and she could hear his frustration.

Taking a deep breath, the throbbing in her head more noticeable, she spun on her heel to face him. "Eli, I appreciate what you're trying to do and that you care enough to not want me doing this, but by hiring someone, you might as well be taking the crop at a loss. It would put us in debt, and then the money from the crop would just bring us back to where we started."

His eyes narrowed, and she could tell by the expression on his face that he was thinking about what she'd said. Crossing, then uncrossing his arms, he said, "But what if I'm willing to do that?"

"Just yesterday we argued about this, remember? I know how you felt then, and what you're saying now is practically the opposite. Why did you change your mind?" she asked curiously, her aggravation slowly evaporating.

"Maybe because I think your wellbeing is worth taking a financial risk for." His voice turned husky and deep. The grayness of his eyes lightened and his heart seemed to fill them. Her breath caught in the back of her throat, but she swallowed, hastily getting a hold of herself.

"I'm not worth that," she whispered.

"I think you are." He stepped into the room and closed in on her. His arms wrapped around her waist and back as he gently pulled her to him. He stiffened as if in pain, but her eyes closed with a silent sigh at the embrace.

Now this is heaven…

"Eli?" she murmured after a few moments, noticing how he slowly got stiffer and his breathing turned shallow and sharp.

"Hmm?"

"You're supposed to be in bed."

A chuckle rumbled in his chest, vibrating through her, and she smiled, glad to finally break the seriousness of their conversation. "And you're a persistent, stubborn woman."

"I guess that's why we go together so well." She leaned back to look up at him. "We're both equally stubborn in our own ways."

"We do go together, don't we?" He grinned, the sight stirring her stomach with butterflies.

"Uh-huh." She nodded, stepping out of his arms even though she never wanted to leave the comfort she found in them. "Now, you get back in that bed, and I'll go change so that I can get those children home."

"Yes, ma'am." He laughed, doing what she said. She grabbed her normal cream blouse and burgundy skirt off the footboard and slipped out of the room and into the girls' to undress in private.

Chapter

TWENTY-SIX

A KNOCK ON THE DOOR ECHOED THROUGH the house the next morning. Scooping up an escaping Jared, Lisa set him on her hip as she hurried across the living room to the front door. He tugged on her blouse, patting her shoulder and babbling in the language that was entirely his own as she opened the door. Jack smiled down at her, and Andrew, Bella's twin brother, peeked around the taller man with a wave.

"Why, hello! What can I do for you two this morning?" Lisa asked with a grin as Jared let out a shriek and reached for Jack.

Without hesitation, he stepped forward and swung Jared off of her hip, resting the little toddler on his arm.

He's going to be such a good father...

Tickling Jared lightly on the ribs, he glanced up as he said, "There's nothing you can do for us, but there is something we can do for you, which is why we're here."

"What?" Lisa's brows raised in confusion.

"Ma told me how she'd been watching the children for you so you could harvest the crop and do all the farm chores while Eli is down," Andrew explained as Lisa waved them into the house. "Jack stopped by the livery yesterday evening, and I told him, so we figured we would come help you out."

"I really appreciate that, but you two have your own work to worry about. I can't let you help me when it would be hurting your jobs," she protested, attempting to take Jared back, but Jack waved her hands away with a smile and shake of his head.

"Phil let me have a few days off just so I can help, and Abe is doing the same for Andrew. You need the help and we're here to give it. Free of charge, mind you." Jack nodded seriously, yet his face cracked in a grin. "Plus if we didn't, we'd never hear the end of it from Bella and Abby."

"Oh, alright. If you insist." Lisa laughed lightly, too exhausted and thankful to protest. Their thoughtfulness filled her with so much gratitude that she was surprised it didn't spill over. "To be completely honest, you both are a heaven send. Yesterday Eli said he wanted to hire someone to harvest the crop, so this is such a huge blessing."

"I'm glad!" Jack smiled, handing Jared to Andrew as the little boy slung himself toward the other man.

"It looks like you two have found a new friend!" Lisa giggled. "It never ceases to surprise me how he likes to be held by everyone."

"He's definitely a people person." Andrew gently bent at the waist, tipping Jared upside down against his thighs. A peal of laughter tore out of Jared as the floorboard creaked behind Lisa.

Her head swiveled to look over her shoulder. Eli stood in the hall entrance, curls messy and four days' worth of a beard shadowing his face. He shook his head with a smile as he saw Jared, happily getting ruffled up by Andrew. Stepping over to Lisa's side, left hand grazing her lower back, Eli stuck out his other hand for Jack to shake. "Nice to see you this morning, Jack. I heard what you told Lisa, and thanks. It's a huge help."

"Don't mention it." Jack waved away the sentiment with his free hand as his other one pumped Eli's. "Well, we better get started. We're burning daylight."

Eli led the brothers-in-law into the kitchen so they could go through the back door, pausing for a second so Lisa could take Jared from Andrew. A grateful warmth filled Eli's chest thanks to their kindness. He didn't know what he ever did to deserve such good friends, yet he'd always be beholden to them especially since Lisa would be spared from the hard work and the money he had saved up wouldn't have to be spent. Jack and Andrew stood patiently, nodding seriously as Eli told them where everything they needed was and what to do in the field. They disappeared out of the door seconds later, and he snagged an empty kitchen chair from the table where the girls were still eating breakfast.

"What are you doing? You're still supposed to be in bed." Lisa reminded him as he slowly made his way to the open door.

"I'm going to sit in the yard and watch them." Eli glanced over his shoulder at her, his expression blank. She stiffened, and he knew she was going to protest.

"You think they need supervision?" Her eyes narrowed slightly as she set down Jared, who was squirming violently to get away.

"No, I think they are more than capable of handling things on their own. I just want to watch. Is there anything wrong with that?" His voice lowered, frustration bubbling up in him. It had been a long three days in bed and he was bored out of his mind, but he didn't admit it because he doubted it would make any difference since she would barely let him leave the bedroom. The only times he had, they'd ended up arguing.

And it looks like we are again.

"No, there isn't, but you're supposed to be in bed resting so your ribs heal." She set her hands on her hips, and his eyes followed the movement. A picture of her wearing his old pants flashed through his mind, and he shoved it away before his thoughts made him blush.

"Doc Adams said I only had to stay in bed for the first several days. And it's been several days," he growled.

"I know, but I don't want to risk you doing something to yourself. I want you to stay in bed at least until the end of the week." She tilted her chin stubbornly, dark eyes flashing angrily.

"Well, your wants and mine aren't the same. And I'm doing my 'want,' not yours." He pointed a finger at his chest as his voice rose. The room was unnaturally quiet, the girls' chatter vanishing. Glancing over at the table, he found the girls silently watching Lisa and him argue with frightened faces. A sigh escaped his lips as he put down the chair and stepped over to her. Gently gripping her upper arm, he leaned in close so only she could hear him as he hoarsely said, "The girls don't need to see us argue. If you want to continue this conversation, and I have a feeling you do, we're taking it outside."

She followed him, her arm still in his grasp as he led her through the back door. A hot, yet gentle breeze swirled around them, stirring his messy hair. The ground was hard beneath his feet and the air moist. It felt good to be outside again, but he had to solve the problem between them before he could enjoy it. He shut the door behind them so the children couldn't hear and turned to face her. He felt the anger boiling in her and it fueled his own. "I know you're fuming and want to yell at me, so go ahead."

"You...you stubborn man!" she exclaimed, jerking her arm away from him. "Why can't you see I'm just trying to make sure you heal and don't get hurt worse?"

"I see it, and I appreciate it. But I haven't been outside since the day of the accident, and I'm about to go crazy!" He tossed out his arms, then cringed as it jerked his tender chest. "You can't keep me locked up forever just because I have broken ribs."

"That's not what I'm doing, and you know it." She glared at him, arms crossed over her chest.

"Well, it sure feels like it." He rubbed a hand over his stubbled cheek. He hated not being clean shaved, yet that was his fault, not hers. She had told him to not bother getting dressed, but staying in his night clothes all day made him feel worse. So, he dealt with the pain and effort it took to change his clothes, yet by the time he was done, he wasn't willing to use any extra energy to shave. Especially since it involved holding his arms up, which caused him more discomfort than he was willing to admit. "All I want is to sit out here for half an hour or so and then I'll go straight to bed."

She uncrossed her arms with a sigh, the angry look on her face dissolving into one of defeat. "Straight to bed?"

"Straight to bed." He nodded, hopefulness stirring in his chest.

She stared up at him silently for a moment, lips pursed in thought. "Oh, alright. I'll get your chair."

Before he had a chance to reply, she opened the door and slipped inside. She was back outside within seconds, his chair in hand. Setting it beside him, she turned to go back in the house, but he reached out and snatched her hand. Her surprised, dark eyes found his. "Thank you, Lisa."

"You just make sure you don't fall off the chair." She shrugged, attempting to tug her hand free, but he pulled her closer. Her eyes widened as he leaned down and brushed a kiss to her cheek. Her sunburned skin was warm against his lips, and as he leaned back, he watched her face darken even further in a blush. A grin broke out despite his attempt to keep it locked away. He loved how she reacted to him, and something inside him wanted to find more ways to get those reactions.

"You know what you remind me of?" he asked, his grin never faltering.

"What?" she whispered.

"A mother hen with her chicks." He raised his brows at her as she shook her head with a light laugh.

"And let me guess—you're one of my little chicks."

"Yep!"

"You're quite large to be a chick, but I'm glad I get to be your hen." Her eyes widened at her admission. She swallowed hastily, pulling her hand from his as she breathlessly said, "I need to get back inside to the children."

She slipped away from him and into the house. His hand felt empty and cold without hers, but a smile played on his lips as he lowered himself onto the chair. Eyes finding the two younger men working in his field he whispered to himself, "And I like being your chick."

Chapter

TWENTY-SEVEN

LATER THAT NIGHT, ELI UNBUTTONED HIS SHIRT and carefully tossed it onto the footboard. Changing into her nightgown, Lisa undressed over by the wardrobe. She was nearly invisible thanks to the darkness cloaking everything. The swish of her nightgown slipping over her head and body was deafening in the silent room. He swallowed hollowly as he climbed into bed as fast as he could without jarring his ribs.

Don't think about it. Don't you dare think about it!

The end of the mattress shifted under her weight as she climbed over the footboard. Crawling like a child, she made her way to her pillow beside his. He smiled, finding her way of getting into bed funny. She'd done it ever since his injury, but he was pretty sure she'd done it a few times before when she had been up in the morning before him.

She slipped under the blanket with a sigh, catching herself before she slid into him. Her warmth spread over to him, and it seeped contentment into his bones. The sheet tugged under him slightly as she scooped her hand across it toward him. Her fingers found his, and she gave them a gentle squeeze as she broke the silence. "It was awfully nice of Jack and Andrew to come help us with the crop."

"Yes, it was." He shifted, pulling the covers up to his chin. "But that's what you can expect from the Askinglys and Klisters—they're two of the nicest families I've ever known."

"That's for sure." Her hair swished across her pillow as she nodded.

A sweet, comfortable silence settled between them, and her thumb drew circles across the top of his hand. The caress shot tingling sparks up his arm, and they swirled around in his chest before settling in his heart. He heard her breathing even out as her circles slowed, and he knew she was drifting to dreamland, yet he still had something he wanted to say to her.

But I hate to wake her up…

Knowing that it wouldn't mean as much in the morning, he whispered, "Lisa?"

"Hmm…" she hummed.

"You awake?"

"I answered you, didn't I?" She slid her hand free from his just enough to lightly pinch his palm near his thumb. Smiling in the dark at her prod, he snatched her hand back and tangled his fingers with hers. "Why did you ask?"

"I wanted to tell you something." She stiffened beside him, and he hastily added, "It's nothing bad."

"What is it? I'm all ears." She yawned.

"I wanted to apologize for earlier," he murmured.

"There's nothing to apologize for." Her voice was laced with confusion, and he knew her brows were likely creased along her forehead.

"I'm sorry I was such a stubborn pain about going outside," he further explained.

Her giggle echoed through the silence. She leaned toward him, propping herself up on her elbow. "If there was anyone who should be apologizing for being a stubborn pain, it should be me. I'm the one who pitched the fit about you going outside when I shouldn't have. I let my worry and stress take over and make me overbearing and annoying. I'm really sorry."

"Don't apologize for caring. It's nice to have someone to care about me again." He smiled, reaching up to caress her cheek.

"Then don't you apologize for being stubborn." She thumped her finger against his shoulder. "It's the type of man you are."

"What, a stubborn mule of a man?" He chuckled, shaking his head.

"No, I won't go that far." She leaned into his palm as she shook her head. "My father was ten times as stubborn as you, so he could be compared to a mule, but not you. You aren't that stubborn."

"Aah, that's where you get it from."

"Ha ha, very funny." She let out a fake laugh.

"I thought it was." He shrugged, grinning.

"You know what type of man you are, Eli Blager?" Her voice deepened and turned husky, and he really wished he could see her face.

"I don't know. What type am I?" A tremble quivered his words as his throat tightened with emotion. Her reply seemed to hold everything.

"A very wonderful man," she whispered.

Wonderful...How can she think so highly of me?

His breath stuck in the back of his throat, and he swallowed to clear it. Tugging her to him, he held her as close as he dared with his broken ribs. Her lips were temptingly close and he wondered if they were as soft as they look, but instead of finding out, he rested his cheek on her hair as he murmured, "And, Lisa, you are a very special, wonderful woman."

"No, I'm not." Her shoulders trembled under his arm, and he knew she was holding back tears.

"Yes, you are, and don't you think otherwise." He squeezed her a little tighter with a sigh as she relaxed against him.

"Thank you." The words were a whispery breath.

"Don't mention it."

If only you could see you're more than just wonderful...

Chapter

TWENTY-EIGHT

"I T FEELS SO GOOD TO FINALLY BE out of those bandages," Eli exclaimed a month and a half later, stretching his arms out on either side of him, his chest pushed forward. Rubbing a hand down his shirt, which covered completely healed ribs, he grinned at Lisa where she sat up in bed, hair a messy, black halo around her face and a smile playing on her lips.

"I'm sure glad I don't have to keep you from doing things anymore," she laughed, pulling her legs up in front of her. She rested her chin on her knees and gazed at him with what he thought was admiration.

Besides her continuing to do his chores for a while since it wasn't as difficult with the crop fully harvested, things had stayed the same between them. Albeit the attraction he felt for her had grown and was harder to ignore, yet they were still just friends. He knew that many people remarried after losing a spouse, and that it was a Biblically sound thing to do, but he felt like it was still too soon to let himself have what he'd shared with Cherish with a new person.

Walking over to the bed, he sat on the edge and leaned toward her. He rested a hand on the blanket near hers, and her fingers instinctively reached for his. Closing the space between them he brushed a kiss to her cheek. A blush heated her skin as he whispered in her ear. "Thank you for doing such a good job at keeping up with everything and me this past month."

"You're welcome." She smiled, her lifted cheek brushing his. He backed up, looking deeply into her eyes, yet not deeply enough for her to see his very soul. He still wasn't entirely sure what to do with the emotions he felt. He wasn't even sure what they were. Everything was so different with Lisa that it often left his thoughts spiraling in confusion instead of straightening them so he could figure it all out.

She lifted her other hand and brushed the curls away from his forehead. Her gaze darted from his hair to his eyes, then his lips, and back to his eyes. She started to lean toward him and he found his body arching closer to her. Everything seemed to slow to a snail's pace as their faces hovered mere inches from each other. But the moment shattered when Cookie tore into the room, meowing his head off, and jumped on the bed. They jerked apart, blinking at each other in surprise. Jared decided to break the tense silence by letting out a shriek. Slipping around him on the bed with a nearly silent sigh, Lisa got down and went to Jared.

Eli raked a shaky hand through his hair, shocked at what probably would have happened if the cat hadn't interrupted.

How did you almost let yourself kiss her?

Guilt swirled through his chest as Cherish's face

flashed through his memory. His mind filled with all the kisses he'd shared with her, and his gut churned. They had been sweet and tender, yet as he glanced over at Lisa where she tended to Jared, he couldn't help but wonder what it would be like to kiss her instead.

"Do you want me to fix you breakfast before you leave?" Lisa's question yanked him from his thoughts.

How can she act so normal when we nearly kissed just seconds ago?

"That would be nice. I probably won't be back until close to supper time, if not later." He nodded, standing up. That day he had to take the grown and fattened piglets to market in the neighboring town of Clearford. The trip would likely take all day, and if he were delayed, there was the possibility that he wouldn't make it back until tomorrow.

"What will it be then? Your wish is my command," she called over her shoulder as she left the room with Jared snuggled against her shoulder.

If only that were completely true…

"Just keep it simple." He followed her into the hall but stepped across to the girls' room instead of continuing on to the kitchen with her.

"How's eggs and some fried ham?" Her voice drifted from the living room.

"That sounds good." He turned the knob on the closed door in front of him, and walked into the silent, dimly lit room. His gaze swooped over the sleeping forms of his daughters as he strode over to the window. He yanked the curtains open, and early morning light seeped into the room. Iris and Cinthy jerked under their blankets as the brightness swept over their faces. Smiling, he called out, "Up and at 'em sleepy heads!"

They all groaned, and a few heads disappeared under the covers. Carefully pulling back the blanket wrapped tightly around Petunia, he scooped her up. In her half-asleep state, she curled into him, burying her face in his neck. He knew that the others would be up within minutes despite their moaning since they strangely thrived off of early mornings, so he made his way back to the doorway. "Lisa is making eggs for breakfast, so you better get up if you want them to be warm."

Iris kicked back the blanket, tossing her arm over her face as she slurred, "Yes, sir."

He walked through the house and into the kitchen. Lisa glanced over from where she stood at the counter, attempting to crack eggs one-handed since Jared was propped on her other hip. Eli slid over to them and took Jared with his free arm. "Here, let me take him."

"Thanks. He wouldn't let me put him in his highchair." She smiled and gently nudged Petunia with her shoulder. "Good morning, hunny."

"Morning, Litha," Petunia whispered, her voice still heavy with sleep. She lifted her head off Eli's shoulder and rubbed her eyes with a fisted hand as he adjusted Jared on his other arm.

Striding across the kitchen, he gently kicked out a chair and sat down. His arms didn't feel as strong as they did before his injury, and he was scared of dropping one of the children. He knew he'd have to work to get the lost muscle back, but it was disappointing to realize a month and a half of taking it easy had weakened him that much. It wasn't just having to take it easy; it was the way he couldn't do anything that would strain his chest and ribs—which was a lot.

"Are you taking all the pigs today or just half?" Lisa asked over her shoulder as she tossed ham slices in a sizzling skillet.

"The first litter are the only ones fattened up enough to sell, so just half." He sat Petunia on the table, patting her on the knee with a smile. "The second litter should be ready to go by spring."

"And then the process starts all over again, right?"

"Yep. Only next year, I can breed two instead of just one. That would give us roughly twenty-eight pigs a year." He nodded, glad that his pig-farming venture was turning out fruitful. If he was successful enough with the pigs, he wouldn't have to depend on the alfalfa crops, which is what he wanted.

"That's quite a few pigs," Lisa laughed lightly.

"It sure is, but I'm not going to complain once my pocketbook is padded nicely." He chuckled.

Pattering bare feet signaled the arrival of the other girls. They poured into the kitchen, hair messy and night-gowns swishing around their calves. Seating themselves at the table, they exchanged "good mornings" with Lisa. She stepped over and set a cup of steaming coffee in front of Eli as he put Petunia down so she could get in her own chair. Lisa's hand brushed across his shoulder, tingling the skin under his shirt. As her hand swished back down to her side, he reached down and gave her fingers a gentle squeeze. Her lips twitched in a small smile before she went over to the stove.

"Do you really have to leave today, Pa?" Tulip's quiet, still sleepy voice pulled his attention back to the table from Lisa's form across the room.

"Yes, but I should only be gone for a day." He nodded, bouncing Jared lightly on his knee.

"I'll miss you," she whispered, her eyes dropping to the table top in front of her.

"I'll miss you, too." He reached across the table and caressed her cheek. "But you'll have fun helping Lisa out around the house while your sisters are at school."

"I wish I could go to school." The moist underside of her bottom lip showed as she pouted. School had started the week before, and not having all the children under foot had been making things a little easier on Lisa.

"You're still too little, but next year you'll get to go." He winked with a smile.

"I still need you as a little helper for a bit longer, and then Miss Melany can have you for a student," Lisa said as she carried a plate full of ham over to the table. Eli got to his feet and put Jared into his highchair.

Within moments, she had the eggs on the table, too, and they were all seated. Silently, Eli glanced from person to person, a sense of contentment and happiness settling in his heart as he watched his family.

This right here is what I've always wanted...

Chapter

TWENTY-NINE

L ISA SPUN ON HER HEEL TO FACE the back door as it was enthusiastically opened. Eli's form filled the doorway, and he tossed his hat on the counter beside him. He'd gotten home the evening before from selling the pigs, which had brought more of a profit than he had expected, yet his merriment wasn't from that. During the past two days since he'd finally gotten free of his bandages, he'd been so happy, and the cheer seeping out of him was contagious. His wide, glee-filled smile delighted Lisa's heart, and she'd never been more thankful to see him elated since she knew being confined to the house had been hard on him. He walked over to her, his hand sliding across her lower back as he looked at the stove over her shoulder. She leaned back just the slightest bit into his touch as he asked, "What's for lunch?"

"Side pork and gravy with some biscuits," she replied, glancing over to smile at him. He gently squeezed her hip before moving over to wash his hands and sweaty face at the sink.

"How much longer until it's done?" His words were warbled as he scrubbed his wet hands over his cheeks and forehead.

"You that hungry?" she laughed.

"No, I was just wondering." He looked over with a grin.

"In about ten minutes." She nodded.

"Good. That gives me enough time to get everything ready." He dried his hands and face with the towel laying on the counter beside him.

"Get what ready?" Her brows scrunched in confusion.

"Tulip has been sad the past few days since she can't go to school with the other girls, so I thought we could do something fun with her, Pet, and Jared," he explained with a shrug.

"What's your plan?" She smiled. He loved his children so much that it never ceased to amaze her, yet it reminded her of her own father, who had been the same way. She'd seen other fathers with their children, and she had realized at a young age that her relationship with hers was different and special, so it had been a pleasant surprise to find out Eli was that way.

"I thought we could have a picnic for lunch."

"But it's too chilly to do it outside." Autumn was beginning to sweep in, and her Alabama-native self wasn't used to the cold.

"That's why we're going to do it inside right here in the kitchen." He waved his hand around the room. His eyes sparkled in excitement, and his features took on a boyish look as he strode over to the table.

If only I could've known him when he was a young man before he married Cherish...

The thought surprised her and she startled, the spoon in her hand jerking. Her imagination took over as she watched Eli shove the table against the wall to make room for a blanket on the floor. He flipped the chairs seat down on top of the tabletop to get them out of the way.

What if I had been his first wife, and the children were mine instead of Cherish's?

Images flashed through her mind of him holding a newly born babe, the grin she loved spread across his face as he looked proudly down at her. It left a sad ache in her heart since it was something that would never happen.

Yet we almost kissed...

She'd been in shock for nearly an hour afterward. Part of her wished she had given into the pull of desire and kissed him, yet she was thankful she didn't. She didn't want to make a wrong move and ruin the best friendship she'd ever experienced. Eli had shifted toward her, but she kept telling herself it didn't mean anything since he was probably just reacting to her—nothing more. Neither of them had mentioned it, and she was glad. The last thing she wanted was to be called out for her moment of weakness.

"Is that extra quilt in our wardrobe still?" Eli's deep, rumbly voice broke her train of thought. Blinking to clear the vision so vivid in her mind, she nodded in reply. His brows raised as he cocked his head to the side. "You alright?"

"Yeah. Why wouldn't I be alright?" The words came out casual, yet her insides churned as she feared her face displayed her thoughts.

"I don't know." He shrugged, shoving his hands into

his pants pockets. "You looked a little far away for a moment."

"Oh, I just got a little lost in my thoughts." She turned back to the stove, her cheeks heating. The spoon in her grasp trembled lightly as she stirred the bubbling gravy on the stove.

"I'll go get the blanket and then everything will be ready." Clicking boot heels signaled his exit from the room, and she released a deep sigh.

"Why does this have to be so hard?" she whispered to herself as she grabbed the plates they would need out of the cupboard. More often than not, she wished she'd never given her heart to Eli without knowing whether she had his. If she had been able to keep their relationship casual, it wouldn't feel like heartache was about to come knocking on her door. Yet as she listened to Eli loudly rummaging through the wardrobe on the other side of the wall, she knew deep down inside that she truly didn't regret it.

Within moments, Eli was back in the kitchen and spreading the blanket out on the floor. Once it was smooth and he'd helped her set the plates full of food on the floor, he went to get the little ones playing together at the other side of the small house. Lisa settled onto the blanket beside the food, pushing aside all thoughts of love and heartbreak so she could enjoy the moment to the fullest, and waited for their arrival.

Tulip and Petunia's eyes widened in excitement as they saw the setup in the middle of the kitchen floor, and Lisa's heart warmed at the realization that this was not just a happy moment for them. It was a memory being made. One which she was glad to be a part of.

Chapter

THIRTY

GRABBING HER ROBE OFF THE FOOTBOARD WHERE she had left it earlier that morning, Lisa slipped it on as she tiptoed out of the dark, quiet bedroom. All the children were sound asleep and had been for an hour.

It had been a good day—a full day, yet an excellent one. Their house picnic went wonderfully, and Tulip had even asked if they could do it again. The older girls had come home from school with pink cheeks from the chilly autumn air and multiple homework assignments. While doing the mending, Lisa had sat at the kitchen table with them after supper and offered her assistance when they needed it. It made them all seem like a real family and that she just wasn't a needed addition.

Lisa's chest heaved in a sigh as she made her way through the house, looking for Eli, who had disappeared after everyone was tucked into bed. She'd been in the bedroom, getting herself ready to slip beneath the covers to travel to dreamland, so she hadn't seen where he went. She didn't know if he was even inside since the house was silent, and she could typically hear him when he sat in the living room as he read his Bible and prayed every night.

Tying her robe strings, she paused, head cocked slightly to the side with a small smile as she spotted the partially opened front door. Her chilly bare feet whispered across the wood floor as she made her way across the room.

Either he's on the porch or someone left the door open.

The hinges squeaked quietly as she pulled the door open all the way. Moonlight pooled onto the porch like a spotlight and shone on Eli where he lay, his legs stretched over top of the steps, his back against the porch floor. He tilted his head back to look up at her.

"What are you doing out here?" she asked with a smile, leaning her shoulder against the doorframe, her arms crossed over her chest.

"Stargazing. Want to join me?" He patted the empty spot beside him.

"No, thank you." She laughed. "I'd rather stay right here where it's warm."

"What's the matter? It's too cold for you?" he joked, continuing to watch her upside down.

"I used to complain about how hot it got back home, yet now I wish it was that warm. Sweating is better than shivering." She shrugged.

"This is only the beginning. Just wait until winter settles in."

"I have a feeling I'm going to be in for a rude awakening." She groaned.

"Yep." He sat up and turned, bending his knees in front of him as he rested his back against the porch railing.

"You aren't supposed to agree." She rolled her eyes with a playful huff.

"And why not?" His brows raised.

"I don't know. You just aren't." She waved her hand at him.

A silence settled between them as she stood smiling at him. He gazed up at her with a tender expression that slowly changed to something more, yet she wasn't sure of what that more was. Her face heated as a tension bubbled up in the small space separating them. Things had drastically changed in mere moments, and she wasn't sure what to do with the emotions churning through her, especially since it appeared that Eli had noticed the switch in the air, too. Her chest tightened as he slowly pushed himself to his feet.

Just breathe, Lisa. Just breathe.

With two strides, he was in front of her. Her arms slipped down out of their crossed position to her sides as he put his hand on the doorframe above her head and leaned down until his face was mere inches from hers. Chest heaving slightly thanks to his closeness, she held his gaze which had turned intimate. He traced her cheekbone with a finger, and a shiver climbed her spine.

"Have I ever told you how beautiful you are?" His breath stirred the loose hair around her face.

"No, I don't think so," she stammered, breathless.

"Well, you are. You're the most beautiful woman I've ever laid eyes on. When I first saw you, I was surprised since I wasn't expecting something that gorgeous to step off the stagecoach. Now I know why Southern belles are always talked about like they're something special." His voice deepened a few tones, and it was like a balm to her soul.

"I wasn't a Southern belle. I was a Southern spinster." She shook her head, correcting him.

"That's all changed now." He cupped her cheek in his hand, and she leaned lightly into his touch.

"But has it really?" she whispered, not truly knowing if she wanted to know the answer.

"I think so." His thumb slid across her lower face, circling around the outer edges of her lips. She trembled as her eyes slipped closed at the caress.

Please, don't let him just be tempting me for the fun of it...

"Eli?"

"Hmm..." His chest rumbled with the sound.

"Don't do this to me." Tears slid down her cheeks, but before they could make it halfway to her jaw, he swiped them away with his fingertips.

"Don't do what?" Confusion laced his voice as he moved his hand away from the doorframe.

"Tease me like this. It's not fair..." Her voice cracked with a held-back sob.

"I'm not teasing you. I meant every word I've said." He tipped up her chin so she'd look at him.

"Really?"

"Really." He nodded, a grin parting his lips. She gave him a watery smile in return, but it turned into a sigh as he wiped the last of the dampness off of her face. Leaning down, he rested his forehead on hers, and his hand gently slid down to rest on her shoulder. His thumb traced a line up the curve of her neck as he whispered huskily, "No more tears."

"No more tears," she agreed, nodding.

He took a step closer until his chest was pressed against hers. Time seemed to stand still as they stood, foreheads pressed together, his hands resting nearly on her throat. Her heart raced, and she could feel his doing the same through his shirt.

Backing up just enough so that they could see each other, Eli reached up and cupped her cheek again. Only this time he leaned down and their faces bumped lightly together as he paused, his lips nearly touching hers. Her hand encircled his wrist where it grazed her throat as his mouth brushed hers.

Finally...

He pulled away, but she snatched the front of his shirt with her free hand, and reeled him back in. His lips found hers again, and he kissed her tenderly. A soft hum of pleasure escaped her throat, but it swiftly ended as their heads angled and his mouth moved against hers passionately. She eagerly met him kiss for kiss, melting under his touch.

His hand left her cheek as she twined her arms around his neck, pulling him closer. He pressed her back firmly against the doorframe, and her knees threatened to buckle from the intensity in his embrace and kiss. Mouth leaving hers, he traced kisses down the curve of her neck. She shivered against him as he shifted her away from the wood at her back. Her robe strings fell loosely to her sides as he slipped his arms inside her robe and wrapped them around her waist, his hands gripping her nightgown at the small of her back.

She curved her body into his as his mouth crashed down on hers once again, taking possession of her lips like he had kissed her a million times and she was all his.

And I am.

He stepped backwards into the house, dragging her with him. The front door clicked shut as his hand slowly moved up her back inside her robe. She tangled her fingers in his hair, and he groaned against her, pulling away. Their chests heaved against each other as they caught their breath. Staring up at him, she watched the shocked look vanish from his face as it was replaced by a wide grin.

Eli kissed her cheek lightly before letting her go. Disappointment swept through her, but it hastily evaporated as he blew out the lantern on the mantel and came back over to her. Stretching his arm toward her, he grabbed her hand, intertwining his fingers with hers. With a gentle smile that she could see in the dark, he led her down the hall and into their bedroom. Once they were in the pitch-black room, he released her hand, but only to reach out and push the bedroom door closed behind him. It shut with an echoing click.

Chapter

THIRTY-ONE

BLINKING HIS EYES OPEN, ELI SLOWLY WOKE up. The room was still as dark as it had been when he'd fallen asleep, so he didn't have a clue what time it was. His eyes adjusted to the darkness, and he could make out Jared's crib along the wall. As always, the little boy had slept like a rock through the night.

Lisa shifted in her sleep behind him, her warm skin rubbing against his bare back. His eyes slipped back closed with a silent sigh. Newly made memories flitted through his mind as he shifted toward the edge of the bed so he could roll onto his back without crushing her. His arm brushed something furry as he settled into a new position, and he glanced over to find the girls' cat curled up under Lisa's chin. A grin broke out across his face.

She likes that cat as much as the girls do.

Lisa was close enough that he could make out her face in the dark. He studied her silently, his pleasure in their night spent together dropping away. Guilt swirled in, taking its place as Lisa's face suddenly morphed into Cherish's.

Flipping back the covers, he swung his legs over the edge of the bed. He hastily tugged his clothes back on as he made his way toward the bedroom door. It opened silently under his touch, and he tiptoed down the hall to the living room.

His shoulders shook as he sank onto the settee. Dropping his face into his hands, he released a deep shuddering breath.

How could I have been so stupid?

When he'd seen her standing in the doorway with the moonlight beaming on her, something had broken inside of him. She'd been so beautiful it hurt. The temptation had been too strong, and what he'd intended to be only a chaste kiss to just get a taste had turned into the whole nine yards when she'd pulled him back for more. He'd thrown all caution to the wind and given willingly–and passionately–into her touch.

A groan tore from his throat as he tried desperately to shove the more than pleasant moment from his mind, yet he couldn't. Not when everything inside of him told him to go straight back to bed to wake Lisa up for more. Part of him wanted to do just that, but the small voice whispering in the back of his mind that he'd done something horribly wrong kept him glued to the settee.

Tears leaked out of the corners of his eyes, dripping down the backs of his hands as he fought with his conscience and his flesh.

Why does something so wrong feel so right? But is it really wrong...

The thought echoed through his mind as Cherish's

smile shone brightly in his memory. He'd never been with another woman besides Cherish, so kissing on someone new felt wrong. Dirty almost. But the time he'd spent loving Lisa hadn't seemed dirty. Intense and passionate, yes, but not filthy.

He was still discovering the differences between Lisa and Cherish, and the hours previously had been yet another example. And once again, no matter how much he hated himself for it, and despite treasuring the old, he found the new better.

I'm so sorry, Cherish.

A sob racked his shoulders at the guilt building up within him. Despite the fact that she'd been gone for over a year, she was still deeply embedded in his heart, and he felt like he had just destroyed what they'd once shared. Needing comfort for his stirred conscience and knowing where to get it, he prayed.

As the last whispered word slid from his lips, he wiped his face dry and sat up straight. He sucked in a deep breath to further calm himself down. Lisa's beautifully freckled face flashed through his mind, and he knew what he felt for her was no longer just friendship. And if the way she gave herself so easily to him was any telltale, he was sure she'd made the same emotional change. Yet he wasn't sure if his feelings were love or just desire born out of sharing a home with her. He'd really hate himself if she were in love with him and he discovered that all he saw in her was something desirable.

Until he figured out the solution to the problem he'd gotten himself into, he decided he couldn't do anything to make it worse. No more resting his hand on the small of her back, hugging her for no reason, and curling into her in bed at night. At least until he could be honest with himself and not be racked with guilt.

Shifting on the settee, he stretched out, arm draped over his forehead. Based on the extremely dim light behind the curtain on the window, he knew he had a couple more hours to sleep, but he didn't dare go back to bed. Not when she would be lying beside him, more of a temptation than he could fight against. He blew a sigh out of his parted lips as he shut his eyes.

Now if only I can figure out this mess inside of me quickly.

Chapter
THIRTY-TWO

LISA SLEEPILY STRETCHED HER ARM OUT, REACHING for Eli on the other side of the bed, but stopped when her fingers met emptiness. Opening her eyes, she found her only bed companion to be the kitten curled up at her feet. She slowly sat, tugging the blanket up to cover her bare skin against the chill in the air as she glanced confusedly around the dimly lit room. Jared's soft breathing signaled he was still asleep, but besides him and the cat, she was alone.

Where did Eli go?

His side of the bed was cool like he hadn't been lying beside her for a while, and his clothes were no longer on the chair like normal. Deciding to go find him, she leaned over the side of the bed and snagged her nightgown from the floor. The thin, soft fabric rubbed against her palms, and a blush heated her cheeks as she vividly remembered the night before. She'd been surprised that he even kissed her let alone actually been a husband to her. Yet she was glad he had.

Tucking the blanket securely under her arms so it

wouldn't fall, she laid the nightgown on her lap. She picked absentmindedly at the small ribbon bow on the neckline as visions of strong arms, smooth chest, and intoxicating kisses flashed through her mind. A grin spread across her face as she basked in the memory like she had his love.

She'd never been with a man intimately before—let alone kissed—so every part of the experience was new. Learning new things was one of her favorite things and it had been exciting, yet part of her couldn't help but wonder whether or not she had disappointed Eli. He'd been married to Cherish for ten years and they obviously had a loving marriage since they'd been blessed with five children.

Did he compare me to Cherish?

The only way she'd ever know was if she were to come out and ask him, and that was something she could never do. It was too awkward of a subject to bring up, and she would rather live with not knowing than going through that embarrassment.

With a deep sigh, she lifted the nightgown and slipped it over her head. The fabric was chilly where it had been on the floor all night, and she shivered as it slid over her hot skin. Flipping back the covers, she disturbed the cat as she scooted across the mattress and swung her legs over.

The floor was even colder than her nightgown had been, and she hurriedly scooted her slippers out from under the bed. Chilly toes tucked into the soft fabric, she walked across the room. She opened the door, pausing to scoop up her robe where it had been carelessly tossed to the floor the night before. Pulling it on, she stepped out into the hall.

The house was eerily quiet as she made her way through the living room. Dim lantern light shone out of the kitchen doorway, and she spotted Eli at the table. His back was to her, but she could tell he had a cup of coffee between his hands.

Her slippers swished loudly in the quiet as she strode into the silent room. He jumped, turning to look over his shoulder. She smiled at him, and to her surprise he didn't return the expression. "Good morning."

"Morning." He nodded somewhat curtly.

"Mind if I join you?" She gestured to his cup.

"Be my guest." His head jerked lightly in the direction of the pot on the stove.

Without a word, yet confused at his nonchalant attitude with her, she crossed the kitchen and filled a mug with the dark brew. The warm cup in her hand, she scooted around him to her seat on the other side of the table. As she rounded the corner, she lightly brushed his arm with her palm like she had many times before, only this time he stiffened at the touch like it made him uncomfortable or startled him. He shifted in his chair until he was out of her reach.

Sitting down, Lisa looked into her coffee as disappointment and hurt swirled through her chest. She had hoped things would've changed between them. She wanted them to have a normal marriage, one that entailed kisses and intimate caresses. But now it appeared he was planning to be standoffish and the farthest thing from what he was the night before.

Her jaw clenched as she fought back tears. An awkward tension filled the small space between them, and she was either going to cry or spill everything she felt.

It's probably best to do neither.

She sent a darting glance in Eli's direction and found

him sitting stiffly in his chair while his thumb circled slowly around the brim of his mug. Desperately needing to crack the silence before she broke, she quietly asked, "What would you like for breakfast?"

"It doesn't matter," he murmured, not even looking over at her.

Stung and slightly offended, she took a drink of her coffee, not even tasting it.

Why is he doing this? Did I disappoint him that badly?

The thought made it even harder to hold back her tears. She set her mug on the table and hastily stood, going back over to the other side of the room. Resting her hands on the countertop, she took a deep breath. It helped a little and once she had control of herself enough that she wasn't about to start sobbing, she opened the cabinet and rummaged through it blindly. She somehow managed to remove the items needed to whip up a quick meal and swiftly got to work.

Eli's chair creaked behind her, and she glanced over to see him stand up. He met her eyes, and she noticed that they were as pain-filled as her own. She opened her mouth to say something, but closed it when a sob threatened to escape instead of the words she wanted to say.

"Lisa…I'm sorry about last night. It won't happen again." His voice was rough with emotion. "I've got chores to do. I'll be out in the barn if you need anything."

He stepped out of the back door, closing it silently behind him.

Tears streamed down her face as she turned back to the food in front of her. Setting down the knife in her hand, she wrapped an arm around her waist as sobs racked her shoulders. Saltwater wetted her lips, but she didn't bother to dry her face—there was no point.

I risked it all and I lost...

Chapter

THIRTY-THREE

"RISE AND SHINE, BIRTHDAY GIRL," ELI WHISPERED a month and a half later as he gently shook Cinthy awake. She groaned and attempted to pull the covers over her head, but with a smile, he stopped the blanket's upward travels. "Oh, no you don't! You've slept long enough. If you stay in bed any longer, you'll have to skip breakfast altogether and wait for lunch. It's already close to ten."

One of their birthday traditions was that the special person got to sleep in later than normal, and Hyacinth was taking full advantage of it. Covering a yawn, Eli stood up from where he had been sitting on the edge of the bed beside her.

If only I could've slept in too.

He'd taken to the habit of purposely getting up earlier than Lisa ever since that night. But it left him more tired than usual since she was an early riser as it was, so he was waking up before the rooster had even crowed.

Things had been tense and awkward between Lisa

and him, yet he couldn't help it. Not when he was still trying to figure out what he felt for her and get rid of the guilt that he'd been drowning in. The guilt was almost worse than the sorrow he'd experienced after Cherish's death. It was all consuming and he wasn't sure if he could ever get rid of it.

But what made it worse was now that he'd experienced loving Lisa, he wanted to do it again.

And again.

Shaking himself out of his thoughts before he got too deeply down a road he didn't want to return to, he waved for Cinthy to get out of bed. "Come on, sleepy head. Up and at 'em."

"Yes, sir," she murmured, doing as she was told. She followed him to the kitchen where the rest of the family was waiting on them. A shout of "Happy Birthday" circled the table as they all caught sight of Cinthy. She grinned with a blush and pulled out her chair. He also took his place at the table with the rest of the children.

Lisa sat a plate in front of her, and the new eight-year-old dug heartily into the kept-warm breakfast food. Walking back to the other side of the room, Lisa glanced at him with sorrow filled eyes. The worst part about all of this was the pain he was causing Lisa. Even though she hadn't said anything, he could tell by her actions and expressions that she was struggling with how things had changed between them. They'd been so close, and now they were farther apart than they'd ever been. Not only were they distant and standoffish with one another, a handful of arguments had erupted since that night. Arguments that were over stupid, silly things, and he hated that he was allowing himself to take his frustrations out on her. Especially since he knew it was only making her feel worse, which was the last thing he wanted to do.

Why can't I just figure this out already?

He wanted to pour out his heart to Lisa and tell her everything he was feeling, but something was holding him back. What it was, he wasn't sure, yet it had a tight hold on him. Everything was a risk, and he feared that he'd only hurt her more if he were to let her see the depths of his heart. It was impossible to show her what he felt when he wasn't even sure what it was himself.

Watching Lisa as she cleaned up the kitchen, he noticed the circles under her eyes. Eyes that had lost their happy sparkle. Not only had they dimmed, but he hadn't heard her genuinely laugh in over a month. A few times when she thought he was asleep beside her, he'd heard her crying late at night. Each of her deep sobs had torn out his heart and stomped on it, and it had yet to mend. Her pain over the situation was stabbing him relentlessly, and he wished it would all stop. And it could stop. All he had to do was say the word, and it would all end–but he couldn't.

On top of not knowing the contents of his own heart enough to put them on display, he feared if she knew about the guilt he felt over consummating their marriage, she would hate herself. And that would be just as bad, if not worse, than what they were going through in the present. She didn't deserve to suffer even more thanks to him.

"When can I open my presents?" Cinthy's voice pulled him out of his thoughts, and he glanced away from Lisa to find Cinthy pointing to the two wrapped items on the table beside her.

"Whenever your pa says you can." Lisa turned with a smile, but it vanished as she made eye contact with him.

"Pa?" Cinthy pulled gently on his sleeve to get his attention since he was once again distracted, but this time it was the tears glimmering in Lisa's dark eyes that made him lose all contact with the rest of the room.

"Go ahead if you want." He nodded, his happy emotional mask pushing up the corners of his mouth in a smile.

"Thanks." Paper was hastily ripped away and tossed to the side. Delighted squeals echoed through the kitchen as the new doll and dress to clothe it with were exposed. Cinthy clutched the curly haired figurine to her chest with a grin so wide nearly all her teeth were showing. She leaped out of her chair and squeezed him in a hug before rushing over to Lisa to do the same thing to her. "Thank you. Thank you so much. I love it."

"You're welcome, hunny." Lisa smoothed Cinthy's hair with one hand as she wrapped her other arm around the girl's shoulders. "Why don't you go play with it in the other room with your siblings while I finish cleaning up the kitchen?"

"Yes, ma'am." Cinthy bounced on her toes and the room emptied as all five children went into the living room, leaving Lisa and him alone.

Slowly standing, he grabbed Cinthy's plate and the paper they'd used to wrap her presents off the table. He slid the dish into the sink as he opened the front of the stove and tossed the paper inside. Lisa shifted around the room, purposely avoiding him as she wiped off the table and countertops.

"Would you like me to help you with anything?" he asked, wishing the painful silence would disappear.

"No, I can handle everything." She shook her head,

not bothering to look up.

"What if I want to help despite that?" He crossed his arms over his chest, cocking his head to the side as he watched her abruptly stop her scrubbing. "It's Saturday, which means you're going to clean as much of the house as you can. Let me help. It'll make things go faster for you."

"I'm fine." She shook her head again.

"It's already later than you normally start. Please, I just want to make things easier for you," he insisted yet knew she'd continue to refuse.

"I said, I'm fine." Her voice cracked and he saw her knuckles whiten as she gripped the washrag in her hand.

Don't push her too hard, Eli. She's already suffering enough.

"Alright," he sighed, the gesture feeling like it emptied his whole body in one breath. "But if you need me I'll be outside in the barn."

Chapter

THIRTY-FOUR

LISA HASTILY CHANGED INTO HER NIGHTGOWN LATER that night and slipped under the covers. Her chest tightened as the door swished open and Eli entered the room. In the darkness, she heard the quiet noises of him undressing and putting his nightshirt on. Tears pricked the back of her eyes as she rolled over and scooted close to the wall. Nighttime felt like it had when they'd first gotten married, but only worse.

Why is he doing this?

All she wanted was him to tell her why he was cutting her off. It hurt nearly worse than losing her family had, and that was something she'd hoped she would never have to experience again. Yet it was happening.

The bed shifted under his weight, and just like every night the past month and a half, she stiffened and made sure she didn't slide toward him. Before their night of love, he would pull her close if she was against or near the wall, but not now. He hadn't even so much as brushed against her, let alone hugged her. That alone was tearing her to bits. She didn't realize how much she loved his touch until it was taken away. It was the thing she hadn't known she needed in her life, and now she couldn't survive without it.

Eli sighed heavily, jiggling the whole bed. She tightened her jaw to keep her teeth from clacking together as she fought down a sob. Like every night, her thoughts flitted frustratingly from reason to reason why he was acting strangely. And one stood out sharply as always.

Did I disappoint him that badly?

If she were a braver person, she would've come out and asked him already, but she was terrified of his answer. Just thinking about him telling her how unsatisfying their time spent together had been for him would have been worse than not knowing anything in the first place.

Waiting until she heard him breathing deeply, she finally let out the sobs building up in her. They came out silently, yet her whole body shook under their force. Her trembling fingers covered her mouth as she sat up, and an overwhelming desire for space filled her. Carefully so she didn't disturb the man sleeping beside her, she crawled to the end of the bed and clambered over the footboard. The door opened easily under her touch, and she silently made her way to the living room.

Collapsing onto the settee a sobbing mess, she curled into herself, feet tucked under her nightgown. She rested her face on her knees in front of her and let the tears flow at their own pace. Her body rocked gently back and forth as she sobbed, and she didn't even try to stop herself.

It had felt like hours had gone by, yet she knew it was nowhere near that when a hand rested on her shoulder. She jumped and spun around, expecting Eli, but instead found Iris's face peering worriedly down at her.

"Land's sake! You scared me, Iris. I didn't hear you," Lisa warbled, her voice thick with tears.

"I heard someone crying and came to see who it was." Iris cocked her head in the dark, continuing to look intently at Lisa. "Why are you crying?"

"I was just a little upset, is all." Lisa shrugged, not knowing how–or daring–to explain the true reason behind her breakdown.

How on earth do you explain to a little girl that you think her father was disappointed in how you did a very specific *thing?*

"You're not just a little upset. You've been acting funny for a while now. And so has Pa." She crossed her arms over her chest. "What's really going on? I know I've only been ten since August, but that doesn't mean I don't notice things. And I'm not the only one. Cinthy asked me what was wrong with you and Pa just yesterday."

"What did you tell her?" Lisa asked, feeling bad that the tension between Eli and her was obvious to the children.

"That I didn't know." Iris shrugged, then pointed to the empty space on the settee beside Lisa. "Can I sit down with you?"

"Sure thing, hunny." Lisa patted the spot. The young girl curled up next to her, scooting in as close as she could get. "I can't really explain what's going on because I'm not really sure what it is myself. But let's just say it's a little mis-understanding."

"So, it will get better then?"

"I really hope so," Lisa whispered, sadness overcoming her.

"When Ma and Pa used to get in misunderstandings, they always got better, so I'm sure that things will be alright." Iris snuggled in against Lisa's arm, and Lisa wrapped it around the girl's shoulders, holding her close.

"How did they act when they had those disagreements?" Lisa asked curiously, wanting to know if Eli had done anything similar to Cherish that he was doing to her.

"Well, Ma would act normal, but her voice would get tight and sometimes her face got serious. Pa, on the other hand, would look like he was happy and feeling fine, but it was fake. Everyone thinks I'm just like Ma, but I'm not. Ma never noticed it when Pa would hide his feelings, but I've always been able to. It was really bad after she died. He always acted happy and like everything was fine, yet when I looked at him–and I mean really looked at him–I could see it was all fake." Iris explained, her voice gentle and quiet.

Cherish never realized he put up a mask? No wonder he was surprised when I noticed it.

"I know this might be nosy, but what types of things did they argue about?" Lisa figured she might as well go all the way since the topic was already opened.

"Oh, mostly things about church. I think the only reason why Pa became the pastor was because of Ma. I was really little, so I can't remember what it was like before he was the pastor, but he's been a lot happier since he quit." Iris casually picked at a loose thread on Lisa's sleeve. "He was so sad after Ma's death, but that all changed when you came. That's why it's almost scary to watch the way you two have been acting. I can't help but wonder if he'll start being sad all over again."

"I'm so sorry that we've scared you." Lisa laid her

cheek on top of Iris's head, her voice catching in the back of her throat.

This was never supposed to affect the children...

"It's okay." Iris patted Lisa's leg, her tone and actions showcasing the fact that she was very mature for her age. "Can I tell you something?"

"Of course. What is it?"

"I'm so glad you married Pa. You've brought so much happiness and love to our family. We'll never be the same without you, and I hope nothing ever takes you away from us like Ma was." Iris tipped up her head to look at Lisa. Tears streamed once more down her face at the sentiment and honesty in Iris's words. "I love you, Lisa."

"I love you, too," Lisa sobbed, pulling the small girl to her chest. After a few deep breaths, she had herself under control again, and she tilted back, wiping away the rogue tears slipping down her cheeks. She smoothed a hand down Iris's messy strawberry blonde hair as she whispered, "Thank you for telling me all this. It makes me feel a lot better."

"You're welcome." Iris smiled in the dark. "My grandparents and uncles and cousins are coming in a few weeks for Christmas, so even if you and Pa are still having this misunderstanding, you better try to hide it. If Grammy sees you looking sad, she'll give you a talking to to find out what's the matter. And Aunt Barbara, well just say she isn't the nicest person around, and if she notices something, she'll be rude about it."

"Thanks for the advice, young lady." Lisa caressed her cheek gently, grinning at her. "But I think you'll have to wait until morning to tell me anymore. It's already after midnight, and you should be in bed."

"How do you know what time it is when it's too dark to see the clock?" Iris questioned, glancing over at the mantel.

"If you pay attention and listen carefully, it ticks louder after the hour hand passes the twelve," Lisa explained. "But if that was an attempt at trying to stall going back to bed, then it was a very bad one. Off to bed now."

"Yes, ma'am," she sighed. "Are you sure you're alright now?"

"Yes, I'm sure." Lisa nodded.

"You'll go back to bed, too?"

"Yes. I'll walk you to your room and then I'll go to bed myself." Lisa stood and stretched her hand toward Iris. With Iris's hand in hers, they made their way down the hall and to the girls' open bedroom door. Lisa brushed a gentle kiss to her cheek. "Goodnight, Iris."

"Night, Lisa." Iris slipped into the dark room, leaving Lisa in the empty hall.

Turning and making her way to her own room, she silently entered the darkness past the open doorway.

She distracted herself by thinking of the depths of the dark surrounding her as she climbed back over the footboard. Eli shifted as she settled back down beside him. She held her breath, wondering whether or not she woke him. He moved again, and his deep voice murmured in the dark, "Lisa?"

"Yes?" she whispered, not knowing what he wanted.

"Is everything alright? I didn't feel you get up."

"I just needed a drink of water," she fibbed. Her cry on the settee and the conversation with Iris were things she wanted to keep to herself.

Why should I tell him anyway? He's the one who's pushing

me away.

"Oh, okay." She could tell by how his voice drifted off that he was already asleep again. Turning to face the wall again, she closed her eyes with a sigh and gladly accepted the invitation dreamland offered her.

Chapter

THIRTY-FIVE

ELI BIT BACK A GRIN TWO WEEKS later as he watched Lisa tap a wooden spoon on the bottom of a pan to get the attention of all the girls where they sat at the kitchen table, chattering amongst themselves and oblivious to everything around them. They all swiftly turned around as she exclaimed, "I know that it's Saturday and that you want to play, but we have company coming in a week. One thing that my mother always did was clean the house until it was spotless before we had visitors, so that's what we're all going to do today. And when I say all of us–I mean *all* of us."

She glanced over at him, a question in her eyes, and he nodded in response. The same awkward tension was still between them, and he'd noticed that she'd started to hide her distress and pain. He wasn't sure why, yet she was. It disturbed him that she was keeping her feelings covered up with a mask like he often did, but he still wasn't ready to spill the contents of his heart to her.

I never thought I wouldn't be able to figure out my own

feelings and settle my conscience, yet here I am.

His lack of discovery over his own self was infuriating, and if he could've taken off his leg to kick himself in the seat of the pants, he would've. Lisa's voice pulled him out of his drifting thoughts, and he concentrated on what she was saying.

"We need to clean every room since your grandparents will be staying with us, so I thought we could split into groups of two and each group will get a room. Iris and Petunia can do the girls' bedroom while Cinthy and Tulip can tackle the living room." She pointed to the girls as she said their names, then looked over at him. "We'll do the kitchen and keep Jared with us. I'll take care of our bedroom when we're done."

"Sounds good." He nodded, surprised that she was willingly wanting his help when they'd avoided working together unless it was absolutely necessary.

Within minutes, they were all in their assigned places, scrubbing and cleaning away. A squeak quietly echoed through the room as Lisa ran a wet rag over the window, and he glanced over from where he was dusting the tops of the cabinets. Water dripped down the inside of her arm from the rag in her hand and a beam of sunlight rested across her face, highlighting her freckles.

She's so beautiful.

Everything in him screamed for him to get down off the chair he was standing on and go kiss the living daylights out of her, but he kept a steady control over himself. That's all he'd wanted to do ever since he got his first taste of what her kisses were like, yet he couldn't have more when he felt guilty over it. That guilt was still burning him up, and it persistently buzzed in the back of his mind.

Lisa looked over and caught him staring. Her eyes softened, making his heart stir, and a smile parted her lips as she asked, "What are your parents like?"

He grinned, relief coursing through him thanks to the distraction and opportunity to have a normal conversation with her.

"Well, Pa is a jolly sort of man. He's been compared to Santa Claus more than once, and he's even got the white beard to match," he chuckled as he thought of his father, who was the largest influence in his life. "I can't tell you how many times he's made me laugh so hard I cried. He's one of those people who you have to meet in order to understand them. But if I were to compare him to anyone, I'd say he's like Abe Askingly, only funnier."

"He sounds wonderful." Lisa smiled brightly. "What about your mother?"

"She's sweet, kind, and will take you under her wing. But she has a spunky side that she shows every chance she can get." He shook his head with a grin. "I'm actually the only one who looks like her. I've been told many times I was just the male version of her."

"I'm sure she's a very beautiful woman then." Lisa's face turned rosy in a blush.

So she thinks I'm good looking...

"You said you had two younger brothers." She cleared her throat, the expression on her face clearly showing her discomfort in her previous admission.

"Yes. Peter and John." He looked back at the cabinet in front of him, giving Lisa time to recover from her embarrassment. "They're both married and have children. They always stay at Granny Lola's when they come for the holidays since it's too many people for a house this size."

"How come they all come up here when it would be easier for us to go to Carson City?" Lisa asked, going back to her window cleaning.

"I honestly don't remember how it started, but for some reason, they came here one year, and they have ever since."

"I can't wait to meet them." The slight bit of a hesitant quiver laced her voice, and Eli knew she was nervous.

"Lisa." He put his dusting rag down and turned his full attention on her.

"Uh-huh." She glanced over and made eye contact with him.

"They'll love you. I know they will." He nodded to emphasize his words. She blinked several times as the first genuine smile he'd seen in two months spread across her face.

They will, Lisa. They will.

Chapter

THIRTY-SIX

"I RIS, WHERE'S YOUR HAIR BRUSH?" LISA CALLED. She was holding Jared on her lap in her bedroom as she attempted to fix Petunia's curls. Iris's boot heels clicked out of the room as she went in search of the item, and Lisa stifled a frustrated sigh as Jared attempted to get down. Besides Iris, none of the children were cooperating with her since they were excited about Eli's family arriving on the stagecoach that day. And he had already left to pick them up, so she didn't have any help.

If she wasn't stressed about meeting his parents and siblings, she would have been fine, but her nerves were putting her on edge. She'd already snapped at both Tulip and Cinthy, and she felt awful for it.

If only I could know for sure whether or not they will like me.

Iris slid up beside her and put the brush in Lisa's hand as she leaned close to her ear and whispered, "Calm down, Lisa. Everything's going to be alright."

"Thank you, hunny." Lisa smiled, letting go of Jared

long enough to reach up and pat Iris's cheek. Iris had become a huge comfort to her ever since the night she found Lisa crying on the settee. Despite the fact that Iris was only ten, she somehow understood Lisa and knew how to console her.

Focusing on the messy brown curls attached to the almost four-year-old in front of her, Lisa made quick work of taming them as Iris took Jared from her lap. She fought to keep her thoughts from drifting to her husband and his parents. She couldn't afford the distraction when there were things to still do before their arrival.

"Alright, you're all done, Pet." Lisa gently shifted the older toddler forward so she could stand up. "Everyone is dressed and has their hair fixed. Now we just need to make sure there aren't any messes anywhere."

"I'll look in the living room. Cinthy, you go into the bedroom." Iris commanded in classic oldest sibling fashion, and Lisa hid a grin. She could remember her oldest brother being the exact same way. Blinking in surprise, it dawned on her that it no longer hurt as badly to think about her family.

When did that happen?

Somewhere in the past eight months since she'd left Alabama, the deep sorrow from their deaths had faded. In its place, she surprisingly felt peace, and as she flitted through different memories, she could finally think on them fondly instead of with tears. She had kept herself from thinking about any of them for so long just to keep the pain away, yet now she didn't have to. Her heart had healed, which was something she didn't think was possible, and she knew it was all thanks to Eli and the girls.

Things were still strange and tense between him and her, but she was learning how to desensitize herself to it all.

In turn, it forced her to pull up a mask like Eli was prone to do when he was upset. She didn't have a choice if she wanted to keep the children from being frightened by whatever was happening between her and Eli.

Silently and with Jared on her hip, she made her way through the house, picking up any scattered things and fixing anything that was messy. Even with deep cleaning the weekend before, seven people lived in the house, so it was impossible to keep it spotless no matter how much she wanted to.

"Everything looks fine!" Iris exclaimed as she entered the living room from the hall.

"It's a good thing, too, because they're here." Lisa carefully lifted the curtain on the window, peeking out into the front yard.

A happy exclamation rippled through the group of girls standing behind her, and she smiled at their cheer despite the nerves that swept in and left her with a trembling jaw. Tightening it so that her teeth wouldn't clack together, she gestured for the girls to go outside. The door banged against the wall as Iris threw it open, and they all bolted out into the chilly December air. Jared shrieked on her hip, attempting to get down to follow, but she patted his leg with a chuckle. "You're staying with me, little man. They'll be in the house in a minute."

The sound of Eli's deep, rumbly voice drifted inside from where he stood beside the buckboard, and its tones melted her heart. Her attraction for him and how it affected her was still as strong—if not stronger than ever—only she couldn't do anything with it, let alone show it. Not when he wouldn't touch her and still continued to act like their night together never happened.

"Alright, everyone in the house. It's too cold to stand out here gabbering all day," a deep voice she'd never heard before exclaimed. The girls swarmed back into the house, several other children following them. A flash of white beard caught Lisa's eye as a tall, broad man filled the doorway. His brown eyes immediately found her, and his mustache parted from his chin hair as he smiled. She smiled shyly back with a small nod.

The room quickly filled with people and Jared was taken from her arms by a curly haired woman who looked like a feminine version of Eli. She pulled Lisa into a hug as she said, "I've heard so many wonderful things about you, sweetheart. I'm so glad I finally get to meet you. I'm Martha, Eli's mother."

Lisa stiffened in surprise but swiftly relaxed into the warm embrace, shocked at how comforting it felt.

"It's a pleasure to meet you, too," Lisa replied, her twangy accent sounding strong in her own ears compared to Martha's soft voice.

"Don't hog our daughter-in-law all to yourself, Marthy. I want to give her a hug, too." The bearded man, who she knew was Eli's father, laughed. Martha let her go, and Lisa was swiftly being squeezed in a bear hug by the big Santa-like man. "Lisa, I know I'm a little late in telling you this, but welcome to the family."

"Thank you, sir." She nodded with a grin, all her nerves vanishing under his tender look.

"To you, young lady, my name is Jared, not sir." He wiggled his white brows playfully at her.

"Yes, sir," she giggled, the habit instilled for her at birth slipping out despite his command. "I mean, Jared."

"Well, since Eli doesn't seem to be giving introductions, I'll do the honors." Jared turned to face the rest of the crowd as Eli's mouth opened and closed before he shrugged with a slow grin. Pointing to a brown haired man standing next to a red headed woman, Jared said, "This is my son, Peter, and his wife, Hallie."

"Hello, nice to meet you." Lisa smiled.

"Their children are the redheaded heathens while the rest of them are my youngest son, John, and his wife, Barbara's." He gestured to the other younger-looking man, whose arm was draped over the shoulders of a woman with caramel-colored hair. Lisa remembered Iris's warning about Barbara, yet her soft features didn't look like they could belong to a rude person.

"It's nice to finally get to meet all of you." Lisa gestured to the kitchen. "I have a pot of hot coffee on the stove if anyone would like some. I'm sure it would help you all warm up after your long, chilly trip."

Chapter

THIRTY-SEVEN

A N HOUR AND A HALF LATER, LISA stood at the kitchen sink, washing the dirtied mugs. Various voices drifted in from the living room, and she smiled, a sense of contentment warming her heart. Eli's relatives were wonderful, and she felt like she was part of a family again. They'd all chatted animatedly over their coffee, laughing often, and it had seemed like they'd known each other for years instead of having just met.

How did I end up so blessed?

Yet despite her many blessings, there was the strained, tension-filled crevice between Eli and her, and just the thought of him made her happiness evaporate into hopelessness. But she didn't get to wallow in the emotion for long since the floorboards creaked. She turned toward the living room doorway, expecting Eli or one of the girls, but was surprised to find Barbara slipping into the room. Lisa watched her drift over to the table and fiddle with the edge of the tablecloth, her demeanor relaxed and calm.

Strange.

Lisa still couldn't figure out how Barbara could be the awful person Iris described her to be. Not with the way she'd held John's hand and looked at him affectionately from time to time while they'd had coffee. Scrubbing the inside of a mug clean, keeping her eyes on Barbara, Lisa quietly cleared her throat and asked, "Is there something I can get you?"

"No." Barbara waved away the offer and leaned her hip against the table. "We didn't get to talk much earlier and I wanted to get to know you a little better."

"Oh, what would you like to know?" Lisa's gaze went back to her dishwater as she absently swirled her finger through the soap suds. Nerves suddenly churned in her stomach, and she wasn't sure why.

A cupboard door rattled, and Lisa looked in time to see Barbara shut it with a condescending expression. Lips pursed, she turned to Lisa, and pointed with her thumb to the cupboard. "Cherish always kept the plates in there, not the cups."

"Eli gave me free rein over the kitchen, so I did a little rearranging." Lisa shrugged, an uneasiness settling in her chest. "Were you close to her?"

"Yes. Cherish and I weren't best friends, but there was an understanding between us." Barbara scooted in a little closer, making Lisa strangely feel like the mouse Cookie had cornered in the living room one day. "You're quite different from Cherish. And I don't mean just in looks."

Her guard coming up, Lisa's head swiveled to the left to look at her. "I realize that, but I can't be someone else."

"I know. I guess I was just expecting you to be different, is all."

"What type of 'different' was that?" Lisa's brows rose.

Maybe Iris was right...

"Well, I figured you'd be a little on the trashy side," Barbara admitted, her voice chilled with a cold tone. Lisa's grip tightened on the mug in her hand.

"Why would I be trashy?"

"Eli did find you through an advertisement in the paper, did he not?" One of Barbara's brows rose saucily. "I was always taught that a woman didn't advertise herself unless she had loose morals and was trashy."

A fiery anger pulsed through Lisa's veins as she took a shallow breath, her heartbeat loud in her ears.

"So you're saying that because I allowed an old family friend to post an advertisement about me in the newspaper that I'm loose?" Lisa's voice lowered to a husky growl.

"Isn't that why you had it posted?"

"No. I would *never* do something like that!" Lisa exclaimed, dropping the mug. Water sloshed out of the sink and splashed her skirt. Tears smarted the back of her eyes, but she refused to let them fall. Not while Barbara was giving her a smug, stuck up look.

"Then why did you do it?"

"Because I wanted to get out of Alabama where memories haunted me. I needed to find a life outside of scrubbing laundry and waiting tables." Lisa stepped away from the sink, intent on escaping the room. "I never did this for any of the reasons you might have thought. My parents didn't raise their only daughter to be that *type* of woman."

Lisa rushed around Barbara, bumping into Eli, who she hadn't seen standing in the doorway as she darted out of the room. Practically sprinting, tears blurring her vision, she made her way to the bedroom. The door slammed as she shoved it closed, and she cringed at the sound. She rested her shaking shoulders against the solid wood and cradled her face in her hands as she sobbed.

Is that what everyone thinks of me? No wonder Eli is acting strange.

Fuming, Eli stepped farther into the room. He'd been standing close to the kitchen only half listening to the conversation between his wife and sister-in-law, but when he heard Lisa's voice turn angry, he shifted into the doorway. The countertop beside him vibrated as he slammed his fist down on it, not caring about the pain, and pointed one finger at Barbara. His voice came out a deep growl as he said, "You had no reason or right to say any of that."

"And why not?" she challenged, her arms crossing over her chest.

"Because it was mean and conceited." He threw out his hands. "You just met Lisa, and you went and accused her of only marrying me to get in my bed."

"Maybe because I believe it's true!" She stood up straighter, her blue eyes flashing with anger.

"You have no reason to! Lisa is nothing like that."

"Then if she isn't, what is she?"

"She's sweet, kind, innocent, and loving." He narrowed his eyes, daring her to contradict him.

"Oh, I see…" she drawled as she cocked her head. "You're just defending her because she's giving you what you need."

His jaw tightened and he fought to keep his temper from exploding, which was no small feat when it was nearly out of unburned fuse.

"And I don't think you're really mad at Lisa." He locked eyes with her, but her gaze darted away, and he knew he'd hit the nail on the head. "Go ahead. I know you're dying to tell me what you think of me."

"Fine I will!" She stomped over to him and stopped when she was mere feet away. "It makes me sick to think that you could replace Cherish so quickly and easily. And the fact that you did it by answering a newspaper ad. That's low, Eli. Very low. Did Cherish not mean anything?"

How dare she?

Everything went dark for a moment as rage ripped through him. His hands shook and he knew he had to tread carefully or else he would do something he regretted. Swallowing deeply, he took a deep breath. "Cherish meant *everything* to me! I never wanted to remarry, but the only reason I did was because my children needed a mother and because Cherish made me promise that I would moments before she died. That newspaper ad was one of the biggest blessings God has ever given me. Lisa has brought *so* much happiness into our lives. More happiness than we've had in a long time."

"I'm sorry. I...I didn't know," Barbara stammered, her face a mask of shame.

"I'm not the one you should be apologizing to." He spun on his heel. Pausing in the doorway, he looked back at Barbara. "If I ever hear you saying those things about or to my wife, you will *never* be allowed in this house again. I'm serious, and I don't care if you're my sister-in-law."

He passed the wide-eyed crowd in the living room, who had heard the conversation, as he made his way to the bedroom. In the privacy of the hall, he leaned his forehead against the closed door, cooling his anger. With a light rap of his knuckles on the smooth wood, he quietly called out, "Lisa, it's me. Can I come in?"

"Yes." Her voice cracked with a sob, and he quickly turned the knob, swinging the door open. She stood by the bed, hands covering her face as her shoulders shook under the force of her silent cries.

His heart cracked, and he forgot his vow to himself about not touching her. Crossing the room, he pulled her into his arms. She stiffened but swiftly collapsed against his chest. His eyes slipped closed as a silent sigh rocked him.

Why does she have to feel so good in my arms?

He slowly rubbed his hand up and down her back and felt her relax under his touch. His self-control leaving him, he brushed a kiss to the top of her head as he murmured, "I'm so sorry about Barbara. I should've known she would have made some sort of scene. She likes to cause problems. To be honest, I don't know why John married her."

"Is that what everyone thinks about me?" she whispered, tipping her head up to look at him. Her face was red and tear-swollen, yet she was still beautiful to him.

She always will be.

"What are you talking about?" he questioned, confusion swirling in his gut.

"Does everyone think I'm loose? Is that what you think about me?"

His heart dropped to his toes as tears filled his eyes. "Never. I've never thought that about you. You're all things pure and innocent, and nothing will ever change that."

"But what about everyone else?" Her voice cracked, and he slid his hands up to her shoulders, which he gently squeezed.

"If anyone thinks you're loose—and no one does—then that would make them the world's largest idiots." He smiled softly.

"You're just saying that to make me feel better," she pouted.

"No, I'm serious. And I've never been more serious." He gave her a stern look to get his point across. She gave him a watery smile before burying her face in his shirt. His heart hammered at her closeness, and he knew he needed to put some space between them before he did something that would rack him with guilt, which had only inflated after what Barbara had said.

I'm still dealing with the guilt from the first time—I don't need to add to it.

"You should change out of that wet skirt." He leaned her back by her shoulders. "Once you're done you can come back out if you want. It's all okay now."

"I can't go out there and be near Barbara after she said all those things about me." She shuddered in his grasp, and it took everything in him to not pull her back against his chest. "I can't face everyone after that. I feel...dirty."

"Hey." He tipped her chin up so she'd look at him. "You're not dirty, and I took care of everything with Barbara. She knows now not to say *anything* like that about you again or else she won't be allowed back in this house. And she won't let that happen because she knows John and I are close."

"You can't kick her out just because of little old me."

Lisa shook her head. "I'm not worth breaking your relationships with your family."

"Yes, you are. I would estrange this family from Barbara in a heartbeat if it came down to it." He raised his brows, then scrunched his nose in displeasure. "She's such a prude. Actually there's a better word for women like her, but I won't say it. Not when I'm in the presence of a lady."

"You're awful!" She laughed, slapping him on the arm.

"But, hey, it made you laugh didn't it?" he chuckled with a shrug.

She let out a slow, deep sigh, but the smile never left her face. "I'll change my skirt and then come join y'all when I'm done."

"Alright. Take your time. And you might want to clean your face, too." He gently swiped away the dampness on her cheeks with his thumb.

"Don't worry, I will." She patted the back of his hand where he rested it on her face. Getting to touch her again after not doing it for a while was more than pleasant, but before he had enough time to dwell on it, she said, "Would you mind leaving the room so I can change?"

"I'm on my way out right now." He winked, moving away from her. His arms felt empty, and he didn't like it. A sudden urge to want to go back to how things had been between them before he unfairly cut her off fought against the guilt attempting to drown him. Yet he wanted her to understand without him not having to tell her everything since he still wasn't sure what that everything was.

Pausing with his hand resting on the doorknob, he looked back at her as he softly whispered loud enough for her to hear, "I'm sorry, Lisa."

"What for?" Her brows scrunched in confusion.

"For the way I've been treating you lately. I'm really sorry." He sighed, hating himself for it all. "I just need a little more time to get some things figured out. Can you be patient with me?"

"Always." She gave him a gentle smile, her dark eyes once again watery. "You're worth the wait."

Chapter

THIRTY-EIGHT

STIRRING AWAKE ON CHRISTMAS MORNING, LISA BUMPED into Eli's back where they lay on a bed made up of blankets in front of the fireplace. Martha and Jared Sr. were staying in their bedroom during the holiday visit, so Lisa and Eli had to sleep on the living room floor. Jared's crib had been moved into the girls' bedroom, and they intended for it to stay there even after their houseguests left.

The house was peacefully quiet, so Lisa basked in the morning silence as she thought about the man lying beside her. After their moment in the bedroom after Barbara's insults—which she'd apologized for—he hadn't touched Lisa again. But his plea for her to be patient put her heart somewhat at ease. Being in his arms again had made her cry harder since it felt like a drink of water after walking through the desert, and it had nearly taken away the sting of Barbara's barbs. Yet at the same time, her chest tightened when she thought about the fact that Eli had said he needed to figure out some things.

What could those things be? Surely he won't...

She never got the chance to finish the thought thanks to Eli rolling onto his back. He gave her a sleepy smile and his voice rumbled in a whisper as he said, "Merry Christmas, Lisa."

"Merry Christmas." She turned to her side, facing him. A cringe flitted across her face as a sharp pain skittered through her shoulders.

"Sleeping on the floor making you sore, too?" He chuckled as he tucked his arm beneath his head.

"It's not too bad." She shrugged one shoulder with a grin. "I just wish the blankets had a little more padding."

"I know what you mean, but it's only for a few more weeks and then we can have our bed back."

"I'm not complaining, but that sounds wonderful." She sighed, rolling onto her back as she looked at the ceiling. Being so close to him was making her heart pound and she knew she'd do something she would regret if she continued to have him right in front of her face.

"It sure does." He sat up and tossed the quilt back. "I'm getting up before I either turn into an old man or everyone else swarms the house."

His nightshirt fell over his knees as he stood up and stretched his back with a quiet groan. Laughing lightly, she shook her head. "I better get up, too."

The blankets were soon picked up and the evidence of their night spent on the floor gone. Making their way into the kitchen, Lisa filled the coffee pot and set it on the stove as Eli pulled out a chair and sat at the table. The quiet footfall of someone walking down the hall echoed into the room. Lisa glanced at the doorway as Martha's motherly form filled the empty space.

"Merry Christmas," Eli rumbled as he stood and went over to hug his mother.

"Merry Christmas." Martha patted his back, looking over his shoulder at Lisa. "Both of you."

"Merry Christmas," Lisa replied with a smile. In the past two weeks that Eli's family had been visiting, she'd gotten to know—and love—his mother quite well. She'd come in and swept Lisa under her wing, and she was the best replacement for Lisa's own mother. Martha's gentle ways were a balm to Lisa's soul.

"Your brothers are going to be here within the next half hour, so you better go get those girlies up. I didn't realize how late we all slept in." Martha gently pushed Eli into the living room.

"Yes, ma'am."

Martha stepped over to the table and gestured for Lisa to follow her as she chuckled. "I really just wanted to get you alone, but don't tell him that."

"Don't worry, I won't." Lisa sat in her chair as Martha did the same across the table. "Why did you want to get me alone?"

What could she want?

"I wasn't sure if I'd get a chance during the rest of our visit. I wanted to talk to you for a moment." She smiled, reaching out to pat Lisa's arm where it laid on the table. "I'm very grateful that you married Eli. You're different from Cherish, but it's a good sort of different. It was what he needed. Even though they never said anything, I could tell that they didn't always get along. Cherish had dreams for Eli that weren't what he wanted, but he did them anyway because he loved her and wanted to make her happy. That's the only reason he got involved in the ministry. I'm sure he enjoyed it to a point since he loves to serve people, yet I don't think he ever was completely happy with it.

"When he sent the first letter telling us about you, I will admit that I was worried it wouldn't work out, yet his other letters pushed away that worry. He's my baby. I know him better than most people, so I could see the happiness and contentment in his words. And I saw it in person when he came to pick us up at the stagecoach. To be completely honest, the man I saw that day was the old Eli from before he married Cherish. Cherish changed him. I never really liked the switch, but you brought back my son. I can never thank you enough for bringing my boy back. I've missed him for a long time now."

Tears streamed down Lisa's face as she attempted to say something, but nothing could get past the emotion clogging her throat. Martha stood up and came around the table, pulling Lisa into a tight hug. "Even though I can tell you two are trying to hide something that's going on between you from us, I know you'll get it all sorted out. You two complement each other perfectly, and I couldn't be happier to have you for a daughter-in-law."

"I...I don't know what to say," Lisa stammered out. Her world had just been capsized, and her mind spun in so many directions she was surprised her brain was still inside her skull. Martha leaned back and looked deeply into her eyes.

"Then don't say anything at all." She smiled, swiping at the tears wetting Lisa's cheeks. "You're a wonderful and very special woman. Never forget it."

"Thank you so much," Lisa sobbed despite wanting to quit crying. She sucked in a deep, shaky breath and calmed herself down enough to say, "And you're right, there is something going on between Eli and me. I can't tell you what it is since it's…uh, a little personal. I don't know what to do about it though. It's been going on now for a while, and I've cried myself to sleep more times than I care to admit."

"Eli has a hard time expressing his emotions, which I'm sure you've discovered, so give him a little more time. I'm not sure you'll work things out–I'm positive you will." Martha patted Lisa's cheek as she bent down and pressed a kiss on her forehead. "Every marriage goes through bumps in the road, and you've just got to figure out how to get past the bump, is all."

"But some bumps in the road can break a wheel or your axle. What if this one breaks us?" Fear trickled through Lisa's veins, making a chill settle over her.

"The thing is to not let yourself think about failure. Go into it with a fiery desire to outsmart and beat the bump, and you'll be less likely to get broken." Martha smiled gently, her gray eyes filled with love.

How did I end up so blessed to get this angel of a woman for a mother-in-law?

"I'll remember that. Thank you." Lisa nodded, her terror calmed, yet her thoughts still whirling.

"Now, you better get your face cleaned up. I hear the girls and Eli and Jared talking in the hall. You don't want them to see a tear-stained face on Christmas morning."

"Yes, ma'am." Lisa stood and walked over to the sink to do as she was told.

Chapter

THIRTY-NINE

"ALRIGHT, EVERYONE, LET'S GO!" ELI'S FATHER EX-CLAIMED as he opened the front door and led all the children outside. Eli shook his head with a laugh as Petunia plowed through her siblings and cousins to get to her grandma, who was already on the front porch. His parents were about to take all the children on their customary buggy ride after a large lunch.

The morning had been pleasant with exchanging presents and just being with family. But his favorite part was getting to celebrate Christmas with Lisa for the first time. Her childlike excitement made him extremely happy and filled his heart with more cheer than he'd felt in a long while.

The house was soon emptied of all but him and Lisa since his brothers and their wives were going back to Lola's Boardinghouse while the children were out on their ride. Stepping into the kitchen where Lisa was elbow deep in soapy water as she washed the lunch dishes, Eli grabbed the towel hanging by the stove and began to dry the clean dishes.

"You don't have to help. I can take care of it." Lisa glanced over at him.

"There's dishes from nineteen people here. It'll take you a good hour and a half to get them all done, so just let me help," he insisted.

"Oh, alright." She sighed with a shake of her head.

A momentary grin spread across his face, and they tackled the chore in a comfortable silence. Eli watched her out of the corner of his eye and wanted to strike up a conversation, but didn't know how.

Why does this have to be so hard? Just weeks ago I could talk to her about anything, and now I don't even know what to say.

Wiping the water from a blue edged, white plate, he flipped through all the conversation starters he knew. Finally settling on one, he quietly asked, "What do you think about my family?"

She stopped scrubbing the bowl in her hand and stared at the suds around it.

Maybe that was the wrong one…

"I really like them." She turned and looked at him, her dark eyes filled with a calm, pleasant emotion.

"Even Barbara?" he joked, raising his brows.

"She's tolerable." She shrugged with a grin. "But really, I do like your family. They're wonderful people."

"I'm glad you think so because I think they're rather great." His shoulders relaxed, and he knew that the conversion he'd started wasn't a mistake.

"Your pa reminds me of one of my uncles. He passed away when I was fifteen, but I remember how he used to give everyone big, strong hugs and always made people laugh." A soft smile spread across her face as she gazed at Eli.

"Ma always jokes and says that Pa's just a human version of a stuffed bear."

"That is actually the best way to describe him. He's the type of person who you could go to for a warm embrace and comforting word." She nodded.

Eli watched her in silence for a moment, and she peered up at him. Sadness filled her eyes, and his heart clenched. Wanting to distract them both from the pain that was sweeping into the room, he asked, "Did my mother upset you earlier? I could tell you were crying when I came back into the kitchen this morning."

"Oh, no, she didn't at all!" she exclaimed. "Your mother is an angel."

"So why were you crying?" His brows creased in confusion.

"You know there's a thing called happy tears." She rolled her eyes, and he bit back a grin, glad that her sass was back. "And don't you ask why. It was between your mother and me. No one else."

"Yes, ma'am." He saluted with the plate in his hand, winking at her. Her head tipped back and the kitchen filled with the sound of her husky laugh. A wide smile pushed up his cheeks and his heart pounded.

How I've missed that laugh...

"You should do that more." He put the stack of plates he'd dried in the cupboard.

"Do what?" she asked, confusion lacing her voice.

"Laugh."

"Oh," she whispered, looking down at the silverware in her hand like it was the most interesting thing in the whole world.

The room slipped into an awkward silence and he wanted to kick himself. The only reason why her laugh had been silenced was him, and he knew that, yet he'd put his foot in his mouth.

A fork clanked off the sink as she dropped it, and he looked closer at her. Her hands shook and her shoulders trembled. His heart sank into the pit of his stomach as guilt swirled through him.

Why do I have to keep hurting her like this?

Nudging her arm with his elbow, he got her attention. She glanced up with tear-filled eyes, and the sight made him feel even worse, which he didn't think was possible. "I'll finish here. Go rest for a little bit. You've been busy all morning and on your feet nearly the whole time."

She nodded, putting the washrag down. Keeping her face turned away from him, she dried her hands and slipped out of the room. The sound of her boot heels on the floor echoed through the silent house as she made her way to the bedroom. The door clicked shut, and his shoulders drooped as tears filled his eyes.

Letting them fall slowly, he stuck his hands into the warm dish water. He wished that he hadn't let himself slip that night, yet the other part of him didn't regret it. His heart was still a swirl of guilt and confusion, and he needed to get it all figured out. He would've talked it over with his father, but despite how close they were, it felt too awkward of a subject to broach, so he was stuck to clean up his mess alone.

I just need a little more time, is all.

Chapter

FORTY

"I'LL BE BACK IN A FEW HOURS," Lisa told Eli two days later as she made her way to the front door.

"Alright. Tell Jack and Bella hi for me." He tossed her a wave before going back to the game of chess he was playing with his father. Laughter seeped out of the kitchen where Martha and the children were making molasses cookies. Eli's brothers and their families had headed home that morning, so they only had two people to entertain.

"Will do," she replied as she slipped out the door.

Pulling her shawl tight around her to shelter herself from the cold air, she headed down the street toward the Klisters's house. A very tired, yet jubilant, Jack had stopped by that morning after Eli left to take his siblings to the stagecoach, and he told her Bella wanted her to stop by for a visit when she got the chance. Bella's baby had arrived on Christmas day, and she wanted Lisa to meet the new babe.

Lisa was happy for the young couple, yet her heart ached at the same time. Part of her had hoped that if she could have given Eli a baby after their time spent together that he would love her, but her monthly little friend had appeared and wiped away all possibility of that. The day she'd found out, she cried so hard she made herself vomit. It felt like the light at the end of the tunnel had been abruptly—and unfairly—blown out. Yet deep down she knew a baby wouldn't have made a difference. It probably would have made things worse considering he already had five children and Cherish died giving him the last one.

He probably doesn't want any more children, anyhow...

A new, dreadfully bitter conclusion filled her mind, and she bit down on her lower lip to keep it from trembling. Since he already had quite the brood, he was likely worried he'd gotten her pregnant, which could've been the reason behind his distant, silent ways.

Realizing she was coming up on Jack and Bella's house, Lisa hastily pushed all dreary and sad thoughts away and put a pleasant expression on her face. The last thing she wanted to do was upset Bella with her problems. Her boot heels clicked on the porch steps as she walked up to their door. It opened before she got a chance to knock, and Abby waved her in.

Lisa was barely in the house when Abby, whose eyes were slightly bloodshot and puffy, yet sparkling with happiness, pulled her into a hug. "I know I'm two days late, but Merry Christmas."

"Merry Christmas, to you, too," Lisa replied, hugging the older woman and midwife back. "How's Bella doing?"

"She's doing well considering she was in labor for over twenty-four hours." A small frown flashed across Abby's face.

"Everything went safely?"

"Yes, thankfully. She had a difficult time, but no damage was done, and both her and the baby are alright." Abby nodded, the relief on her face showing her thankfulness.

"I'm so glad." Lisa smiled, knowing how hard it had to be for Abby to watch her daughter in pain.

They both turned as Jack stepped out of the bedroom and into the living room. He saw Lisa and waved in her direction. "Hello, Lisa. I'm glad you could come by today."

"I wanted to see that little baby of yours as soon as I could," she laughed lightly.

"Well, Bella's awake, so go on in and see her." He gestured to the door behind him as he walked over to pour himself a cup of coffee at the stove.

Knocking lightly on the doorframe as she paused in the doorway, Lisa called out quietly, "Can I come in?"

"Oh, Lisa! I didn't expect you today." Bella's voice was laced with tiredness, but she smiled widely. "Do come in."

"And how are you feeling, little mama?" Lisa asked as Bella patted the side of the bed for her to sit down. Carefully lowering herself onto the mattress, she reached out and gave Bella's shoulder a light squeeze as she leaned in to peer at the baby nestled against her chest.

"Exhausted, but very happy." Despite dark circles under her eyes, Bella's face shone with glee. She reached up and pulled down the blanket covering her and the babe a bit to expose the little one's face. "We named her Noelle Eleanor."

"That's a wonderful name." Lisa's heart clenched with sadness, but she hid it with a smile.

"Would you like to hold her?"

"I don't want to hurt her." She shook her head.

"Lisa, you take care of five children on a daily basis." Bella rolled her eyes as she shifted the baby off her chest and lifted her toward Lisa.

"But they aren't delicate newborns. I've never held a baby this small before." Lisa carefully took Noelle and cradled her in the crook of her arm, treating her like the most breakable china that existed.

"Well, there's a first time for everything. You aren't going to break her. Just relax." Bella sank into her pillow with a laugh.

Noelle opened her eyes with a small coo, and Lisa's heart melted. Gently running a finger across her little chunky cheek, Lisa whispered, "She's beautiful, Bella."

"She looks just like her pa." Bella reached out and fingered the soft blanket Noelle was wrapped snugly in. "But I'm not complaining. She's everything I ever wanted. Dark hair and eyes included."

"She has so much hair!" Lisa shook her head in amazement, brushing the dark locks tenderly.

"That's a Klister family trait," Bella giggled. "All Klister babies are born with a head full of hair. And most of the time it's dark, too."

"Well, that's a very good trait to have. I was bald when I was born." Lisa looked down at the young woman with a grin.

"So was I."

"I've held her long enough now." Lisa handed Noelle back. She knew if she had the little baby in her arms any longer she was likely to cry.

"But you've barely held her," Bella protested, yet

gladly took her back.

"It's alright. She needs her mama, not me."

"Is something wrong?" Bella's blue eyes searched Lisa's face intently.

"No, everything is fine," she fibbed, not about to tell a nineteen-year-old girl the problems with her marriage. *Not when she has everything I've ever wanted.*

"Are you sure?"

"I'm sure." Lisa nodded, emphasizing her point.

"If you say so." Bella narrowed her eyes, giving her a suspicious look. "How was your Christmas?"

"Really good." Lisa glanced away from Bella, eyes drifting across the room to the lacy curtains covering the window and small, yet sturdy table under it as she thought about the previous holiday. "We had a wonderful day with Eli's family."

It had been a good day until her time in the kitchen with Eli had turned into her in tears thanks to the predicament they were in. She'd spent nearly half an hour crying then a good ten minutes cleaning up her face to destroy the evidence. But after that, everything else had gone smoothly until that night when Eli had wrapped his arm around her waist in his sleep. The tears had flowed once again as she scooted carefully against him without waking him up. They'd slept like that nearly the whole night, and she hated the fact that no matter how hard she tried not to, her patience was wearing thin.

"I'm glad. His family are some really good people." Bella's eyes darted away sheepishly. "Well, except for his one sister-in-law."

"You've heard about Barbara?" Lisa asked,

surprised.

"Nearly everyone in town has." Bella rolled her eyes, her hand rubbing careful circles on Noelle's back. "She made a huge scene several years back in church when Eli was still the pastor. Her husband had to reprimand her in front of everyone, and I don't think I've ever seen someone's face so red in embarrassment and anger before."

"She's definitely something," Lisa giggled. Bella covered a yawn with the back of her hand and her shoulders slouched. "I better leave you alone so you can get some sleep. You need your rest so you can get back on your feet, and me gabbering to you about a not so nice sister-in-law is not letting you do that. I best be on my way back home now."

"Alright. Thank you for stopping by." Bella smiled, the expression slipping in her exhaustion.

"You're welcome." Lisa stood and leaned down to give the new mama a hug. "I'll stop by sometime soon."

"See you then." Bella nodded, her eyes already beginning to slide closed.

Chapter

FORTY-ONE

ELI SETTLED ONTO THE FLOOR, CROSSING HIS legs under him Indian style as he stuck the small pot of popcorn kernels into the fire in the fireplace. He glanced around the living room at his mother, father, Lisa, and Iris, who were the only people still awake. A kernel in the pot sizzled before it let out an echoing pop.

"Thank you for letting me stay up with you all, Pa," Iris sighed as she curled up into her grandpa's side on the settee.

"You're welcome." He nodded with a grin. "I was ten when I got to stay up till midnight to bring in the new year for the first time, so I figured we could continue the tradition with you."

"When do you think that popcorn will be done?" his mother asked from where she sat in the rocking chair, knitting in her lap.

His pa clucked his tongue and good-naturedly shook a finger in her direction. "Miss Impatient, hold your horses.

He just stuck it in there."

Lisa hid a smile behind her hand as she tucked her legs underneath her on the other end on the settee, snuggling Cookie into the bed made of her shirts. Eli caught her gaze and rolled his eyes at his parents' antics. She shook her head at him, but her dark, soulful eyes sparkled with mirth.

"It will be done in a few minutes, Ma." He shifted the pot as the kernels began to bounce off the inside of the lid.

"If you don't mind, Lisa, I'll go melt some butter to douse it in." She tucked her knitting safely onto the seat of the rocking chair as she stood up.

"Be my guest. Buttered popcorn sounds better than just plain popcorn." Lisa waved for her to go into the kitchen.

"That's what I thought, too." She patted Lisa's shoulder as she walked past on her way to the most used room of the house.

"I don't know if Eli told you or not," his pa said, turning to Lisa, "but we have a little New Years' Eve tradition that we've done for years."

"No, he didn't mention anything. What is it?" She watched him curiously.

"Well, we each share something that we want to accomplish in the new year." He nodded before placing a kiss on top of Iris's head.

"Oh, that sounds nice!"

"Pa, you get to go first like always." Eli pulled the popped corn out of the fire as his mother came back with a small bowl of melted butter and a spoon.

Lisa stood up, taking the dish from her, and between him and her, they served out the popcorn in the bowls they had sitting on the coffee table. The sound of munching filled the room, and he secretly watched Lisa as his pa told his resolution.

Her cheeks were a rosy pink from the warmth of the fire and the cheer of the night, and despite the late hour, she didn't look tired. If he squinted just right, he could almost imagine what she looked like as a teenage girl. At twenty-nine, she was stunning, so he didn't doubt that she had many young men knocking on her door in her debutante days. He was more than glad that she hadn't accepted any proposals or else she wouldn't be his.

If only I had met her first...

Unsure of where the thought had come from, he was glad for the distraction when his ma told him it was his turn to share his resolution. Caught off guard and unprepared, he came up with an answer hastily. "I would love to make double the profit that I did with the pigs next year. I should be able, too, if I breed two of them instead of just one."

He swallowed a proud grin. His answer was quite a decent one for coming up with it so instantaneously.

"That would be nice." Lisa nodded, her lips pursed in thought. "I haven't really put much thought into something I'd like to accomplish in the new year, but I would just like for it to be a good year like this one has."

He caught and held her gaze. She gave him a slow smile and his heart fluttered at the sight. Yet it quickly dipped with sadness.

She's had a good year until the past couple of months thanks to me.

He vowed to himself that he would do anything he could to make her life happy and as pain free as possible. It was the least he could do, yet he found that he wanted to be able to do the most for her. She was too special for a small effort.

Way too special.

"Goodbye!" Eli's parents called as he snapped the reins over the horses' backs and put the buckboard in motion. Lisa and the children waved from the porch, and Eli could see tears streaming down the girls' faces. It was hard on them to only see their grandparents once a year. He'd considered moving back to Carson City multiple times, especially after Cherish's death, yet he couldn't. Half Circle Creek had his heart, and he didn't think he could ever leave.

Cold air swirled around them as they made their way into town. The ride was silent since they were all sad to have to part once again. Every time his parents went back home, he always wondered whether it would end up being the last time he ever saw them. Carson City was over fifty miles away, and life could change in the blink of an eye.

The platform where he had picked up Lisa months before came into view, and he pulled the buckboard to a halt as they came up beside it. Holding the reins between his knees for a moment, he took a deep breath to calm the emotion swirling through his chest. His father jumped down and helped his mother down, and Eli swiftly tied the strips of leather to the brake.

His boots hit the ground and he snagged their bags out of the wagon bed as he walked over to them. His father pulled him into a hug before he had a chance to put them on the ground, but he felt them taken out of his hands as he was crushed in the familiar embrace of the greatest man he'd ever known. Patting his pa on the back, he blinked back tears. As was their custom, he joked, "Don't you think I'm a little too old for you to be squeezing the living daylights out of?"

"No, my son will never be too old for me to hug." His voice cracked, and Eli snapped his eyes shut before the tears fell.

Letting go, his father held him at arm's length, and he gave him a manly slap on the back. "You take care of yourself and your family now, you hear."

"Don't worry, Pa, you can count on it." He smiled despite the unbidden salt water droplets slipping down his face. "And you take care of yourself, too."

"You know me. I always do that." His pa winked with a watery grin.

"Alright, you let me have my turn already, Jared. The way you're carrying on, the stage will be here and I won't get to say my goodbyes." His mother tapped her husband on the arm, one hand on her hip.

"Yes, ma'am." He let Eli go and stepped away, swiping at his face.

She pulled him into a tight hug, and he rested his chin on her shoulder, the embrace bringing back memories of all the times he'd done it. Her hands rubbed gently up and down his back as she sobbed lightly against him. He squeezed her tight, not wanting to have to see her go. "We'll see you again soon."

"What, a whole year? That's not what I call soon," she huffed.

"Well, no one said you only had to come once a year," he murmured, wishing they would come more than that yet knowing they wouldn't.

"You know what I think of traveling, plus we have the mercantile to tend to." She sighed, pulling back to look him in the face.

"I know."

Her hands slipped up to his face, and she cupped his cheeks, wiping at the tears dampening his skin. "Eli, you've got something really special back home, and I don't want you to mistreat her or break her heart. She's too precious for that. I know that there's something standing between the two of you, and I hope you get it figured out soon for her sake. To be honest, I think she's the greatest thing in your life, and you shouldn't take that lightly. Don't just treat her right–love her. She deserves and needs your love more than anything else."

He nodded, not sure what to say.

I'm trying, Ma. I swear I am.

She tugged him down toward her and brushed a kiss to his forehead. With a final pat to his sticky cheek, she pushed him gently away, raising one finger to point at him. "Now, don't you let those grandbabies of mine grow up too fast."

"You know I can't do that," he chuckled, glad she had turned the emotional conversation around with a change of the subject.

"Here comes the stagecoach!" his father called from where he was standing over in front of the post office with their luggage.

"Well, it looks like we have to go now." She gave him a sad smile, her gray eyes still shimmering with tears. "Remember what I said."

"Don't worry. I will." He nodded, walking her over to

the just-parked stage.

He helped her in and gave his father one last hug before stepping back out of the way. Lifting his hand, he waved until they were out of sight. His voice cracked lightly as he whispered to himself, "Keep them safe, Lord. Keep them safe."

Chapter
FORTY-TWO

HUMMING LIGHTLY UNDER HER BREATH, LISA SLID her needle in and out of the dress she was mending. It had been two weeks since Eli's parents had left, and things had gone back to normal, including the way Eli was treating her. Her patience was wearing thinner and thinner, yet he'd still not said anything to her.

A spew of unintelligible words echoed through the living room, and she glanced up from her seat in the rocking chair to find Jared still at his game of carrying wooden blocks from the coffee table to the settee. She would be forever grateful that he was easily occupied by simple things or else she wouldn't be able to get anything accomplished.

The older girls were home from school since they were still on winter break, and they were playing with their new dolls in their room. The day had been going rather smoothly with Lisa and Eli in their regular routines.

"Iris, where are you going?" Tulip's voice drifted down the hall from the open bedroom door. "Iris?"

Lisa glanced up, wondering why Tulip sounded so worried. Iris stumbled into the living room, her face flushed. Bundling up her sewing, Lisa tossed it on the chair as she leaped to her feet. She was at Iris's side in the blink of an eye, bending down to peer into her face. "Iris, hunny, do you feel alright?"

"I feel like I'm going to be sick." Her hand went up to her mouth, and Lisa rushed her toward the kitchen where a bucket sat on the floor. But they didn't make it, and a mess was soon on the floor.

Iris's shoulders shook as she sobbed out, "I'm so sorry, Lisa."

"It's alright. I can clean it up." She rested the back of her hand on Iris's forehead, surprised to find it hot to the touch. "Does anything else hurt?"

"My head and my throat." She shivered against Lisa, her teeth clacking. "And I'm cold."

"Well, let's get you to bed." Lisa started to lead her back out of the kitchen.

"But what if I puke again?" Iris slurred, her eyes glassy with fever.

"I'll put this beside your bed." Lisa snagged the bucket and hurried her back to her bedroom. She shooed the other girls into the living room and tucked Iris into bed. Inspecting the girl, she discovered a red rash traveling up her neck and onto her face. Her heart hammered in her chest as worry stirred in her. "Open your mouth so I can look at your throat."

She complied and Lisa saw that her throat was red and raw, but something else made her breath catch with shock. Iris's tongue was white with red spots dotting it. Lisa's eyes slipped closed as she took a deep, calming breath.

Please, not scarlet fever.

Lisa's oldest brother had gotten scarlet fever as a young adult, but she and her other brothers were sent to a friend's house before it could spread.

"You lay here and rest. I'll be right back." She smoothed the hair away from Iris's forehead.

Hastily making her way through the house, ignoring the mess on the kitchen floor, she bolted out the back door, and sprinted across the yard to the barn. The door was open and as she ran inside, she shouted, "Eli!"

"Lisa, what's wrong?" Eli's form rushed down the loft ladder.

"It's Iris." Tears streamed down her face, and her voice cracked.

Peering worriedly into her face, he grasped her shoulders. "Calm down. What's the matter with her?"

"She's burning up and complaining about her throat hurting. When I looked at it, it was red, but her tongue is white with red spots. She also vomited and says that her head hurts," she explained in a rush. Eli's face paled and he blinked a few times, apparently taking in what she'd said.

"Oh, dear God," he whispered as he pulled her to him and wrapped his arms around her. She buried her face in his shirt and listened to his pounding heart. His heavy breaths and trembling shook her to the core. They both knew that Iris had scarlet fever, and dread filled the air around them. Eli's chest vibrated as he quietly spoke. "Scarlet fever took Cherish's parents and it almost stole her, too. I got it too, but not as badly as they did."

Lisa's heart dropped, yet a sense of determination to

comfort and reassure him filled her at the same time.

"Eli, look at me." She tilted back, grabbing his face so he'd do as she said. "Iris will be fine."

"But what if she isn't?" His voice shook and teardrops rained onto her fingers. "I can't lose her, too."

"You need to go get Doc Adams. He knows how to treat scarlet fever the proper way and he'll help us." She wiped away the moisture from his face.

"I want to see Iris first and then I'll go." He nodded, gripping her wrists like she was the only thing keeping him from falling apart.

"I hate to have to say this, but you might want to pull on your mask before you go around the children. You'll only scare them if they see you like this." She smiled gently despite her own worry and fear. He was near panic, so he didn't need her terror to feed his.

"You're right." He nodded, taking a deep breath.

She watched him for a moment, waiting for his tears to slow and for him to loosen his hold on her. She didn't mind his tight grip, and she knew it was only him trying to not lose it completely. But she wanted it to loosen since it would mean he was calming down. Brushing her fingers through the hair falling across his forehead since he wasn't protesting at her touch, she said, "Everything's going to be alright."

"I know." He nodded again, but his tone gave away the fact that he was unsure.

"You look at Iris real fast and then go get the doc." She pulled her hands away and immediately regretted it. She hadn't touched him in weeks, and she missed it horribly. Wiping his face dry, he followed her back to the house. He slipped into the girls' room as Lisa grabbed the scrub brush and bucket from the corner and began cleaning up Iris's mess. The front door swished open, then closed with a click moments later, and she knew he'd left.

Pausing her scrubbing, she stared unseeing in front of her. All the worry and fear swirling around in her stomach solidified into a hard lump, and she blinked back tears. They were in for a rough time with the possibility of death with scarlet fever in the house.

Now if only the rest of the children don't get it...

Her grip on the brush tightened as she decided to do whatever it took to keep the others healthy, including moving them out of the children's bedroom and into the living room.

Doc Adams gestured for Eli and Lisa to follow him into the hall. Eli's heart had yet to slow its worried pounding, and he was terrified at what Doc had to say. Once they were in the hall, Lisa slid up close beside him, and she slipped her hand into his. The gesture surprised him since they had rarely touched in the recent months, yet he squeezed her hand back, grateful for the comfort in the gesture.

"I'm afraid your assumption was correct," Doc Adams sighed. "Iris has scarlet fever. We'll have to put your house under quarantine, and I'll stay here until it runs its course."

"Do you think the rest of the children will get it?" Lisa asked, her voice hushed.

"Since they haven't had it, there's a high chance that they will, but only time will tell. I know Eli's had it since I was the one who tended to him, but have you?"

"No, I've never had it." She shook her head.

"Well, that makes you susceptible to getting it, too."
He took a deep breath, looking intently at Lisa. "We can't
have anyone leave the house but I'm going to have to ask you
to stay as far away from Iris as possible."

A heavy silence fell over the hall as Eli closed his eyes
briefly, taking a shallow breath.

Why couldn't she have already had it?

"No!" came Lisa's answer seconds later, her head
shaking. "I refuse. The only thing that matters is Iris, and I'm
not letting my risk stand in the way of her getting better."

"Alright." Doc Adams nodded. "I don't like it, but it's
your choice."

Pushing all emotion out so he could concentrate, Eli
asked, "What will we need to do for Iris?"

"Scarlet fever gives you a high fever with chills, so
we'll need to keep her temperature down. We'll also need to
keep her hydrated. Those two things are the most important."
Doc Adams rubbed a hand across the back of his neck. "It's
likely she'll vomit again, so the bucket will need to be handy.
There's also a possibility that she could have a hard time swallowing, but let's hope that she doesn't get that bad. In a way,
scarlet fever is like a severe cold with a few different symptoms."

"I'll get a bowl of cool water." Lisa let go of Eli's hand
and went to the kitchen.

"What do you want me to do?" Eli watched her go,
feeling useless.

"Don't panic." Doc Adams rested a hand on Eli's
shoulder. "Just help out when you can and don't let yourself
think about what could happen. That's the worst thing you
can do in a situation like this."

"Alright, I'll try." Eli nodded.

Hours were spent tending to Iris, but they were interrupted when Tulip fainted in the middle of the living room. She was hastily examined and tucked into bed, her diagnosis being the same as Iris's. Throughout the rest of the day, one by one the rest of the children came down with it.

Eli paused in the doorway of the children's room as he brought fresh water and watched Lisa and Doc Adams wipe the brows of his shivering, feverish children. His heart cracked with fear and an overwhelming love for them all. He couldn't lose them–they were everything to him. Prayers had been sent heavenward all day, and he didn't intend to stop until everyone was out of the woods.

They have to be alright.

Chapter
FORTY-THREE

LISA SLOWLY WALKED OVER TO THE KITCHEN table, cup of coffee in her hand. Eli was already seated, and his eyes had dark circles under them, testifying his exhaustion. It had been a week and a half since Iris had first gotten sick, and all the children were now on the mend.

Doc Adams had made Lisa and Eli take a break since they'd been going nonstop, barely sleeping or eating. Lisa collapsed into her chair, her coffee nearly sloshing onto her hands. Her eyelids drooped and she fought to keep them open.

To just go to sleep and wake up to this all being over...

The children had been delirious, vomiting, shaking with chills, or complaining of a headache by turns, but it was slowly letting up. Yet all Lisa saw was wet cloths and flushed faces covered in red rashes, and she was about to break. It was all too much, but she couldn't quit. The children still needed her.

Hot liquid rolled down her throat as she took a drink

of her coffee, and she cringed as it surprisingly stung. Running her fingers up her neck, her skin felt hot to her touch, but she didn't think anything of it since the house was stuffy.

Eli shifted beside her, pillowing his head on his arm. His eyes slipped closed, and she knew he wanted to sleep as much as she did. She lifted her mug to her face once again, but hastily set it down as nausea swept through her.

Standing up, she went over to the back door, needing cool, fresh air. The outdoor breeze smacked her in the face, driving away her nausea, but not the burning heat filling her. With a quick movement, she undid the top button on her blouse to let the chilly air lick her bare neck.

She blinked rapidly as her vision blurred and the room tipped slightly. Her hand shot out, and she braced herself in the doorway.

It's probably just because I'm really tired.

The scrape of a chair being scooted on the floor echoed over from the table, the sound of it distant and like her ears were plugged. Boot heels clicked loudly, and a hand rested on her shoulder. "Lisa, are you alright?"

"I'm…I'm fine," she stuttered, her mouth not wanting to cooperate.

He turned her to face him, and as her hand left the doorframe, she swayed. His hands gripped her shoulders tightly as his worried eyes darted across her face, studying her. "Are you sure? You don't look so good."

"I'm…" The room spun and began to darken. A cry escaped her throat as she exclaimed, "Please, make the room stop."

"What?"

"Why is everything getting so dark? Did someone

blow out the lantern?" Eli's worried face slowly disappeared in the darkness as she pitched forward, her legs giving out.

"Lisa!" Eli caught her as she collapsed. His heart pounded frantically in his chest, and he hurriedly carried her into the bedroom. "Doc, come quick!"

"What's wrong, Eli?" The older man rushed into the room. "Oh no, not Lisa."

Eli gently laid her down on the bed, and she didn't so much as stir. The sight of her flushed face sent panic through him, and his eyes filled with tears. She looked so small lying in the big bed by herself as Doc Adams brushed his hand across her forehead and felt her neck with knowing fingers.

"She has it, too, doesn't she?" Eli croaked, his voice clogged with emotion.

"I'm afraid so. I was hoping she had just collapsed from exhaustion, but she's burning up and a rash is already breaking out on her neck and cheeks." He shook his head slowly. "She needs to be cooled down before the fever does damage. She feels hotter than any of the children have been, and they've reached some high temperatures."

"I'll get some water." Eli turned to leave the room but stopped as one of the girls in the other room let out a cry.

"Go get that water. I'll tend to whoever that was." Doc Adams slipped past Eli. "All of the children will be fine. Lisa needs your attention right now more than they do."

"What do you want me to do?" Eli ran his hand over his face, desperation erasing all thoughts except for worry over Lisa.

"Once you get the water, strip her down to her chemise and drawers. If she starts shivering, put a light blanket over her, but don't put her clothes back on. They'll hold in the heat she needs to lose." Doc Adams gave Eli's shoulder a firm squeeze. "I'll be back as soon as I've tended to the children."

Eli nodded and made his way to the kitchen to get the needed items. Within moments he was hovering over Lisa's inert form. His hands shook as he set the bowl of water on the nightstand and reached for her. The buttons on her blouse slipped free under his fingers, and he gently pulled it out from underneath her. Her boots came off easily as did her skirt and many petticoats, but he paused as he came to her corset. The lacing was at the back and he didn't want to move her more than he had to, so carefully sliding his fingers between the thick, stiff fabric and her thin chemise, he slipped open the metal clasps on the front. Shifting the undone garment out from under her, he tossed it to the side.

His breath caught in the back of his throat as he saw the telling red lines of scarlet fever drawn on the inside of her arms. The rash that was scattered across her face made its way down her neck and disappeared under her chemise. He didn't doubt that it was covering most of her body.

Dipping a clean cloth in the water, he tenderly wiped the coolness across her hot forehead and made his way down her neck. His finger traced a path over her flushed cheek as he swallowed down a sob. "Please, don't leave me, Lisa. I need you."

More than anything else.

Chapter

FORTY-FOUR

ELI HELD LISA'S HAND IN HIS AS he watched her worriedly from the chair he sat on beside the bed. It had been several days—how many, he wasn't sure—since she'd fainted, and instead of getting better like he wanted, she was worsening. She'd only opened her eyes once, but it had been in delirium.

He let his own eyes slip shut, but they shot back open as she moaned in her sleep. Leaning his elbows on the mattress, he smoothed a hand over her sweaty forehead. Her teeth clacked quietly as her whole body shivered, and he frowned, wishing he could take it all away from her.

Her face scrunched into a look of pain as she murmured something unintelligible. Her hand skittered across the blanket, like she was searching for something. He gently grabbed her fingers in his, squeezing them as he whispered, "I'm here, Lisa."

She tossed her head back and forth on the pillow, her shoulders arching up. A sob escaped her throat as she cried out, "Eli. Where are you? Please, don't leave me!"

"I'm right here, honey." He moved from the chair to the edge of the bed, cupping one of her cheeks in his palm while he held tightly to her other hand. Everything in him begged him to crawl into bed beside her and hold her tight, yet he was terrified it would only make things worse. "It's alright. I won't ever leave you."

Her voice slurred as she talked, but he made out something about being a disappointment and no baby. His brow scrunched in confusion as he bent over her, murmuring softly to calm her, yet it didn't work. She continued to sob, and tears poured past her lashes as her eyes stayed shut.

Why does this have to be happening?

A hand rested on Eli's shoulder. He glanced up to find Doc Adams watching Lisa with a worried frown. Reaching out his other hand, he felt her forehead, and shook his head. "She's too warm. If we don't get her temperature down soon…"

His voice trailed off and his unspoken words echoed loudly in the room.

She'll die…

"Can't you do something?" Eli begged, his throat clogged with held back tears.

"The only thing I can do is continue to give her the willow bark tea like we have been. And you know how that went the last time." He rubbed a hand down his weary face. Lisa had barely been conscious, yet conscious enough for the tea to come back up. Her getting sick would only make matters worse, not better. "But we can try again. If we can get even a little bit to stay down her it would help."

The older man left the room to whip up a cup of the

nasty tea. Lisa called Eli's name again, and he gripped her hand tighter, but it was no use. She was too delirious to hear or feel him.

Drawing slow circles on the back of her hand with his thumb, he watched her through tear-filled eyes. Tears slowly rolled down his cheeks as he leaned forward and gently kissed Lisa's brow. Not sitting back up and instead letting his face rest lightly on hers, he realized like a blow to the stomach that he loved her.

More than anything in the whole world.

The thought had flitted through his mind multiple times since she'd gotten sick, but he'd been too busy to really dig into it. Yet now that there was a large possibility that she wouldn't make it, he let it wash over him with its fullest force. A sob racked his shoulders as he realized he had loved her for a while and that he'd stupidly not realized it.

How could I have been so blind?

"I'm so sorry, Lisa," he whispered, his tears wetting her skin. "I'm so sorry for being an idiot."

Boot heels clicked on the floor as Doc Adams entered the room, and Eli sat back up, wishing Lisa would open her eyes and be completely better. Doc Adams set the cup of steaming tea on the nightstand but the spoon he still held clattered to the floor as Lisa jerked, her whole body stiffening.

She began to shake uncontrollably, and Doc Adams grabbed her arms, keeping them pinned down so she wouldn't hurt herself. "I had a feeling this would happen."

"Will it stop?" Leaping to his feet, Eli watched her body twist and writhe. It took everything in him not to cry as a solid lump cut off his airway and tears filled his eyes. He wished he could wake up from this horrid dream.

"Yes. It already is," Doc Adams sighed as her body slowly relaxed. "Thank God."

"How much more of this does she have to take?" A sob slipped out with his words, yet he didn't care.

"I'm not sure. I really wish I didn't have to tell you this..." His shoulders drooped and his chin bobbed toward his chest. With a slow movement, he looked up and caught Eli's gaze. "I will be very surprised if she makes it. Her fever has been too high for too long, and she's dangerously dehydrated."

Eli's heart shattered into a million tiny pieces, crumbling down to his boots as the wind was knocked out of him. It took all his strength to stay on his feet and not collapse onto the floor.

"No!" Eli shook his head, tears streaming down his face. "She has to make it. I can't lose her. I just can't!"

Doc Adams stepped forward and grabbed Eli's arm, pulling him into a tight hug. Eli's face dropped to the older man's shoulder as deep sobs wracked his body. A strong hand slowly rubbed up and down Eli's back, and it made him cry even harder.

"Why? Why is this happening to me?" Eli leaned away from Doc's embrace, taking a step back as he swiped at the tears violently running down his cheeks to his stubbled chin. "He already took Cherish. Why does He need Lisa, too?"

"I don't know, son. All we can do is pray for a miracle." Doc Adams wiped away the moisture dampening his own face. "Now that she seems to be resting, I'll leave you alone with her while I go check on the children."

Eli nodded, his sorrow strong, yet not consuming

enough for him to not be thankful that all of the children were practically well again. The doctor slipped out of the room, shutting the door behind him.

Knees hitting the floor, Eli knelt by the edge of the bed. He laid his head beside Lisa's on the pillow and gently stroked her cheek as the salt water continued to drip from his eyes. "Please, don't leave me, Lisa. I know I haven't been treating you right, and I'm *so* sorry. You have to get better. Our life together has barely started, and I want to live that life to the fullest."

His eyes slipped closed as a sob escaped his throat, and he prayed harder than he'd ever prayed before.

Please, let me keep her, Lord...

Chapter

FORTY-FIVE

"ELI, YOU NEED TO GET SOME REST." Doc Adams rested his hand on Eli's shoulder where he sat in the chair beside Lisa many hours later. It was a new day, yet he'd never gone to sleep.

Eli shook his head, peering up at the older man in the dimly lit room. "No, I'm fine."

"You'll only make yourself sick. You need rest," Doc Adams insisted.

"Lisa needs me more." Eli looked back at his wife where she lay still burning up with fever and shivering violently.

"If you get sick, it won't be any help to her. You're on the verge of collapsing as it is. I've seen you sway in that chair multiple times even though you tried to hide it." Doc Adams crossed his arms over his chest, giving Eli a serious glare. "I don't want to have another patient when I finally only have one. Go take a nap on the settee. I'll stay with her."

"I'm not leaving the room." Eli gently grabbed Lisa's

hand in his.

Doc Adams let out a long, deep sigh. "You're one stubborn man, and I can't help but admire you for it. If you're going to insist on not leaving the room, then at least get into bed beside her."

"It won't disturb her will it?" Eli's head swiveled around to glance up at the doctor, relief swirling in to mingle with his distress. He'd finally been given permission to do something that he had wanted to do for days.

"I'm afraid nothing is going to disturb her right now. I'll be out in the living room taking a nap myself. If there's any change, come get me immediately." He nodded and slipped from the room, his shoulders drooping from exhaustion and what they were sure was to come.

Slowly standing, Eli swayed, but he caught himself before he fell.

He was right. I am close to collapsing.

He carefully shifted overtop Lisa's legs to get to the other side of the bed, and he gently collapsed onto the empty pillow. Not wanting to bother her, yet needing to touch her, he slipped his hand under hers and enclosed her small fingers in his. His eyes threatened to close before he was ready, but he leaned up and brushed a kiss to her flushed cheek as he whispered, "I love you, Lisa. Please, don't leave me."

Letting his eyes close, he fell into a light, fitful sleep. He wasn't sure how long he slept or what woke him up, but he blinked, his eyelids heavy with sleep. Holding still and listening, he waited to see if he had heard something.

I must have woken myself up somehow.

The tiniest shift from Lisa drew his full attention. He propped up himself on his elbow and leaned over her, peering worriedly at her face. She was no longer shivering, her breaths were shallow, and she was drenched in sweat. His hand shook as he reached out and tenderly touched her cheek, a sob welling up in his throat. He nearly jumped out of his skin when her eyes fluttered open.

"Li…Lisa?" he stammered out, completely shocked.

The corners of her mouth twitched in the smallest of smiles as she looked at him with eyes that were no longer glassy. His palm went to her forehead and found that her sweaty skin was cool.

Her fever is gone!

Eyelids heavy with exhaustion, Lisa watched Eli hastily sit up beside her. He bent over her and cupped her face in his hands as tears streamed down his cheeks. Her mind was foggy, yet she still knew the tears were over her.

"Don't cry," she croaked, her throat tight and dry.

"I'll cry all I want, young lady. I thought I was going to lose you!" he exclaimed, his voice cracking with a sob.

"Can't lose me…that easily." The words were hard to get out, but she managed somehow.

"Thank God." His hands trembled against her, and she attempted to reach for him, but she was too weak. He must have seen her hand move because he let go of her face to grab it. He raised it to his mouth and kissed the top of it. "You sure gave us all quite the scare."

She wanted to apologize, but the tiny bit of energy she had was spent. He shifted and climbed over top of her to get out of bed. He smoothed his hand over her forehead as he whispered, "I'll be right back. I'm going to get Doc Adams."

He practically ran out of the room, and she let her eyes slip closed, only wanting to go to sleep, yet keeping herself awake for Eli's sake.

The floor creaked and a cool hand pressed against her cheek then forehead. She attempted to open her eyes, but all they did was flutter.

Too tired...

"You're right. Her fever is gone." Doc Adams's voice seeped into her, the sound of it echoey. "It's nothing short of a miracle."

Chapter

FORTY-SIX

A MONTH LATER, LISA LAY ON THE settee with a napping Jared curled in her lap. She was back on her feet, yet still weak, and Eli wouldn't let her go back to her regular chores. She understood why, but it made her feel worthless.

After her fever finally broke, it had taken her a week to just get enough strength to sit up. She had hated having to stay in bed feeling so weak that she'd wanted to cry, but Eli had never left her side, so she was never lonely. Abby and a few other women from the church helped out with the children and house chores so he could be with her, and she would never be able to repay their kindness.

Things had changed between Eli and her, but not in the way she wanted. He was always giving her tender smiles and gentle touches, yet he'd never said anything about feelings or emotions. She figured considering she'd almost died, it would have drawn something out of him, yet it hadn't.

But he has been extremely busy...

The whole time she was bedridden, he'd helped her do everything since she'd been too exhausted to even carry a conversation, and he only slipped away to do his farm chores that the ladies couldn't do. As soon as she was on her feet and no longer had to be in bed at all times, he took over all the chores. He'd been nonstop, and he fell asleep at night before his head even hit the pillow.

She felt awful that he was wearing himself thin because she couldn't carry her own weight. But it was worse to think that nothing had changed between them. The time he'd said he needed surely had passed.

How much time does he need?

Jared squirmed against her as he woke up, and she smiled at him as he blinked sleepily at her. "Hello, little man."

She would be forever grateful that out of everyone who had gotten sick, she was the one who got the worst. Losing one of the children would've been harder on Eli than her death. She could be easily replaced, but not the children.

If she had died, she was sure Eli would have moved on quicker than he did with Cherish since he had loved her. It made her heart heavy to think of him not loving her when he meant everything to her. Tears came to her eyes as Jared slid from her lap and walked into the other room with the rest of the family. Thankful that her back was to the kitchen doorway she let them stream down her face.

Why did it have to turn out this way?

Slipping into his nightshirt later that night, Eli stepped over to the bed as Lisa pulled down the covers on his side. She scooted over toward the wall, tucking the blanket under her chin as she rolled on her side. He sighed silently as he climbed onto the mattress.

At least she's facing me and not the wall.

She'd been acting odd ever since that afternoon, so he figured she would ignore him and just go to sleep. He couldn't have that happen that night. Not when he planned to tell her he loved her.

It was long overdue, but every time he'd tried, something had happened and he didn't get the chance. At first, she'd barely been able to keep her eyes open, and he wanted her to be able to understand what he was telling her. But since then, he'd been so busy, someone had been around, or he'd fallen asleep too fast, yet he was determined to tell her. She'd had to wait all too long, and it wasn't fair to her. Yet he wasn't sure what she felt for him, but he was willing to take that risk and tell her everything.

Reaching a hand across the blanket, he brushed her arm as he whispered, "Are you awake enough to talk?"

"Uh-huh. I'm surprised you are. You're typically asleep by now."

"Well, I've been rather busy, and that makes a person tired." He grinned despite the fact that she couldn't see it in the darkness. His stomach churned with nerves as he licked his lips. Not knowing how she'd respond to him saying how he felt was terrifying. Especially since she meant everything to him.

"I'm sorry you've had to pick up my slack," she apologized, shifting closer to him as he grabbed her hand.

"Don't be. You still need rest." He gently squeezed her fingers before intertwining them with his.

"But I'm practically better!" she insisted. "I can do the dishes, take care of the children, and fix meals now. I don't need to be catered to."

"And what if I think you need to be catered to?"

"I'm not worth that," she whispered, her voice barely a breath.

"Lisa…" His words got cut off as a high-pitched scream ripped through the air. He kicked off the covers and heard Lisa's feet hit the floor as she followed him into the girls' bedroom. Iris stood over a sobbing Cinthy, trying to wake her up.

"I've got her." Eli shifted Iris away and she went to Lisa, who wrapped her in a hug. He gently shook Cinthy awake and she sat up reaching for him in the dark. Scooping her up, he sat on the edge of the bed and held her close. "It's alright. It was only a nightmare."

"No, it wasn't!" she sobbed violently. "Ma died! She's gone forever."

His heart clenched in his chest as sorrow swept through him. Cinthy had nightmares about Cherish frequently after her death, but it had been months since the last one. He rocked her and rubbed a hand up and down her back.

Lisa stepped over, kneeling at his side. She reached up and stroked Cinthy's hair with a murmured word. A beam of moonlight shone through the curtains on the window, and he saw tears glistening off of Lisa's face.

Knowing Cinthy would be calmed down within a few minutes and that he was going to sit with her a while, he nudged Lisa with his knee to get her attention. "Why don't you just go on to bed? I'll take care of her and you need your sleep."

"I'll be fine." She shook her head.

"Lisa, please. We went through this many times before you came, so I'll be able to get her calmed down. Just go to bed. I can't have you getting sick again," he insisted.

"Oh, alright," she sighed, standing up. She wiped her face with the sleeve of her nightgown as she crossed the room to the door. "If you need me, come get me."

Chapter

FORTY-SEVEN

CLIMBING BACK INTO BED, LISA COLLAPSED ONTO her pillow with a deep sigh. The bed felt empty without Eli, yet she knew he would be back beside her soon. How soon, she wasn't sure since Cinthy was pretty upset, but she was glad she'd just had a nightmare and wasn't hurt.

Poor thing.

Even in the dark, Lisa was able to make out Cinthy's face, and she'd looked like she'd seen a ghost. Which was probably close to the truth since she'd dreamed about her dead mother. Lisa had woken up in a cold sweat more times than she could count thanks to similar nightmares, so she knew what it was like.

Pushing loose hairs away from her face, her thoughts drifted to her interrupted conversation with Eli. The way his voice lowered several pitches made her wish that Cinthy hadn't had a nightmare, and not just for the girl's sake. She didn't have the least idea what Eli had been about to tell her, yet she dearly wanted to find out what it was.

But what if it wasn't what I'm thinking?

She sat up abruptly, her trembling fingers covering her mouth.

What if he was about to tell me that he doesn't love me—that he never can?

Her brain was still a little foggy from her sickness, so she wasn't sure if she was thinking straight. Yet the thought wouldn't leave. Tears streamed down her face as her chest heaved with held back sobs. She would let herself cry, but she didn't want Eli to hear and come see what was wrong. The last thing she wanted to do was spill all her feelings to him when he likely felt the opposite. That would be impossible to bear.

She scooted to the edge of the mattress and got out of bed. Avoiding the spots on the floor she knew squeaked, she made her way to the kitchen in search of a cool glass of water to calm herself down. With the glass clasped between her hands, she slowly sat in a kitchen chair. The chilly liquid nearly choked her on her first sip, but she got it down without spewing it all over the table.

Laying her cheek on the tabletop, she took a deep, shuddering breath as her tears wetted the wood under her. Her voice croaked as she whispered to herself. "What am I going to do?"

A small voice inside her replied, "Leave…"

She squeezed her eyes shut as her head shook.

I can't leave…

That same tiny voice argued with her, making her sit straight up. She could leave if she wanted to. Yes, they were married, but if he didn't love her and only needed a cook and nanny for his children, why would he oppose her leaving? All he would have to do was hire someone if he really wanted the help. They would still be married, yet she wouldn't have to be tortured by seeing him every day knowing what it was like to be treated like a real wife by him.

I just need to get away.

Yet how far was far enough? She didn't have the desire–or strength–to go all the way back home to Alabama where there was nothing for her, but she wasn't sure if there were any other options. Staring absently across the dark kitchen, she stood up and walked her glass over to the sink. Half Circle Creek was surrounded by other towns, some of which were miles away yet close enough to travel to within a day. She didn't want to travel a large distance since she was still weak from the scarlet fever, yet she wanted to be far enough away that there wouldn't be a chance of running into Eli somehow.

Running through the names of the towns she knew about, she paused when one stood out.

Virginia City.

It was roughly fifty miles away, which meant the trip could be made in one day. And on top of being far enough away to stay clear of Eli, she would be close to Eli's family should she need help. Even though she would be separated from him, she didn't doubt that they would help her if asked. But, despite how much she liked them, she hoped she would never have to ask for any aid. She would get some sort of job in Virginia City. She wasn't sure of what type of job that would be yet, but she would take anything that came her way. Going back to the lifestyle she'd left behind in Alabama was the last thing she wanted to do, yet it seemed like a better prospect than living with a man who didn't return her love.

Mind made up, she slipped back into the bedroom. Eli was still in the girls' room, so she had successfully avoided him. With one quick, silent movement, she slipped back into bed and tucked the covers under her chin. Not wanting to have to talk to Eli lest she change her mind, she closed her eyes and gave into the exhaustion that was her constant companion.

Tiptoeing through the house the next morning despite the fact that the oldest girls were at school, the younger children with Abby, and Eli out in the barn doing chores, Lisa packed some clothing into her carpetbag. She had decided to only take the bare minimum so she wouldn't be loaded down with luggage.

Tears pricked her eyes as she placed the last folded item in the bag. She didn't want to leave. She loved the children and Eli too much to be parted from any of them, yet she needed space. Living in the same house as Eli was too hard and painful. Her heart couldn't take it anymore.

The paper lying on the table caught her eye, and she swiped the tears off her face as she walked away from the bed. No matter how much she wanted to, she couldn't leave without a trace. It would worry Eli, and that was the last thing she wanted to do.

The pencil shook in her hands as she wrote him a letter explaining as briefly as possible what she was doing while excluding her destination. The last thing she wanted was for him to follow her for some reason. Tears dotted the page despite her attempt to keep them in check. Her chest heaved as she laid the pencil down and grabbed the carpetbag off the bed.

Hustling through the house, she went out the front door, enough money in her pocket from the jar they kept their savings in to cover the stage ticket and a few nights in a hotel. She almost felt like she was stealing, yet she reminded herself that it was rightfully her money, too. Her breath clouded in the cold air around her as she walked toward town, the stage station her destination.

No one was around when she stepped onto the wooden platform that she'd last seen the day her life changed forever since she'd had no reason to go to that side of town and had stayed home when Eli dropped his parents off. She paused, her blurry vision taking her surroundings in as memories of that day assaulted her. Eli's smile and rumbling voice echoed through her head, and a soft grin parted her lips as she remembered how his voice surprised her. Knowing she was only stalling, she sighed as she pulled herself out of the past and headed in the direction of the ticket booth window.

"Good morning, Mrs. Blager." Luke Fabre, the telegram operator and man in charge of the mail and stage station, greeted with a bright smile. "How are you feeling?"

"Quite better, thank you." She nodded, hoping he didn't notice her watery eyes or strained voice.

"What can I do for you? Do you need a telegraph sent?" He pulled out a pad of paper from somewhere on his desk.

"No. I actually need a ticket for the next stage going to Virginia City," she explained.

"Virginia City?" His brows rose.

"Yes." She nodded again. "When's the next stage?"

"There are actually two stages stopping here that are on their way to Virginia City. The first one should be here in about half an hour, and the other in about two hours. Which one would you like to take?" His pad of paper was hastily replaced with a ticket.

"The first one please." She smiled, handing over the correct amount of money in exchange for the ticket. "Thank you, Mr. Fabre."

"Just doing my job, ma'am." He grinned with a nod. "Have a safe trip."

"Thank you." She walked away and sat on the empty bench against the building wall. Her head lightly knocked against the siding as she leaned back with a deep sigh.

Here goes nothing...

Chapter

FORTY-EIGHT

"Lisa?" Eli stepped through the back door and tossed his hat on the countertop beside him. He listened for the click of her heels on the floor, but his ears were met by silence.

Strange.

"Lisa?" He tried again as he walked through the kitchen to the living room. His eyes darted through the cozy room to no avail. The dark-haired woman was nowhere in sight. There were things he had to tell her, which was one of the reasons he'd taken the youngest children to Abby's.

His footsteps sounded loud in the all-too-quiet house as he made his way to the bedroom. Sticking his head in the open doorway, he found it to be empty as well. Panic started to build up in his chest when he didn't find her in the girls' bedroom either. He swiped a hand through his hair as he thought of the other places he could look. She hadn't been in the barn or the backyard since that's where he had just come from.

The front porch…

He sprinted through the house, expecting to find her sitting on the porch swing, only to be disappointed when he burst out onto the porch to find it as empty as the rest of the house. His gaze took in the yard, but was met with grass and nothing else.

"Where could she have gone?" he thought aloud. "Surely she didn't go to town without telling me."

Remembering the reticule she always took with her on errands, he rushed back into the bedroom. His heart beat wildly in his chest when he didn't find it in its usual place on the table. Eyes blurred by tears, he sank into the chair and plopped his head into his hands.

Why can't I find her?

Thumbing the moisture from the tops of his cheeks, he sat up and exhaled deeply. His eyes caught onto a written on piece of paper lying on the table inches from where Lisa's reticle normally sat.

How did I not see that?

He snatched the paper and a sigh escaped his parted lips as he recognized Lisa's familiar handwriting. But as her words registered, he sucked in a breath so sharp a pain shot through his side. Hands shaking, he reread the letter, trying to understand what he desperately hoped wasn't real.

Eli,

Thank you for everything you've given me. I have to leave. I hope you understand. As soon as I get a steady job, I'll send you the funds you'll need to hire someone to do your cooking and to watch the children.

Farewell,

Stunned, he let the paper flutter to the floor. His breath came in gasps, and he felt like he was drowning without the help of water. Blinking away tears, he set his trembling hands on his knees and tried to pull himself out of the panic overtaking him long enough to think.

He knew it was his fault she left, but that didn't mean he couldn't try to get her back. He loved her way too much to let her get away. His intention had been to tell her that when he came in the house, yet now it looked like his plans had changed a little.

I'm coming to get you, Lisa.

Not even bothering to pack any clothes, he blew out all the lanterns in the house and snatched enough money out of the jar in the kitchen to rent a horse from the Askingly Livery. The front door slammed behind him as he rushed out of the house and down the road. His plan was to stop at the Askinglys' house and ask Abby if she could watch the children for a few days. Who knew how long it would take him to find Lisa. It was a big state—she could be anywhere.

And what type of job does she expect to get?

He doubted she could find something honorable considering she'd run away from her husband. The only way she could do that is if she were to quit wearing her ring and never mention the fact that she was a married woman. Just thinking of her in a frilly dress and serving tables in a saloon with the men all over her made his blood boil.

The first man to touch her…

Coming up to the Askinglys' house, he pushed the

thought to the side as Tulip ran out of the door. He scooped her up and continued into the house. Abby came toward him from the kitchen, a smile on her face that vanished when she caught sight of his taunt worried expression. "Eli, what's wrong?"

"Can I talk to you alone for a moment?" he asked as he put Tulip down and gestured to the front porch.

"Of course." Her brows scrunched, but she followed him outside without another word. But as soon as the door clicked shut behind them, blocking the children's ears from their conversation, she turned on her heel and peered up at him worriedly. "What's going on?"

"Lisa left." He broke eye contact with her and looked down at his boots. A gentle hand brushed his arm, and he glanced up with tear-filled eyes.

"What do you mean by left?" she questioned, her tone and look as tender as her touch.

"She's gone. She packed up and left this morning sometime between the time that I got back home after leaving here and when I started my chores." He scrubbed a hand over his face. "It's all my fault."

"How's that?"

"I...It's hard to explain since it's rather personal between the two of us, but to put it simply—I was an idiot. A silent, pushing-away idiot." He shook his head, his deep voice trembling as tears leaked down his face.

"Do you know where she went? Or did she leave without any word?" He glanced over and found her giving him a sympathetic, patient look.

"She left a note, but I don't know where she went." Rubbing the back of his neck, he saw her handwriting flit before him. "I came to tell you because I needed to know whether you could watch the children for a few days."

"You're going after her then?" Her question sounded more like a statement, and she nodded with a small smile.

"One thing I won't do is let her get away. I love that woman more than I ever thought I could, and I've been a fool to never tell her. But I plan to fix that as soon as I find her."

"I'll watch the children for as long as you need me to." She patted his arm, turning him toward the porch steps. "Now you better get a move on it so you can get Lisa home as soon as possible."

"Thank you so much, Abby. I really appreciate it."

"Don't mention it. You get your love back and that will be more than enough thanks." She grinned with a wave as he took off down the street.

His steps were fast along the dirt road, and he made it to the stage station in record time. Thanks to the information given to him by Luke Fabre, he soon discovered Lisa's destination. Crossing town to the livery stable as quickly as possible, he rented a fast horse. As he swung into the saddle, a note tucked in his pocket telling the stage station in Virginia City to use the horse on the returning stage, he whispered to himself, "I'm coming for you, Lisa, whether you want me to or not."

Chapter

FORTY-NINE

S TUMBLING DOWN THE STREET THAT EVENING, LISA leaned on a beam supporting the roof over the wooden sidewalk as her head spun. She hadn't eaten since breakfast that morning, and it was catching up to her. She had yet to find Virginia City's hotel since she'd gotten off the stage less than an hour before, and the town was unfamiliar and quite large.

I just need to sit down for a moment, and then I'll be fine.

Laughter spilled out of the building behind her, and she glanced over at the accommodation with a mixture of disgust and curiosity. Without even having to read the painted sign above the wooden, swinging doors, she knew it was a saloon. The smell of booze drifted heavily out of the openings above and below the typical short, washboard-shaped doors, and her nose crinkled at the stench.

The doors swung open, and two men—one big enough she had to tip her head to see his face and the other average height—stepped out of the place. The large man slapped a ten-gallon hat on his head as he laughed loudly at something the other man said. She watched them, not caring that she was staring. She felt too bad to give anything much thought, let alone the fact that she wasn't being polite.

The shorter man, who sported black hair and an outfit just as dark, caught her looking, and she darted her eyes away. Her face heated, and she let go of the beam to walk away before he could question her, but she only took one step before she swayed. A warm hand grasped her arm as a smooth baritone voice tickled her ear. "Are you alright, ma'am?"

"Yes," she stammered, glancing over expecting to find the dark-haired man, but instead was met by the broad chest of the bigger man. She leaned her head back to look him in the face and was surprised by the genuine worry in his light blue eyes.

"Are you sure? You look awfully pale." His blonde brows scrunched together.

"I'm just tired." She smiled, knowing the gesture likely appeared as drained as she felt and sounded.

"I don't think I've seen you in these parts before." The dark-haired man stepped out from behind the big man, who still had a light grasp on her arm. "Do you need help getting anywhere?"

"I was looking for the hotel. I arrived in town on the stage not long ago, and I will admit to being a little lost."

The blue-eyed man grinned softly as he let go of her arm and took the carpetbag from her hand. "My brother and me will take you to the hotel. You look like you need a good, soft bed to take a nap in. I'm Hank Milton by the way, and this is my big brother, Aaron."

"Thank you. And nice to meet you both." She offered her hand to first Hank, then Aaron. Her exhaustion muddled her brain, making her not think completely straight about what personal information she was giving these men as she replied, "I'm Lisa Blager, but please just call me Lisa."

"Where are you from, Lisa?" Aaron asked as he offered her his arm when she swayed once again. She walked in between the two brothers as they led her through town to the hotel.

"Half Circle Creek. It's about fifty miles north of here." She glanced over with a smile, feeling a little awkward to be on another man's arm besides Eli's. But it was unfortunately the only thing keeping her upright. She wanted to at least get into the hotel room before she collapsed if she was going to.

No sense in being a burden to complete strangers.

A small grin tugged up the corners of Hank's mouth, displaying a small gap between his two front teeth. "Our younger brother and pa went up there this past spring to get some mares bred at the Askingly Livery. Jesse met a man by the name of Jack Klister last year when he came to Virginia City on business that went very bad. Jess wanted to see Jack again, plus apparently the fella who owns that famous stallion is his father-in-law."

"Yes, Jack Klister is married to Abe Askingly's daughter. Jack and Bella are…I mean, *were* my neighbors." Lisa smiled, yet a sadness seeped into her heart at the realization that she'd never get to see Bella and baby Noelle again like she promised the younger woman.

"Well, ma'am, here's the hotel." Aaron gestured to the building in front of them. "If you need anything at all, just tell

338

the clerk to contact the Miltons."

"Thank you for your kindness, but I'll be fine." She bid them goodbye and made her way into the place that would likely turn into her new home for several days, if not weeks. Her legs were still wobbly under her, but she somehow made it up the stairs without falling after getting a room.

The door came open easily after she unlocked it, and once she was in the room and the door closed behind her, she leaned her back against the solid wood. Her carpetbag fell from her hand and smacked the floor as she slowly slid down the door to sit in front of it. Letting her head fall into her hands, she let herself cry as the need suddenly arose inside her.

What have I done?

She thought she would be fine on her own in Virginia City, yet now she wasn't so sure. She was exhausted and hungry, and she found that more than food or sleep, what she really wanted the most was to be wrapped in Eli's arms. In his arms, she felt safe and comfortable, yet now she wouldn't get that ever again. And it was the worst feeling, especially when she loved him so much it hurt. The thought of just getting back on the stage and returning home flitted through her mind, but she shoved it away.

It's too late for that.

She was positive that Eli wouldn't take her back after this shenanigan, and she didn't blame him. She wouldn't take back herself either.

Slowly standing back up, she made her way over to the bed on the other side of the room and flopped down on it. Too exhausted to take off her boots, she just curled up on top of the blanket and gave into the pull of sleep with the hopes of escaping her problems for a few hours.

Chapter

FIFTY

IRGINIA CITY BEGAN TO DARKEN AS THE sun set in the
early evening as Eli stepped down from the stagecoach.
His eyes darted back and forth in the dim lighting as
he searched for Lisa's form on the streets. There were many
ladies walking back and forth, but none of them were the
dark-haired woman who held his heart and more.

I'm sure she probably got a room.

Not sure where the hotel was because the only time
he'd been to Virginia City was the year Tulip was born and it
had grown considerably since then, he headed down the sidewalk with hopes that he would find it soon. The air was chilly
through his thin coat, and he was more than a little worried
about Lisa. She was still weak from being sick, and for all he
knew, she could be lying somewhere unconscious. His boots
picked up speed as the thought flitted through his mind.

He kept his eyes on the wooden planks under his feet
and was startled to run into someone. He stumbled and a
large hand grabbed his arm to steady him. Eli glanced up into

the face of a tall man wearing a ten-gallon hat. The blue-eyed man slowly grinned as he said, "Sorry about that, mister."

"It's alright. It was my fault. I wasn't paying attention," Eli apologized, his cheeks pink from more than just the cold.

"You look like you're searching for something. Can we help you?" A dark-haired man stepped out from where he was hidden behind the tall man. He offered Eli his hand, which he shook with a nod. They both looked vaguely familiar, yet Eli didn't have the concentration to give it deep thought. "I'm Aaron Milton and this is my younger brother, Hank, by the way."

"Nice to meet you. I'm Eli Blager."

"Hey, Aaron, wasn't that the name of the little lady we helped to the hotel earlier?" Hank turned to look at his older brother, who was surprisingly the smaller of the two.

They've seen Lisa?

Eli's heart hammered in his chest as he hastily asked, "Did she say her name was Lisa Blager?"

"Yeah. She was about yay high and had black hair and dark eyes." Hank gestured to his chest to Lisa's height. "She looked exhausted and pretty pale when we found her."

"Do you have any idea where she is now?" Eli looked eagerly between the two of them but was surprised when their faces morphed into expressions of suspicion. He quickly realized why and added, "She's my wife. I don't have any intention of hurting her."

More than I already have...

"Just keep going down this sidewalk, and then turn on the corner and the hotel is the first building on the left." Hank nodded, pointing over his shoulder with his thumb.

"Thank you." Eli reached out his hand to shake the large man's once again. "I'm glad I ran into you, or else it probably would've taken me all night to find Lisa."

"You better go find her in the hotel. She didn't look too good earlier when Aaron and me helped her." Hank frowned. Eli nodded, then took off down the street in search of the hotel.

I hope she isn't passed out in her room or something.

Pushing the thought to the side, he stepped through the large door of the hotel. The clerk glanced up with a smile as he greeted, "Hello. How can I help you?"

"I'm looking for a lady by the name of Lisa Blager. I was told she got a room here." Eli rested his elbows on the countertop, letting the large desk hold his weight.

"Yes, she got a room here." The clerk flipped the page in the record book laying open on a lazy susan in front of him.

"What room is she in?" Eli's heart hammered as thankfulness swept through him.

She really is here...

"I'm not allowed to give out that type of information to strangers." The clerk's expression went from cordial to stern and tightlipped.

"I'm her husband," Eli hastily explained.

"How do I know that? Do you have proof?"

Eli panicked internally. He didn't have any other way of proving that they were married beside his word, and that wasn't good enough for the clerk. Making eye contact with the fancily dressed man, Eli slowly shook his head. "No, I don't have any proof. But I swear I'm her husband. I wouldn't have followed her here from Half Circle Creek if that wasn't the case."

"I'm sorry, but your word just isn't enough." The clerk raised a dark brow in a look that was serious, yet saucy. Hank's words about Lisa not looking well echoed through Eli's mind, and a determined angriness pulsed through his veins.

This city fool isn't keeping me from Lisa!

Before the clerk could react, Eli reached out and spun the lazy susan around to face him. His eyes darted across the page until they found her name and room number. He was halfway up the staircase behind him before the clerk could say a word. "Hey! You can't do that! I'm getting the sheriff!"

Let him get the sheriff. I'm not doing anything wrong.

Eli hurried down the hall, eyes frantically searching the numbers on the doors as he passed them. Finally finding the right room, he stopped and caught his breath. Lisa was on the other side of the wooden door, and he hoped not on the floor. With a hand that was shaking, he reached out and knocked on the door, calling, "Lisa! Lisa, are you in there? It's Eli."

Lisa stirred awake on the bed, the dimly lit room around her unfamiliar. Blinking away the panic pressing against her chest, she heard another knock on the door. An extremely familiar voice called her name through the door. She sat up with a start, her head spinning lightly.

What is he doing here?

She hadn't told him where she was going in her letter, so she didn't know how he'd found her. Sliding off the bed, she stumbled over to the door. The key lay on the floor beside her carpetbag where she'd dropped them, and she bent to pick up the carved piece of metal. With one quick motion, she stuck it in its appointed hole and turned it, locking the door.

The last thing she could do was see Eli. Not when she was way too close to breaking and sobbing out everything through the piece of wood that was the only thing separating them.

"Lisa, are you in there? Please answer me!" His voice was panicked, and she knew he was close to breaking down the door. Only he wouldn't be able to since it was locked. The door knob rattled, and a loud thump vibrated through the door. "Lisa!"

"I'm in here, Eli." She rested her forehead against the wooden trim beside the door.

"Finally! Why didn't you answer, and why is the door locked?" His voice sounded breathless, and she knew he was releasing a deep breath.

"Eli, please just go back home," she begged.

"Not until you tell me what all of this is about." The door knob moved again, and she reached down, gripping it in her strangely sweaty palm. She was too weak to stop its wiggling, so she dropped her hand to her side.

"Just go home. Please…" Her voice trailed off with a barely held back sob.

"Lisa, I know I haven't been treating you right, but give me a second chance. I know I don't deserve it, but I don't intend to mess up this time." His words rang with truth, yet she couldn't let her heart get broken even more than it already was.

"Leave. Just leave." She took a step away from the

door, and the room spun. A sharp breath pierced her lungs as she threw out a hand toward the wall to catch herself. The cool surface of the wall steadied her. But it only lasted for a moment. Her head filled with air as a ringing so loud she couldn't hear Eli anymore filled her ears. Black dots flashed before her eyes, and the already dim room began to darken even further. Her hand slid down the wall as she called out, "Eli, help me."

Chapter

FIFTY-ONE

LI PRESSED HIS EAR TO THE DOOR, heart pounding, as a solid thump followed Lisa's frantic words. His hand reached for the door knob despite the fact that he knew it was locked. "Lisa? Lisa, answer me!"

Dropping to the floor, he peered under the door, but the room was dark and he couldn't make out anything through the tiny gap. His fist pounded the floor as panic rose in his throat.

Why'd she have to lock the door?

He sprinted down the hall and nearly fell as he ran down to the first floor, skipping every two steps. His eyes darted over the clerk where he stood talking to an older man with a silver star pinned to his vest.

He really did get the sheriff.

Not caring about what would happen to him since Lisa was all that mattered, he stopped in front of the two men. His chest heaved and he had to swallow down the worry before he could demand, "I need a key to Room 8. My wife's door is locked and she's fainted or something and needs help."

"I can't give you the key." The clerk tilted up his chin, looking down his nose at Eli with a snobbish gleam in his eyes. "It's against policy."

"I don't care about your policy. I want that key." Eli's hands fisted at his sides. His face heated and he knew he looked like an angry bull about to charge since it was exactly how he felt. The woman he loved was lying on the floor of a hotel room behind a locked door, and he'd do whatever it took to get to her.

"Well, you'll have to prove that you're really her husband and not just a man chasing after her. You've already admitted to following her here." The clerk crossed his arms over his chest.

The sheriff cleared his throat, saying, "Why don't I unlock the door and take a look before you go in?"

But Eli barely heard the words over the pounding in his ears as a growl rumbled in his chest. He darted around the clerk's desk, snatching the extra key from its hook on the numbered wall. The clerk exclaimed for him to stop, but Eli sprinted back up the stairs, stumbling into the wall as he reached the top floor. He heard footsteps following him, but he paid no mind to them. All that mattered was getting the door open and helping Lisa. The key slid into the lock easily, yet he stopped himself before he threw the door open. The last thing he wanted to do was hurt Lisa by smacking her in his haste. Instead he slowly pushed it inward, and it bumped into something. Carefully pushing it against what he was guessing was Lisa's unconscious form, he got it opened far enough for him to squeeze into the room.

Face scarily pale, she laid in a crumbled pile on the floor. His knees hit the carpet beside her as he carefully slipped an arm under her shoulders and the other under her legs. Lifting her light form, he cradled her against his chest as he stood and carried her over to the bed.

Voices filled the hall and the door was shoved open even further. It loudly smacked against the wall as the clerk rushed into the room. He pointed at Eli, glancing at the sheriff, who stood beside him. "Arrest him! He stole my key, violated the policies of this business, and has been stalking that woman."

"Hold on a minute, Jerry." The sheriff smoothed down his mustache. "Let me assess the situation before I do anything. As suspicious as this seems, everyone deserves the benefit of the doubt."

The clerk began to say something but sputtered to a halt as an angry look flashed across his face.

Turning away from the two men, Eli gently patted Lisa's pale cheek as he whispered, "Lisa, please wake up."

"Son, do you think that she needs a doctor?" A gentle hand rested on Eli's quivering shoulder, and he glanced up to find the sheriff's face in a look of compassionate worry.

"Yes," he breathed, his head nodding vigorously. "She had scarlet fever about a month ago and is still not fully recovered."

"I'll send for the doctor. He'll be here within minutes." The sheriff turned to leave, but Eli reached out and stopped him.

"You can do whatever you want to me, but I have to make sure she is alright first." Eli's eyes filled with tears, and he blinked to keep them in check. Crying in front of a complete stranger was something he didn't want to do, yet Lisa was more than worth those tears.

"I'm not going to arrest you." He smiled gently. "Jerry tends to overreact, and I don't think you would have stalked that little lady. It's obvious you care for her and that you aren't dangerous."

"Thank you so much, sir. I don't know how I'll ever repay you." Eli's chin quivered against his will as he reached out to shake the older man's hand.

"Now, I'll go get that doctor and keep Jerry out of your hair." He left the room, dragging the clerk with him. The door clicked shut, and Eli left Lisa long enough to light the lamp on the table across the room. It was too dark for him to see her properly and he needed to make sure she was alright.

Brushing flyaway hairs off her forehead, he leaned down and gently kissed her cheek. Her lashes fluttered, and he sucked in a breath. "Lisa?"

Her brows scrunched before her eyes were even fully open. He smoothed the crease with his thumb as she looked up at him with dreary eyes. Tears leaked out of the corners of his eyes, and he let them roll unhindered down his face. "You gave me quite the scare there, young lady."

Instead of smiling like he hoped she would, she turned her head away with a small sob. Tenderly cupping her cheek, he shifted her back. "I won't ask you why you left until after I've found out if you're alright, but please don't look away."

She nodded, her lips trembling as she fought back sobs. His thumb traced them as he whispered, "Someone once told me that God gave us tears for a reason, so don't waste that gift."

Her chest heaved under the force of a deep cry as she

reached for him. His heart soared with a love so strong it made him each of his heartbeats echo with a throbbing ache. He gladly shifted closer, and her shaking hands found their way to the back of his collar. He carefully rested his face against her shoulder, and he listened and felt her let all her sorrow out. Tears of his own dampened her blouse, but neither of them noticed. No words were spoken, but the emotion escaping from both of them was loud in the quiet room.

He didn't know how long they held on to one another, but a sudden knock on the door brought him to his feet. Swiping his face dry on his sleeve, he turned to open the door. The sheriff stood with another older man, who he assumed was the doctor if the black bag in his hand was any telltale. With one gesture from Eli, they entered the room. The doctor went immediately over to the bed where Lisa lay looking small and pale against the coverlet.

Extending his hand to the sheriff, Eli said, "Thank you again, sir. Your help was much appreciated."

"Glad I could be of help, I just wish we could have met under different circumstances." He nodded. "I'm Sheriff Dave Perry, since Jerry didn't have the common courtesy to introduce us."

"I'm afraid that wasn't possible anyways. I never told him my name," Eli chuckled lightly despite the worry still heavily pressing against his chest. "I'm Eli Blager from Half Circle Creek."

"I got to meet your deputy last year, and from what I've heard it's a nice little town."

"That it is." Eli glanced over his shoulder at where the doctor was quietly talking to Lisa.

"I can tell you want to get back to your wife, so I'll

leave you be." The sheriff smiled, stepping back into the hall.

"Thank you." Eli nodded, then shut the door. Hurrying back over to the bed, he stood on the opposite side as the doctor, and his still-frantic eyes darted from the older man's face to Lisa's. "How is she?"

"Well, apparently this young lady thought that it would be fine to go all day without eating when she was already in a weakened state." He shook his head with a small smile. "As soon as she's gotten some wholesome food in her stomach and a good night's rest, she'll be fine."

Eli's shoulders drooped in relief as a smile pushed up his cheeks, and his sight became hazy with tears. Lisa glanced over at him but didn't make eye contact. He could tell she felt awkward and embarrassed by the way her eyes darted from thing to thing instead of looking at him or the doctor.

"I'll stop downstairs and have them bring you both up some supper on my way out." The doctor nodded as he gathered up his things. He headed in the direction of the door, and Eli followed him.

"How much do I owe you?" Eli asked.

"I didn't even do anything but ask a few questions and take her pulse. There isn't a charge. Just make sure she eats most of her supper and that she gets at least five hours of solid sleep." He smiled, opening the door and striding into the hall. "I wish you both the best."

"Thank you, sir. I'll make sure she follows your orders. And thank you for having our supper sent up to us." Eli shook his hand.

"No problem. I can tell you don't want to leave her, and to be honest, I don't think she wants to be left." The doctor flicked the brim of his hat and turned on his heel to walk down the hall. Eli watched his dark jacket until it disappeared down the staircase.

Closing the door with a sigh, he glanced over at Lisa. Her eyes shifted away as he caught her watching him. The thud of his boots on the floor was loud in the silent room as he strode across the carpet to the bed. She shifted and slowly sat up, swaying slightly. He steadied her with a gentle touch, and her chin quivered as she stared at the coverlet beneath her. With his thumb and forefinger, he tenderly tipped her face up so she'd look at him as he softly asked, "Care to explain yourself?"

Her dark eyes filled with tears and she pushed his hand away with trembling fingers. He let her and carefully lowered himself onto the edge of the bed beside her, giving her space, yet still close enough should she faint again.

"Can we wait until I've eaten something, or at least until I don't feel like the room is spinning?" she whispered so quietly he had to lean in to hear it.

"Of course. I'll wait as long as you need me to." Her eyes slowly rose to meet his and he smiled softly. "You're worth the wait."

Chapter

FIFTY-TWO

FIFTEEN MINUTES LATER, LISA SAT IMPATIENTLY FIGHTING tears as Eli stood by the window, absently tapping on the windowsill with his thumb. She wanted this awkwardness to be over with so that they could move on with their separate lives. He was being so patient with her, and she wasn't exactly sure how she felt about it. She expected him to rant and rave at her for running away, yet instead he was doing everything in his power to comfort her. He'd even gone so far as to echo her words about tears and being worth the wait.

It's not fair of him to say things like that when he doesn't mean it.

Something was different about him, but she couldn't put her finger on what it was. His look was filled with an emotion she couldn't place, and she wanted to know what it meant. But she refused to talk until after eating, and it wasn't just because of the spinning room. She needed to be able to keep a level head and her tongue in check, and she couldn't do that when she felt like she would pass out again if she moved too fast.

A quiet knock sounded on the door, and Eli crossed the room, giving her a small smile as he went. The door opened easily under his touch, and a teenage boy stood in the hall, a plate full of food in each hand. Eli's voice was too low for her to catch what he said to him, but she watched him dig in his pocket for the money to pay for their supper. The plates were exchanged, and the door shut once again.

Eli's boots made a shuffling sound on the carpet as he strode over to the bed. With a soft, tender smile, he carefully placed one plate on her lap. Her lips twitched up as she murmured a "thank you." He circled the bed, and the mattress tilted slightly under his weight as he sat in the empty space beside her.

Reaching over, he patted her hand where it lay on the fancy coverlet. She darted a glance at him and found his gray eyes filled with worry and yet again that emotion she couldn't figure out. "Don't eat too fast. You don't need to get sick on top of everything else you've been through today."

"I won't." She nodded, her voice hoarse from holding back the tears threatening to consume her. Blinking to clear her vision, she picked up her fork where it rested on the side of the plate and scooped up some of the gravy-smothered mashed potatoes. Her eyes slipped closed, and a small moan escaped her throat as they hit her tongue.

"Taste that good?" Eli chuckled beside her, jiggling the bed.

"Uh-huh." She nodded, humming the answer around a mouthful of tender roast beef.

"It does taste pretty good, but I like your cooking

better," he quietly admitted.

She nearly choked. Clearing her throat to remove the blockage, she looked over at him. "You're joshing."

"Nope. I'm one hundred percent serious." He cocked up a brow.

"This is way better than anything I've ever fixed you," she insisted with a shake of her head.

"Well, I disagree." He leaned to the side, setting his barely touched plate on the nightstand beside his side of the bed.

"Aren't you going to finish eating?" Her brows scrunched in confusion.

He always finishes his meals.

"I'm not really that hungry." He shrugged.

"But you're always hungry." She laid her fork down, her stomach not wanting any more. Knowing she'd hate herself for it in the future, she reached out and touched his shoulder where he sat on the edge of the bed angled away from her.

"Well, maybe finding out your wife left you because of your stupid mistakes makes you lose your appetite." He glanced over at her, his voice hollow and his eyes glimmering with tears. She looked away, not able to handle the overload of emotion coming from him. His shoulder trembled under her fingers, and she pulled her hand away. Shifting her plate off her lap, she carefully swung her legs over the edge of the mattress.

Eli's deep voice met her ears. "Don't you get out of bed. You'll hit the floor. I can see you shaking."

Knowing what he said was true, she stopped before standing up. She sucked in a deep breath, letting her shoulders droop. She wanted to curl into herself and disappear from the mess they were in.

Why did I ever let myself fall in love with him?

"Lisa?" His voice cracked, and she snapped her eyes shut, fighting the well of tears that had opened.

She wanted to answer him, but instead she started to sob, realizing there was no way she could tell him the truth since she would only end up hurt even more. Not caring what he thought, she flopped sideways onto the bed. She buried her face into the coverlet and her arm, sobbing violently. The mattress shifted and gentle hands pulled her up. Strong arms wrapped around her, and she clung to Eli, wishing he'd never let her go.

"I'm so sorry, Lisa." Part of her hair tumbled down as he intertwined his fingers in it and tucked his face between her neck and shoulder. "This is all my fault. I never meant to hurt you, but I did."

Gasping for breath under the force of her deep sobs, she shook her head. "It's my fault."

She was shifted back, and through her tears she saw Eli studying her face with a confused expression. His face was as wet as hers, and it sent a pang through her heart. "How on earth is it your fault? I was the one who treated you unfairly with my silence."

"It's fine." She dragged a hand across her cheek, attempting to dry her face, but failed as it was quickly soaked again. "I just need to stay away and everything will be alright."

"What on earth are you talking about? I don't want you to leave! My silence has nothing to do with you. It was all me." He cupped her face in his hands, his fingers trembling against her skin. "I was letting Cherish's memory make me feel guilty for loving you, but I was wrong. She's gone, and with her, everything we could have shared. After that night we spent together, I felt guilty, like I had somehow cheated on her. But you can't cheat on someone who isn't even alive."

"What are you saying?" Only one word stood out to her.

Loving. He loves me?

"I pushed you away because I felt like I had done something wrong and because I was trying to figure out whether or not what I felt for you was love or just desire. I didn't want you to hate yourself–because I knew you would– if you found out I felt guilty for making love to you. Yet I did more damage by not saying anything. I'm really sorry. I put you through the wringer when you didn't deserve it." He swiped at her fast-falling tears. "When I almost lost you from scarlet fever, I realized that I loved you."

"You love me?" she choked, not sure if she was even awake at this point.

"Yes." He nodded with a grin, his face still damp and red. "I love you and need you more than anything else in the world. I let you in, and you saw me at my worst. And when you did, you didn't push me away, you pulled me closer."

"But I'm so different than Cherish."

"I know, but I like what I have now. Yes, a small part of me will always love Cherish, and our time spent together will forever be a treasured memory because how can it not be? I have five wonderful children thanks to those ten years. But at times, we were like oil and water. She wanted things for me I didn't desire, yet I did it anyway to make her happy. There was a side to her I only saw. A side where she would pout or give me the silent treatment if she didn't get her way. You're nothing like that. You have a good sort of stubborn streak that matches my own. To be honest, we complement each other so well that it could have only been God's doing that brought us together." He smiled, his gray eyes shining with love.

That's what that emotion is—love. Love for me!

"I didn't disappoint you that night?" she asked, the question burning her up so badly she was surprised she wasn't scorched or a melted puddle.

"Never," he whispered, his voice turning husky as he pulled her closer, resting his forehead on hers. "You can never disappoint me, Lisa Marie Blager. Not when I want you so much that it hurts. I love you more than I've ever loved anyone. In fact more than I did Cherish. And I'm not about to lose you."

"Eli…"

"Hmm."

"I've loved you for so long." She backed up, lifting a hand to caress his cheek. "I thought you didn't love me back and that I disappointed you that night. I was so scared of getting my heart broken that I did the cowardly thing and ran."

"I'm so sorry, Lisa. It was all my fault that you thought those things. Can you ever forgive me?" His brows raised.

She watched him for a silent moment, fiddling with the collar on his red-checkered shirt. A slow, mischievous grin spread across her face as she teased, "Maybe."

"Maybe?" he exclaimed. "I just poured my heart out to you—which was no small feat, mind you—and your reply is maybe?"

"I forgive you, young man." She nodded, her grin

nearly painful.

"Good thing," he growled, "because I was going to kiss you anyway."

He leaned down the short distance to her. His mouth moved across hers like he was trying to make up for lost time, and she met him eagerly kiss for kiss. He tugged her closer, and she willingly gave into his touch, basking in his love that he was pouring on her by the bucketful.

Chapter

FIFTY-THREE

ELI GLANCED OVER AT THE BED AS Lisa shifted. She rubbed her hand across her still sleep-filled eyes and looked over at him with a small smile. "Good morning, Lisa."

"Morning." Her voice was huskier than normal thanks to just waking up.

"Did you get a good night's sleep?" he asked as he pulled one arm into his shirt sleeve.

"You know I did," she laughed lightly, swinging her legs over the edge of the mattress. "You were right beside me the whole time."

"I was sleeping myself, so how was I supposed to know whether or not you were?" He joked as she walked up to him, her legs surprisingly steady underneath her unlike the night before. He pulled her into a hug, and she leaned against his chest, her cheek pressed against his bare skin where it showed through his unbuttoned shirt. "You ready to go back home today? Or do you want to stay in Virginia City for another day to make sure you feel up to the trip back?"

"I feel fine. Stop worrying about me." She looked up at him with a grin. "I want to go back home today. Abby doesn't need to watch the children longer than necessary."

"You're right. But it is nice just you and me here without any of the littles ones under foot," he whispered, sliding his hands up to cradle her face between his palms. Her face bloomed in a blush as a smile twitched her lips upward, scrunching her freckles together. "Maybe I could send Abby a telegram telling her I haven't found you yet, and it could give us another day."

She smacked his arm, a light laugh escaping her throat. "You're awful! And, no, you're not doing that. We're going to go home today."

"Yes, ma'am." He nodded, slowly lowering his head toward her. She raised slightly up on her toes and met him halfway. He buried his hands in her loose hair, and she deepened the kiss. A shiver crawled up his spine as she slid her arms around his waist inside his shirt.

A low hum vibrated in the back of his throat, and he backed Lisa up a step. She arched into him, and he thought he would melt. He'd never drank any type of booze, yet he was sure he was intoxicated.

She's my whiskey, and I can get drunk on her whenever I want.

He let go of her long enough to tug his shirt off his shoulders, but she put a palm on his chest over his hammering heart, stopping him before he could kiss her again. Her breath was ragged, cheeks flushed as she said, "We need to get ready to go so we can catch the next stagecoach."

"You're right," he groaned, yanking his shirt back on.

"But I wished we didn't."

"So do I," she whispered as she stepped away from him.

After eating a quick breakfast, they gathered their things and headed hand-in-hand down the street toward the stage station. Eli bought their tickets, grateful that the next stage for Half Circle Creek was within the next fifteen minutes. Even though he'd love to be alone with Lisa for a little longer, he missed the children. It was the first time he'd been away from them overnight since Cherish's death, and he wanted to see their cheerful faces again.

Surprisingly right on schedule, the stagecoach pulled into town. Eli helped Lisa into the box-like contraption, thankful they were the only passengers. He took his seat beside her after tucking the carpetbag on top, and she curled into him with a sigh. Wrapping his arm around her shoulders, he pulled her close as a shout and snap of the reins signaled their return home.

Lisa watched Eli knock on the Askinglys' door. Her stomach churned with nerves at the thought of facing Abby, who knew she had deserted Eli even if it was only for a less than a day.

What does she think of me?

The door opened before Lisa had a chance to give it much thought, and Abby smiled at them. With a wave of her hand, she said, "Come on in. I'm glad you both were able to make it home so soon."

Eli gently tugged her along behind him into the house.

Her breath caught in the back of her throat in panic as Abby pulled her close in a hug. "Welcome home, Lisa."

"Thank you, Abby," she whispered, her vision hazing with tears.

How did I end up with such good friends?

"Lisa! Pa!" Lisa turned just in time to see Cinthy barrel into Eli's legs and Iris coming in her direction. She bent to hug the girl and was met with so much warmth, the tears she was desperately holding back nearly started to fall.

"Mrs. Askingly said that you and Pa had to take a short trip, and I'm glad you made it back so soon. She wasn't sure when you'd get home," Iris explained, her whole face one giant smile.

"Yes, we tried to get everything we needed to figure out as fast as possible so we could get back to y'all." Lisa looked up at Abby, hoping her thanks was shining out of her eyes. She had really hoped Abby hadn't told the children the real reason they had left town, and she would forever be grateful she hadn't.

Eli shifted closer to Lisa, murmuring in her ear, "Are you up for the walk back home? If not, I'll go get the buckboard."

"No, I'm alright." She smiled, squeezing his hand. He nodded, the corner of his mouth lifting.

"I think we'll get out of your hair now, Abby. Thank you so much for watching the children for us." Eli picked up Jared and grabbed Petunia's hand. Lisa gathered up the three oldest girls and began to lead them outside.

"You're welcome. Anytime you need someone to watch them, just stop by." Abby waved as she slowly shut the door behind them.

Walking the distance back to their house, Lisa slid up beside Eli and whispered, "I've never told you before, but your children are one of the biggest blessings in my life, and I'm so thankful you've let me be a part of their lives."

"You're welcome. And for your information, they're *our* children." He raised his brows at her, then leaned down and pressed a kiss on her forehead as they walked side by side.

Her eyes filled with tears once again, and her smile wobbled. He sent a wink her way before switching Jared to his other side. He grabbed her hand in his, intertwining his fingers with hers. Swinging their joined hands gently between them, they strode up through their front yard, a new, happy life before them.

A life that I'll enjoy more than words can express...

Epilogue

Half Circle Creek, Nevada
Late March, 1868

"**A**LRIGHT, GIRLS, TIME TO GET A MOVE on it. You don't want to be late for school." Lisa waved for the three oldest girls to put their plates in the sink. A lot had happened in the year since Lisa ran off to Virginia City. Tulip was in school, Jared could talk their ears off if he got a notion to, and Petunia's lisp had completely disappeared.

"Goodbye, Pa." Eleven-and-a half-year-old Iris scooted over to Eli where he sat at the table, nursing the last of his coffee. He brushed a kiss to her rosy cheek, doing the same to the other two as they came up for the customary school days farewell.

Lisa smoothed a hand across the top of Jared's messy, red curls where he slapped a palm on the table as Iris wrapped her arms around Lisa's waist from behind. She turned around to hug her daughter from the front, hoping the girl wouldn't notice the slight swell in her stomach under her apron and blouse. "Goodbye, hunny. Have a good day in school today. And remember, don't worry about your test. Just do your best and your pa and I will be proud of you no matter your grade."

"Thanks, Ma." She stood on tiptoe to plant a kiss on Lisa's cheek. "Can we still make that pie when I get home?"

"You bet! Now scoot, little missy." She smiled, the sound of the 'ma' from Iris's lips still making her heart patter with love and pride even though the children had been calling her it for a year. She'd never take being their mother for granted, and she would forever be thankful she asked Miss Prudy to add her to the list of women in her mail-order bride agency.

I can't even imagine how my life would be if I hadn't.

She caught Eli's eye across the table as the older girls ran out of the back door, their school books tucked under their arms and lunch pails swinging from tight grips. He sent her a wink and slow grin. Her cheeks heated in a blush as her stomach fluttered. She never thought she could have loved him more than she did when he came in search of her in Virginia City that day, but she'd proved herself wrong. She loved him so much she could barely keep it contained. And he felt the same. Never a day passed that he didn't tell her he loved her or that he needed her. She woke up every morning to the words whispered in her ear and fell asleep to them vibrating on her cheek where it rested against his chest. He was her better half, best friend, lover, shoulder to cry on, and person to rant and rave to if the need should arise.

My everything.

Lisa lifted Jared off his chair since he could never get down without falling on his face and sat the wild two-and-a-half-year-old on the ground. He ran over to Petunia where she sat at the table about to get up. "Play with me, Unia."

"Go on, Pet. I'll take care of your plate." Lisa laughed, scooping the empty tin plate off the table.

"Thanks, Ma!" She leaped to her feet and grabbed Jared's hand. They disappeared into the living room as Lisa carried both Petunia and Eli's empty plates to the sink. Scraping off the food remnants into the slop bucket at her feet, she plopped them one by one into the sudsy water.

Eli's chair creaked behind her, and she glanced over her shoulder to find him putting his mug on the table. A small smile tilted the corners of her mouth up as he looked over at her. "Would you like some more coffee?"

"Nope." He grinned, cocking one brow up. "But there is something you can do for me."

"And just what is that?" she asked, wiping her hands clean on her apron.

"Come here." His gray eyes sparkled with mischief and love. She was by his side in a breath. Gentle fingers encircled her wrist, slowly making their way up her arm as he pulled her onto his lap. He wrapped an arm around her waist, scooting her in closer against him with a low chuckle. "Now that's better."

Lisa laughed, snuggling down into him. She rested her arm around his shoulders and leaned in. His lips caught hers eagerly, and she let her eyes slip closed with a hum of pleasure. His grip on her tightened as he deepened the kiss, and she melted completely against him.

Now this is heaven…

They pulled apart, breathless and grinning. She intertwined her fingers into the hair at the nape of his neck, tugging at it playfully as she asked, "How soon do you have to go to town to deliver that side of ham to Luke?"

"In about an hour." He slipped a piece of hair behind her ear. She'd woken up late and hadn't had time to pin it up, but she knew he liked it when she wore it down.

"Good. I can have you all to myself for a little longer." Eli had been making so much of a profit from the pigs that he no longer had to raise alfalfa to make up the difference. They had so many pigs that they had to double the size of the corral behind the barn. And on top of selling live pigs at the market in Clearford, Eli butchered and smoked others. He was an extremely successful pig farmer, and Lisa couldn't have been prouder of him.

"What do you have planned for today?" he asked as she laid her head down on his shoulder. He smoothed a hand over her hair, letting his fingers slide down her back until he stopped at her waist.

"Oh, just the usual. I was thinking about making fried chicken for supper. Would you be a gentleman and kill the chicken for me?" She fingered a button on the front of his red checkered shirt.

"Of course." He brushed a kiss on the top of her head. "But why fried chicken? You only make that when we have visitors or if it's a special occasion."

"We have some celebrating to do." She smiled, her cheek lifting on his shirt. A warmth filled her chest at the secret she'd been keeping from him since the day before. She'd wanted to tell him in private since she knew he'd likely get emotional, which was something he still didn't like to do in front of the children.

"What for? Did something happen that I missed?" He gently nudged her back and looked down at her with a confused expression.

"No, you didn't miss anything. I just haven't told you yet." A grin so big it hurt spread across her face as she moved Eli's hand from her hip to cover her stomach. He tilted his head to the side, eyes going wide.

"Are you sure?" His voice cracked as tears turned his gray eyes into a watery mess.

"Yes," she whispered, overcome with emotion. "I went to see Abby yesterday, and she said yes."

"Oh, Lisa!" He pulled her into a tight hug, tears raining into her hair. She clung to him as he quivered with fear.

He's terrified.

And she knew he would be, which was one reason why she wanted to tell him when they were alone. She gently trailed her fingertips up his back, and he tugged her even closer in response.

He suddenly leaned her back again, eyes frantically taking in her face. His fingers gripped her shoulders lightly as tears continued to stream down his cheeks. She wiped them away with trembling fingers as he asked, "Do you feel alright?"

"I'm a little queasy in the mornings, but I've only been sick once," she reassured him. She'd been feeling a little odd for the past three months, but it wasn't until she realized that her monthly little friend hadn't visited her during any of that time that she decided to drop by Abby's for a visit. And Abby had confirmed Lisa's suspicion. It had surprised Lisa that she hadn't gotten pregnant sooner thanks to her and Eli's habits, but she figured it was from her fight with scarlet fever. That fight had put her down for a while even after she came home from Virginia City. It took her a large portion of the year to get back to her normal self.

"I don't want you doing anything that would hurt you or the baby, you hear?" His grip tightened slightly on her shoulders.

"I hear you." She nodded with a small smile, knowing how worried he would be.

And he has every right to be.

"Eli, I'll be fine. I'm strong and Abby said everything is going wonderfully." She cupped his cheek in her palm, making him look at her. She needed him to believe she would survive the pregnancy.

"I know. I just can't help but be scared," his voice dipped to a rough, emotion filled whisper. "I can't lose you."

"You won't! You hear me? You won't." She pulled him close and rested her forehead on his. "We'll make it through this. I'm not that easy to lose."

A sob racked his shoulders, and she wrapped her arms around his neck, squeezing him tight against her chest. He slowly calmed down, and his voice was muffled as he said, "I love you so much, Lisa."

"And I love you." She shifted him up until his face was level with hers. He gave her a weak smile, but it vanished as she placed a kiss on his mouth. His arm tightened around her waist, and he kissed her tenderly back. Breaking away after a few moments, she looked deeply into his eyes. "Are you happy about the new baby?"

"Of course I am! How could I not be?"

Thank goodness!

"I just wanted to make sure." Her eyes darted down, and his fingers gripped her chin gently, tipping her face back up. "I will admit I was a little scared you'd be mad or upset since you already have five children."

"Lisa Marie Blager, I couldn't be happier to have a baby with *you*." He cupped her face with one hand, drawing slow circles with his thumb on her cheekbone. "I've imagined it more times than I can count. I'm thrilled and excited, but at the same time terrified. I can never have too many children, yet if they risk your life…"

"I'll be fine, Eli." Her voice turned husky thanks to the tears streaming down her face. His words had put all her fears to rest, and now she hoped she could do the same for him.

"I know. I believe you. I just can't help thinking about it."

"Then don't. If I know you're worrying, it will only make me worry about you. So please don't." One side of her mouth lifted in a smile, and he shifted his hand, swiping his thumb around her lips.

"I can't promise anything, but I'll try my best." He murmured, dipping down to kiss her softly.

Lisa nuzzled into his chest with a sigh, intertwining her fingers with his as he rested his hand on her stomach again. She had dishes to wash, but she was content to sit on his lap, cradled in his arms for as long as she could before he had to leave or one of the children needed her. A light kiss brushed her temple and her eyes slipped closed.

Perfect. That's the only word to describe this—absolutely perfect.

Author's Note

When I started coming up with the idea for Eli and Lisa's story, I knew I wanted it to be different. I've read quite a few romance novels that dealt with a widower or widow getting remarried for convenience's sake, and it almost always seemed like they moved on with their new love rather quickly. But that always felt a little unrealistic to me, especially if they loved their first spouse a lot and grieved deeply for them.

Life is rather black and white when it comes to things like this, so I wanted to add a bit of color to it. I attempted to do that by having Eli and Lisa's love bloom slowly. Even though I didn't like having to put them through pain, I wanted that guilt, longing, and fight for true love to be there, and now I can only hope that I did a good job.

Not only was this the very first time I've ever written about a married couple, this is also the first time I've written a slow burn romance, and let me tell you, it was a lot of fun!

The pining, stolen looks, small touches, and almost kisses are some of my favorite things to write, and watching Eli and Lisa's relationship go from being strangers, to best friends, then to lovers was one of the best experiences ever. Even though it's like picking a favorite child, their love story is my favorite out of all the novels I've written so far.

I realize this story–specifically the strength of the romance–isn't for everyone, but I love it. I sincerely hope that if you got anything out of this story, that you see how much of my heart I've put into it. Many hours of work and moments of nervousness and self doubt were dished out for this story. The Blagers at times were hard to keep up with as they slowly came to life since there are so many of them, but I wouldn't trade this little family for the world!

Thank you for welcoming Eli, Lisa, Iris, Cinthy, Tulip, Petunia, Jared, and Cookie–because he counts and is actually based off one of my childhood cats–into your life. I hope they touched your heart and that you fell in love with them just like me!

Acknowledgments

This book is dedicated to my little brother, Eli, for many reasons, but one in particular is the most special. As we've grown up, we've gone from fussing and fighting with each other to him sitting in my room until nearly midnight as we chat about the most random things. And during one of those late night talks we discussed the plot for *Worth the Wait*. There were many eye rolls and laughs since he thinks it's weird I named a character after him, but it was a lot of fun to bounce my ideas off of him and hear his input. But, of course, quite a bit of it was funny because not only is he a teen, he's probably the most hilarious person I know, and even though he annoys me sometimes, I'm grateful to call him my brother. Thanks to this book and our sometimes giggle-filled conversations, we've grown closer than ever before and I love that.

So, this book is for the guy who knows how to make me laugh until I cry when I'm having a bad day, teases me for being shorter than him, acts ridiculously immature with me in the kitchen while we do dishes at night, and most importantly, makes my life so much better by just being his weird, goofy self!

But obviously, I can't wrap this book up without thanking some very important people:

Thanks to them being my biggest supporters, my parents get the first shoutout.

Sarah, Jessica, Billi, Lilly, and Janessa–thank you so much for beta reading this novel and helping me turn it into what it is now. Sarah, I wouldn't have been able to do this without you–a million thank yous!

I can never thank L. Taylor enough for everything she does because let me tell you, she does way more than just edit my books! She's my personal cheerleader and hype woman and I love her to bits. Thanks so much, girlie.

Thank you Ariana and McKenna for making the inside of this book gorgeous! I wouldn't have been able to put it into reader's hand without you.

I'll forever be grateful to everyone who has encouraged me in this journey. You guys keep me going!

Now for the biggest thank you: I wouldn't be able to do any of this if not for the talents God gave me, so He deserves all the credit.

Last, but not least, thank YOU! Thank you for giving Eli and Lisa's story a chance. I really hope you enjoyed it as much as I enjoyed getting to watch it come to life.

About the Author

Millie Shepherd is a twenty-year-old author and second generation homeschool graduate. *Worth the Wait* is her second novel. She has been a storyteller her whole life, but it wasn't until after her eighteenth birthday that she began to pen down the stories that filled her mind. Creating new characters and getting to tell their stories is something that makes her the happiest. When she's not writing or plotting out a new story, she's likely watching old westerns or anything starring Michael Landon, sewing, reading, or dabbling into photography and digital design. Millie lives in the mountains of West Virginia with her family. You can find her on Instagram at millieshepherd.author and on Facebook at Millie Shepherd.

Made in United States
North Haven, CT
22 June 2023

37962925R20232